MW00445891

ANGOLIN

C. E. TAYLOR

ANGOLIN

CamCat
Books

CamCat Publishing, LLC
Fort Collins, CO 80524
camcatpublishing.com

This is a work of fiction. Names, characters, places, and incidents are either products of the author's imagination or are used fictitiously.

Hardcover ISBN 9780744306750
Paperback ISBN 9780744306774
Large-Print Paperback ISBN 9780744306811
eBook ISBN 9780744306798
Audiobook ISBN 9780744306828

Library of Congress Control Number: 2023940696

Content Warning: This novel touches upon the subject of homophobic prejudice and may be disturbing to some readers

Cover and book design by Olivia Hammerman (Indigo: Editing, Design, and More)
Map illustration by C. E. Taylor
Artwork by Pixabay.com and Aerial3

5   3   1   2   4

To my husband, whose love and support helped make this work possible, and who has believed in me always.

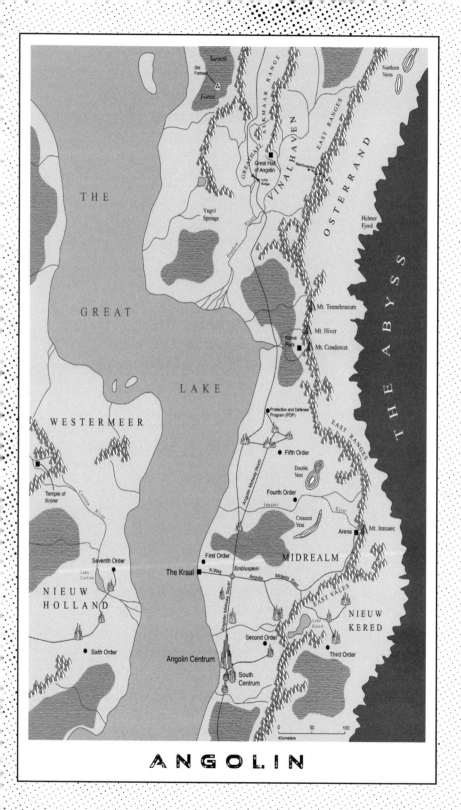

ANGOLIN

PROLOGUE

The war room uprights were filled with maps and data blocks. General Gennet knew the suns were setting behind them; daylong cloistering and covered windows hadn't dulled his senses. But the battlespace awareness points and strategic possibilities held his attention so deeply that he didn't bother to turn to his Fifth Order counterpart entering the room.

"This is our objective, I take it?" said General Estes. Even after decades of friendship, he never was one for hellos.

"It is," Gennet answered, darting his eyes back and forth over the information updates and absorbing every refresh. "This is Negara, our enemy's new target for a stronghold. It's three hours south-southeast by standard M-7 gunship, much less if we get the new troop transports I requested. And good evening!"

"The *new* transports? The ones equipped with TimeSpace drives? I wouldn't count on it," said Estes. "TS might have been common-place technology to our ancestors, but we're still relearning it. High Command won't release it for combat before it's ready."

"I beg to differ, Eldric, and so should you. I think you know they will." Gennet peeled himself from the uprights. "We need to get down there undetected, past the enemy's primitive satellites and surveillance craft. HC knows this and so does Parliament—the Kraal will grant what I ask."

"Mmm," Estes said with a bit of a sniff. "I've read your reports on the matter, Vieron. I also hear every councilor and legate in Angolin has visited you on this—the Seventh Order will become the *new* Kraal if you're not careful. But help me understand why we're doing this.

Negara is down in the Mare Vresel, six thousand klicks away. It's halfway around the hemisphere. If the enemy wants a foothold down there, why not let them have it? By the gods, this makes no sense."

Gennet eyed him, mystified. "Did you read all my reports or just those involving you and Fifth directly? You know what's at stake as much as I do. You have to."

The uprights' shifting hues danced across Gennet's deep-brown skin and Estes's pallor. In lieu of a response, Gennet received a blank stare at his hand resting on his sword pommel. He was one of few in the Angolin Guard to wield the time-honored weapon.

"Last month"—he unhanded his sword and continued—"the Kraal received a diplomatic message. In short, it warned that the enemy is planning permanent troop installations on this end of the Abyss. We both know why: after all this time, the Carmogen finally know about Angolin. They're searching for us, and harder than ever."

"After nearly a millennium? I doubt it," Estes said. "We're called the Hidden Realm for a reason. The ancients were more than thorough in our concealment, and we've excelled at it since. We can't jeopardize that by rushing outside the Cloak for this kind of operation, we'd do better to stay put and remain unseen. Why waste lives and resources on the Kraal's useless whims?"

"The enemy is headed in this direction, Eldric. Isn't that enough? If even a portion of our technology gets into their hands, they'll over-run this entire planet, starting with us. Angolin will be neither safely hidden nor *safe* any longer."

"This diplomatic message," Estes said, narrowing his eyes, "who sent it?"

"The foreign secretariat of Lena. Who else?"

"Lenans! We're listening to them now? They may have unparal-leled intelligence services, but they've never been reliable allies in or out of combat."

"They've always done what we asked, if only just," Gennet rebutted. "They've also never betrayed our hiding. It's us who keep to ourselves. We can't blame anyone but ourselves for that."

"I recall reports of Lenan aid being tepid in past operations."

"And *I* recall them providing it anyway," Gennet threw back. "We would have lost the Campaign of 1370 without them. Their help allowed us to remain hidden. I was there. You weren't."

Estes sighed hard, eyes flitting across the uprights-illumined floor. He removed his cloak, tossed it across a chairback, and loosened his collar as though it was strangling him . . . His jaw quivered. He eyed Gennet before closing his eyes in a single, recognizably tight blink indicating he was receiving an incoming call.

"Do you want to take that in private, Eldric?" Gennet asked.

"No! It's not important." Estes straightened. "So you trust the Lenans then?"

"Not *trust*, exactly—I wouldn't go that far. I understand their position. That's the distinction."

"From one containment op back in '70? And now, they've conveniently stoked our fears to get us down into the Vresel to do what they could achieve themselves. What else could they intend with this beyond securing our protection?"

Gennet marveled at the hastily cobbled calm's collapse. "Look past that intent to see their role in this. Carmogen inroads over here won't stop with Angolin. Lena is equally vulnerable: huge army but no energy weapons or timespatial shrouds to protect it. We have these advantages; they'll provide whatever assistance we require, regardless of who's protecting whom. Simple. Try to add sight of that to your pleasant mood this evening—"

"You know this won't be a garden stroll," Estes interrupted. "Negara will be our biggest operation in decades and instigated by a people we know little about."

"Or have little faith in, Eldric. That's your real meaning," said Gennet. "But this isn't about Lena, it's about our survival on this world. We depend completely on stealthtech now that the enemy is developed enough to cross the Abyss and reach this side of Tentim. TS-shrouded ships, Angolin's Cloak—if they get hold of the technologies we've revisited . . ." He leaned in, eyebrows lifted. "They discovered the Kay Allendë three years ago, look what happened there. A proud warrior culture more advanced than the Carmogen is now a race of battle conscripts and slave labor. We'll suffer worse if we *don't* go to Negara."

"And you and HC believe a handful of TimeSpace drives barely out of workups will spare us from that fate somehow?"

Gennet sighed annoyance. *Is nothing at all being heard?* "Right now, the enemy thinks the Angolinian Rise is down in the Vresel. We can keep it that way if we take this opportunity and don't squander it."

"Whether we do this or not, Vieron, what about the collaborators?" Estes asked, shifting tack after apparently having run out of arguments. "You told me a while ago—insisted, actually—that you suspect plotting right here to aid the Carmogen. If that's true and if it finds its way to Negara, how do we stop it? How do we fight the enemy and our own people at the same time?"

"You expect me to have all the answers. I don't, of course," Gennet said. "But I don't intend to let Angolin fall to invasion"—he peered into cold eyes icing over the strangely inscrutable wiles the other brought with him—"or treason." He turned to the surrounding uprights. "Close all files and end."

Real windows replaced informational ones. Gennet looked beyond Nieuw Holland Valley toward the Great Lake. Far away on its opposite shore, he could just make out the Parliament Pavilion and High Command buildings atop the Kraal. Beyond the government citadel, fading sunlight rendered the Angolin Centrum's skyscrapers as pastel needles against the East Ranges. Civilian traffic plying the sky lanes glinted like snowflakes on winter winds . . .

Movement below caught his eye. A crowd filled the base entrance court around two officers, unequal in rank but in a heated exchange. Their shouts couldn't penetrate the windows' translucent metal, but their mouths definitely moved in argument. And bystanders intervened when words led to shoves.

"I understood you ran this base with a nemurite fist, Vieron," said Estes. "Is this what passes for discipline here at Seventh?"

Gennet ignored the sarcastic quip of a question as he watched the men spar. He had grown accustomed to their altercations. And now, he *counted* on them.

The subordinate officer turned and walked away. A sword much like Gennet's hung from his belt, an immediate identifier. "That must be Dharmen Tate. I've heard about him," Estes said.

"No doubt," Gennet replied. "Excellent officer. Highly capable. A bit rough-edged, though. And that whole package makes him the perfect choice for my plans. You asked how we'll handle traitors and the enemy at once? He's it."

"Him? You can't be serious," Estes said. "How do you expect to root out collaborators with that hothead leading your efforts? I smell another gamble here, Vieron. You have a few of them tonight. His dossier is impressive and he gets a lot of praise, but I don't care if he *is* Nüren Tate's son, he's a standard-issue boot if I ever saw one. I've seen more professionalism in cadets."

"That's a snap assessment on your part, of which *you* have a few tonight. But it won't matter at all if he succeeds. I'm not worried." Gennet raised his chin, comfortably settled in his convictions as he continued to look down below. "And believe you me, if treachery really has seeped into my ranks, the lieutenant is just the man I need to flush it out."

CHAPTER 1

NEGARA

ave you heard the rumor, Rem-E?

If you are referring to the upcoming campaign, sir, I have.

Campaign. Interesting term. Why not call it a containment operation like last time? What's High Command up to?

"Containment" may not adequately describe the operation's scope, Lieutenant. The information I have compiled indicates that this will be—

A big one. The enemy's getting closer and closer to us. I'd like to be surprised, but I'm not.

Do you require anything further before I enter rest mode for the night, sir?

Just one thing, Rem-E: What combat survival files do you have for tropical *warfare?*

❂

HOW IN THE BLAZING SUNS did we get into this?

Dharmen wiped sweat from his eyes and tried to focus. He and his comrade fought heat, flies, and fear with every fleeing step. *Gods, you brought us to this crazy jungle rise. Do you have to prey on us like this too?* He dismissed the paranoid blasphemy and snatched a glance behind him. They had managed (he hoped) to lose the enemy, but who could be sure? And especially with all this seemingly aimless meandering.

"Theus, is this really the way?"

"Course it is, Lieutenant. Trust me. Don't you recognize that tree over there, the big one with the two trunks?"

"How can you possibly tell one tree from another *here*?" Dharmen replied.

"Just believe me for once, Tate. You can't always be in control of everything," Theus said, nearly breathless as he hacked a useable path through the bush. "I'm sure this is the way back to the river. It has to be!"

"If I wasn't reassured before, I am now. Thanks for that." *Hear that, you bloody Carmis, Theus is sure!* Dharmen would have shouted it, but they had already been discovered once and barely escaped. If the Netherlords wanted them, he wasn't about to make it that easy.

He looked to his side, then forward. Theus instantaneously appeared far ahead and then quickly faded from sight. His personal TimeSpace generator's temporal interruptions were randomizing again. He vanished entirely, then reappeared alongside and bumped into Dharmen. Both PTS fields flashed.

"Lower your setting," Dharmen said in a low voice. "If I can't see you, neither can the enemy. You don't even show up through these damn synth lenses. What idiot engineer thought these could penetrate an artificial gravity well anyway?" He turned his attention to his internal and gave a thought command: *Rem-E, deactivate.*

Theus's barely visible hand went to his controller. "PTS output decreased by fifteen percent. Let it be enough. We can't get caught here. I don't want to see a POW camp just yet."

"You will if we get separated," Dharmen said. "For now, I need to know where you are. This is the last place I want to end up alone."

Theus moved on without reply—exhausted or afraid, Dharmen couldn't tell. "When we reach the river," Theus finally said, "we can follow it north to the ford and head back to camp from there. Stick with me, and we'll be there by dinnertime."

"Sticking with you got us separated from our team," Dharmen said. "The general trusted us to relay enemy strengths and positions. Now what do we do? The others better make it back on their own, 'cause we'll never find them like this."

Dharmen hid his fright in the overgrowth, but he couldn't calm his rushing thoughts. *Why did Gennet send us here? The Guard has superior tracking abilities. An advanced post is about as necessary as these stupid new interstellar naval ranks. We still have ground wars to fight, we're not going back into space right this minute! And why us? Theus and I don't have this kind of experience, why put us out here alone with two shipman recruits barely out of basic?*

An hour ago, the four of them were manning their post when they spotted Carmogen troops approaching. Dharmen and Theus ordered their fresh-out enlistees to remain as silent and still as base micromice. Hopefully with PTS running, the enemy would move on past them. One SR obeyed. The other panicked and fired before anyone could stop him. A hail of return volleys—*particle energy volleys*—had followed from weapons the enemy shouldn't have had. The team had to scramble before their makeshift hideout was blown to pieces.

Now they were separated and on the run. Wonderful! And Theus's ranging skills weren't helping. Neither was the dense Negaran forest. Its wildly variegated foliage created an explosion of blinding colors eased only by sun shading in the otherwise useless synth visors. Dharmen assumed it was a beautiful place, if only he could stop to appreciate it without being visually overwhelmed—and shot dead in the process. And like the flora of Angolin, most of the plant life here was motile—pulling, tugging, and wrapping wiry prehensile tendrils around unwary limbs. Body armor synth cutters and membrane herbicides couldn't keep up. Dharmen was glad he had left his sword behind for a field machete.

The suns had just left the sky, and the landscape grew easier on the eyes. Small comfort for being lost behind enemy lines. He pushed on, thought of the recruit who had nearly gotten them all killed. *Yes, he disobeyed orders, but he's just a kid. Angolin's isolation hasn't prepared any of us for this. What more could I have expected? If only his twin sister had been assigned to us instead of to Intel Company Bravo off-rise. Now she's a* real *soldier!* He pictured himself back in his enlisted days, taking orders, making mistakes, and making more mistakes, all while downplaying his position as the son of the famous General Nüren Tate, and just doing his duty. The memories put a razor-thin smile on his lips.

Then he froze in his tracks.

Voices. They traveled up the path behind him and then ceased. He crouched and listened. Nothing. He looked around. "Theus?" he called as softly as he could. "Thee, where are you? Lieutenant Tarkala!"

No answer, and no return on internal AI trace. Theus's PTS had put him too far ahead again in the twilit, increasingly moving forest growth. Dharmen's mind raced. It felt cowardly, but he wished he were back at Seventh. Its peacetime comforts and daily routines were downright heavenly compared to this. Even his superiors' accolades would have been welcome for once. A "pillar of honor" and a "rock of courage, much like his father . . . when his temper's not in the way". The lauds that filtered back to him were embarrassing though not undeserved. Dharmen fit every one of them beyond his own self-awareness.

But that was before Negara. Before the sweltering heat and bizarre landscape that compounded every discomfort, and an enemy that was always too close despite all the latest (and unreliable) stealthtech.

He felt his heart pound up through his temples. *What are my options? Shoot? Run? At what? To where? . . . How 'bout calm, first and foremost?* He took a deep breath and quietly readied his pulse rifle, settling the butt into the pocket of his shoulder. He focused his hearing on unnatural sounds—*people sounds*—in the bush.

A harsh cackle reverberated about thirty meters away. Talking followed. He knew it wasn't the rest of his team. Even fresh-outs wouldn't make this much noise in a war zone for anyone to hear. This group sounded hostile and too large, whoever they were.

Dharmen quietly backed off the path, dodging thick, undulating stalks to move behind a reasonably wide tree. He increased PTS output and peered around the tree's shivering, creaking bole as the voices approached. Heads moved through the bush single file. He could hear their speech clearly now: a mixture of Lenan and Angolinian Standard. There was a woman with them. She couldn't have been Lenan; their brigades had no female soldiers. But there were no other Guard postings behind enemy lines. Who was she?

He heard a male voice, too annoyingly familiar to be anyone else's. *Lieutenant Commander Armetrian! What in the Netherworld?*

They were nearing. Dharmen checked himself. He was too visible, even for dusk conditions. He set PTS output to full, instantly adding cloaking and temporal interruption to his camos' natural light-bending fibers: the hair of the East Ranges *taroc* provided outstanding natural camouflage. The wooly animals were champion steeds and expert climbers, but they were fearful of everything. Physiological reactions rendered them invisible when threatened, and with good reason, considering their high-mountain predators. Dharmen's own fear response activated the camo fibers a fraction. He hoped PTS would compensate.

Silently, he watched. Several were in the group, including two very short figures moving to the sounds of chains.

"Keep walking!" an Angolinian voice ordered.

They were in front of him now. His heart resumed its race. He stood still, trying not to give himself away with accidental noises or movements that PTS couldn't cover. The last figure passed. He crept from hiding and checked for stragglers.

No one. Just the sickle forms of Kiern and Dasha, Tentim's inner-most moons casting a dim glow on the path from the darkening sky. He thought of getting back to the Allied line. But what about this Lenan-Angolinian mix? *And Armetrian*—what were they all doing out here? Hesitating for a few heartbeats and double-checking PTS status, he edged along the path, following their tracks.

He came to a break in the forest and saw all of them, about ten people standing in the clearing. All but four were Guardsmen, partially PTS-blended into the night. Two deathly pale men—one young, the other much older—were obviously Lenan. The remaining two were fettered and naked.

Dharmen took position behind a cluster of static tree ferns, tread-ing cautiously as he recalled the general's comments about his ques-tionable woodcraft.

The woman in the group swung around and activated a wrist-mount field torch, Guard-issue. It alarmed the prisoners, who mut-tered something unintelligible and rattled their primitive Lenan-made shackles. Dharmen held still, narrowing his eyes to slits as the passing beam enveloped his entire body in spite of the foliage. But it revealed nothing. PTS and light-bending taroc fiber hid him excellently.

"Shut that off, Vara!" Armetrian ordered. "They're due any minute, and *they* don't need light."

She lowered her torch but left it lit. "I'm from the Fifth Order, Lieutenant Commander, not the lowly Seventh. You're not my CO. Don't give me orders."

"Forgotten your place, soldier? I still outrank you," Armetrian shot back. "We don't know who else might be out here, so cut it!"

"Forgotten yours?" she said. "We're not exactly on Guard-sanctioned duty at the moment."

He stepped toward her.

Wordless, she deactivated the torch right when they were nose to nose.

Dharmen sensed the friction between them—no need for light to reveal that, and no surprise at all. Armetrian got along with almost no one. *But what on Tentim is this about?*

"We don't have time for this, Armetrian. Can't you do something about her?" said the elder Lenan. "You know what our associates think about women, especially *your* women. You should have left her back at your encampment or at least not brought her here in uniform."

Vara turned on the man. "No one *brought* me here, and that'll be enough from you! I've put as much on the line for this as any man present, so don't—"

All attention went to figures emerging from the bush. Three were in the forefront.

"You have no control over her at all." One stepped forward and scoffed at Armetrian. "In Gragna, we know what to do with them."

His speech was coarse, but he spoke Standard surprisingly well. Dharmen sighed, glad for this little benefit. Despite years of use, Guard earplant lingua mappers still struggled to translate anything more foreign than Lenan speech. Regardless, the rough, smoky hiss in that voice was unmistakable: Carmogen—enemy combatants—and out here meeting clandestinely with Guard soldiers and Lenans—who were supposed to be Angolin's allies.

"My gods, *what* is going on here?" Dharmen lightly mouthed.

The lead looked the group over. The dim moonslight revealing his scaly gray skin over a flat, noseless face and ridged skull reaffirmed his east-of-Abyss heritage. "Which of you is Armetrian?"

"I am Lieutenant Commander Armetrian. And you are . . .?"

The gray man sneered. "I might have known. I hoped you would be someone else. What man takes back talk from a female? And she wears a uniform. Do not tell me she is a soldier."

"That's not important," Armetrian said across Vara's protest. "What we're here to discuss *is*."

The Carmogen studied the others. "Interesting to finally *see* all of you. It makes a change from fighting foes who step in and out of shadows like cowards."

No one responded.

The gray man grunted. "Right, then, if *pleasantry* is what this side of the world requires . . ." Luminous yellow eyes peered down nostril slits at Armetrian. "I am Lord Naul, First Lescain of the Ninth Army of Carmogen. These are my inferiors." He nodded a near-acknowledgment to two aides standing behind him.

"Glad to meet you in person," said Armetrian. "Uprights—or *televisors*, as you call them—do us no service. Now that we're all here in the flesh, we can talk business."

"*All* is the operative word, Armetrian, and finally," the elder Lenan said. "You've kept my aide and me in the dark from the beginning as you've smiled and sung your own praises from the other side of a screen. What is *our* role in this enterprise, and how will *we* benefit from it, exactly?"

"All will be clear soon enough, and you'll benefit through coalition," Armetrian answered. "Angolin is old, tired, and complacent. My people sit sheltered and unseen behind artificial disguises, with our leaders insisting on total seclusion. They keep us captive out of fear that we'll rise up and go out into the world to discover what it really holds for us. But my associates and I will change that. We intend to bring Angolin out of isolation to join the rest of the world. There's great opportunity all across Tentim and more yet to be had if we all work together."

Dharmen kept still, ears open and eyes round with surprise.

"Work together toward what?" the Lenan pressed. "A better life for all involved, or just for you?"

"Toward a partnership," replied Armetrian. "Angolin is the most advanced society on this planet. Lena and Carmogen are great empires. They would become even greater with the technology we'll share with our esteemed colleague here and with you. Operation Dawn Fire will see to that."

The Lenan cocked his head. "Dawn Fire? Labeled this little scheme, have you? And still without our input?"

Lord Naul stepped forward, bare gray arms folded across his chest. "Names mean nothing to me as long as they set the stakes no higher, Lieutenant Commander. My people have conquered most of this planet, but we are at constant war to keep it. I want assurance, not empty words."

"What you would gain goes beyond Carmogen's wildest dreams," Armetrian said, and began strutting among the group. "And we've already armed you well for this fight as a sign of our good faith. What further assurance could you need from me?"

Armed? That's how our weapons are getting into their hands? Dharmen was frozen to his spot at hearing this. He was certain he made noises as he shifted uncomfortably in place, but no one appeared to notice.

"Keep your part of this deal. That will be satisfaction enough," answered Naul. "And I know you have the ability—I have seen your knowledge. You have controlled energy weapons instead of shells. You also have the ability to hide your bodies, your equipment, and even your whole rise from our eyes. Some kind of devices our scientists are still trying to comprehend; our best intelligence forces cannot locate you. At least not yet. And I hear you are beginning an impressive space program, though you likely come from elsewhere to begin with. You Angoliners conceal every part of your existence."

Naul surveyed the group. "Money is no issue. We can pay billions, and no doubt we will, but I demand to know if we will receive what we pay for. Can you deliver Angolin's technologies to us as promised? You and your superior, wherever he is? His absence from this meeting has not escaped me."

"You'll get what you want. Don't worry about that," Vara said in Armetrian's place.

The heavy, stifling air went quiet. Even the night sounds of the surrounding wood seemed to hush as Naul wheeled on her. "You dare address a high commander of the Carmogen Army, woman! In my homeland, you would be ripped to pieces and thrown into the Great Nothing for that!"

"She meant no disrespect, Lord Naul." Armetrian eyed Vara. "Did you, Lieutenant?"

"No, sir. None at all."

"A female warrior. Pitiful!" Naul muttered. "Well, Lieutenant Commander, what do you say? Do I have your assurance?"

"Of course," Armetrian replied, "and don't concern yourself further. I swear to you that my people will give the information willingly."

"And if they do not, Angoliner, then what?"

A sick smile formed on Armetrian's face that even the night couldn't hide from Dharmen. "Then my associates and I will break Angolin. We'll deliver its secrets to you if it means delivering the Hidden Realm itself. You have my word."

Naul perused him. "Excellent! I look forward to our growing relationship. And I am curious to see how you will react if your people do *not* cooperate."

Armetrian raised a hand and motioned.

The chained captives were yanked forward. Dharmen could make them out clearly now: two short, broad-statured men with green-brown skin and bone-straight hair hanging from their heads like shadowy bowls. Negaran natives. The moonslight was just enough to reveal intricate tattoos and gold nose rings on panic-stricken faces.

"To satisfy that curiosity in the meantime, take these gifts as a small token," Armetrian said. "I've heard of the high price exotic races bring in Gragna's slave markets. You should do well with these two."

"Add this fiery beauty, and I will accept," said Naul, looking at Vara. "It is a long journey to the empire, and I could . . . use her."

Vara's lid blew before Armetrian could clamp it down. "I'm a free woman, not some foreign army whore! You're a long way from home, Carmi. Don't forget it."

Naul moved just one step before her rifle raised. His men readied weapons.

The Guard contingent countered.

Dharmen watched, unblinking.

Only Armetrian kept his rifle stowed. He ordered his people to lower theirs.

"My whore you would be," Naul said, smiling at Vara through razor-sharp teeth. "As God wills . . ."

Dharmen's chest grew hot as the collaborators wrangled on. The misogyny, slave trading, and collusion were bad enough, but Armetrian was handing his own people to the enemy. Under any other circumstances, Dharmen would have screamed and shouted at these people for what they were doing. He wished he could do that here. He couldn't, but the notion to end this right now gripped him. They were huddled, it would be quick and easy. But there had to be more of them. And the captives—risking gunning down innocent people, especially over something like this, sickened him. He wrestled with the decision . . . and decided he had to try. Other traitors would have to be found later. These were going down now.

He increased his rifle's beam width setting and aimed. Targets locked, he fingered the trigger and left his fern cover. A thick vine wrapped around his ankle and yanked him off his feet. His back smacked the hard ground, damaging his PTS generator. A thin ripple of PTS light dishearteningly indicated he was no longer concealed.

Vara's torch arm found him first. Weapons clicked and pointed at the lone officer on the ground. Dharmen couldn't take all of them on in a gun battle. He quickly untangled himself and jumped up to flee into the darkness. The blast to his side hit right between his armor's protection zones. He yelled and recoiled at the burning sensation from the particle beam, impulsively wrapping his arms around his middle as he fell. He rolled over to find himself facing mud-splattered boots and staring up rifle barrels.

"Looks like we've got an eavesdropper," Armetrian said, stepping on and securing Dharmen's pulse rifle. "This is no lounge, Tate, get up!" He grabbed Dharmen by the collar, pulling him to his knees.

Dharmen struggled to hold on to his pierced abdomen.

"It was a mild shot, soldier. Your internal's already on it; don't be so weak. Though I guess your kind isn't accustomed to pain."

"My kind? What is that exactly?"

"Shut up! You're in deep as it is." Armetrian rounded him and snatched the PTS generator from his belt. "Be more careful now that you have no protection, though discretion's not your strong suit either, is it? How much did you hear just now?" He put his face in Dharmen's. "And what are you doing out here, alone?"

"I could ask you the same, *traitor*," Dharmen came back. "We've been fighting them for weeks with you right beside us, and all this time you've been supplying them. That has to be the worst thing imaginable. Though why am I not surprised to find you of all people destroying your honor and selling us out? Is it because you have none to begin with?"

Armetrian backhanded him. "You're speaking to a superior, Lieutenant, show some respect! How many times have I had to tell you that?"

"As often as I've needed to make you. *Sir*! Show your officers some; maybe we'd return it—oh, and do you think you'll gain any from this?

You've betrayed your own; respect is forfeit for good! And don't think powder face here'll give you any either." Dharmen took the hatred-turning-to-fear on Armetrian's face and ran with it. "The collaborators get taken too, Lieutenant Commander, even if they're last to go. Think about that when you end up in the same slave markets as your *gifts* here."

Naul bent down and leveled his face with Dharmen's. "This is a waste of my time!" They drilled stares into each other: the Carmogen's trying to intimidate and Dharmen's having none of it. Naul rose, glared at Armetrian. "Want to show me your true worth, Angoliner? Here is your chance! In my ranks, he would already be dead."

Dharmen watched a vein pulsate across Armetrian's sweat-drenched forehead. He braced as the rifle lifted to aim between his eyes. Considering who was holding the weapon, he had no delusion at all over what would come next.

"Well enough for me," Armetrian said in a deadpan tone. "'Bout time I carried out my instructions anyway."

Dharmen peered curiously at that.

"Tate," Armetrian continued, "you don't know how long I've waited for this . . ."

Blinding light pierced the darkness. A thundering rumble knocked everyone to the ground. A second airborne beam hit a tree, cleaving it in two. Another hit much closer. Flying debris struck the elder Lenan and felled him on the spot.

"High-yield energy weapons—Angoliner attack. Move out!" Naul ordered his men.

Dharmen seized the only opportunity he knew he would get. He snatched up his pulse rifle and bolted, making it to the edge of the bush. A shot fired past his head. *Not good at distance targets, are you, mate?* he thought of Armetrian. Beams hit the treetops, incendiary ones in rapid succession. The surrounding forest ignited. It was all

Dharmen could do to hold his wounded side and escape as flaming branches dropped around him.

KEEP GOING. NO TIME TO—KEEP going! Dharmen's mind raced faster than he could run through the moving forest. Fear, pain, and living branches reaching and darting at him didn't stop him. He had to reach camp. That meant crossing the river, wounded or not.

The ground began to slope downward. Dense, undulating brush gave way to peacefully immobile reeds. He heard the sound of moving water. Before him, the forest opened up to the wide, silvery band of the Nabreac River, the dividing line between opposing forces. Running all the way to the ford was no option. He had to cross here and now.

Dharmen dove into the fast-moving river. The water was surprisingly cold for such a hot, humid place. Pain gripped him. Each stroke was a biting chore as he struggled with the current and with his wound, but he forced himself to push on and get to safety. He was determined he was not going down, no matter what. Explosions filled the forest behind him. Agitated voices followed.

A pulse beam shot above his head. Another hit the water. He ignored them and kept stroke, despite strong currents that threatened to sweep him downstream. Smoky eruptions snaked across the water's surface. The river was wide and fast, but not quite turbulent enough to make him such a difficult target, even in darkness. He couldn't believe he was still alive. Armetrian's marksman skills were laughable.

He reached the opposite shore and plowed up the muddy bank. Shaded by undergrowth, he collapsed to the ground. He heaved and coughed up water, trying to regain strength. He heard movement in the brush, far too close. Scrambling to get his pulse rifle into position, Dharmen hoped its nemurite housings had remained sealed against the water.

"Tarkala, don't shoot!"

"Theus?" he sputtered.

"Affirmative, Lieutenant. Are you all right?"

"No, absolutely not!" Dharmen rose to his feet. The riverside growth rustled. Camos approached, hacking at dangling vines and joined by another face Dharmen was glad to see.

"Thee, what's going on?" Dori Secár demanded, and then sheathed her machete. "Dharm, is that you? Where on Tentim have you been? I was about to order a search team."

"With the enemy, Commander," Dharmen reported, "and not just the one from the East. We need to get back to camp, ASAP. You won't believe what I've just discovered about our good comrade, Armetrian."

THE SWELL OF UNIFORMS AMAZED Dharmen. The frontline outlier staffed by a single platoon just two days ago swarmed now. Seventh Camp had relocated—all of it. *Hopefully this* campaign *will end soon,* Dharmen thought. *In spite of everything tonight.*

Dharmen was taken to the infirmary tent where his wound was hastily treated. It was examined, particle-depurated, and stitched by a medi-synth assistant that proved more effective than the human medic and his detached cotside manner. Dharmen couldn't stand external AI—synth or robotic—but he had to admit his wound looked and felt better. He sat up slowly on the narrow examination cot, cursing at the nerve suppressor's wearing off as Theus and Dori entered.

"What were you saying earlier, Dharm?" Dori indifferently asked as though perusing the NewsMesh after morning muster. "Something about Lieutenant Commander Armetrian? Honestly, you two at it again. What's he done now?"

Dharmen got to his feet, ignoring the medi-synth's protests. He relayed everything from beyond the river, including his escape.

"Man, did the gods watch over you tonight!" said Theus. "If you hadn't gotten away when you did, all this would've gone to the box with you, and Angolin would be invaded before it knew what—Commander, what do you make of this? Commander?"

Dori stood motionless, arms crossed and chin resting on one hand. A pursed-lipped frown preceded her reply. "Dharm, are you sure about all of this? Are you certain you heard them correctly? I know Armetrian's a taroc's ass and all, but this is over the top. Meeting with the enemy, lifting weapons and tech? And captives? It's all . . . well, it's a stretch to say the least. It really is an incredible story."

Dharmen couldn't believe what he was hearing. "Incredible story? Try an incredibly painful truth, Commander, one I just took a hit over. But you don't believe a word of it, do you?"

"I'm not sure what to believe," Dori said.

"All the years we've known each other, longer than you've been my ISIC," Dharmen said, "and you think I'd make up something like this?"

Dori watched him silently. So did Theus. So did infirmary staff who probably hadn't heard the full conversation but saw the fire in Dharmen's jet-black eyes and felt the heat in his words. His signature plainspoken directness had followed him even to Negara.

"I just uncovered the worst thing ever and barely escaped to repeat it," Dharmen continued. "We're in serious trouble if Armetrian and these people succeed. If you don't believe me, at least see that!" He stared at her. *If you're listening to me but not hearing me, what more can I say?*

Dori was an excellent commanding officer: fair and usually dependable. But she could be self-absorbed and in her own head at times—traits too common among Angolinians. And this was the wrong time for it.

"I don't know what else to tell you, Lieutenant—these are serious accusations," she replied. "By the sun goddess herself, if this is real . . ." She turned and paced the tent without another word.

"Then we're SOL if we don't get on this fast, Commander. Wouldn't you agree?" said Theus. "There's no time for debate by the sound of it. If it *is* real, then we have to one-up these traitors."

Dori spun on him. "Not so fast, Thee. We need to know what we're dealing with first before we dive into anything. We were sent here to repel the Carmogen, not to accuse our own people of conspiracy without real proof."

Dharmen's anger charged the tent's dehumidified air. "I'm the proof, Commander. I heard everything said, I saw the 'gift' Armetrian gave to the enemy, and I got particle-sliced for it. I already know what we're dealing with. I don't need doubt spread all over it!"

Dori's mouth opened then closed at that.

"Ma'am!" he added.

"We'll discuss it later, Lieutenant. Much later," Dori said sharply. "It's nearly nineteen hundred, and—"

A dutiful, excited shipman burst through the tent's opening, saluted, and relayed a message: all personnel were to convene outside in ten minutes, general's orders.

"Hear that, soldier?" Dori said to Dharmen. "We're about to make the plunge, for better or worse. You've got ten to continue this."

His gaze smoldered and darkened. "Permission to spend each one of them alone, Commander."

"Your wish, Lieutenant." Dori turned and left.

Theus sighed, gave Dharmen a quick slap on the shoulder, and followed her out.

Dharmen sat back down on his cot. *Guess I know my next move, Commander*, he thought. *Because you've just handed it to me.*

"I CONGRATULATE YOU ALL ON a job well done, but it's not over yet," boomed General Gennet. The particle fire lighting the night and the blasts shaking the ground seemed to affect him much less than it did the assembled companies. "The enemy has strengthened their line on the Nabreac's south bank. We will engage them across the river and break their defenses. Then we will continue into the mountains. You'll all have your orders shortly; I want the entire ridgetop taken tonight. By dawn, we'll have Carmi's ass dangling over the edge of the Abyss. Now, if there are no questions . . ."

A hand rose high from the very last row. Dharmen had taken a rearmost position to get a command view of the assembly. "General, have you noticed that we're taking on fire from our own weapons? How can we fight effectively if we're not sure who we're shooting at?" Dharmen knew whom to shoot at more than ever now, but he couldn't mention the meeting beyond the river in this setting.

"Lieutenant, I don't care who they are or what they're using, if someone shoots at you, shoot back!" Gennet bellowed.

Chuckling rippled through the crowd, but murmurs mixed in. Dharmen wasn't the only one concerned, even if he was the only one willing to voice it.

"But if this goes as planned, the enemy will spend the night running, not firing," Gennet continued. "Now lastly, several people from both orders are suddenly missing tonight, with internal AI comm and trace functions offline." He recited a list of names, and it wasn't short. "And has anyone seen Lieutenant Commander Armetrian?"

No one answered to this or to the roster from the Fifth Order. Of no surprise to Dharmen, it included Lieutenant Vara.

Voice thundering and both hands raised, the general disbanded the assembly. Camos dispersed like an insect army losing its chemical trail. Once orders were received from COs, they scattered in animated precombat preparation, deactivating synth DRASH, gathering provisions, reworking supply lines, loading weapons—chaos, but efficiently organized chaos typical of Seventh. Dharmen found comfort in it. His side was about to advance, and the enemy would counter. It was normalcy he could understand and handle. He wanted badly to sound the warning on what he *couldn't* understand, but there was too much to do at the moment.

And most importantly, who could be trusted?

He looked around. It took him a few seconds to notice, but the hordes of camos swirling around him had thinned, and not from assuming stations. Dozens had vanished, undoubtedly with TimeSpace. He ordered Rem-E to raise synth lenses and scanned the forest behind him. No one, not even with heat sensing at full. Not that he expected to find anyone. *Hmmph, I don't have to wonder whose side you've all slipped off to.*

THE GUNSHIP'S ROLL AND PITCH sickened Dharmen's stomach. The small craft hadn't been airborne for a minute before taking on enemy fire that, judging from the blows, was energy based. Its shields would have easily repelled shells, but the particle fire rocked the vessel like a child's tub toy. TS curiously provided no cover, and the pilot compensated by slowing their approach to both soften the blows and prevent the blasts from breaching the shields, potentially tearing the ship apart. But it allowed more enemy fire to find its mark.

My Lord Krone, have mercy on us, Dharmen prayed to his patron deity. *I'll be the best soldier I can be, just get this hunk of nemurite on the ground!* He looked out a viewport. Beams fired from the formation's support sloops. Within seconds, all enemy fire ceased. Dharmen wasn't very religious, but he thanked the god of war immensely for the assist. He just wished he knew what all of the uplords had in store for them tonight.

Most of his company—including the SR who had exposed the advanced post—spun a cursing web deadly enough to match the Negaran summer heat clashing with the Abyssal gases below. Dharmen joined their rant. Silently. He felt himself rise in his seat. The ship was descending; it lurched and shuddered before landing. All hands unstrapped and stood, pulse rifles at the ready.

Dori shot up from her cabinside jump seat as the deployment hatch desynthed: "Go! Go! Goooo!" she ordered with a push to exiting backs.

The company stormed out into the night through the bush covering the low foothills. Gunfire answered, bullets mixed with particle fire. But the Allies were in force, pushing forward against the opposition.

Something curious caught Dharmen's attention. Distance to hostiles and darkness lit only by fleeting beams couldn't hide subtle differences in troop movements and tactics on the enemy line. Troops and volleys were positioned in staggered bundles instead of their usual continuous single-line formations. That matched the Guard's combat style too closely. Dharmen saw movement. He tracked the targets and magnified synth lensing. It defied night vision training, but he had to know the truth. He fired—not at the enemy, but *past* them.

"Don't I know it," he muttered to himself. "And right where I expected you to be."

His shot illuminated what he had dreaded: several figures, all in Guard camos, positioned among the enemy forces. They hadn't even bothered to use PTS. He groaned at the realization. *So there is more to this than Armetrian and a few stray rogues. A lot more.* Focusing squarely on his duty, he reset lensing, took a deep breath, and channeled his disgust into his trigger finger.

Night passed with enemy fire retreating ahead of the Allies, but not without casualties. Scores had been hit by Carmogen and by their own comrades. It was quickly understood not to be friendly fire. The number cut down by particle fire was too high and the targeting too precise. A handful of the renegades were apprehended. Those who couldn't be captured safely were shot.

The Guard had a new internal situation more threatening than Carmogen bands nosing too close to Angolin, that much was clear. Dharmen wondered how centuries of peace in his homeland could suddenly have degenerated into this, but small comfort came in the form of victory. General Gennet's strategies had prevailed, the Carmogen line broke, and their forces were routed. If treason threatened to destroy Angolin, it wouldn't happen tonight.

BLACK SKY MORPHED INTO THE brilliant red of Tentim dawn. Companies from Fifth and Seventh stood with Lenan brigades in silhouette along the high ridge that split Negara in two. Smoke rose from fires all across the slopes. The nightlong pummeling had thrown the enemy back to the far side of the rise as Gennet predicted. Spirits were cautiously high, but Dharmen was too exhausted to be relieved. The shelling was over, yet his teeth chattered uncontrollably, and he couldn't stop trembling. His ears rang with phantom gunfire and explosions, and his eyes remained open by adrenaline alone.

There would be no rest yet. The Allies were preparing to advance down the mountains and finish the enemy for good. Dharmen was ready despite his combat fatigue, but one thing had to be done first, and it wouldn't be stopped by—

"You s-saw what just happened out there, Commander. S-still need proof?" he stammered through his condition as Dori and Theus approached.

"I'd order you at ease, Lieutenant, if you weren't there already," Dori said.

Dharmen was unmoved.

"Look, if we can talk for a moment, not as superior and subordinate, but as friends, then . . . Well, I just want to say that—"

"Please forget it, Commander!" Dharmen knew she would have called him on his insubordinate tone had he not been right about the traitors, and had so many Guard lives not just been lost at their hands. "Now if you'll both excuse me . . ."

He left them, forgetting his shakes and still throbbing abdominal wound, and wishing he could forget the entire night. He found his target and moved with confidence he had rarely felt before top silver. Distrust would have to wait.

General Gennet turned as he approached. "Problem, Lieutenant?"

"Sir! Permission to speak." *Candidly.*

"Granted."

"General," Dharmen addressed respectfully but firmly, "I have something urgent to report."

CHAPTER 2

DHARMEN'S DAY

wonder, Rem-E . . . ?

Still about the general? I would not, sir. He is conferring upon you a great honor.

Honor? Hmmph! How 'bout putting Armetrian in detention where he belongs, that would help more than anything. For me, and for Angolin. What do you suppose is Gennet's motive?

Motive, sir?

Sometimes . . . most of the time, actually, humans have personal reasons for doing things. Reasons that are usually dishonest.

Would sir qualify paranoia as a reason for his own doubts about everything and everyone of late? It would be advisable to control them and leave mental room for what is to come. As for Lieutenant Commander Armetrian, I think time will neutralize his transgressions.

I think you think too much, Rem-E.

❂

DHARMEN STOOD AT ATTENTION, LAST in line. General Gennet reached him and stopped. "Forward, Lieutenant!"

He complied, aligning himself face-to-face with his superior.

"Dharmen Nüren Enri Tate," Gennet recited, "as Head of the Seventh Order of the Angolin Guard, I hereby promote you to the field commission of Lieutenant Commander, with all rights, responsibilities, and privileges of that rank."

He tapped at a hovering upright, and a new chevron synthed on Dharmen's collar. A thin smile broke through his rigid bearing that Dharmen instinctively didn't return. They saluted before Dharmen stepped back into line.

"Fellow officers, recruits, and assembled guests," Gennet announced to the audience in Seventh's entrance court, "I present to you twelve men and women who have gone beyond the call of duty. They were instrumental in our victory on Negara and have served Angolin with the highest distinction. Put your hands together for the Guard's finest new leaders!"

Dharmen barely noticed the applause. He was too fixated on his partner following everyone toward the court's center. Willem came over and curiously offered a hand for a shake. "Mr. Tate, it is an honor to make your acquaintance and congratulate you on this great achievement," he said in a flippantly deadpan tone.

Dharmen took his hand. *Oh, uplords, why not? It's only in front of the whole base!* He pulled Willem close and kissed him.

"That was unexpected!" Willem said, looking stunned but pleasantly surprised. "Are all my efforts to try and loosen you up lately working?"

They weren't, but after Negara, any sign of cheer in Dharmen was an improvement. Even he knew it.

"Don't get carried away before the nuptials, you two," Dori joked.

"They're not getting married tomorrow, Commander," Theus said. "Though let us know when you do take that plunge. I'll need time to figure out a gift. It's hard enough shopping for a man and woman. What do you possibly get for two old men in their declining—"

"Something for yourself instead since you're older than both of us, Thee. Isn't forty coming up soon?" Dharmen volleyed, silently clinging to his own thirty-six years.

Everyone around them laughed.

Theus didn't. As usual, embarrassed silence took the place of a good comeback.

Dharmen smiled what constituted one for *him* and looked across the crowd. A glare returned that could have killed had it taken solid form. "And just when life tried to look up . . ."

"Tate, well look at you!" Armetrian said, walking over with his usual entourage obediently in tow. "I see you're elevated now, too bad. I won't be able to give you orders anymore. You've no idea how much I'll miss that."

"With Dawn Fire keeping you busy these days, you won't have time to miss it," Dharmen shot back. The silence that followed seemed to suck the air from beneath the bioshield dampening the afternoon's high winds.

"And your manfriend has come all this way to support you. Good to see you again, Mr. Hanne," Armetrian continued with a sideways look at Willem. "We crossed paths constantly before you two moved off-base together. Strange that we've never actually met until now."

Willem's smile disarmed like a subtle, silently cast spell. "We never had need to, Lieutenant Commander. There's nothing *strange* about it."

"Beg your pardon?" Armetrian asked with a layer less audacity.

"Forget it," Dharmen cut in. He always enjoyed his mate's ability to cover verbal punches with a warm demeanor, but this wasn't Will's fight.

"Right," Armetrian said, expressionless. "So all this time being one of the general's favorites has finally gotten you a promotion, Tate. You'll match your father soon. You're following in his footsteps and blazing his trail, if nothing else."

"I'm honoring him and my realm. Any trail I blaze will be my own," Dharmen said.

"So you say, but surely you of all people can't deny the legend of General Nüren Tate. He was all I heard about when I was commissioned. You really think you can live up to his reputation just because you're his son?"

"Sons live up to their fathers' reputations all the time, Armetrian," Dharmen said, thrilled at no longer having to call the man he hated more than anyone *sir*. "My father led a force of thousands in 1370, and he led it well. Yours deserted the Guard and hasn't been seen since. I guess treason runs in your family as much as honor does in mine."

Beneath his facade, Armetrian looked ready to explode. "Another time, Tate. Another time!" He and his company glowered at both Dharmen and Willem before turning and heading indoors.

Willem gave Dharmen a wry smile. "Did I say too much?"

"Probably. Definitely," Dharmen said, nearly grinning.

"Oh bother. I really didn't mean to."

"Oh bother, you certainly did, love. You know you did. So did I," Dharmen returned. "And it was awesome. Nothing's better than watching that scum squirm in his own—"

"Will wasn't the one talking too much, soldier. And I wouldn't gloat if I were you," Dori said. "That was over-the-top, and you know it."

"On Armetrian's part," said Dharmen. "And he asked for it as always."

"Still, be more careful, especially in your first few minutes at midlevel," Dori insisted. "There are fewer toes to step on higher up, but they're a lot longer and harder to avoid. And if what you said about Armetrian is true—"

"Then he deserves whatever I give him," Dharmen replied. "And I can take care of myself, Commander, don't worry about that."

"I guess it's time to pull up synth stakes. Some people just can't be told!" Dori looked to Dharmen's more agreeable half. "See what you can do with him, Will, we need him in a presentable mood for the party tonight. If that's possible."

"Party, Commander? What party?" Dharmen asked.

"The one in your honor, mister. Don't pretend you've forgotten."

"A civvy party for an officer?" Dharmen groaned. "That thing's not for me, Commander, it's for Aremel. She'll use any excuse to throw a large social do, and Will's her cousin, so my promotion gives her the perfect one. That's all there is to it."

"Dharm, you'd turn a festival into a funeral, if you could," Dori said, running her fingers through her short, spiky red hair. "Yes, she loves to entertain, and she can be a handful most, well, all of the time. But the invitation specifically mentioned you. It'll be a fun night for a change—even you can't deny Aremel knows how to put it on." She eyed Theus. "Everything all right, Lieutenant? Life agreeing with you at the moment?"

"Certainly, Commander."

"This is a special day for Dharmen, we can't have you backing out of the party too. That's in his brain, so I know it's circling round yours."

Theus sighed. "Is my presence really necessary?"

"Is it ever, Thee?"

"Commander, you know what Aremel's like. She'll be too busy surrounded by important people smiling and talking about nothing all night to notice us. I'm a soldier, I have no use for yet another Hidden Realm Who's Who."

"A who's who with lots of women, Thee," Dharmen enticed. "Young, beautiful, single ones mostly—that's what her parties attract. Remember?"

That nearly floated Theus right out of the assembly area as expected. "Fine, I'm in," he said before looking back to Dori. "But what will you do, Commander? Most of the men will be *your age* and not quite so eligible, much like the stiffs you've dated lately."

"Shut up, you," Dori said with syrup on her tongue and eyes narrowed in a prickling smile. "Anyway," she continued to Dharmen, throwing Theus to the wind beyond the bioshield for the moment, "you're moving up in the ranks, you have a great life, and tonight, you're being honored by one of Angolin's most prominent women, who just happens to be your partner's kin. How much more good fortune could anyone want?"

Good fortune! Dharmen rolled his eyes to the heavens. "Oh, a little more maybe, just a wee bit: Safety and security over useless celebrating would be a good start. A military career not spent fighting my own comrades would be another. And friends who believe me when I have something vitally important to tell them, especially when lives depend on it—that would be the best of finishes. I can go on till Angolin's thousandth birthday, Dori. Would you like that?" It needed to be said, though maybe with less peeve. Attack first and think about (regret) it afterward was Dharmen's sorely unending wont. He wished he had the people-patience for the reverse. "Sorry, ma'am."

"Save the vinegar for Armetrian, Dharmen. I'm on your side," Dori said. "But hold off on it this evening. He's on the guest list, if you can believe it. Let's pray the gods find him something else to do. We don't need any drama tonight."

"Aremel's the hostess. That'll be your drama whether he comes or not," Dharmen said and received a disapproving look from Willem. "But relax, he won't be there. You'll never find Armetrian attending anything honoring me."

DHARMEN WATCHED THE SUNS SET behind the northwest marches' distant mountains. Blue Rior trailed red Lothnë in fading light as they descended beyond the broad valley beneath the ballroom terrace. Kleve Park, Aremel Hanne's estate, was fit for royalty (and in the Outside World, she would have been). Its perch at Mount Condorcet's feet overlooked the bend of the Vale of Angolin, framed on either side by highland forests brushed with the brightening shades of second autumn.

Above the tree line, the East Ranges' white peaks enthroned the Heavenly Pantheon on Tentim beneath the red and blue Lady and Lord of Light, watching and kindling life from the daytime sky. On the Bent Valley's curving floor, skippers plying the Great Lake lowered sails as approaching twilight chased the classic vessels back to harbor.

Dharmen had never seen most of what the Hidden Realm's freshwater spine connected: loosely knitted conurbations, entertainment districts, industrial centers (kept well out of sight), farming cooperatives tucked in the western finger plains and pocket vales, and unknown communities shrouded in dark matter. He *had* seen the Great Hall of Angolin up north many times. After nearly a millennium, the old fortress and administrative center of his homeland's founders still sat concealed among tree-covered ridges: a well-hidden, defensible base to an army as mysterious as the faraway galactic empire that had planted it.

He went to the Great Hall whenever he could. It was the one place where he felt the life force of his forebears and their sacrifices fill him. "Because so many built, fought, and died there for the protection of their own, I want to be a part of it," was his explanation for anyone questioning his sojourns there. But with what was seeping into Angolin now, he wondered if his people still honored the ancients, or just coasted on their labors, ready to abandon everything in a heartbeat.

Alone on the terrace in his stuffy dress uniform, he looked southward. Fog rolling up the valley surrounded the distant Angolin Centrum's skyscrapers. Their slender, darkening forms and the dim glow of their stabilizer beams floated on a twilit sea of mist. It was peaceful and breathtaking at once, but it didn't calm Dharmen. Beyond the high ranges palisading the Angolinian Rise, the land dropped fifty thousand meters into the deadly brethyl gas and liquid methane seas of the Abyss, a barrier that no longer held back the enemy. *When the Carmis discover us, what then?* Dharmen wondered. *Our society, our lives, everything we've built and done here. Will it all end just like that? Lord and Lady of Heaven, will we lose it forever?*

A dark spot caught the top of his eye. A double-wing-set high flyer wheeled overhead in threatening silence. Dharmen shuddered. He was certain the giant airborne predator's sharp eyes caught sight of him. Soon, it would leave its mountain aerie for the micro season in search of warmer continental rises. Right now, he just hoped Aremel's ground shields were fully raised.

The great bird sped off. A shimmer of lights leaped across the southern sky behind it, followed by a telltale whoosh. The lights floated in the air as they rushed northward, rounded the valley, and continued behind the mountains in connecting triangles morphing into one solid, dimly luminescent form. Dharmen stilled. He had seen Angolin's Cloak activation only a handful of times in his entire life. This one was the second in a week. Definitely in no mood for mingling now, he decided on a quick exit. He turned to go; he'd find an excuse later. Or not.

"Ready to join the party?" Theus asked, with Willem standing silently beside him. "Or are you just going to stand out here and avoid it all night?"

"Got my own going for now if you two don't mind." Dharmen gestured around the empty terrace. "Can't you tell?"

"Some people do mind, actually." Willem glanced up toward the faint shimmer filling the sky but said nothing of it. "Aremel's been asking about you all evening. She wants to introduce you to her guests."

Dharmen never liked Willem's stop-fighting-and-give-in tone. "Do I have a choice?"

"You always have a choice!" Willem glowered. "And the choice right now is to stop standing out here brooding."

"And celebrate being midlevel now," Theus put in. "That, and Armetrian and his goon squad skipped tonight. Thank the uplords for small favors."

"Small people if anything," Dharmen said. "And what's it to me if they're here or not? I'm not afraid of them—it's their *plans* that scare me. Negara was weeks ago. Krone only knows how much damage they've done since."

"Is this really the right time for this?" said Willem. "I was hoping you'd *join* the party, not cast a dark cloud over it."

"We're in a dangerous situation, love. There is no *right time* anymore."

"All I'm suggesting is that you try at least once, in the midst of it all, to live a normal life and have a little fun."

Dharmen ignored Theus's uncomfortable look and stared at Willem. "Fun? After everything I've told you about what's coming? You and Dori are exactly the same. Your world is about to cave in on you, and all you can think of is . . ." He turned, looked out into the approaching night. "Well, enjoy yourselves now while you still can, because if someone doesn't listen soon, all this will end. The Carmis will be on us while you two and the rest of Angolin are looking for a good time." Before anyone could challenge that, he slammed his hands on the terrace's wide marblite railing, cursed, and lowered his head.

Theus flinched.

Willem didn't. "*Told*?" he said. "Ranted, more like. And just because my back isn't as easily put up as yours doesn't mean I'm not concerned." He took Dharmen's arm and turned him so that they faced each other. "I've heard you, I believe you, and when the time comes, I'll be with you one thousand percent. So will Theus here."

He nodded behind them. "And so will Dori. She'll come around, I'm certain of that."

Dharmen sighed at yet another successful deflation of his negative moods by his partner. He capitulated, let Willem's warm-as-Lothnë's-morning-light smile coax him from the terrace and into the party. *I'll snatch a few appetizers and* then *make my exit,* he considered.

Inside, the spectacle invaded his senses. Every tunic, cloak, and gown was decked in unending embellishments. Angolinian mode on display and in force—everyone wore their festive best: women in warm colors in honor of the Red Sun Goddess, and men donning the Blue Lord's cooler shades.

And the showstopper of the evening by far was the hostess. Aremel Hanne always dressed to match her dynamic personality. Tonight, her gown's enhances glowed and changed tone by the half minute, making her an ever-fluctuating kaleidoscope. To complete her ensemble and literally outshine all others, she had the same tiny flames of holo-light programmed to dance around her head and upturned locks, finished with a tiara that caught every light from her and from the room. The hostess, her guests, and all the dress uniforms present made the whole event look more to Dharmen like a mad costume ball than a formal engagement. Though being coupled with a Hanne had accustomed him to these affairs. He still hated them, but he knew now to spare Willem's ears and grumble inwardly.

"You see the two foreigners over there?" asked Theus.

Dharmen found them: two platinum-haired, morbidly pale men huddled with Aremel, General Gennet, and a handful of heavily medaled legates. "Lenans, Thee, not foreigners. This was their planet first."

He looked more closely. One was pushing elder years, but he was affable and charismatic, and even more garishly outfitted than the other guests. He wore a deep-red suit with a high collar. His entire coat was threaded in intricate gold patterns, as was his thigh-length cloak, fastened at one shoulder. A fist-sized gemstone hung from a heavy gold chain around his neck. His much younger counterpart dressed in near-equal ostentation, though he didn't exude the same preeminence. Nor the same grooming. The thin white fur covering nearly his entire face advertised his lower status. Only highborn Lenan men removed it, leaving behind human-style beards.

Dharmen sniffed. "That must be Lord Balaneth and one of his aides. I've heard about him. He's the first ambassador to Angolin in eight hundred years—this really *is* a special event."

"Apart from the Sun Goddess's colors, someone should've told him to leave the woman's cloak behind," said Theus.

"It's standard Lenan wear," Dharmen said. "It has the emblem of their third royal house woven into the material. Don't you remember it from the elite corps officers we worked with on Negara?"

"I don't have your eye for that kind of detail, Dharm, sorry. And regardless, it's still too short and skimpy for a man."

"For an Angolinian man, which he isn't. A minor cultural difference, Thee, along with everything else about him. Watch your manners," Dharmen said, with a raised eyebrow of support from Willem.

Theus whipped his head distractedly from the Lenan. "Huh?"

"Stop staring!" Willem hissed through smiling teeth.

Dharmen eyed the northerners with discretion that escaped his colleague. He wondered why the palest people from Tentim's coldest, snowiest rise wore such bold colors. On Negara, even their combat uniforms were gold-trimmed to varying degrees, and not to indicate rank. They instead denoted class distinctions that Dharmen was glad Angolin didn't have. He remembered the two Lenans in the forest . . . and before that thought could swirl to dark places, his traveling eyes met the last pair in the room he wanted to engage.

With sudden bright-eyed enthusiasm that outshone her outfit, Aremel came over, parting with the relieved-looking top silver but bringing the Lenans with her. Dharmen cringed. Escape was never an option with Aremel.

As the preeminent troika arrived and before their feet ceased movement, "Dharmen, *dear,* what a *magnificent* day this is for you, receiving such an honor for your courage and *outsstannnding* service to our great society! It's so *wonderful* to have you at Kleve Park this evening, and I *do* hope you know just how *happy* I am for you. *I'm just so simmmply . . .*"

He was glad that she looked at him for once and not over his shoulder in search of someone more important as she usually did. But her hyperextroverted harangue left him light-headed, with no idea of how to stop it, calm it, or jump in and steer it toward a true conversation. All he could do was smile and hope that she might come up for air soon.

"And by Lord Rior himself. Cousin, *you* are *truly blessed* to have such a *brave* man in your life!" she declared to Willem. "Though I *must* say, why we sent troops down to that *gods-awful*, horrid place *completely* escapes *me*. We Angolinians have our *own* matters to attend to. We should find proper use for you soldiers *at home* rather than have you tramping *uselessly* in the world without—*wouldn't you agree?*"

Her words were as florid as her outfit, and her opinions as provincial as Dharmen had come to expect from his people. Centuries of isolation had its effects. He caught himself backing a few paces away from it all, though he did finally manage a few responses through momentary fits of blindness from the glare of Aremel's ensemble, and that ridiculous thing on her head. Her gaudy adornments and the rock dangling from Lord Balaneth's neck made him hope there were no jewel thieves around.

"And my *dear, Dharmen*, I've *so* wanted you to be a part of my little social tonight, but since you've managed to keep to yourself for most of it, I thought I'd bring the guests to *you!*" Aremel introduced the ambassador who was nearly as animated, though in a much more formally measured fashion.

Dharmen extended a hand. Lord Balaneth took it haltingly and with the artificial smile Dharmen discovered to be common among Lenans. *Just as phobic of an honest handshake as to teamwork on the battlefield!* The younger man couldn't have been more aloof if he'd tried. Gallin, as he was called, washed him with a dark stare before looking away. Dharmen wondered where he had seen him—where in combat—because he had never met a Lenan outside of Negara before now.

The trio eventually (and thankfully) moved on.

"Aremel's a blast as always, but the general doesn't look too pleased tonight. Or he didn't before she released him anyway," Theus said, scattering Dharmen's musing.

"Eleven hundred of our people KIA on Negara, many of them by traitors. That's probably put a few things into his mind."

Theus snorted. "On that note, how on Tentim did Armetrian and his stooges get away with their story about being 'captured'? And do they really expect anyone to believe the Carmis had internal AI knowledge, enough to conveniently disable trace functions only? That's the worst alibi I ever heard."

"I have no idea, Thee. None." Dharmen shook his head. "You'd think seeing our people take out their own would open our general's eyes to reality, but after everything, they're still walking around base clinging to their new leader. That everyone with the same tale is connected to Armetrian ought to tell Gennet something."

"Right, but what did he say about what you overheard that night? You did tell him?"

"I did, and it didn't go well," Dharmen replied, ignoring Willem's annoyed look.

"He didn't say anything at all about Armetrian and the traitors? He must've had some opinion," Theus said.

"Not really. Our meeting was short. I told Gennet everything I saw and heard about Armetrian, the Lenans, the captives, the enemy—all of it." Dharmen sighed, flicked the front edges of his dress cloak over his shoulders, and folded his arms.

"And?"

"I asked him again about being shot at with our own weapons. 'Battle after battle taking particle hits—that was no friendly fire,' I said. 'The enemy has our armaments, likely handed to them by Armetrian himself.' I told him all I knew, and I don't think he took a word of it."

He lowered his voice; people were beginning to stare. Dori stood nearby with their friend, Doctor Yos Andren, and a colleague of his that Dharmen had met once before. Brona was her name if he remembered correctly. Both were university physicists and newly appointed members of Angolin's fledgling space commission. They waved.

Dharmen nodded quickly and continued: "All I could get from Gennet was that he and General Estes already knew about the weapons, but he wouldn't say more. I asked him point-blank what HC was going to do about it. He said the Kraal was aware of the situation and not to press further."

"*Aware of the situation*? That's it?" Theus said. "So what happened next?"

"Same thing that always happens next with me, Thee. I got angry. You know how I am. Runaround boils my blood—I'm no good at not pressing further. 'Our leaders have done everything possible to keep us hidden and keep our technology out of the wrong hands. Now look what's happened,' I told Gennet. 'The Carmis'll have every advantage we do, and soon. That's not what our ancestors wanted!' At that, he told me to check my attitude before I went too far. That was the end of it. Before I left, I asked if we could at least have another meeting. He said he'd grant it. That was two weeks ago. Where have we gotten in that time?"

"*You* got a promotion out of it," said Willem. "The general has faith in you from what I can tell."

"He promoted me to shut me up and to add another midlevel now that the Guard's scrounging up more recruits to make up for losses on Negara," Dharmen flatly replied. "Gennet needs managers. He isn't interested in my abilities or anything I told him by the look of it." He grunted, pushed his dark, wavy hair backward with one hand. "I'm standing here with a meaningless extra rank while Armetrian's out there plotting our lives away. I tell you, Angolin's in serious trouble, and not just from the Outside—"

A hand touched his shoulder. "That was a rousing speech," Yos beamed. "Beyond congratulations, how've you been? I haven't seen you since you left for combat. Still keeping things tidy at Seventh?"

The placid, carefree smile that Yos floated through life with was as present as ever, but beneath it, Dharmen detected a shadow he was unaccustomed to from the man. And he wished he had paid better attention before letting his emotions run his mouth. "It's a long story."

"We know. We heard it," Yos said with Dori standing purse-lipped beside him. "And none of it surprises me in the least."

Dharmen heard himself ask, "What do you mean?"

"Haven't you noticed a change in how people think around here, especially younger people?"

"It's been a while since any of us were in school, Yos. Enlighten us," said Dharmen.

"Surely you follow the NewsMesh. Students all over Angolin have been staging antigovernment protests for some time now. I've had long arguments with some of my own who say they intend to leave Angolin and live in the Outside World in spite of the law."

"That's been going on for ages," said Willem. "Your students can't seriously believe they'd do better in the East. The slave markets would snatch them up the minute they stepped a foot off this rise, if the Abyss didn't swallow them first. Anyone with sense knows that."

"Who said anything about sense?" Brona spoke up. "And why would anyone spread false, negative rumors about our government that can't be proven true?"

"Probably to use anyone who listens as foot soldiers for their purposes. Your students will fall into that trap easily," Dharmen replied.

Brona scrutinized him. "And they'll do it with military help, I'm sorry to tell you. I think some of your people are conspiring with our Protection and Defense Program staff."

Dharmen's eyelids lowered. "The agency responsible for Angolin's cloaking systems? I thought you were part of the Space Commission?"

"Oh no, that would be Yos," Brona said. "I've been approached, but one thing at a time for now. The university and PDP have me rushed as it is." She leaned into the group but kept eyes squarely on Dharmen. "Lately, several of my team scientists have been seen escorting Guard soldiers in and out of restricted areas."

"What's unusual about that? The Guard works very closely with government agencies," Dori broke in.

"Yes, but only in highly controlled capacities. Research, Development, and StealthOps areas are strictly off-limits to all but those with proper security clearance. No one else of any description should have access to them," said Brona. "In the past few weeks, several PDP data sets containing sensitive cloaking and TimeSpace information have been lifted, including some of my own. And I'm certain the files have found their way into enemy hands"—she looked around the group—"via the Angolin Guard."

"But how can you be sure it's all part of some plot to steal secrets and compromise Angolin's security?" Dori sounded irritated.

"I'm not. I have guesses, not answers, but I won't discount what I've seen, and from the look of things, neither should anyone in the

Guard." Brona looked to Dharmen again. "You, Yos, and I, we must talk. Soon."

Dharmen nodded. Brona's candor was refreshing, but the disclosure was anything but. He had assumed the plot went well beyond Armetrian and the Guard. Now it likely included those who controlled Angolin's defenses. The Cloak not only rendered most of the rise undetectable; its energy subbarriers also shielded it from attack. Any part of the grid lifted at the wrong moment . . .

"We'll definitely talk," Dharmen said, "and figure out what to do, and quickly."

The huddle quieted in stark contrast to the rest of the party. Dharmen watched Dori. She looked exasperated, and he knew why. News of a subject she still appeared to doubt was one thing, but parties were her chance to be a center of attention without need of rank for once. Brona had stolen that show.

"Isn't this a lively group!" Dori said and made steps to leave.

Willem cuffed her arm and smiled. "We'll get the good times going for you again, D, don't worry." He located Aremel and waved her over.

She complied, moving arm in arm with Lord Balaneth, who gave her an endearing but weary look. Gallin stayed put with his back to a pillar, surveying the room.

"It looks like Aremel has a new friend," Dori beamed, apparently regaining her festive spirit.

Dharmen exchanged a chilly stare with Gallin. "And the rest of us have a new enemy."

Dori eyed him quizzically, but he understood fully. He and the Lenan *had* met. Weeks ago, that night in the Negaran forest. He clenched his fists at the thought: Armetrian hadn't needed to bother with the party. Dawn Fire was there without him.

CHAPTER 3

NIRO WAY

Sir, when you are ready, we need to discuss treatment.

Treatment for what, Rem-E? Aggravation over these gods-damned traitors? That's about all I need help with right now.

For your Combat Stress Disorder, sir.

Come again?

Combat Stress Disorder, or *shell shock* as your ancestors called it. You have endured it for weeks now without improvement.

Probably because it's not really a problem.

Definitely because you are ignoring the problem, sir.

My problem right now is getting though this joke of an assignment— that and stopping Dawn Fire. Think you can help me there?

❂

"SHIPMAN VINC," SNAPPED A VOICE from across the gunship deck. "Shipman Vinc! Irzek!"

"S-sir!"

"You're thinking out loud again. The ride's not that bad. Stop whining and shut up!" Sublieutenant Ciros ordered.

Snickers filled the cabin as though no one else's nerves complained about the turbulence.

Dharmen ignored his own. "Sublieutenant, copy that one for yourself. Same for the rest of you. That's an order!"

Everyone quieted but Ciros. He complied about two seconds late and with a quick, roasting glare. An instant adversary from day one and another seedling in the traitors' lot. Dharmen had felt it the moment the sublieutenant stepped foot on base and immediately gravitated to Armetrian's brood. But this was his command, and Ciros had better realize it.

As for SR Vinc—awkward, bumbling, and perpetually on edge— Dharmen knew he wouldn't handle this assignment any better than he'd handled the advanced post on Negara. His twin sister, Leatra, was a nonissue, but wherever Irzek went, calamity great, small, or just plain annoying followed.

Please don't turn an already crap posting into a disaster before it can even begin, kid. We can't afford it, Dharmen thought. He looked out the viewport for a mind refresh even if there was nothing to see. The ship had just left clear purple sky for choppy plumes of brown haze: toxic but natural cover allowing for TS conservation. Bemin Spaceport, their destination, was in the upper troposphere, level with the Angolinian Rise. It was Dharmen's second time over. They would land soon, but he wished the trip would take longer. Hours would do! He pictured the world beyond the viewport's transparent metal.

Tentim was a bizarre planet: a gas dwarf of sorts with rocky, carbon-nemurite landmasses jutting high into a band of breathable nitrogen and oxygen. Dharmen recalled wide-eyed schoolteachers describing the world as a spiny ball akin to a pincushion, with Angolin perched atop one of the pinheads, thousands of meters above Abyssal Sea level. Lena, Carmogen, Kay Allendë—all of the planet's population centers sat on other "continental" rises; some larger, some smaller, many long and narrow like Angolin's—the result of millions of years of brethyl-methane erosion leaving high, rocky quills and a small but intense gravity core.

Childhood instructors could salivate about the Outside World all they wanted. What did they know? Not one of them had ever left home to experience any of it. Dharmen had crossed the Abyss and fought above it more than once, but there was no time for combat memories or old science lessons now. The assignment that no amount of daydreaming would call off was about to begin. But why had he been chosen for *this*?

Gennet promoted me and sent me as far from Seventh as he possibly could. Fine! Exile one complaining officer to Angolin's farthest end if that's your tactic, traitor. Dharmen's thoughts swirled with the dark, billowing gas clouds holding his attention. *But I'm not going without a fight.*

"Our CO doesn't seem afraid of any of this, maybe I should get over it too." Irzek's fright from the turbulence had found his tongue again. "I just hope I'm not assigned to this duty permanently."

"For both our sakes, brother, I hope not too. We need the quiet." Leatra's tone was harmless, but it didn't stop Ciros and the others from laughing.

Krone, did I not order mouths shut? Dharmen wondered how brutal he could make his reprisal—

"Why did Tate of all people get this post?" came the question, hushed. "He's the last person Gennet should have picked. How does he get to be chief when others—"

"Narond, you know our new CO has special talents. Maybe he's been showing them to the general." Ciros hadn't bothered to whisper.

Dharmen seethed. Insults about his sexuality had been rare in his career and usually by accident rather than intent. Ciros was obviously different there, and the seed had sprouted close to the tree, considering the mentor. *But good information—nice to know who and what I'm dealing with,* came a more calming thought. *If only the little shit would open his mouth enough to expose his link to Dawn Fire. All in good time.* "Don't hear well, Sublieutenant?"

"Sir. I . . . apologize."

"Disobey me again," Dharmen said, "and *I'll* have to apologize!"

The hull shuddered, ending all chatter beyond Irzek's swearing. Faint shadows passed upward through the cabin. The ship had entered the cloaking grid's outer layer, with defensive undershielding lowered for arrival. There was no visible shimmer or distortion. Dharmen marveled at the spaceport's stealthtech: a dark matter cloak far more advanced than mainland Angolin's gargantuan stealth system.

As Yos had explained it, dark matter was invisible and disruptive to normal matter. But on Tentim, it bonded with a native particle substance little understood even by the ancients, but harnessable in its altered form. It was used to permeate all matter, living and nonliving, on the small island rise below.

Up in Angolin, EM spectral deflection, nanotechnology, false image projection, metamaterials, and only PDP knew what else concealed natural and built environments. But here, inundated in dark matter nothing existed for all intents and purposes, including people. It made Dharmen feel queasy. He didn't like being "permeated" any more than he liked Yos's vacant-smile description of it.

He ordered all hands to activate synth lenses. Nothing and no one here would be visible otherwise. The shadows retreated to reveal clear sky above and a scene below as incredible as it had been on his first briefing trip.

Sprawled as far as the eye could see was an array of compounds and facilities larger than anything he'd ever seen beyond the Angolin Centrum or the factories in the industrial far north. Buildings raced beneath: hangars and maintenance bays, storehouses, research centers, and control towers standing like glass needles before landing berths housing newly built spacecraft. Impossibly slender service gantries spanned great distances over parked vessels. Maintenance synths hovered around them, shuttling materiel and performing repairs—white-hot sparks illumined their labors. Approaching ground revealed legions of hurrying uniforms. Port personnel coursed through the complex like insect hordes during a second-spring swarm.

A hush greater than the Abyssal murk blanketed the gunship. Even Ciros and company were quieted. Youthful assumption plus one lengthy campaign on Negara were no substitute for the reality below: they were still in Angolinian territory, but far from its familiar mainland environs. The Hidden Realm was full of surprises, even for its own inhabitants.

The retros fired right before that palpable thud signaling flight's end, and the ability to escape airborne imprisonment for firm ground. The spaceport-and-chief installation of Angolin's space program was ready to receive them: thirty raw recruits and a handful of petties and juniors rounded up for a tour of the isolated island rise facility, with little about their assignment communicated even to their freshly promoted leader. Dharmen wanted to be anywhere but here, wanted to get to the bottom of the conspiracy and not waste time with this distraction. *But until then,* he grudged, *it'll be an honor to do . . . whatever it is we're here for.*

The deployment hatch desynthed. Dharmen rose and took the center of the broad opening with full military bearing: posture upright, arms at his sides, uniform neatly ordered and flawlessly fitted. His 1.8-meter frame didn't make him tall by Guard standards, but his broad build, hard-as-nemurite demeanor, and probing black eyes beneath his father's shadowy brows rendered him formidable in spite of it. "On your feet!"

Camos shot up from seats and stood at attention with far more ado than acceptable. Dharmen ordered them out to the tarmac. After a blistering rebuke on their poor formation, he introduced his people to the waiting port security administrator and gave what information he could on what to expect during their facility tour. And wished he *had* solid information to give.

"As you've probably noticed," he bellowed, "this is quite an installation. It's huge, to say the least, and in some areas, very strange. You'll see things you're not used to, and more often, *you won't*. So keep an open mind, and if we're placed here indefinitely, keep it confined to your . . . What was that, Sublieutenant? I didn't hear you!" He stepped fast, stopping just centimeters from Ciros's face.

"It was nothing, sir," the other said, startled but still managing a smirk that Dharmen would've loved to have put professionalism aside to rip from his face.

"Nothing? You opened your mouth and wooords came out, soldier! Even after ordered twice now to keep quiet. Since you're so determined to talk, let's hear it. Now!"

"All I said, sir, was that this place isn't the only thing—"

"The only thing strange. Yes, I heard that bit, but I want everyone else to hear it too. You don't approve of your assignment, I take it. Tell us, what else don't you approve of?"

Ciros's smirk evaporated.

"What else!"

"You, sir. You haven't told us what this posting is about or how you got it over Lieutenant Commander Armetrian. He works hard. Bemin should've been assigned to him." His voice cracked. Exposure was his weakness; Dharmen was glad to discover that.

"He does work hard, in ways you couldn't imagine, Sublieutenant. *Or maybe you could.*" Dharmen burrowed eyes savagely into him. "And no, I haven't told you exactly what the assignment is. Last time I checked, I wasn't required to tell my subordinates anything I didn't see fit to. Understand that, soldier?"

"Sir! Yes, sir!"

Dharmen moved in front of the rest of the company. "And I'll inform all of you further after my superior informs me. Plain, simple direction isn't a luxury always given in the Guard. We deploy with our orders and do as we're told, we're not asked to like it. Am I clear?" he yelled.

In unison and correctly for the first time since he took command, the entire company responded affirmatively.

"Excellent! And while I'm on the subject of following orders—"

A shockwave rumbled beneath his feet. Falling metallic debris pinged in the distance. Port personnel hurried past the company toward the explosion. Dharmen had no time to contemplate. He ordered everyone to follow and assist—and to stay alert.

They arrived at a small, one-story structure with a single broad door. The bunker-like building stood beside what had likely been its twin, completely leveled by the blast. Black smoke poured from the chasm and from flaming material strewn across the ground. The intact structure appeared harmless, but no one was willing to risk venturing inside.

"Everyone keep back!" Dharmen ordered. He turned to a port maintenance attendant dressed in coveralls. "What is this, exactly?"

"It *was* the entrance to the primary power exchange underground, the control center for this quadrant's power grid." He pointed a shaking finger at the intact bunker, panic filling his eyes at the smoke seeping from the doorframe. "That one leads to the backup exchange."

"The security administrator came this way before the blast. Do you know where he is?" Dharmen asked.

"Last I saw of him, he'd gone down into the backup to—"

"Down in there?"

The other nodded furiously. He and Dharmen tried to contact the administrator. No response, and Rem-E couldn't locate him. Dharmen ordered his people to a safer distance.

Just as one of them ran heedless toward the bunker door.

"I said back, Shipman!"

"But sir, can't you hear him screaming? Somebody has to do something," Irzek said. And before Dharmen could stop him, he bolted for the door and accessed its control panel. It slid open.

Dharmen saw only the recruit's silhouette when the bright yellow oxygen-seeking flames billowed out at him. The surge sent Irzek stumbling backward. He fell to the ground, gripping his face. Dharmen and Leatra rushed in and pulled him away before he could be engulfed in the fire.

"What have I repeatedly told you about obeying orders, Vinc, especially in an emergency?" Dharmen barked.

Irzek moaned and coughed. "Sir, I was only trying to—"

"Quiet! Getting us shot out of our post on Negara wasn't enough. You want to get killed here too?"

A harshly berated child could not have clamped shut faster. Irzek pulled his hand from his badly burned skin, yelping in agony.

"Stay calm, Shipman. We'll get you to the infirmary, stat. Port's medical facilities are some of the best. This is treatable no matter how bad it looks." Dharmen forcibly removed the anger from his voice, though roughness aside, Irzek was a soldier, and the kid needed to realize it sooner rather than later.

He left Irzek to his sister and a port staffer to see him safely away. He looked around, eyes narrowed. "This is definitely no accident, someone's—" He saw them, a short distance away: two small craft rising rapidly above Port. He'd been in enough troop transports and seen enough takeoffs to know these pilots were in a hurry. Their liftoff speeds were far faster than tolerable and their ascent much too steep.

One ship disappeared for a split second, and reappeared far above its initial position. *TimeSpace!* Dharmen realized as both vessels shot into the sky and out of sight, apparently without the cloak's undershield raised to stop them. He located a port security officer. "Do you have landing berths over there? I don't recall any from specs."

"Negative," the woman replied.

"Then where did those ships just leave from?"

Her eyes flitted between him and the point where the sky swallowed the vessels. "I'm not sure, unless they took off from—"

"From a rooftop," he finished for her, "on a weapons store just before activating TS!"

Emergency crews in protective suits and helmets appeared in force, armed with portable deoxygenators to douse the power exchange entrance's flames and extract the security administrator's body. Dharmen had no time to think about that. Via his internal, he summoned Guard reinforcements from the mainland to augment Port's pursuit vessels. Whoever was on those fleeing ships couldn't be allowed to escape.

IRZEK'S TEETH CHATTERED AS HE walked the South Centrum's wet ways. His bare hands were shoved into his pockets, and his shoulders hunched nearly up to his ears. The rain had stopped, and the fog had retreated beneath a damp, frigid first winter night, bathed in the faint silver light of Tentim's outer moons.

Young couples passed him, absorbed in each other and seemingly oblivious to the weather. He watched the mood pavers glow in peaceful shades beneath their passing feet. The hues beneath his were more anxious. He was far from content, which the whimsical sidewalks announced.

Irzek pulled out his hands and blew into them, thinking of the elderly woman who had stopped him minutes before to inquire about his facial biopress and lack of gloves.

"I have gloves," he had replied.

"Where are they, then?" she had pressed.

"Um . . . in my bag."

"Oh," she had said with raised eyebrows and pursed lips, "they'll be very warm there!"

He snorted. *Why does everybody, even strangers, pick at me? I already have* three *parents: an uptight mother, grumpy father, and increasingly nosy sister. Who needs more than that?* Frustration quickened his pace. "Meddling old *meler*, two teats short of a . . ." He stopped muttering. Comparing the woman to a bovine kept him no warmer than sounding like his father complaining about his livestock, the *grochlaroot* harvest, unwanted relations visiting from distant farms, and whatever else occupied the old man's bother stream on any given day.

He refocused so hard on reaching the rendezvous point that his feet found every cold puddle along the way. Images of the spaceport bunker, that taroc's ass Ciros, and the whole Bemin incident flashed through his mind like a mad synth circus. Even after four days, he could no more dodge the montage of events than escape the damp chill frosting his breath, drenching his hatless head, and seeping through his flimsy, unheated jacket to find his thin bones.

And what does Ciros have against Lieutenant Commander Tate? He's not such a bad CO to work under, he thought as he wiped rainwater from his face. The sky had cleared, but overhead traffic continued to spray him. "He's deadlier than the Abyss if you make him angry. Even Lord Krone must notice. But he's always been fair to me and my sister. Well, mostly my sister."

A passing woman eyed him curiously.

He was talking to himself again. Something more penetrating than the dropping temperature gnawed at him: he had been yelled at in front of everyone when he thought he was helping, and insulted by Ciros beginning to end. He appreciated neither. *Is this what military service and honor are about?* he thought. *A man's life needed saving. Doesn't my superior get that? Doesn't anybody?* He wondered how he had become Seventh's punching synth in less than a year's enlistment.

He scanned the way as he walked, taking in the mix of stately pod house clusters sprinkled among some of Angolin's tallest towers. It was a fascinating neighborhood. He usually liked these walks. He liked anything that let him escape the Westermeer's farmlands and, lately, Seventh. But tonight was different. Second autumn's ubiquitous flowers had shriveled on the trees, and once-fiery leaves, now morbid dark purple, hung limply in the cold, wet wind. No warmth, no color, no energy, nothing. Just dark limbs creaking in the dampness to make him feel as empty on the outside as he did within, alone in a place that was small and shrouded, but right now felt too big for him.

Even his sister was changing. Since the day they enlisted together, they seemed further and further apart to him. Leatra was doing well in the Guard. Irzek wasn't, and he could feel it even if he couldn't admit it. To make things worse, she was becoming inquisitive, and at times, critical of his every move. She had asked him where he was off to on such a miserable night.

"Nowhere," he had told her. "And what's it to you, anyway?"

"Don't lie, Irz. You're going someplace," Leatra had insisted. "Someplace you shouldn't be. We've grown up with the same face and nearly the same mind. You think I don't know you by now?"

He looked down at his soaked shoes, wishing his sister would live her new, near-adult life on her own and stay out of his. And everybody else, too, for that matter. He crossed a canal, passed beneath a broad metal arch between two enormous, beam-stabilized megatall towers, and reached the appointed intersection. He looked up at the holographic way signs: "Ursula" and "Niro," they glowed. He waited, shivering more now that he was standing still. He hopped up and down in place—Thaeg, Lord of Winters, was busy tonight!

He peered down Niro Way for some sign of his friend. It seemed dimmer than normal, and not from the night's lifelessness or the micro season. Darkness enveloped the street in a way that public lighting seemingly couldn't penetrate. Dull, nondescript houses lined both sides. They were definitely pod types; he could see the interlock clamps and antigrav propulsors at their bases. But they were separated, arranged not in clusters of a few to a few hundred like the rest of the neighborhood's residences, but oddly side by side behind untended, immotile bushes.

Beneath their anciently styled bell and step-gabled rooflines, they revealed nothing to the Outside World. Most of South C's buildings stood in resplendent pride as if declaring their right to exist on their prominent avenues. These hid in plain sight. He stood staring. He had been through here often. How had he not noticed them before?

"Where is he?" Irzek and Kerbentha Duraan had grown up together, and it was great to still have a friend outside the Guard. But he was always late, and it didn't help that he'd made the evening sound so mysterious.

"Adventures better than anything the Hidden Realm can give are coming," Kerbentha had said.

Irzek wondered who put such grand talk into his silly, idle mouth.

A blazing red glow approached beneath a trio of shady-looking young males. Kerbentha's yearlong growth spurt gave the only indication of who they were. "Ho, Irzek!" he called from between the other two.

One hushed him and muttered something about keeping a low profile, too loudly for his own request.

Irzek's stomach sank. Kerbi did say they might come, but he had hoped to Krone not. *Damn!* "Ciros, Narond," he greeted civilly.

"I'm still *Sublieutenant* to you," Ciros said. "Tate tried to bust me back to ensign, but he couldn't get authorization for it. He said I insulted him and challenged his authority on Bemin. Damned faggot has no sense of humor."

Irzek blinked. "Damned what? What's a—"

"Nothing, Vinc. Forget it. Just an ancient term I picked up from Lieutenant Commander Armetrian," Ciros replied. "So you're here after all. I s'pose that's good. Didn't think you had it in you."

"We just came from a rally in the Falconerplein!" Kerbentha excitedly interrupted. "A big one. It filled half the square. It's the very first in a whole series they have planned and . . . Irz, what happened to your face?"

"They? Who's they?" Irzek asked.

"Students for a New Angolin, that's who. And they've got some great ideas," Narond said. "The government's kept us holed up here for centuries, but no more. We're going out there to experience the real world and turn this place upside down if the Kraal interferes."

Irzek's heart raced. "Sounds like some kind of anarchy movement." *And not what Kerbi alluded to at all.* He backed away from the whiff of stale sweat coming from the three of them.

"If it has to be," said Narond. "And don't look at us like we're crazy, Vinc. Those old has-beens have run our lives long enough. It's time we controlled our own destiny. Krone knows we're young and more than ready for it."

"And gain the power that's rightfully ours," Ciros added.

"I thought this was about ending isolation," Irzek said. "You planning to overthrow the government, too, Sublieutenant?"

"Only if Parliament stands in our way, in which case the Guard can settle things," Ciros said. "There's already plenty of support through the ranks, and more will come with so many students behind us."

Irzek felt his face flush, even in the cold. "But that's treason. That's not what I signed up for."

"It's not treason, you idiot," Ciros spat. "It's money. It's status. It's leadership change, or it will be if we don't get what we demand. We three intend to be part of it. You'll make four if you know what's good for you."

"There's nothing to worry about, Irz. This is for everyone's benefit," Kerbentha half-assured. "Angolin should be part of the world, not hide from it. Don't you think?"

"No, Kerbi, I don't think. Not like this. And you know why we hide from it. It's evil. My father says he's heard—"

"Your father's never left this rise and neither has mine, Vinc," Ciros said. "And if he did hear about the Outside World, who told him? His melers? Do they moo these things in his ear while he milks them? Our parents don't know a thing, and they ought to spend more time freeing Angolin and less time talking up nothing. They never will, so it's up to us."

Irzek couldn't find a rebuttal. Venom aside, Ciros had a point. The four of them stood in silence, waiting uncomfortably for who knew what.

"So when's he coming?" Narond asked. "It's brutal out here. Hard to believe Angolin is surrounded by boiling gases when it's this cold. And where's all that Carmogen pollution that's supposed to rip holes in the ozone layer and fry the planet? I could use some of that right about now."

"Buck up and find some patience, soldier," said Ciros.

"*He* who? Who are we waiting for?" Irzek demanded. "I thought it was only going to be us four."

"You'll be disappointed then. We're meeting our fifth," Ciros replied. "He'll come past. We'll follow. Simple."

"F-follow him to where?" said Irzek.

"If you're this scared of everything, Vinc, why even bother to show up?" said Ciros. "You should have stayed back on base with your equally mouthy sister."

"Leave her out of this." Irzek didn't like where this was going, especially with Ciros and Narond in whatever it was. And the fresh raindrops weren't helping. "We've been here a while now. Are you sure he's coming? It's week's end, let's go to the gamers' centers up in Mid Realm. The AirTransit terminal is up the next way." He looked to Kerbentha. "Wouldn't that be better than standing here getting wet?"

"I'm bored with all that. Who needs SynthWorld games when reality's about to give us so much more?" Ciros said past Irzek to the others.

"You two heard everything in the Falconerplein tonight. Do you want to have at it or keep wasting your youth on kid games?"

"I have a better idea!" Kerbentha beamed. "Forget fantasy worlds. Let's go to East Vales for something *truly* real, if you know what I mean."

"I'll go for that," Irzek chimed in.

Ciros gave them a vacant look.

"Oh, come oooon!" Irzek said. "Every man in the Guard's been to the brothels. It's all I've heard about since I enlisted. Now it's my turn. We'd just have to keep General Gennet and Lieutenant Commander Tate from finding out."

"Kerbi's too young," said Ciros.

"I'm seventeen. I could pass for eighteen easily," Kerbentha protested.

"*You* could, but your ID nano couldn't," Narond said. "We'd be detained the minute we stepped off the transport, and that the general would find out, not that he's all that apt."

"What's that supposed to mean? Our general is one of the Guard's best leaders. He commands an order," Irzek said.

"And his latest command decision was to hand Bemin to Tate?" Ciros countered. "Look what happened over there. The best assignment we could've hoped for, and he bollixed it for us."

"The station was saboed, probably from inside, Sublieutenant. It wasn't our CO's fault. He's a good leader," Irzek said.

"Really, Vinc? You up in his ass just like that?" Narond said with the tenderness of a razor-tooth high-mountain *borbol*. "And who other than our man-loving CO said anything about sabotage? It's a new spaceport with a lot going on. Anything can happen."

"And in case you've forgotten, we're meeting someone here," Ciros said. "He'll have more than games and prostitutes for us, I promise you that!" He added Kerbentha to his peruse. "And the East Vales wouldn't do you two any good, anyway. Scrawny farm boy twigs with no money—what woman would have either of you? Though maybe Tate would be willing if you are."

"Willing for what, Sublieutenant. What are you saying, exactly?" Irzek asked, annoyed.

"I'm saying people like him don't belong in the Guard or anywhere else in decent society, period," Ciros came back.

"That one come from Lieutenant Commander Armetrian too, or did you conjure it up all on your own?" Irzek said.

"You're lucky we're on week's end leave, Shipman. I could put you on report easily."

"And add yourself to it for treason, sir."

Ciros glared heat. "Armetrian says Tate's lifestyle is depraved and not the way of the rest of the world. I think we ought to listen to him."

"If Armetrian told you jumping off the fjord line into the Abyss was the way of the world, would you take him up on that?" Irzek shot back. *Please do us a favor and say yes!*

"If it was the key to my future and everyone else's, I just might! You'd do well to follow," said Ciros. "And as for Tate, I don't need anyone else's reasons to hate him. All he ever does is get in everyone's way—him and that stale old soldier honor of his. We're headed for a real life in a world ripe for the taking, and he'll do anything to keep us from it. Well, what's coming is coming, and if he tries to interfere—"

Kerbentha jabbed Ciros on the shoulder and pointed his thumb at a passing figure: a man wearing a heavy gray cloak. Its broad hood was pulled over his head. He walked up Niro Way, slowed, turned his head slightly, and gestured as if to say, *What are you all waiting for?* He went up to a darkened house, stopped at the door. It opened silently without his having to ring. He disappeared across its barely lit threshold.

Stiffening legs carried Irzek alongside the others. He wanted to turn back, but he didn't want to appear a coward. He'd had his fill of that. And deep within, desire for something new and exciting took him so covertly that he didn't perceive that his cold feet had suddenly warmed. He wanted answers, wanted to know more about the life the others insisted they all deserved. And well, Kerbi didn't seem scared, so why should he be?

They followed the stranger into the house. The door shut behind them—an old manual wooden door on hinges, not an automatic. Little was visible in the small foyer beyond bare pockmarked walls illuminated from above by a dim, spherical, floating light bot. A man, a different one, stood beneath it. Only the top of his head and shoulders, and a faint glow in his eyes, were fully visible.

"Greetings." His tone said, *I'd rather have anyone in but you lot.* "Into the sitting room, please."

Irzek's stomach reknotted. He thought he would have lost his dinner, if he'd had any. The group filed in tentatively as if entering some dark, unknown cave in a remote corner of Angolin, instead of a harmless urban live-in. The floor softened slightly beneath Irzek's feet. An area rug filled the middle of the room, strangely patterned and a bit threadbare in places. The room was otherwise sparsely decorated with what was probably not real furniture. Little appeared to be permanent. Synth furnishings were popular in Angolin, but their use here inferred temporary living over mode. The small room's mustiness suggested likewise—not an unclean odor as much as a barely lived-in one.

Irzek looked over, found the hooded man from outside standing in a corner by a curtain-drawn window. The aura around him, if it could be considered such, was as off-putting as his companion's. "A little more light, my friend. We don't have your eye for darkness," the covered man said. The host commanded the bot to increase output. The man in the corner withdrew his hood.

Irzek's mouth opened.

"Lieutenant Commander!" Narond gasped in his place and jumped to attention.

Irzek fumbled a salute but said nothing. He had seen enough of the man on base, but they had never properly met beyond the other's scolds and insults.

The Terror of Seventh, as new recruits called him, looked to Ciros, who wore a darkly satisfied smile. Armetrian was expected.

The raised light level unveiled the host. Luminous yellow-green eyes stared out from a face of thin white fur. Irzek frowned. *What in the blazing suns is a Lenan doing here and working with—*

"Evening, everyone," Armetrian greeted. "I see you had no trouble getting here. I just hope you didn't arouse suspicion. You were loud enough out there for the whole way to notice." He looked to the Lenan. "This is my associate, Gallin. He's done a fine job at maintaining a discreet presence here. We want to keep it that way, so be more careful in the future. At ease, Shipman Vinc. I won't bite if you don't make me."

Irzek's eyes flickered. His anxiety practically displaced the room's dusty odors; even he felt it. Something was up. Armetrian wasn't his usual self tonight. He was *smiling*.

"I heard about what happened on Bemin, Vinc," he said. "That was a bold move on your part."

Irzek's vocal cords broke free of their bondage. "Sir, I know I disobeyed orders, but I didn't mean to! Lieutenant Commander Tate—"

"Forget him," said Armetrian. "Poor excuse of an officer. Can't even recognize true bravery when he sees it. You tried to save a life. You acted selflessly and showed no fear. That's what's important. Our task needs someone with that level of honor."

"Vinc doesn't want honor. He wants whores," Ciros said. "He tried to get out of this meeting by suggesting we go *Up East*."

"Want women, eh, Vinc?" said Armetrian. "Of course, why not? Other than Tate's kind, who wouldn't?" He sat on the low sofa, beckoning the others to find seats also. He leaned forward with his hands clasped and elbows on his knees toward Irzek and Kerbentha. "And I can make that happen for you: beautiful ones, not the hags you find over in Nieuw Kered. But their services aren't free and neither are mine. You two will have to prove your worth first. Join me. Follow my example, and you'll be set for life, in and out of Angolin."

Kerbentha was practically drooling. Irzek was more cautiously intrigued. "You said there was a task, sir."

Armetrian raised his eyebrows. "The goal is liberation. The task is achieving it. My colleague and I intend to ensure that we can all leave this tiny nation someday and gain our share of the Outside World. That requires work."

The Lenan stood quiet and motionless as Armetrian nodded to him. He contributed nothing beyond an unreadable stare.

"You wouldn't believe the wealth available to men like us on the Outside, and especially with military power to back us up. The student movement is just the start. With Dawn Fire at the forefront, there are no limits." The flame in Armetrian's eyes softened Irzek and rendered Kerbentha barely able to sit still.

"What would we have to do?" the teenager asked.

"Keep your minds open to every possibility," Armetrian replied. "And be ready to follow my commands. Stick by me, and we'll all benefit, not just us but all of Angolin."

"What about those who stand in our way?" asked Ciros. "Not everyone's on board. Tate's been against us from the beginning."

"Everyone will come over to our side sooner or later. And you four will become instrumental in that, don't worry. As for Tate . . ." Armetrian lost his amiable facade and reverted to the salty officer everyone was used to. "Ah, Negara. Negara! Nearly twice in one night—the man's got too many lives. But we'll fix that soon enough."

"Sir?" Irzek asked.

"Tate knows too much, Shipman, and he's as stubborn as he is interfering. But what he doesn't know is when to quit," said Armetrian. "He'll have to be dealt with when he gets in our way. Because I know he will."

THE FOUR YOUNG GUARDSMEN LEFT the house with more encouragement from their new leader, and a deigned Lenan goodbye. Back at the corner, they picked up nearly where they had left off. Kerbentha could barely contain himself over the student movement, and he was so eager to work for Armetrian that he even suggested enlisting. "I hear you boys are recruiting. That would get me some quick experience! I'm as brave as anyone. Maybe I could become a soldier and join you three."

"Maybe not!" said Ciros.

Narond was nearly as animated, but Irzek was subdued. He didn't know how to take it all. He had spent his youth dreaming of far-off greatness. Now it was promised to him. But would he really have to work with Ciros and Narond to achieve it? And under Armetrian too? And what about his duty? He was a Guardsman, and he had sworn an oath to protect Angolin and uphold its laws. What would happen to that now?

Caught between what was right and what he wanted, he abruptly left the others and hurried up Ursula Way, ignoring Kerbentha's loudly reiterated plea for East Vale pleasures. He left in as thick a mental fog as the one he had arrived in, and just as cold. He looked back, saw Ciros headed in the opposite direction. His steps were too purposeful, even for excitement over revolution. And carrying him in the wrong direction, off alone to the brothels.

CHAPTER 4

THE GENERAL'S OFFICE

Are you afraid he won't pass muster, General?

A blasting on Negara and sabotage at Port his first day in command there? Not exactly confidence inspiring.

But I understood he was doing well, sir. Outstanding performance in combat operations and a promotion, followed by his own command and prompt action in an emergency situation. I fail to comprehend your concern over his abilities.

His abilities aren't the issue, Chlö-GE, it's him *that I'm concerned about. And I'm fully entitled to that. Officer or not, he's the only son I have.*

❂

"VINC, WATCH YOUR PARRYING. ANALYZE your opponent's actions and counter," Dharmen ordered as he moved between dueling student pairs. "And remember to move and use your whole body. You're not a stationary robot, don't just stand there battling in place!"

Irzek *was* watching his parrying. His blocking. His whatever. It was the third time that morning he'd been told about his damned parrying, what other choice did he have? His sparring partner was doing just fine. So was the rest of the class beyond stray criticisms, but each time "Vinc" was called, he knew it meant him rather than his sister. Across the gym, Leatra handled her synth sword effortlessly.

When the Vinc twins enlisted, most of their village, including their parents, said learning the ancient combat methods would separate them from the crowd and help turn their service into lasting military careers. And having two Ergyres—instructors of the ancient Ergive battle arts—right on base was an unheard-of opportunity. "And it beats farm work, anyway," was Kerbi's input. "Unless you'd rather spend your lives milking melers and putting up with your father!"

Two months later, Leatra was at the top of the class. Likewise at Bemin. Irzek was another story, and right now, his increasingly impatient Ergive instructor and new CO wasn't helping.

"It's lunge, parry, retreat on your hind leg, Vinc, not the other way round," Dharmen said on his next walk by. "When you advance, advance properly. Don't back away scared and then rush up to your opponent with no attack plan. That's not sword fighting!"

I did lunge first. Or maybe I didn't! Irzek's head spun. Yet another fog filled with the Niro house meeting drifted over his already limited attention span. Everything that he and Dawn Fire wanted, Tate was working against.

And if only he could concentrate on this and sword handling at once—his opponent countered his every move, if they could be called moves. He couldn't get a single opening. Every feeble effort got him a level-four hit in return, not fatal but still unacceptable in this stage of training as Tate constantly reminded him. He had already taken hits to the left shoulder and both arms. In a real battle with real swords, he'd be limbless now, but this gave his attention no fuel.

Lieutenant Commander Armetrian was right, he thought through his multitask of battling his opponent and himself. *I did show courage. Why should I have to prove that to anybody?*

He felt a mild pushback. His opponent's synth blade passed right through him. His eyes widened at the sight of the simulated cross-guard traveling from the back of the other's blade right up to his chest. He looked down at his opponent's hand across the grip. He shouldn't have. He shouldn't have been close enough to allow a complete ram-through to begin with. He cut an eye across the gym. Every hit, especially life-threatening registers, were recorded by the instructor's internal.

And pacing the gym floor with his floating personal upright of student icons in tow, Dharmen stopped, frowned, and came over immediately: "Through the left lung, centimeters from the heart—near fatal, Vinc. Keep your guard up and focus on your opponent like I've told you."

"But—"

"No buts, Shipman. Focus!" As quickly and hotly as they came, Dharmen-and-upright left to observe the rest of the class.

Irzek *had* focused: on the Bemin incident, on the Niro house, on coming into his own soon, as Lieutenant Commander Armetrian promised. A new life awaited him . . . and he wouldn't get it with a sword. *Who needs this outdated training anyway,* he thought, staring over at Dharmen. The disapproving look he got back was intended to return his attention to his opponent, where it belonged. He didn't take that meaning. His thoughts were in a new place now, and as dark as Gallin's house. He ignored his opponent and studied the synth sword in his trembling hand, feeling its simulated weight and glancing back to his instructor . . . right before getting another ram-through.

DHARMEN STOOD OUTSIDE GENERAL GENNET'S office, waiting to be admitted and going over what he wanted to say. He had never met with any officer so senior in his career, but that didn't unnerve him at all. *Can Gennet be trusted? Am I wasting my time on a traitor who already knows everything I want to tell him?* Those thoughts hadn't left his head since he adjourned class. An intercom signal sounded followed by an all-base announcement . . . and he shut his eyes rather than listen, trying to control his sudden quaking. It didn't occur often, but when it did, the faintest ping sent tremors through him. He would be fine one minute, but then suddenly, the simplest sounds triggered his CSD.

Rem-E, it's happening again.

"Yes, sir, I am working on it."

Can you work on it a little faster?

"I can on one condition."

Which is?

"That you stop resisting my efforts and meet me halfway, as you humans say. Calm yourself and relax."

All right, Rem-E, you win.

The door slid open. "Enter!" came the order from within.

Dharmen flinched. He opened his eyes and straightened his posture as he stepped in and stopped just across the threshold as required. He saluted, opened his mouth to address his superior, but the scene before him took his words.

The room buzzed with automation. Images and diagrams flashed through every wall, window, and table surface. Instruments trilled and hummed endlessly. He grunted, not anticipating all the noise. At the room's opposite end floated the general's desktop with icon arrays and open data windows spread across its surface, and still more on personal uprights. A holo of the Bemini Rise oscillated above. It held Gennet's complete attention, bathing him in undulating light.

Dharmen was quietly amazed. He had finally been granted a proper meeting with the general instead of a hurried talk in a corridor, but he hadn't expected to find a mini command center in place of a standard military office suite. "Reporting as ordered, sir."

Gennet deactivated the holo and dismissed two hovering assistant bots. "Come forward, Lieutenant Commander."

Dharmen rolled eyes at the mechanical annoyances as they whizzed past him and out the closing door. He deemed his internal irreplaceable. Robots were better out of sight. He moved into the center of the room and stood firm, hands clasped behind his back.

"At ease," Gennet ordered. "And let me get right to it. I received word this morning that two cargo sloops were found on a small rise a hundred klicks east of Bemin. They're the same two ships that fled Port the day your company arrived. There was no damage to the vessels but no sign of life either. Our saboteurs escaped, and hastily."

Dharmen held his surprise at the news and at how openly it was given.

"They left behind their entire plunder: particle cannons, pulse torpedoes, ship-mounted shield emitters," Gennet continued. "No signs of handheld or light weapons of any kind. It was all heavy ordnance and equipment housed on Bemin for deep space travel." He turned one of his hovering uprights to Dharmen. "With skill and a lot of improvising, these armaments could easily have been retrofitted for atmospheric and land-based use."

Dharmen scrolled through the manifest. "These weapons could've taken down every ship the Guard has, even with shields at maximum strength. And even cloak undershields could've been breached, Bemin's as well as Angolin's."

"Most definitely. But though our thieves got away, at least their cargo didn't, and now"—Gennet's eyebrows lifted—"now we have the proof of smuggling that we desperately needed."

"Sir?"

"I couldn't approach HC with suspicions alone. I needed solid evidence. Sabo of our largest port installation and stolen ships full of heavy artillery—the Kraal can't ignore this now."

"Can we be sure of that, sir?"

"We can't be sure of anything, but they're alerted at least. HC has been hounding me all day, and I've received communiqués from four members of Parliament. Sit down, Mr. Tate. You wanted a meeting, so let's have one."

Dharmen complied, feeling odd to be doing so. It was the first time he had ever sat before top silver.

"I'm sure you've wondered why I assigned you to Bemin."

"I have, sir."

Gennet lowered his eyelids a fraction. "And?"

"I wasn't quite . . . I was uncertain as to why you assigned me to Port when there are other, more sensitive areas that need safeguarding, like the intermountain cloaking generator stations or PDP itself."

Gennet was silent. Dharmen breathed tensely and examined the space around the man. His desktop was in order with hardly a solid item on it. His sword was propped against the floating slab's back edge, with only the hilt visible from a visitor's perspective. Behind him stood a full suit of armor complete with helm, hauberk, and shield, all emblazoned with a high flyer with unfolded wings across a long dagger: the venerable emblem of the ancients.

"I had to keep my purpose secret up to now," Gennet finally said, "but given events since your company's first day at Port, I think you now know the reason for the posting, and why Bemin is as crucial as PDP or any other part of our defenses."

Dharmen felt the scrutiny. The same level of diligence expected of Ergive students was demanded of him. "We weren't sent to protect Port itself as much as the heavy armaments stored there."

"Exactly," Gennet said. "Angolin is dotted with arsenals, but Bemin houses our most advanced, most powerful munitions. It's the only complement substantive enough to overcome our own defenses. The Carmogen want it badly; that's why our thieves fell over themselves trying to secure it for them. I needed someone there watching. Someone I could trust."

Dharmen felt a ray of hope, like a door opening in his wall of wariness. And finally, some information was walking through it! "I'm glad to know my posting wasn't just another arbitrary change from HC, sir."

"Change? Oh, there's plenty enough of that coming. Now that we're venturing out into space again after a thousand-year hiatus, much of the Guard will find itself manning ships, not bases. You've witnessed the updated enlisted and low- to midlevel officer rankings, and soon"— Gennet paused, and *cringed*—"soon you will address me as Admiral."

Dharmen's eyes widened. He envisioned the general in the plumed bicorn hat and gaudy shoulder epaulettes he had seen in historical synth texts. He would have laughed out loud in lesser company. Gennet's expression indicated he would not be similarly amused. "Our ancestors were a space-faring people, sir. It's only natural for us to eventually—"

"Perhaps, Lieutenant Commander, just perhaps. Let's leave it at that."

"With permission, General."

"Granted."

"I'll do whatever it takes to keep the weapons safe, but what about the traitors? Sir, I came to you about Lieutenant Commander Armetrian back on Negara. He's right in the middle of all this. Why has he been allowed to keep his commission for nearly four months now without the slightest action taken? He and his accomplices should've returned from combat to base brigs, and not left free to continue working with the enemy." Dharmen slowed his breathing and calmed himself. He didn't want to go into a tirade now.

"Mr. Tate, if you were as long on patience as you are on anger . . ." Gennet said it without disdain and with the very cool Dharmen sought for himself. "I hear you, but there was no good way to approach it.

Even before you told me about the conspirators, I had seen the signs: the particle fire from the enemy, and the strange behavior within the ranks, even up to a few of my peers. The jittery councilors sitting where you are now, feigning ignorance of the situation but looking like trapped borbols at my every word. This all started long before Negara, but I couldn't do anything about it. Until now. Solid evidence, as I said earlier—a man in my position doesn't march up to the Kraal armed only with words from just one of his officers."

Dharmen balked, but Gennet raised a pique-dousing hand.

"It was a tough call," said Gennet, "but I had to have more, and in the meantime, I needed to keep an eye on the collaborators. All of them."

"You mean Armetrian's following here at Seventh."

"And in other orders too, Lieutenant Commander, precisely. Hauling them before the Judge Advocate, even giving the slightest hint of suspicion too soon would have shut down my efforts faster than a high flyer snatching up a West Ranges shepherd." Gennet cast eyes about the immediate area in casual reference to his wider command. "Traitors are like weeds, Mr. Tate. Uproot one bunch and more sprout up in their place. I wanted to keep watch on all those spreading in *my* field; identify as many as possible and uncover others elsewhere before they could do real damage." Gennet sighed. "But now, there's the dead Bemin security administrator. I knew there'd be a smuggling attempt there eventually, but I didn't expect such lengths to achieve it. As for your situation up to now, Angolin's safety is more important than one officer's discomfort, no matter how extreme. Let that be clear."

"Aye, sir." Dharmen exhaled raw emotion. He wished he could reverse every moment he had let outrage control him where discretion had been called for. Dark clouds were lifting, and if these months had been filled with nothing but fear and doubt— "I understand completely, but what role do I take in this going forward?"

"The same role you've been in: the vigilant, hotheaded, truth-seeking soldier I've discovered you to be, similar to the ancient who wore this metal suit behind me," Gennet answered. "And as my eyes and ears in this situation, which we both know is only just beginning. As administrator of this order, I don't have the same ability to keep watch over every corner of my command as you do. It's not easy to uncover traitors when you're in meetings all day, running this base one minute and dealing with bureaucrats the next."

"By the gods, sir, I'll do my best!"

"That, you will."

"Sir, one last thing. Back on Negara, Armetrian mentioned carrying out his *instructions*. Would you know anything about that?"

Gennet raised an eyebrow. "I beg your pardon, Lieutenant Commander?"

Dharmen remained silent.

"That brings one suspicion to mind. Can't say I'm surprised," Gennet said too casually.

Dharmen didn't like it.

The general gave him a seconds-long perusing. "Dismissed."

Dharmen stood, saluted, and turned to leave.

"And Tate . . ."

"Sir?"

"Be careful. Very careful."

Dharmen nodded an affirmative and left the office.

GENNET STOOD AS THE DOOR slid shut. He paused all imagery on his office surfaces; there was too much on his mind and he wanted audible and visual quiet. A message floating before him from his wife, Audra, blinking in standby mode was the room's only movement, and all he was willing to permit at the moment. It wasn't marked urgent. It could wait just a little while longer. He turned to the window, closed the data files on it and looked down to the entrance court, watching the bustle of base's late-afternoon activity as he often did. It was one of few things in his life now that granted him peace. But his calm visage frowned in the pane. "Admiral, indeed," he muttered to his half reflection. "Hmmph!"

THE DINE-IN CLANKED WITH PLASTIFORM as Dharmen cleared the first course and placed the soiled synthware on the refuse platform. With everything carefully piled and the command given, platform and contents vanished, sending the food scraps to the communal sublevel compost. Willem came to the table with the second course stretched across both arms.

Seated at the head of the table, Dharmen's father received the first plate. "I see someone's done this before," he said, smiling gently to Dori and Theus seated toward the opposite end.

"I spent half my school years working in restaurants. I learned a thing or two," Willem replied indifferently.

"*You* waited tables?" the elderly man inquired.

"That and other jobs, yes. I had no sponsorship, so tuition had to be covered somehow."

"But you're a Hanne. You're from one of Angolin's wealthiest, most prominent families."

"So I'm told," sighed Willem, "and it hasn't helped one iota. I didn't follow the family line and go into politics, I chose civic service instead. Father was outraged. He cut me off, and that was that. Are you comfortable, sir?"

"Nüren, Will, not *sir*. I won't have my son's mate standing on ceremony after all this time." He furrowed bristly white brows. "How long has it been for you two, anyway?"

"Almost four years," Dharmen cut in, arriving at the table with a decanter of Vinalhaven Valley red. "And no one's standing on ceremony, Father. Will's just looking out for you. You've only been out of VetsMed a day. We want you to get well."

"Good Krone, why all the fuss?" Nüren said. "I had far worse scrapes in the Guard. Now I miss a step and fall, and suddenly I'm rushed to a pen full of sick people. Can't an old soldier just get normal medi-synth homecare and be done with it?"

"You fractured your leg in three places, sir. That's more than medi-synths should be trusted with," Dori said. "And I *have* to call you *sir*. You're still our superior."

Nüren grimaced, turned to Dharmen. "She's almost as rigid as you, m'boy: every little thing so neatly tended to and put in place, up to and beyond Guard standards."

"I don't know what you mean, Father, and neither do you."

"Oh, no?" Nüren looked to Willem. "Does he still do that odd thing with his clothes at night before bed?"

"No," Dharmen answered in Willem's place.

"Yes, actually." Willem grinned. "I just assumed he was continuing basic training."

"Basic? Certainly not, Dharmen's been doing that since he was a child," said Nüren. "His mother—may Lady Xoraen keep her in the afterlife—found it funny. She would sneak into his room at night and rearrange everything—move the arms and legs into all sorts of gestures. You should've seen his reactions in the mornings, wondering why his clothes were saluting him! Gave us a laugh every time, watching him get dressed in a huff and stomp off to school angry. He was Rior's fire then and still is!"

Theus chortled and promptly stifled it. Guests at the same dinner table notwithstanding, Nüren was still one of the most renowned military leaders in Angolinian history.

"I'm sorry you missed Dharmen's promotion, sir," Dori said. "I understand your reasons, but I'm sure everyone would love to have seen General Nüren Tate in the flesh again."

"And steal my boy's moment? No way. This is his army now, and the time is his and yours to shine." Nüren leaned close to Dori. "And retirement is what it is, Commander, but if I were thirty years younger, just thirty years—"

"Have another helping, Father!" Dharmen heaved a generous serving of grochlaroot spiced the way he and his father liked onto the man's plate. "You need real food to regain your strength, not the tablets and strips you've subsisted on up to now."

Nüren ignored that and asked Theus, "Lieutenant, how *is* the Guard these days? It's been a long time since I commanded the First Order. I get scarce little news now."

"Not bad, sir. Not bad at all," Theus answered, startled.

"Not exactly good either," Dori said.

"How so, Commander?" Nüren asked.

"Well, sir . . ." Dori sat back and sighed. "Our people today aren't what they were when you were in command. Discipline's fading, and the threat we're facing has even the officer corps recruiting younger. We'll be pulling them out of middle school soon if we're not careful."

"What threat do you mean, Commander? I didn't know you perceived one," Dharmen said. "Something change for you since Negara?"

"You're not the only one who sees trouble coming, Dharm. You were just lucky enough to have overheard a good part of it and escaped to report it," Dori explained. "And I've already told you I'm on your side. I believed you back then, but hearing that your homeland is under the gun from its own is a lot to process, especially before a major offensive. *A situation* couldn't begin to describe it, so do me a big favor and let somebody else feel for something for a change."

"Good advice for yourself, Commander," Dharmen pulled from his comeback file.

Dori ignored that and continued: "And then there's Bemin. That didn't happen on its own. I heard the two escaped ships were found fully loaded. I assume that's what you and General Gennet talked about this afternoon." She gave Nüren a dreary look. "Treason in our ranks, unrest on our streets—all these centuries of peace just to come to this? Krone only knows what's next, sir."

"You sound as though it's hopeless, Commander," Nüren said. "It isn't. It's not new either."

"Father?" Dharmen queried.

"This happened in my day too. It's been going on since Angolin was founded. You can't cut eighty million people off from the rest of the world and expect them to accept it indefinitely. That number plus the millions living in dark matter pockets whom we still don't know about."

"But, sir . . . but Nüren," said Willem, "this isn't just discontent. Lives have been lost—nearly Dharmen's too—and it'll only get worse by the look of it. Where's the hope in this?"

"We've been isolated for too long, Will. This was coming eventually. Great peoples don't exist in a vacuum, and we *are* a great people, even if we don't always know it or act like it." Nüren paused, studied each face. "We will join the larger world, for better or otherwise. And a lot of blood will be spilled in the process. It won't be easy."

The table went quiet, all but Dharmen. "But the Kraal has made our hiding law, Father. When some of our people defy it to *join the larger world*, what position will that put the Guard in? Besides the traitors, the protests are increasing. When they finally boil over, how will Dori, Thee, and I be expected to handle it? Are we expected to be the *otherwise* part? I don't know about my colleagues here, but I signed up to defend Angolin from the Outside World, not from itself. I'll protect the people. It's up to them to run their society."

"And is that the speech you'll give them if they don't?" Nüren said.

"All I'm saying, Father, is if our people can't control themselves, then they deserve what their choices get them. I'm a soldier, not a babysitter."

"Son, as long as you have a Guard uniform on your back, you'll go where you're needed and do what's needed, whether it's down the Vresel or down the block. Angolin needs your service now more than ever. You will uphold your honor and protect this land in whatever way required. Get ready for diaper duty if that's what it takes!"

Dharmen simmered with an energy outside of anger that he couldn't place. "Yes, sir."

"Each of you," Nüren said, surveying the table, "keep our homeland as safe under your charge as it was under mine, but be mindful. Uphold the law, but respect the will of the people. And above all, don't let need for power infect you as it has some of your peers."

"Excellently put, sir," Dori said. She raised her wine vessel. "To the Hidden Realm and its safety, and to leaders who remind us of our duty."

Vessel in hand, Nüren stood shakily, refusing help. "To Angolin's future," he added, "to the well-being of friends and family, *and* . . . to my son and future son-in-law!"

Dharmen choked on his wine that he had already begun sipping.

"You two do intend to marry, right? I'll be highly disappointed if you don't. Been a long while now, this messing about. Time to get serious." Nüren's chuckle brought some cheer back to the table. "And for Krone's sake, be quick about the wedding. I'm not getting any younger!"

Willem smiled. He tapped an icon on the table to warm the plates a bit. A spark in the console made him retract his hand. "That's odd, what could have . . .?"

"It's probably a short in your dining system," Theus said with his mouth full.

The console sparked again and hissed. The icons degraded to faint rings and disappeared. Willem frowned. "What in Rior's name?"

The hiss grew loud and shrill. Dharmen's eyes twitched from combat stress, but he ignored it. "Get back!" He grabbed Willem and Nüren and pulled them from the table.

The tabletop detonated. Dori and Theus dove to the floor. Dharmen, Nüren, and Willem turned to a wall, shielding heads with hands. They had no time to take cover. Flying debris sprayed them. They carefully peered back to find the dine-in table scattered around the room in twisted chunks.

Smoke and melting plastiform filled Dharmen's nostrils. "That was no short, someone's tapped into our household systems!"

The light bots flickered and then shut off. Dharmen activated an upright to access the systems through his internal only to find that Rem-E's patch-in to them was being blocked. "Somebody somewhere is trying to—"

"You saw the delay. It had to be a low-level signal," Theus said as he and Dori got up from the floor. "Your perp is an amateur, and probably close by."

Out of the corner of Dharmen's eye, he caught movement. He looked to the dine-in window. The room's darkness illuminated the outside. A face that wouldn't have otherwise been visible bobbed above the sill. The trespasser's eyes met Dharmen's for an instant, and quickly disappeared. The stomping thuds of fleeing feet came from the narrow passage between pod houses.

Dharmen snatched his gun from his trouser leg holster and darted through the floating upright. He commanded the front door open, instinctively aiming as it slid aside. He went out and quickly scanned the area. A figure ran fast down the pavement and turned onto the bridge over the wayside canal. Dharmen set off in pursuit, hearing Theus and Willem yelling after him before their voices faded.

The other crossed the bridge with a sizeable lead. He slowed and turned, likely to see if he was being followed. He looked young, possibly a teenager, though very tall . . .

And those few seconds were enough. With a clear line of sight and his target briefly facing him, Dharmen fired. But the other turned in the same instant and stumbled. He grabbed the side of his head; the blast had barely clipped him. The lanky figure righted himself, cut a sharp left, and darted around the end of a pod cluster. Dharmen followed. He knew there would be little chance of a second shot now. The way was broader and much busier; even Rem-E's targeting assist would be of no help under these conditions.

Dharmen realized the other was headed toward the Zuidenmarkt. South C's open-air bazaar of shops and entertainment venues would be teeming at this hour. He refused to let that stop him. This was no common prankster. *Got me in your sights personally now, Armetrian? You should've been man enough to do this yourself!*

He ran on anger-fueled adrenaline, dodging others on the gently glowing pavers. Some weren't fast enough to avoid him. His attacker fared little better through the increasing mass of ambling bodies. He was also clearly not used to a chase. His inability to make quick maneuvers or control his long limbs gave Dharmen ground, but not enough to close the gap. The other reached the market and headed down its main promenade.

Dharmen's chest burned, but he refused to give up. At the market entrance, he turned in, only to find exactly what he'd dreaded: hordes of people moving aimlessly, and no sign of his attacker. Even the kid's great height didn't distinguish him in the crowd. And the market itself hid him. A breeze of laughter and conversations joined blaring music, flashing lights, roving ad bots, and scrolling banners, all competing for attention and covering the fleeing youth's footfalls.

Dharmen's whole body shook. It was happening again. He kept control as best he could, let his internal intervene and entered the throng. Onlookers stopped and stared—and quickly backed away, not as much from the crazed look in his eyes as from the sight of the large, bright nemurite gun in his shaking hand.

"Rem-E! Public ID!"

In front of Dharmen's breast pocket appeared a holo-badge with his portrait beside the Guard Standard: a shield bearing the stars of Lothnë and Rior shining above Tentim, spread across the breast of a high flyer. The floating insignia glowed on a field of Guard gray-blue, clearly visible and properly identifying him before the sea of puzzled faces and jumpy market security.

He scanned the crowd. No sign at all of his target. He snarled and slammed his free hand against a hovering kiosk. It beeped in protest, and everyone close by cleared away at once. Then he heard his name.

Theus rushed up beside him with winded, heaving breaths.

"Dori's not with you?" Dharmen puffed, still catching his own.

"Negative. She stayed behind to . . . keep an eye on . . . Will and your father. She didn't think it would be safe . . . to leave them—"

"I know, Thee. I know." Dharmen groaned. He was relieved at Dori's quick thinking and put off by his own lack of it. *I abandoned my family in a dangerous moment for a traitor. How could I be so stupid?*

Theus contacted Dori. She relayed that base security had been alerted and were minutes away. She hadn't bothered with the conurb police; she didn't think they'd respond quickly enough.

"Great," Dharmen muttered. "A patrol sloop sitting in front of my pod half the night. That'll have the neighbors talking!"

Theus looked around uselessly. "See any sign of him?"

"Course not!" Dharmen wanted to slam his head into a wall as awareness seeped in. This wouldn't be Dawn Fire's first attempt on him. And it didn't matter because it was on. Definitely on! He stowed his weapon and let out a frustrated breath. "We may as well go back and wait for the MPs, Thee. Our big-little bomber has gotten away."

CHAPTER 5

LATE NIGHT TREACHERY

ix-L, TimeSpace status.

Functioning normally, General.

Communications block.

Still active.

Tracking.

Dampening of all onboard signatures is at maximum strength.

The lieutenant has outdone herself on this one, no one can find us . . . Or almost no one. Distance to srθ's last known position?

Approximately seven hundred kilometers aft, if rumor of their existence is accurate, sir.

Good. I have one more task for you: erase your identity signature. It's the only thing at this point that would give us away. I know you were reprogrammed with that ability.

I was, sir, but that action is unlawful. Article 26A-7 of Guard Code strictly prohibits suppression of or tampering with—

I am your user, Nix-L. Carry out my order!

❀

GENERAL ESTES ACCESSED HIS INTERNAL and found a newly arrived message flagged high priority. He supposed he should have waited until he was alone to listen. He supposed too late; he had already sent playback to his earplant.

Through the crackle of interference, General Gennet's voice updated him on the investigation into the Tate house incident. The murder attempt on the lieutenant commander had not only failed, but it had also caught his romantic partner—a Hanne of all people—along with two active Guardsmen, and one highly decorated, honorably retired one. Estes shut his eyes at the thought: *Nüren Tate. This is the last kind of attention we need. Damn Armetrian and his juvenile helpers!*

"Is there a problem, General?"

Estes opened his eyes to black-flecked yellow ones and a semblance of lips curled into a thin grimace. "No. Everything's fine."

"Excellent. I trust things are well back in your little realm. I hope the message you just received reported nothing troubling. As your host, I would not want anything to burden you during your visit." Naul smiled with rows of sharp, silvery teeth. "Pity though your Seventh Order counterpart is not with you on this. He proved an excellent battlefield strategist on Negara. Such formidable ability considering the cloistering of your people. When you return to Angolin, give General Gennet my regards."

Estes wondered through his surprise if the Carmogen were capable of levity. He peered out a window. Naul's compound was amazing. Even Hanne estates in the Condorcet foothills weren't as opulent. And it was a far cry from the ride in. Devoid of the simplest antigrav technology, the transport that delivered them rolled across the ground on plastiform cylinders and emitted a smelly gaseous vapor from the archaic contraption's rear. It had sickened his stomach and worsened a mission that was no more escapable than the conveyance itself.

After months of clandestine telecons, Estes had gone from negotiator to gunrunner in one very long trip: an hour flying undetected through Mare Vresel's gases and three more across that obscure sector of the Abyss intimately known but little mentioned by top silver. He was the first Angolinian to venture this far out in centuries; srθ must have been alerted to his presence. But they had curiously done nothing to hinder him. Were the tales just that? He didn't really believe in luck.

After programming his sloop's concealment on the rendezvous rise, he was flown secretly to the eastern hemisphere in a flimsy craft that pitched and bounced more than any Angolinian vessel, and required high flyer-like metal wings to stay airborne. But he was here now on the unknown other side of the world. Everything Angolin would never provide: wealth, power, prestige, freedom—the effort demanded whatever he could accomplish here.

That realization pushed his overworld trip out of his mind, along with the ground transport that circumvented Gragna to reach Naul's massive abode. And the "refreshments" offered to him went unnoticed as his attention circulated around his host's lavish drawing room. Every square meter of marblited wall was trimmed and appliquéd in precious metals, and the room contained more furnishings than he had ever seen in one place.

"Is it all real?"

"Pardon me, General?"

"This furniture, these pedestal sculptures—none of this is . . ." Estes clipped his words. He had gone to great lengths to conceal nonweapons synth tech, including leaving all traceable devices behind in his ship. He hoped by the mercies of Krone that his host hadn't noticed the slipup.

Naul had. "If you mean artificially rendered, General, no. Everything in this house is real and quite valuable. The chair in which you sit is worth fifty slaves alone," he said with a casual glance to his footman. "I am familiar with the Angoliner ability to create matter from nothing, and I do hope to discuss this technology someday very soon. But you have come a long way, and arms are today's business."

Estes wanted to crumple in his seat. Striving with Naul's wily intelligence was as difficult and demanding as managing what weapons tech to offer him. He beckoned the servant holding his case of presentation materials. The encumbered man scowled at him and waited for Naul's approval before complying. From the case, Estes produced several documents containing schematics of Angolinian weaponry, all on paper to avoid using synth media. He explained the use, energy yield, and mean outcome of each inventory item, from shoulder-mounted weapons to ship-mounted heavy cannons.

Naul listened, inspected every schematic, and asked pointed questions in rapid succession.

Estes felt worn and whittled.

Naul inquired about a particular particle emission system. "Yes. I believe this was used in the Negaran conflict," he said to his guest's increasingly slowing explanations.

"They were, actually," Estes affirmed too quickly and openly. "This design was mounted on our Class LR-2 Gunships. Their upgraded housings and components are lightweight enough to not compromise the ships' flight and hover capabilities."

"Hovering craft? I was not aware of their use on Negara. In several weeks of battle, I saw not one."

"You wouldn't have. They and the rest of our heavy materiel were spatially and temporally cloaked with a combined . . ." Estes swallowed his remaining words, jaws quivering and sweat that had beaded his forehead now flowing in rivulets down his face.

"Cloaked? How so, General? Do go on," the other said and handed him a handkerchief.

"Lord Naul, I came here to discuss weaponry, so if it's all the same to you—"

"If it is all the same to *you*, General, my people have great interest in this technology. You would do well to share it with us, at least some modest portion of it if you desire our continued fellowship."

Estes tried to turn an uncomfortable heave into a casual sigh.

Naul smiled dryly. "When you are ready, of course," he said, and pressed the matter of stealthtech no further.

They spent the rest of the morning discussing shipments, timelines, and possible rendezvous points. Naul consistently gravitated toward armaments that would offer his forces the fastest military offensive results. Estes noticed that even through his fatigue, but he was too mentally exhausted and too eager to coact at once to give much resistance.

"And General," said Naul, "make sure that we receive the deliverables we paid for this time. The Lescainate was highly displeased with your last attempt at shipment, and since I represent them in this relationship, their umbrage is understandably heaped on me. In the future, I trust you will find pilots who will not ditch their cargo and run at the first sign of pursuit. A repeat of the Bemin situation will not behoove your efforts."

Estes was astounded at Naul's knowledge. He'd had pilfered quantities of light munitions funneled to Carmogen for months and never once mentioned where they came from. He'd never mentioned Port either; how could Naul possibly know about Bemin?

The meeting ended as it began: in surface pleasantries as though part of a routine, sleepy diplomatic junket. Naul reached over to a bulky device beside his chair, retrieved a part of it attached to a plastiform cord, and spoke into an apparent mouthpiece. "Send them in."

The double doors opened. In sauntered two women. Estes couldn't believe his vision, though the day was beginning to numb him to surprise. Their nakedness embarrassed him, but they were stunning. Flawless. The dark-skinned woman bore an uncanny resemblance to his wife, Coraia. As for the other, he had seen more Lenans lately than desired. He thoroughly despised them, though he had to admit, she, too, was lovely. And thankfully not furry like Lenan men.

"General," Naul began, "accept these beauties as a token of our continuing friendship. They will comfort you enormously during the remainder of your stay." He ordered the women to escort their guest to his apartments.

Estes gulped. Prominent Angolinian men weren't accustomed to such "gifts." Visibly unnerved and unwittingly communicating such, he was unaware that his every reaction was being noticed.

Naul's baleful smile receded. "In the empire, it is considered poor form to refuse the grace of one's host."

My beloved Coraia, can you possibly *forgive me?* Estes was caught. Saying no would jeopardize this entire deal. Saying yes was unthinkable . . . though knowing of his wife's zeal for their new future, she just might look the other way if she knew. He managed to give the women put-on interest for now. It became genuine once they joined him. Reluctance slowly evaporating, he slid arms around their bare waists, savored the perfume of the dark woman's beautifully slender neck, and whisked both out of the chamber.

NAUL EYED THEM AS THEY left, adding his observation to his mental file. "I would remember your taste in the future, Angoliner," he murmured as the doors were shut behind the trio, "if indeed you had one."

Dearest friends,

You are cordially invited to spend the week's end of the thirty-fourth with me on the Mount. My beloved Lord Balaneth, esteemed ambassador of the Dominion of Lena, will join us, and we'll have wonderful news! Please reply at your earliest

convenience, and do bring friends. We welcome all. I know you
will have a grand time, and I do look forward to your company!

With sincerest regards,

Dame Aremel Hanne
Kleve Park Estate of Mount Condorcet

"Damn it to Krone!" Dharmen swore hard enough for his breath
to briefly scramble the message holo suspended in front of him. "Two
months of guard duty on this rock and now this? Week's ends are all
I've got now!"

Port personnel passing in the distance stared.

He stopped venting out loud and deactivated the upright. Aremel
meant well, but Dharmen could only take her cloying personality in
small doses, and as seldom as possible.

He watched his breath swirl on the cold wind sweeping the landing
berth toward its steam-shrouded control tower. The day was ending.
Lothnë had retired, and Rior departed Bemin's rocky landscape in a
deep blue glow across the drizzle-soaked tarmacs. It had been a cold,
damp afternoon typical of second winter's last days. But despite dreary
weather and inconvenient invitations, Dharmen was glad to be alone
for once and not constantly watching for sabo with one eye and Ciros
and Narond with the other. He squinted through the wind and pulled
his cloak around his shoulders. One last meeting on assault vessel
prototypes (at the ass end of shift, naturally), and he would be aboard
the transport for home.

Will's seen the invite. He'll naturally want to go, he thought, and
managed a smile at the reaction he knew would greet him later.

"Did you see Aremel's invitation? We'll have to request leave for
this one!" Dori yelled as she hurried across the tarmac with Theus in

tow. "Mountain vistas, downhill skiing, and all at the start of second spring. Krone knows we need the retreat!"

"Don't forget taroc riding," Theus said.

"I *will* forget it, Lieutenant. I'll enjoy myself thoroughly while forgetting it," Dori said. "You can have Aremel's smelly animals all to yourself. Will and I will stick to the slopes. Dharm, aren't you excited? I know your better half will be."

"Screaming at the thought, Commander," Dharmen said, expressionless.

"Screaming at the thought of week's end relaxation in Aremel's care," Theus jabbed.

"You can relax for me, Lieutenant. You're good at that lately," Dharmen retorted. "Just how are the East Vales these days?"

"East Vales? W-what do you mean?"

"Yes, Thee, what *does* he mean?" Dori said.

"Well . . ." Theus stammered, "Up East is where . . . lots of people go for—"

"For entertainment," Dharmen put in for Theus, trying to save his hapless friend from screwing himself into the pavement with a botched excuse. He luckily had no time to concoct more.

"Sorry I'm late! Security's hard to clear nowadays," puffed Yos, running up to them with an umbrella floating above him.

"Even with your credentials?" Dori said.

"Afraid so. Sabotage and theft will do that, even to the great Yos Andren. What are you two doing here? Did Dharm snatch you up for backup?"

"My company was posted to augment the lieutenant commander's— strictly a precautionary measure," Dori answered.

"Because some believe I can't handle the assignment myself," Dharmen interjected.

"You can, obviously. And why would *you* listen to Armetrian and his latch-ons?" Dori said. "The attack on the station warranted additional personnel. You know that. But if it helps, I'll look the other way when you kick Ciros's and Narond's asses across Port. I know that'll come eventually."

"Excellent for me in any case," said Yos. "I'm glad to have all three of you here. Your presence will make my job easier."

"Nice to accommodate you. What job, exactly?" Theus asked.

"I cannot divulge particulars yet, Thee. But after that last incident, the Space Commission has granted my request to work here on a special mission of my own. I may have to cancel classes next semester to accommodate it." Yos looked around. No one else was within earshot; the wide, empty tarmac gave them plenty of space away from potential eavesdroppers. "What I *can* say is that Brona and I have been brainstorming, and we've come up with plans to help neutralize an enemy attack if and when it comes. I'll need some of Bemin's particle-emissions labs to test them."

"Is that all you two have been doing?" Theus asked, sounding mildly irritated.

Dharmen knew why. *Developing a new crush, Lieutenant?* "Ask Brona that at month's end, Thee," he said. "I'm inviting her and Yos as my guests at Kleve Park. Aremel did say we could bring friends, and there's more than enough room." He ignored Theus's suddenly gaping mouth to that news and looked to Yos with eyes pleading, *Help me pad this thing with more people to offset Aremel!* "You'll come, won't you?"

"L. Vinc to Tate . . ." Leatra's voice transmission displaced Yos's reply in a distressed whisper. "Come to berth twelve-center immediately! They're moving heavy ordnance onto a ship. It has to be another theft attempt. Over."

Dharmen blinked comm acceptance. "Hold your position, Vinc! We'll get someone—"

"I can't, sir! They've seen me. I have to get—"

The gun blast blaring through Dharmen's earplant made him flinch. Shakes through his entire body immediately followed. *Not now, damn it!* He ignored them as best he could, opened an emergency channel to Security, and quickly relayed what had just happened. Dori and Theus had no choice but to follow as he set off toward the other landing berth while ordering Rem-E to copy them on the distress call. He heard Yos yell after them that he would be in Main Command. *Krone, let her be all right. Not one more death over this, please,* he thought as he ran.

The trio arrived at twelve-center. It was empty except for a figure lying unconscious.

"Get medics here quickly. She's down!" Dharmen ordered to Guard and port security rushing in. He floated an upright above Leatra's torso for a preliminary exam. She had been stunned, but heavily. "Where's the ship that was here?" he asked a port staffer.

The man had no answer, at least none to give willingly. Another call came in on general comm.

"Andren to Secár, Tate, Tarkala," came Yos's voice. "Come to MC as quickly as possible!"

THEY FOUND YOS IN THE ops hub: a wide, oval section of workstation uprights forming one of the room's four duty islands.

"We need to access capital inventory. There's a ship missing," Dharmen said as he joined him.

"Not just one, Dharm. Three Heinlein class frigates, and they've just launched without authorization," Yos explained. "They're moving fast, and their TimeSpace drives have been altered. They're nearly untraceable. This has to be another weapons lift, a massive one judging by the size and type of ship."

"Commander, sensors just located them, only for a millisecond, but it was enough," a shipman apprentice working with MC staffers reported to Dori. The recruit studied the floating information and shook her head. "Scan of interiors indicates heavy artillery of various grades in their cargo holds, with tonnages exceeding weight limits. It appears each ship is packed solid, ma'am."

Yos's eyes oscillated between Dori and Dharmen. "You've got to get your people after them!"

"We will. Don't worry," Dori said.

"Shipman, contact Seventh Command. Have them dispatch interceptors," Dharmen ordered. "Tell them to launch from the Nieuw Holland–side pads and forego the shipyard. Lieutenant Commander Nirya is the yardmaster on duty tonight. We don't have time to go through all his taroc crap." *And he's one of Armetrian's lot—we can't trust him,* was what he thought and wished he could have said aloud.

"Aye, sir," the SA replied. "Seventh Control's already on alert, but I'll— Sir, General Gennet is on the line. He wants to speak with you, and he sounds a bit tense."

"Patch him through to my internal," Dharmen ordered. *Rem-E, put the general on standby.* He ignored the SA's puzzled look as she complied. He then quickly left the room, ordering Theus to accompany him.

DHARMEN AND THEUS SCRAMBLED TO a ship, with Dharmen hurriedly briefing General Gennet's floating semblance.

"Lieutenant Commander, why did you choose to bypass Port security craft for ships all the way from Seventh?" Gennet demanded.

"I'm not bypassing them, sir," Dharmen answered. "Bemini ships have more accurate TS tracking capabilities, but they're not all fast enough for pursuit. The traitors won't let this end easily. We'll need backup from base if we want them caught."

"You have people on it?"

"Affirmative, sir." Dharmen neglected to say whom.

"Understood, Tate. I trust you urged them to use caution. Gennet out."

Dharmen closed the channel and glanced anxiously to Theus, his lone "people on it," as they ran. They reached the nearest vessel: an M-4 patrol sloop with only medium-range firing capabilities. It would have to do.

"Hold it right there," huffed the lead of three Port security guards blocking their path. Their stares were rigid but uncertain. They had been hastily dispatched. "No one's allowed on any ship without pursuit orders, is that clear?"

"Pursuit's the intention," Dharmen came back, "so unless you plan to assist, stand down." The other was unimpressed. "We don't have time for this, those ships are dots by now. You want that on your conscience? Or better yet, on the report I'll make to your superior detailing your interference?"

The Bemini trio eyed Dharmen and Theus with hands hovering over holstered guns. "I'm in charge of security for this quadrant," the lead said. "This situation has to be tightly contained. Threats won't help."

"Neither will inaction, Captain," Dharmen said.

"Inaction, my left nut! Ops has been trying to track them since this began, but TS detection is being suppressed. If *we* can't find them, how do you expect to?"

Dharmen stood adamant. "Just let me worry about that."

The other studied him for a few brittle seconds. "Right then. But if you're so sure you can take this one, don't come back empty-handed!" He ordered his internal to release the ship's hatch.

Dharmen and Theus entered immediately once he stepped aside.

"And Lieutenant Commander?" said the lead.

Dharmen turned.

"Krone be with you both!"

Dharmen gave a fast salute and closed the hatch. He strapped in, took the conn, and nervously recalled his flight training. Theus took the copilot's seat. After a hastily run preflight sequence, Dharmen fired propulsors and had the sloop airborne.

"When was the last time you flew?" Theus asked.

"Never you mind!" After a hard ninety-degree yaw, Dharmen accelerated, leaving the Bemini Rise for the open Abyss. "Scan the area, Lieutenant. Two-thousand-klick sweep. Report any TS anomalies."

Theus set sensors for a broad-vector search, joining timespatial distortion with nemurite hull signatures in the scan criteria. The twelve-second results seemed like forever to Dharmen as he navigated through plumes of brown-red haze.

"I've located them," Theus reported.

"Lock onto their signatures using the program I had Rem-E upload to Nijs, and send out a gravity well disruption signal. We need to fry their TS drives for good if we can."

Theus accessed his internal. "Done. All three ships visible now. They're on vectors headed east by northeast at these coordinates." He had Nijs transfer the information to the conn.

Dharmen eyed it quickly. "Either our thieves have well-armed R & R planned, or they're headed for Carmogen."

"Gennet to Tate. Just what do you think you're doing, Lieutenant Commander?" the general inquired sharply over the comm.

"Attempting to intercept our smugglers, sir."

"I gathered as much, mister. You neglected to mention that you were carrying out the pursuit yourself."

"Sir, there was no time. I had to get moving, and I needed someone I could trust for the job. Lieutenant Tarkala and I are on it."

"Commander Secár already has Bemini ships in the air, Tate, and their staff is better trained at this. When they reach your position, return to Port and let them do their jobs."

Dharmen slammed his fist on his flight seat arm. *No way am I going back. Dawn Fire's already struck once under my watch!* "Traitor bastards. Not this time." *Oops, that was out loud!* "We've already done it for them, sir. TS drives of escaping ships neutralized thanks to a few—"

Beeps sounded on Theus's console. "Other ships closing. Four echelons, according to sensors."

"Stand by, General," Dharmen said into the comm. "Backup from Bemin already, Thee?"

"Negative. They're coming in from the east, possibly intercepting the frigates. Configurations: winged, jet-propelled fighter craft."

"A Carmogen escort and right on time," Dharmen said. "Number of hostiles and ETA to the frigates?"

"Sixteen vessels and moving fast. They should reach the frigates in seven to ten minutes. We'll be there in three, given your flying."

"Did you copy that, General?" Dharmen asked.

"Affirmative, and Bemini security will handle it, Lieutenant Commander. Stand down!"

"Sir, the Port contingent's too small and too far behind me to be effective. I have to go forward for this to work. We won't get another shot at it."

The pause on the other end of the channel was excruciating. This was no time for conference and debate.

"Do what you must, Lieutenant Commander. Brief me upon your return. Gennet out."

His superior's sign-off tone was recognizable. Dharmen wasn't looking forward to a discipline lecture, but he meant what he said, unless Bemin and Seventh wanted to chase the thieves into the heart of

Carmogen defenses. He tracked the escaping frigates' positions, adjusted approach vector, and closed in. "Ready forward cannons, Lieutenant."

"Sir? There are too many fighters. We can't—"

"The enemy isn't the target, Thee. You have your order."

Theus complied, arming the ship's weapons as Dharmen gave a distance countdown . . . and in an instant, the stolen vessels disappeared from scanners. Theus tapped furiously at his panel. "Damn it, what the . . .?"

"They're as tricky as we are, just as I anticipated," Dharmen said.

"I'll have to recalibrate sensors to locate them, if there's even time to retrace their TS signals."

"How 'bout something better and quicker? Rem-E, enter sequence 6-Echo into particle-emission control, four-second bursts."

Theus turned his head from his panel. "Lieutenant Comm—"

"Trust me, Thee."

Theus monitored as Rem-E accessed onboard ops, entered a short encryption series, and activated the sloop's emitter, sending its beam in a wide sweep.

Sensors located the escaping ships almost immediately. "There they are, Lieutenant. Right where you left them," Dharmen said.

Theus scanned again. "And TS and shielding are now inoperative on all three. Nice!"

Dharmen resumed countdown. "One minute fifteen . . . ten . . . five . . . one minute. Ready, Lieutenant?"

"Affirmative."

"I have visual." Dharmen realigned pitch to intercept the fast-moving frigates. "Target the lead ship and fire!"

"Aye!" Theus locked on, deployed cannons.

The blasts hit dead-on. Dharmen jinked the sloop and accelerated to avoid the fireball. The g's from the maneuver pressed him hard into his seatback. He fought to keep his breath as he decelerated and brought the sloop about.

The two remaining frigates' pilots hadn't been able to make similar compensatory flight corrections. Within seconds, both were mortally struck by flaming debris from the lead ship. Internal explosions claimed one ship, blowing out its forward viewports. Heavy blasts ripped the other to airborne shreds. The flaming-hull trifecta fell from the sky, black smoke trails marking their journey into the void below.

"Hooaaah!" Dharmen bellowed. "Excellent shot, Lieutenant! You gave us exactly what we needed."

"Actually, it was your move that did it," said Theus. "Firing on the lead? You must've known the ordnance in its hold would ignite and take out all three at once."

"I didn't know, Thee. I hoped and prayed to Krone." Dharmen glanced upward with a smile in the heavens' general direction.

"But how did you program Rem-E to convert ship's energy reserves to gravitons? I've never been able to do anything that advanced with Nijs and wouldn't try to. And I'm supposed to be the technical one here."

"You deal with traitors long enough, you learn a few tricks. It was just something I had prepared for this very situation after the last time."

"Sensors detect the Carmogen force closing rapidly on our position," Theus reported.

"Right, Lieutenant, engage TS." One patrol sloop couldn't match sixteen hostiles no matter how primitive their weapons were. Dharmen banked and retreated toward the Bemini ships. He was ready to *pull Guard* and have them stand down and return to Port. Double-checking the sensors, he confirmed the number. He hadn't anticipated this many of them; that extra weapons complement gave him a better idea. He ordered all ships to maximum TS and to await the pursuit force from Seventh.

Theus monitored the enemy. Their fighters halted their advance and circled the smoke over the stolen frigates' terminal position. Dharmen joined the Port fleet and waited. Nothing for just a few . . .

The sky filled instantaneously with TS-exiting ships. They raced past at breakneck speed, heading straight for the enemy armada. The backup force from Seventh had arrived.

Theus disengaged TS as Dharmen powered up and joined the Bemini force forming the combined assault's rear guard. Once in position, all ships opened fire on the Carmogen. The enemy fighters had no time to put up a defense; they were blasted to pieces. Metal wings separated violently from fuselages as the entire Carmogen fleet was downed.

BEMIN'S CLOAK UNDERSHIELD DEACTIVATED JUST long enough for all ships to land. With the rest of the joint pursuit force, Dharmen and Theus emerged to a tarmac erupting in hoots and shouts.

"That was amazing! You two are heroes, you know that?" Yos yelled above it all. "The traitors will think twice about what they're doing now. You just consigned their whole cargo to the Abyss and an entire enemy force with it!"

"I don't know about *heroes*," Dharmen said. "I think we'll end up on report instead."

"It worked, but it wasn't exactly regulation, Yos," added Theus. "Neither was taking out so much capital equipment."

"Forget the worries for now, boys," said Dori. "I've been in contact with Seventh from the beginning. The general supports your actions. Don't count on commendations just yet, but disciplinary action is off the slab." She had other news: Port was on lockdown. Per General Gennet's order, all companies were to remain on Bemin to begin an immediate investigation.

Dharmen didn't want to spend the night without Willem, but he couldn't ignore the scene around him. All of Port seemed to join in. Adrenaline fueled him, enough to not care about the cold drizzle drenching his face and hair. He was looking to the stars twinkling in the few clear patches of darkening sky when a whoop suddenly went up around him and Theus. Both were hoisted onto shoulders. Dharmen eyed the man carrying him around.

"Great job, Lieutenant Commander. I knew you wouldn't disappoint!" the security lead from earlier yelled up to him.

"No problem, Captain. We owe you for that," Dharmen said as he and Theus were paraded around the landing berth.

He watched the sea of happy, shouting people beneath them. And found two stony faces within. Ciros and Narond glared venom before threading the crowd and leaving. Dharmen's euphoria cooled. Tonight was more exhilarating than anything he had ever experienced, but it changed nothing. This wasn't the first theft attempt, and it wouldn't be the last. He was sure of it.

He looked over to Theus. "We have a long night ahead of us, don't we, Lieutenant?"

I CAN'T STAND THESE UPPER-LEVEL platforms, why don't they put outbound lanes on the ground? Willem's sky-side wait for an airtram home was packed. He hadn't been the only one working late.

Nearly every square meter of standing space was occupied except for the end of the platform, where three teenage boys took turns hurling themselves against the edge-side force field. Their shouting, guffawing spree sent flashes across the field's entire length. Bored commuters became annoyed onlookers.

An elderly man asked them to stop. One of them said something back. The man raised his voice. The kid raised a fist. Several people immediately stepped in, with more joining them. Outnumbered and shame-faced, the boys backed off.

"Kids today. I don't get it," Willem said to a woman beside him. He meant it.

Angolinian youth were typically well-behaved, because Angolinian adults tolerated nothing less. But lately, they were increasingly causing trouble. Pulling mindless, increasingly dangerous, pranks and getting arrested for senseless things was becoming common. Dawn Fire's threat was growing. Angolin's future needed looking after now more than ever. Willem wondered if its youth would become part of the solution or join the problem.

His communicator signaled a waiting message. His cousin's invitation improved his spirits. Finally, a welcome respite. *And Dharmen will warm up to it eventually*, he thought, *if I start on him tonight.*

A new message followed: a holo. He watched and listened to Dharmen's hazy, rain-drenched image relaying what had just happened: another theft, but worse, the spaceport lockdown would keep everyone there overnight. His heart sank. Dharmen had upgraded their household security grid after the dine-in explosion, but tonight would be Willem's first night alone in the house since . . .

Gasps swept the platform. Light cascaded across the deep twilight; the Cloak was being raised. Murmurs swirled around Willem. He sighed, drawing no comfort from being the only one on the platform to know the reason. He looked toward the arriving airtram. A man stood at the platform's edge farther down. He wore a thin, hooded jacket that looked far too light for the season. *Aren't you cold? Can't see where that hood is any help, either,* was Willem's fleeting thought through his own worry. The hood turned toward him, slowly and purposefully. Willem looked away. The tram stopped, and the doors desynthed. Willem boarded his hovering car, his mindset quickly shifting to the commute.

It was dark when he reached South C. As he walked the quiet, wet ways, he shuddered. After three weeks, he still couldn't get it out of his mind. The bombing of their dine-in that night was obviously intended for Dharmen. It had worried him every day since, but now his dread was more immediate.

They're watching everything, probably have been for a while, he thought. *I should listen to Dharmen more. I should listen to him, period. Yes, he complains too much, but he's usually right. He's a curmudgeon, but he's my curmudgeon and a perceptive one. Oh never mind, just walk!*

Willem looked around. Windows glowed with early evening life, and here and there, people passed above the soft light of the mood walks that South C's leadership found so amusing to dot the neighborhood with. Willem would normally have been warmed by it all.

He edged closer to home, his legs feeling heavy, his gait slowing to an idle. Stopping to catch his strangely labored breath, he looked up the way. There was no one in sight but him. And a slight hint of footsteps; he wasn't alone.

He forced himself to turn and look behind him. Someone was approaching—not fast, not slow, but moving deliberately. It was a man . . . the one with the thin clothing from the tram stop. His hood was still drawn far over his head, shadowing his face.

Willem wrenched himself from the spot and began to walk, slowly at first, then faster. The footfalls behind him kept step. Willem forced himself to put one leg in front of the other and fight the urge to freeze completely. His mind raced faster than his feet. He crossed a bridge over one of the neighborhood's many canals and moved briskly. It occurred to him to remain on the mood walk side of the way to stay lit and publicly visible.

He crossed another bridge, turned down his own canalside way. He looked over his shoulder again, right at the stranger, appearing and turning with him. The pavers flashed crimson beneath both of them. Willem quickly looked forward and glanced across the narrow, hemmed band of water. The canal's typically lazy flow was high and fast tonight. The sluice fields were down to direct melting snow from the East Ranges through the canal system and into the Great Lake. Willem wanted to find peace in the sound of the rushing water. But the noise mockingly resonated hollow in his ears, drowning out all other sound, including footsteps.

Ignoring his churning stomach, Willem hurriedly crossed the next way. He was on his own block now. Home was just doors away.

But he couldn't risk going in. The house sat near ground level with only a quarter flight of stairs. *I might, just might, get up the steps and command the door open in enough time,* he considered. *But then what? This isn't one of Angolin's once-in-a-long-while muggers you hear about on the NewsMesh. Even if I make it inside, he'll get in right behind me. Blasted! Why did Dharmen have to be held over? Why tonight?*

And it occurred to him: a major incident—any incident on Bemin lately—was enough to detain Dharmen. Tonight had been planned with Willem's isolation carefully crafted into it, and his mood-paver-lit pursuer was preparing to finish the job. *Armetrian, you scheming, conniving . . .*

With a painful lump in his throat and absolutely frightened, he passed his own home. He wiped away the cold sweat trickling into his eyes and searched for options. The next cross way was a major thoroughfare with good foot traffic. Five pod clusters down. *If I can just get there, I can run into a shop. There are plenty open at this hour, right? Right!*

Praying to Rior to make it to the end of the block, he cut an eye behind him. The mood walk glow that had advanced beneath the stranger and broadcasted his every move was gone. He turned completely around. There was no one, neither behind him nor across the canal—

Faint light flashed a split-second before he could react. A jacketed arm wrapped around him and a blade pressed against his neck before he could react. The metal against his throat was unmistakable.

Fright froze him. How had the man so quickly and quietly crept up to him? From the corner of his eye, he noticed they were parallel to a service way between pod clusters. It was too convenient a place to be pulled into from plain sight.

"Back up as I do, and don't dare try anything!" his attacker huffed. With his grip tight and the knife blade making painful contact with Willem's throat, the man gestured toward the darkened passage with his free arm. In that brief moment, Willem noticed a tunic sleeve peeking out from the flimsy jacket. It was bright red and trimmed in gold. He didn't know what to make of that and had no time wonder about it.

The man pulled. Willem hesitated.

"Move!" he growled.

A tear ran down Willem's face. "I'm going to die. I don't believe it—he's going to cut my throat right here. I'm going to die," he thought out loud.

"Quiet!" the other ordered as he dragged Willem from view. "You'll live if you cooperate, but either way, you're coming with me."

That voice. And that accent! Willem had heard it only once before and in a very different setting, but he definitely knew it. He couldn't let this happen and hand them a win, not when Dharmen had worked so hard against them. Kidnapped? Or worse? No way, not like this! He moved in step with the man, frantically turning over in his mind the self-defense techniques Dharmen had insisted on teaching him.

Now . . . or never.

Carving a mental path through his fright, he reached up, grabbed the man's knife hand, and yanked it downward from his neck, holding the other's fist in place on his own chest just as he'd been instructed. Quickly, Willem ducked backward under his attacker's arm, and tugged with both hands, forcing the man's arm behind his back to the sound of a pained groan. Willem grabbed the knife handle and wrenched the weapon out of the other's hand. The knife's clanging on the pavement was music to his ears. Surprised it worked but with no time to gloat, he shoved his attacker as hard as he could, sending the Lenan to the pavement.

Willem dashed for the corner, turned, and ran down the busy way. Chest burning and heart pounding right up through his throat, he looked left and right for a safe place to duck into. He realized he had a direct comlink to General Gennet—he would be a lot more effective than the conurb police! But what if he didn't answer right away? Willem dropped that option and continued searching for safety.

He found it through the doorway of a new, wonderfully noisy restaurant and burst in. He tried to speak but collapsed against the startled host's floating podium. He heaved painfully, unable to put breath to words. The host stared, puzzled, first into Willem's frightened eyes, then gapemouthed at the sight of his neck.

Willem clasped a hand to it and felt a trickle of warm blood. "Contact . . . the police!" he finally, breathlessly gasped. "I've just been attacked!"

CHAPTER 6

MOUNT CONDORCET

That place again! I'd keep walking, if Lieutenant Commander Armetrian hadn't said something about another assignment. Can't he just upload instructions through the DarkMesh and let me forge him a pathway for the information he wants? Who needs to be cooped up in that stuffy old house on a warm day like this?

Sir, whom are you speaking with? And where is "that place"? You have once again disabled my geolocation functions. I can only detect that we are in transit.

I'm talking to myself, Na-Voort. And never mind. Just package those security decryption files as I requested.

❂

"LIEUTENANT COMMANDER, YOU OBVIOUSLY DON'T see very far, so let me broaden your vision," General Estes said as his flickering image filled the live-in. "This operation has to succeed, and Tate is sinking it for us. We can't let that continue."

"Agreed, sir," Armetrian returned.

"And why was a teenager trusted to take him out? Couldn't you have found someone a little older and more experienced?"

"General, our youth are the most skilled at revived technologies. Kerbi here is just what we need. This is too important for tinkerers who don't know what they're doing. But mistakes will happen, of course."

"That's right . . . um . . . General," Kerbentha bumbled. "The link was solid, and the timing was right, but somehow my patch-in to their dining system lagged. I used all the right commands, so I can't explain why detonation took so long."

The irritation on Estes's face leaped through the upright. "Oh, I can. You didn't work hard enough at the task. You didn't understand its importance or the subtlety of hand needed for it. And if Tate wasn't aware of our efforts before, he is now. We need him silenced. I'm no hotshot young tech-head, but anyone can access and handle such simple systems. Your procedure should've worked for the average Angolinian dwelling, but he must have recoded and reinforced his household security grid a while ago. The man's alertness is incredible. It's the last thing about him we should underestimate."

"Regardless, sir, I see a minor mishap, nothing more," Armetrian contended, "and maybe an ironically fortunate one. We only wanted Tate and his manfriend. We didn't know two more officers *and his father* would be there too. If we had killed Nüren Tate, all of Angolin would be after us now. We'd be uncovered and on the run, not standing here having this polite conversation from opposite ends of the Abyss."

"That point was understood long before this 'polite conversation,' Lieutenant Commander," Estes said. "And it could have been avoided altogether had you killed Tate on Negara when you had the chance. Why the blazing suns didn't you? I worked so carefully to have his advanced post discovered and herd him toward your meeting, and instead of taking him out, you plugged him once, then let him get away. Now he's causing us all kinds of headaches, and you still can't get the job done! What's the problem, Armetrian, then *and* now? Were your instructions unclear?"

"No, sir, but—"

"And while I'm at it, what about Willem Hanne's abduction? That was a botched mess too, thanks to your other accessory back there." Estes nodded toward Gallin sitting in the stuffy room's rear and who, up to now and as usual, listened but said nothing. "Was that also just a minor mishap, Lenan, or couldn't you take down one unarmed, defenseless civilian?"

"My colleague is more than capable. He's the only one of us with real experience in this," Armetrian said, defending Gallin.

"Does the man not speak?" said Estes. "Or does that escape him as easily as his targets?"

Gallin stood. "That *defenseless civilian* has some skills of his own, likely taught to him by his mate. And if you disrespect me again, General, I'll show you *my* skills when you return. I'm not one of your subordinates. Never forget it."

The eyes on the upright rolled. "In any case, Lieutenant Commander, this is two in a row for you. These persistent failures have to stop. Our friends on this end expect much more than they've received so far, and with them breathing down my front and the Kraal breathing down my back—"

"Here's another twofer for you, General," said Armetrian. "The Bemini weapons lift the day Tate's company arrived at Port was seized after the pilots—your people—fled the scene, and this latest one, which you also arranged, was intercepted and shot down by Tate himself. I'm not the one who has some retooling to do."

Estes's simulated head jerked to one side and glared at that.

"And your weapons tasks were higher profile than any you've given me up to now. I'm sure your Eastern contact has noticed," said Armetrian.

"My contact and I have already discussed this latest situation over the Abyss, Armetrian, and the next one *will* succeed. Count on it!" Estes said.

"If you mean Lord Naul, General, he's also contacted me. There'll be another shipment, but this time, he and I agree that I will take charge of it." Armetrian looked to the faces around him. "My own associates and I will more than meet the challenge. Oh, and you may want to check your internal, as I'm sure Naul's sent word of this by now."

Estes's image sat still. No surprise or rage at the news crossed the upright. Armetrian silently matched the brinkmanship. "Don't get too far ahead of yourself, Lieutenant Commander. Estes out."

Gravelly groans flew at the cleared upright. "How will we accomplish anything with him running this?" Ciros said. "Isn't it time for the Carmogen to chuck Estes for good and put you in charge, Lieutenant Commander? You've done more for us than that moron ever will."

"The general has his own views on how things should happen, even if they don't fit reality," Armetrian said. "That's what being a fossil in your job gets you. Just be patient. You too, Shipman," he said to Narond's disgusted grunt. "Everything will work out, one way or—"

"Maybe, but we've all done our share. When's Vinc going to do his? Wasn't he also put on Bemin to contribute?" Ciros said.

"Sublieutenant, you talk too much. It's all being handled. Leave it at that." Armetrian cut an eye over to Irzek. "Did you gain access to the security codes I requested, Vinc?"

Irzek stopped glaring at Ciros for a second. "Affirmative, sir."

Armetrian nearly smiled. "Great! Keep Tate off your back, and we'll be well prepared for our next move."

"DHARM, YOU COULDN'T HAVE BEEN sneakier about it," Dori said.

"About what, Commander?" Dharmen said, leaning casually against one of the garden terrace's freestanding columns.

Avalanche sensors and medium-yield shield emitters were likely concealed within. Aremel spared no effort in protecting Kleve Park from the beautiful but deadly slopes above.

"You know what I mean: inviting Yos and that friend of his. This was supposed to be a relaxing trip *away* from Angolin's troubles. I was hoping to just be at ease here and enjoy all this fresh mountain air, but that won't happen now with you, Yos, and that Mona or whoever, talking Dawn Fire and playing counterrevolutionaries the whole time. Couldn't you three have planned your thing elsewhere?" Dori closed her eyes and inhaled. "And just smell the cleanliness of that air!"

"Smells no different than South C to me, Commander. One bit of Angolin ozone is as clean as any other," Theus interjected.

Dori turned to him with a grimace and jabbed a finger into his midsection for that. "And you were in on this too, I'm sure."

"After this last gunrunning attempt, I should think you'd want to join in and help," Dharmen said. "Yos and *Brona* might appreciate that."

Dori angled her head indignantly, and he imitated it.

"There's plenty to do here and more than enough real estate to get you away from us serious folks if that's what you want. Hike down to the Great Lake and have Aremel's skipper take you sailing. Go taroc riding in the hills instead of riding my ass about our friends the whole week's end. Do something besides gripe in all this fresh mountain air."

Dori's eyebrows shot upward, and her mouth dropped open at the notion of Dharmen accusing someone else of complaining. "You know I'm not getting on one of those animals. I couldn't stand them on parade as a recruit, and I wouldn't remember how to ride one now even if I could see the thing."

"Taroc hair bends light at specific EM spectrum wavelengths and only under fear response, Commander. If you don't scare them, you'll see them," Theus said. "And our camos are mostly made of the stuff. You were practically wearing a taroc back on Negara."

"Oh, I know all that, Thee, stop trying to make sense!" Dori moaned.

"Go skiing then," Dharmen said, glancing up to Mount Condorcet's snow-covered summit. "And take Will. He'd love that. He and Aremel are Highlanders; they were practically raised on skis." He sighed gravel and clenched his fists at what entered his mind next. "And it might take his mind off what happened to him the night we were stuck on Bemin."

Dori sighed. "Slopes or no slopes, this getaway just won't be the same is all."

"Pretty soon, nothing will be the same. Haven't you gotten that by now?" Dharmen said.

"Whatever, Dharm, I'll make the best of it. And I still wish Yos's friend would stay home and play with her particles or something, but if she really has to come, then— Oh, hi!" Dori quickly reset her face and tone as Willem, Yos, and Brona came up the terrace steps.

Theus fumbled a reintroduction attempt at Brona and bumped a tray of wine vessels brought by a floating server synth.

Brona smiled amused politeness as the synth lowered, extended several of its limbs, and quickly removed the broken glass from the ground. "Yos and I know all about your Guard's battlefield PTS," she said to Dharmen. "We're looking forward to your company tonight, so try not to disappear on us."

"You'd have no trouble finding us, if we did," Dharmen returned. "Didn't you and your team at PDP help resurrect that technology?"

She smiled.

Dharmen leaned over to Theus. "That was your line, mate. Look alive!" he whispered.

"Ready for the week's end, Thee?" Willem cheerfully asked.

"Most definitely! Peace and quiet, *voluntary* outdoor time without combat, and no threat of wigbigs here for once. It'll be my kind of R & R."

"I think the ancients called them *bigwigs*, Thee," said Dharmen. "And just so you know, Aremel's apartments are full for this stay.

There'll be a few of them around, plus she and Lord Balaneth are attached at the hip now, so he'll be in attendance tonight. I hope you brought dinner attire."

"Dinner attire?" Theus croaked. "Nobody said anything about that for this trip."

"Nobody had to. This is an estate. Dinner is always formal here. You didn't pack the proper wear?" Dharmen knew the answer, but he just couldn't resist.

"I don't have proper wear, just my dress uniform back at base. And quit constantly picking at me!"

"Second nature, sorry."

"Dharm, you stew me up every chance you get."

"Only because you give me the pot!"

Theus looked ready to melt into the flagstones.

"Come on, Thee, let's go find Aremel's head footman and see if he can have something synthed for you," said Dharmen.

"But I—"

"Lieutenant, relax! That's an order for the rest of this week's end." Dharmen ushered him down the hedge-lined stairs and out of sight.

NO SOONER THAN THEIR HEADS had lowered beneath the pavement, Dori asked, "Will, how've you been holding up?"

"Fine. I think."

"What do you mean, you think?"

"I know who attacked me."

"Really? Who?" Yos asked.

Willem looked down to the entrance court. His face shadowed. The others followed his gaze to two men talking beside a large, rather gaudy gold hover car.

"Aremel's pilot?" Dori asked bemusedly.

"No."

She looked more closely. "But that's . . . Oh, Will, you can't be serious!"

"I am."

"You're saying the ambassador's aide assaulted you on the street?"

"That's right." Willem craned his neck just in time to meet Gallin's eyes. They stared at each other across the distance. "I couldn't be more sure of it."

"But why would anyone want to go after you? And why a diplomatic attaché of all people?" Dori asked.

"To get to Dharmen, of course," Willem said. "He's become a threat to them. Armetrian and Gallin wanted to use my kidnapping to silence him. That's how I see it. But I didn't give them what they wanted." He moved away from the ivy-covered railing, dodging a leafy tendril reaching for his wrist. "And Dharmen and Theus stopped a major smuggling attempt that same night, so it'll all get much worse before it gets better."

"Aside from the conurbs, have you told Dharmen any of this?" Yos asked.

"Of course not! Dharmen would cut him to pieces if he knew. The last thing we need is an international incident, and the last thing I need is my partner in detention."

"Will, how the blazes are you going to handle this?" Dori asked.

"Don't know yet." Willem massaged the slit healing across his neck. "I'll leap that abyss when I come to it."

Heads turned, startled. Dharmen mounted the steps, went to Willem. "We'll leap it together, love."

DHARMEN'S DEEP, STRAINED THOUGHT ROOTED him to his seat like *saaryl* pines on the heights above. The scene beyond the dining hall's high windows helped calm it. Lothnë had retired, leaving Rior to bathe the estate's rear gardens in cool, pretwilight shades. Evening's serene approach came in stark contrast to the dinner table's forced manners degrading to revelry.

Aremel had spent the last half hour laughing at Lord Balaneth's recital of a cleverly comedic but long Lenan folkloric tale. Her latest guffaw wrenched Dharmen back to reality. Ten were present, including the ambassador as expected, Gallin unfortunately, and Princess Nien, the youngest daughter of the Lenan king: an acerbic little creature wearing a jarringly bright, gender-inappropriate green gown and an apparently permanent sneer. She dismissed anyone who tried to engage her; even Willem gave up. Dharmen watched him. Willem smiled back, and then, when he thought Dharmen wasn't looking, he glared at Gallin for the fourth or fifth time that evening.

"I'm so *glad* to have only the *best* of company here for a change!" Aremel said, breaking Dharmen's musings a second time. "Such a *pleasant* alteration to the usual mass-unwashed that tramp into my engagements. And, my *dear Willem,* you were so *brave* in fending off that animal the way you did. *Imagine* such a thing happening in *Angolin* of all places! Just what *in the Realm* is wrong with our youth nowadays?"

"It was no youth, Mel." Willem cut Gallin another hard eye.

It was returned with equal frost.

"Oh, *really*! Well, it was courageous of you just the same, cousin. And you, Dharmen—*dear Dharmen*—I must say what a fearless man *you* are, going after those thieves down at the space station."

"That incident's classified, Aremel." Dharmen was surprised at her knowledge and chagrined at having it spoken before a traitor, though the man likely knew of it. "And I did what had to be done, courageous or not." He nodded to Theus. "We both did."

"He's being incredibly modest, Aremel. Forgive him," Dori beamed. "These boys brought down the stolen ships and destroyed their cargo before the enemy could collect it. And I'm proud of them both."

Dharmen shot her an alarmed look. "Commander!"

"The Bemin events are common knowledge to this group, Dharm. Don't worry," Dori said.

"Well, you don't say," Aremel fluttered in astonishment toward Theus. "How *commendable* of you also, Lieutenant! And may I compliment you on your choice of dinner attire. Never realized you knew such fashion, dear."

Theus smiled, glanced down at his dark-blue jacket's neatly pressed sleeves.

Dharmen hoped the ensemble's synth generator would hold its signal through dessert.

"My *word*! Three honorable, *heroic* men at one little table, including a most *prominent* officer of the Lenan Diplomatic Corps." Aremel moved loving eyes from Balaneth to the irascible slip of a woman opposite him. "Princess, we are in *excellent* hands tonight."

"Beyond the three, not so much," Willem muttered.

"What was that, Mr. Hanne?" They were Gallin's first words all evening. "We didn't quite catch it."

Willem took a sip of wine and perused him. "I think you did. And may I compliment *your* dinner attire, Gallin. Such an interesting color. Don't see many men in red in Angolin. Though I did see one recently. On my own canal two weeks ago, I believe."

Gallin betrayed no surprise at the implication. "I'm aware of the idiosyncrasies of Angoliner fashion, but we Lenans live in a cold place. We appreciate warmth, even in dress, which is more than I can say for—"

"Angoliner? Wonder where you picked up that term?" Dharmen interjected.

Lord Balaneth stood, wine in hand. "A toast to the valor of Angolin and of Lena. Now that our two cultures are getting to know one another again, may we continue to work in peace and lasting friendship." He raised his vessel.

The rest, save Princess Nien, followed suit.

With plastiform to lips, Willem and Dharmen exchanged barbed glances with Gallin.

"And to our fine officers here of both lands," Balaneth continued.

Dharmen did a double take at him.

"You and my aide have something in common, Lieutenant Commander. He also fought on Negara."

"Oh, is that so?" Dharmen edged eyes to Gallin and retorted. "Running round the jungle with the rest of us, *whoever knew*?"

"He co-commanded our Tenth Infantry Brigade," Balaneth said. "And finished up a submajor before resigning his commission and entering my service. My Gallin is a quiet man, but he's steadfast and full of surprises."

Dharmen's eyes bored hot enough into Gallin to redden more than his clothing. "I don't doubt it!"

The two stared each other down long enough to uncomfortably silence the rest of the table. Clinking flatware was the room's only sound as server synths busily cleared the course.

Dharmen sat back as his plate was removed.

"By the Norgods, Meester Dharmen, is thees any way to treet a peer," said the princess in her heavy Lenan accent.

Dharmen postponed his peeve before the dinner guests. "It's Mr. Tate, Your Highness. Or Lieutenant Commander if it suits you. As for His Lordship's aide, I'm sure he's full of interesting talents"—he peered back at Gallin—"which we'll all discover before long."

Dori cleared her throat, but Dharmen ignored it.

"It seems you have an ally, my dear Gallin," Aremel said obliviously.

"Or an adversary. Who can be sure?" snorted the princess.

"I'll drink to that one!" said Willem.

Aremel rose from her seat. "My, my, what *interesting* discourse we've suddenly fallen into, and I *do* hope to return to it in *just* a moment." She chuckled nervously, fanned her face with a neatly gloved hand. "But *right now,* I have an *important* announcement." She looked to Balaneth, took his hand in hers. "My Lord, we've had such a *wonderful* time these last months. I've been *so* happy, and I *know* you've been as well, and I think the time has come for me to tell everyone—"

"Rubbeesh, indeed!" the princess said with eyes rolled to the ceiling.

"Pardon me, m'dear?" said Aremel.

"You and your tiresome theatreecs, Miss, are plague enough. But these two," Nien said with a poisonous look at the male couple across from her. "They've been most eensulting to our Gallin all evening. Is thees how your realm honors eets guests?"

"What I consider honor, Princess," Dharmen replied, "is something you wouldn't understand."

"Dharmen!" Dori hissed.

"My dear Highness," said Balaneth, "I am certain that our friends meant no offense to Gallin or to any of us. In my time in Angolin, I've experienced only the utmost appreciation for us and our work here." He squeezed Aremel's hand affectionately.

"My Lord, how can you be so horribly naive at your age? Do you really mean to attach yourself to her?" the princess cracked.

"Your Highness, I of all people cannot deny the hospitality I've received." Balaneth smiled into Aremel's eyes. "Particularly here at beautiful Kleve Park."

"And does hospeetality include bivouacking in thees drab little finca with thees mountain woman? She's not even royalty. They don't have royalty in thees gods-forsaken land." Nien sat back and folded her spindly arms across her tiny chest. "Really, Lord Balaneth, what would your wives think?"

The room stilled. With eyes like synth saucers and mouth wide open, Aremel turned sharply on Balaneth, who sat quivering and staring down at the table.

A gasp broke the silence. All eyes went from Aremel to Brona and then to Theus, who sat hunched over the table with shoulders up to his ears and hands covering his bare chest. He looked down, and shot them quickly to his lap. His dinner attire's synth generator had apparently malfunctioned, and along with his newfound confidence, his illusion of clothing had vanished.

THE SOBS AND WAILS FROM Aremel's apartments drifted shrilly across the courtyard and into Dharmen and Willem's windows. Dharmen lay across the bed on his back, hands clasped on his stomach and feet lightly brushing the floor. He thought long and hard about dinner and how to handle—

A crash on the terrace below jolted him up. He heard Balaneth try to calm Aremel's screaming.

"I hope that wasn't her delftware porcelain vase," Willem said. "Mother gave her that when she graduated from university. It's been in our family for generations. The ancients brought it when they settled here. Priceless can't begin to describe it."

"Priceless pieces would now," Dharmen quipped and lay back again.

"Shut up, Dharmen, this is serious! Mel's seen much worse than Balaneth and Princess Big Mouth. She'll bounce back soon enough. But regardless, tonight was our fault."

"I don't know about that, love." Dharmen got up and joined Willem at the window. He took his hands and looked deeply into his eyes.

"You knew it was Gallin all along, didn't you?" Willem said. "You knew it before you overheard me this afternoon."

"Not completely. I suspected when you told me how he suddenly appeared. Only TimeSpace produces the effect you described. I knew someone with PTS access was involved, but until today, I'd convinced myself that it was another Guardsman."

Willem sighed.

"Why didn't you tell me it was him, earlier?"

Willem let go of Dharmen's hands "I couldn't bring myself to. I know how you are, and this is supposed to be a peaceful week's end retreat. I didn't want to ruin it, at least not before we could even settle in. Though I'm surprised you haven't torn Gallin apart by now. I'm amazed he made it to the dinner table in one piece."

"I left my sword at home, like you asked," Dharmen said with open palms and a thin smirk.

Willem reached down, patted Dharmen's pant leg, and located the handle of the assault knife he always carried in a hidden pocket. "You didn't leave this at home."

"Don't know how that got there. Netherlords must've snuck it in when I wasn't looking."

Willem went over to Dharmen's travel pack, rummaged through its compartments, and carefully pulled out a holstered gun. "I suppose you don't know how this got in here either?"

"Okay, you're right! I just might've put Gallin down, and still might, though I won't need weapons for it." He ignored Willem's rolling eyes and continued: "We've already been bombed once, and you were nearly kidnapped. There are more of them than one Lenan traitor. Don't you think we need *some* protection?"

Willem shut his eyes and flinched at Aremel's latest screaming wails. "Yes, but for defense only, please. I don't want anyone else to get hurt, even if it is—"

"What I do for a living? It makes you uncomfortable, I know, but I'm not as rough as you think. I can show restraint when I try." Dharmen looked into disbelieving eyes. "I won't kill him. I promise."

Willem lowered his shoulders.

Dharmen smiled, raised an eyebrow. "Not tonight anyway, love." He kissed Willem deeply. Willem's arms wrapping around him felt so wonderful that he forgot all else from the night. Barely noticing the noise filtering in from their aggrieved hostess now, he removed his trousers, pulled Willem toward the bed, and commanded the light bots out.

MIDMORNING SHONE WARM AND BRIGHT over Kleve Park. The East Ranges' forested feet had finally shed their purple-black winter foliage for a more cheerful second spring raiment. High above, Condorcet's summit met the Heaveners with a snow-capped piercing gleam through thin, silver-white clouds.

Willem had taken Dori and Theus skiing with him. Caution warnings from the avalanche sensors simply couldn't hold him back. That left Dharmen, Yos, and Brona to their own business on tarocback racing upslope. Dharmen had the wind in his hair and, for a few fleeting moments, no cares. *I could do this forever. And why don't I?* his mind questioned as the leafy, yellow-green world flew by. The trio found a small clearing and stopped.

"You did tell Will not to go too far up the mountain, right?" Yos asked. "The trees that high up—"

"Are carnivorous. Yes, he knows," Dharmen said.

"Then he knows to lookout for borbols too," Brona put in. "The saaryls are deadly enough, but the snow beasts . . . Well, he should avoid the heights. He can't render himself invisible like a taroc."

"No, but he has instincts like one. He grew up in these mountains," Dharmen said. "But he promised me he'd take them cross-country only and keep low. Don't worry."

Yos sniffed and looked around. "So how've things been on Bemin lately? I haven't been able to get back down there. Been too busy with midterm exams, though if my students' grades don't improve, I may chuck academia and join the Space Commission exclusively."

"Port's been strangely quiet. Too quiet," Dharmen replied, reaching down and stroking his peacefully grazing taroc's bushy mane while avoiding its sharp, stubby horns. "And I don't like it one bit. I'd rather be *fighting* traitors than sitting around waiting for their next move."

"You may well get that chance," said Brona, "and if you don't, I just might. Last week, I caught one of my colleagues with one of your people prowling around my section. I had them removed immediately, but when I accessed my workstation files—my secure partition files—half of them had been opened and sifted through. I told the director. He said he'd look into it. My colleague's been flitting about since with no apparent action taken. No investigation, no word of one, nothing."

"I'd like to know who that Guardsman was," Dharmen said. "Did you get any information on him?"

"Her, actually," Brona replied. "And no I didn't, though Ian, my colleague, did call her by name. Something beginning with V."

Dharmen blinked savagely. "Vara, by chance?"

"That might've been it."

"What did she look like?"

"Hmm, dirty-blond hair, surly expression. She looked at me like she wanted to bash my head in when I asked what they were doing. You know her, I take it?"

"Oh, we've met," said Dharmen. "Back on Negara, with me at the wrong end of her rifle."

Yos frowned. "Dharm, please don't tell us—"

"She's part of the semper knife and trying to get stealthtech secrets to the enemy now."

Yos kept his frown. "Semper what?"

"Backstabber, Yos. And the absolute worst kind."

"Dharmen, this is getting dangerous. This and shuttling weapons to the enemy . . ." Brona trailed off, looking troubled.

"More weapons, actually," Dharmen said. "They succeeded at least a few times down the Vresel. I was shot at with more beams than bullets."

Brona fiddled with her taroc's reins as the animal stamped at the mossy turf. "And now they've infiltrated PDP, and it hasn't stopped with that one incident. A few times since, file information on the Cloak has abruptly changed right before my eyes, with time stamps suddenly appearing backward in time and no reasonable explanation for it."

"You know the cause, Brona. TimeSpace," said Dharmen, "used while dumping the information onto personal media to not risk detection by sending it through your program mesh. Your traitor would be more expert at that than ours."

"But he chose the busiest times of day to lift the data. It makes no sense," said Brona.

"Oh, it makes sense," Dharmen said. "Ian would've had to dodge more bodies, but more activity would help hide visible timespatial distortions."

"He's right on that, Bron," Yos said. "That minor flash here or ripple of shadow there wouldn't hold your attention for long with lots of people and bustle around to occupy your senses."

"I know all that, Yos. I know," Brona said. "I've done my share of applied research on light-bending and temporal displacement. I just never expected to see PTS used for this purpose—to steal information literally from under everyone's noses, including mine. There's more to this than running guns. The traitors are trying to neutralize the Cloak or help the enemy do it. I think we have an invasion coming from *both* sides of the Abyss, and if the Carmogen and Dawn Fire are mobilizing, then we have to counter. Yos, were you able to access those schematics we discussed?"

Dharmen narrowed eyes at both of them. "What schematics?"

"Of heavy particle artillery," answered Yos. "Our most powerful weapons housed on Bemin that the collaborators have been scrambling to get hold of. The Carmogen could never mount a successful invasion with their own primitive weapons. Even our lightest shields would repel them. They'll come here with energy weapons and lots of them, so we'll need an effective match."

"Yos and I are working on ways to detect and render inoperable anything used by the other side that could compromise us," Brona said. "We'll need every advantage possible."

"Our ancestors had those abilities," Dharmen said. "Any old files you can locate on particle energy suppression would be more than a bonus."

"Already have," said Yos. "Now Brona and I just have to study them, work whatever's of use into our plans, and hope for success when the time arrives."

Dharmen reached down again, patted his taroc to ease its sudden restlessness. His fingers became entangled in the animal's thick, wooly coat. "You'll need Guard help, the bit that can be trusted. I still think that's most of us. I've met with my superior on this, and when you're ready, I'll discuss strategy on our end with him. The three of us can't go up against these bastards alone."

At that instant, Brona's taroc reared and let out a screeching howl that Dharmen knew meant another of its kind was nearby. The other two nearly discharged their riders.

"What's the matter with them?" Yos asked. "What do they sense?"

"There!" Brona pointed to a low ridge just above them.

Dharmen saw it too: a faint play of light and shadow that couldn't have been made by a tree. "I wondered if we were alone up here. Rem-E, graviton burst, three-fourths yield, now!"

What could only be described as a rumble of thin air flew from Dharmen to the ridgetop. A man appeared, looking stupefied and trying to control his own mount: a full-grown longhorn nearly twice the size of the other steeds.

Yos leaned over toward Dharmen. "Isn't that—"

"Gallin!" Dharmen growled. "And using PTS, as I suspected." *Didn't take into account your animal's cooperation to keep it functioning, did you, traitor scum?*

"What the Netherworld is he doing up here?" said Brona.

Dharmen grunted. "Eavesdropping. And who knows what else—"

Instinct screamed at him to duck. The blast shot between him and Brona, hitting a large stone and reducing it to flying shards. The trio on the lower ground could barely control their mounts. Gallin aimed for another shot. Dharmen's was faster and surer. It hit Gallin dead-on. He lurched backward, and his weapon flew from his hand. But Dharmen's had been set to stun, and apparently not high enough to affect a Lenan. Gallin righted, turned his steed, and kicked it into a gallop.

"After him!" Dharmen yelled. He prodded his mount out of the clearing and broke for a path leading up to the ridge.

Yos and Brona followed.

It was far, but the distance shrank quickly beneath the animals' multiforked hooves. Dharmen had ridden before but never with such velocity up such steep slopes. He had heard about the speeds alpine tarocs could reach, thanks to a marriage of strong, agile limbs and superior climbing abilities, but the experience was beyond his wildest imaginings. He held on for his life and yelled to his companions to do the same.

They passed Gallin's lookout and rounded a narrow bend. They caught sight of him through the trees, riding hard ahead of them. Dharmen spurred his steed on, ducking as moving branches stretched farther and lower across the path.

The trail rose, twisting into sharp curves and dropping into narrow but deep ravines in places. The tarocs' leaping abilities more than covered the distances, though their mountaineering prowess did little to calm their riders.

Brona yelped as she nearly fell from hers at its last landing.

"Hold on tight!" Yos shouted. "This is the wrong place to fall. We don't want to lose you!"

"You won't get rid of me that easily, Professor. Just keep going. I'll manage!"

They went higher. Tree limbs bent and reached for them. Noticeably. Guiding his mount with one hand and thumbing his gun's energy setting higher with the other, Dharmen fired at a heavy bough directly ahead. It severed clean; the entire tree shuddered in recoil.

"We can't go much farther!" Yos yelled. "The higher you go, the bigger and more dangerous they become. Not enough of a nutrient base up here, so they rely on—"

"Animal protein!" Dharmen shouted back. "I remember my high woodlands training, Yos. Calm down!"

Dharmen halted his steed suddenly; his companions nearly slammed into him. They looked around baffled. The path, clearly visible up to this point, dead-ended. Throngs of moving trees larger than any they had encountered below blocked the way. The mounted, racing, yelling strangers had caused a chain reaction, with more and more limbs thrashing fiercely toward them and into each other. They barred any possible passage.

Terrified of the flailing branches, the tarocs snorted and wailed. Dharmen looked down. His was nearly invisible. He could see his boots through the animal's hide. *Now that's a fear-reaction. They never said it was this strong when they handed us the camos.* He scanned the area, listened carefully through the melee. No other taroc sounds nearby—no animal sounds of any kind, just the anger of the moving forest. And no hoof tracks to follow.

"Where could he have gone?" asked Yos. "He couldn't possibly have gotten past all this."

Dharmen's eyes searched. Rem-E's graviton burst had been enough to scramble any portable gravity wells. Unless he had a small army of engineers handy to reprogram his generator, Gallin's PTS was completely disabled. There had to be something they'd missed. "He'd better stay wherever he went for his own sake." Dharmen rose in his stirrups for a look around, though he knew it was useless. Then he plopped down, cursing and further unsettling his already terrorized mount.

Brona flinched, blushing at the spewing invectives. "Looks like he's gotten away."

Dharmen put his hands to his face and threw his head back. "For now. And if I have anything to do with it, not for long!"

CHAPTER 7

THE TEMPLE OF KRONE

hat are your calculations on religion, Rem-E?

I find the subject to be an interesting construct of the religious, sir.

Hmm.

◉

"WEAK. USELESS! I ASKED THESE Angoliners for just two weapons shipments, and they botched both!" Lord Naul paced his office like a penned animal. He gave the letter in his hand another disgusted look, crumpled it, and threw it onto his desk. "Any house slave could have done better. If I ever see Estes again, I will snap his alien neck!"

"What did my Lord expect from such a passive race?" said Naul's senior aide, Daio. "Sneaking around betraying their own people, filling a man's war with women soldiers, allowing every kind of Angoliner to fight equally without proper and necessary segregation? How much more inferior can a people be?" He looked to Eldo, who nodded agreement.

"Anyone allied with the Carmogen Empire has neither the option nor the luxury of failure," Naul grumbled, "and my newest Angoliner lead had better produce more than his predecessor." He stopped at the windows, looked across his compound. "Though he did give us great prizes in the Negaran forest ten months ago. The proceeds from the sale of the two jungle savages will buy my firstborn son's place in the army. He will make as fine a warrior as his father."

"And a better one than that pink-face on Negara, regardless of his gifts," Daio snapped. "That paltry excuse of a soldier will never be of any real use to you."

"Keep your baseborn opinions on my choices to yourself, Daio," said Naul. "This Armetrian is my best hope. My only one apparently. And for one of such a filthy race, he is strangely bright. He has had three operatives at their spaceport for some time now without his superior's knowledge. They do the work while he conceals himself behind their labor and well out of the Kraal's sight. The tactic befits a Carmogen." He turned to his two aides. "Do either of you know what is in that letter?" he said, pointing to the mangled piece of paper on his desk, not waiting for an answer. "It is from Supreme Command. My commission is under review over this arms situation—many in the Lescainate seek my removal over it."

"Surely not, my Lord!" exclaimed Daio.

"Surely so. The council would have my head over one Angoliner general who delivers nothing beyond smiles and promises."

Eldo, his junior aide, bowed for acceptance of his low-caste input. "I recall his visit, my Lord. His shadow would have been braver. That is what undermines your designs."

"And he tried to refuse willing whores when he was here. That is not warrior behavior. Are men not men in the West?" Daio added.

"Estes is like a frightened child alone at night on a low-sector Gragnan street. And that is only the tip of it," said Naul. "He was the wrong choice. He comes from naive, gullible people. I see clearly now the glacial, worry-free lives Angoliners enjoy. It is a weakness I will gladly exploit!" He clapped a gray hand onto each man's shoulder. "I hate these creatures, but I need their war technology if I am to continue heading the Ninth Army. When all is done, the Carmogen Empire will become Tentim's one and only dominion as God wills, and the Lescainate will have no choice but to make me supreme overlord of all imperial armies."

A page entered and begged his Lord's pardon, through Eldo with head down and voice low. House slaves were forbidden to speak to their master or to his senior aide directly. He handed over a slip of paper and hurriedly left the room. Naul took no notice. "Eldo, open the Angoliner communication channel and inform me when you have a secure connection. I want to speak with Armetrian immediately and without Lescainate eavesdropping."

"My Lord." Eldo handed the page's note to Naul and said, "The connection is already established. The alien has just contacted us."

DHARMEN HAD BEEN A SOLDIER for half his life, so he naturally looked forward to Kronaas, the fifth month of the Angolinian year, named for the god of war. He revered its sanctity. He appreciated the end of the winters. He did not appreciate the sudden heat that accompanied the holy month. Second spring sped by like a fleet-footed taroc stag, carrying the memory of the Kleve Park excursion with it. First summer would be brief, but scant comfort that was.

It was nearly two hours before morning muster. Lothnë had barely peeked above the eastern heights with thin but waxing light across the circular walkway surrounding the Temple of Krone, and it was already oppressively humid. And forecasted to last the next three weeks without a break, longer than the micro season itself. The MeteorologyMesh had already dubbed it the "Long Hot."

The stifling misery of Negara, all over again. Wonderful! Even the environmental cells embedded in Dharmen's uniform couldn't handle the heat as he fanned himself and swatted uselessly at insects swarming around him. Leaning against the balustrade and staring blankly outward, he hoped for some meditative peace of mind along the temple's frontages before venturing in.

Krone's house sat atop a low green hill overlooking one of the west marches' countless pocket vales. Falls roared over high bluffs above, emptying into a moat-like channel that isolated the massive building from its surroundings. A broad stone bridge provided sole access.

It was an oddly serene setting for a place built for soldiers, but Dharmen hadn't come to admire nature. He needed all the help he could get—spiritual included—to face what loomed on the murky horizon far beyond the Angolinian Rise. But he hadn't been to temple since his enlisted days and could barely remember the simplest ritual. Would his Lord lend an ear to one so absent for so long? Would Krone hear him? In spite of the heat, he trembled.

He moved closer to the falls, hoping their spray would repel the heat and flying nuisances. It worked. Winged things thankfully refused to follow, and the gentle, roving mists cooled and refreshed. He went from being hot and afraid to just afraid. *This isn't R & R, soldier! Are you going to do this or not*, he self-challenged.

He pried himself from the shelter of the walkway and entered the building. Across the threshold, he bowed clumsily as he accidentally cleaved through a small but close group of monks.

The temple interior was a sharp contrast to its bright outdoor environs. The circular sanctuary was huge, dimly lit, and strangely quiet for a structure perched beside so much rushing water. Thin breezes flowed between the massive piers supporting its dome. Dharmen was relieved to be out of the rising suns, but the sheer expanse of the space made him feel tiny. He had forgotten how much larger the sanctuary felt on the inside. The stories-high statue of Krone at its center reduced him further. Fear stole his nerve before his patron deity's likeness.

Glancing timidly up to the nemurite idol, he put his fist to his heart in holy salute and knelt. Too quickly. His scabbard chape struck the polished marblite floor, echoing metal through the chamber. Worshippers seated before the monument ceased chanting and turned with annoyed looks.

He rose and stifled curses as he bumbled past them, holding on to his clanking battle gear (and remembering the storage lockers made available to soldier-worshippers in the complex's satellite buildings). With furtive micromouse steps, he headed toward the great space's side chapels. He reached the low entrance of one and halted, unsure of what to do: holy salute before entering? Just go in?

Two approaching figures caught his eye. A man and woman, austere in appearance and seemingly at great peace, glided silently along the curving colonnaded passage between sanctuary and chapels. Their dark robes were edged in the script of the ancients. Their sword pommels glinted with every soundless movement. Few Ergyres remained in Angolin—these two were temple rectors, at least. The sight of them stirred memories of Dharmen's earliest days of worship, and the sword fighting instruction he had received from his father.

Suddenly remembering protocol, he placed his open right hand firmly to his chest and lowered his head.

"Welcome, child," said the man with untroubled calm.

Dharmen lifted his gaze to two formidable middle-aged faces. The eyes looking back seemed to hold stores of wisdom far beyond their bearers' years. The man was tall, with frost streaking his temples and beard, and a deep knife mark across one cheek. The priestess, of no less height, had dark-brown skin and straight black hair that hung neatly above her shoulders. Her deep, probing eyes pierced Dharmen's trepidation. Never before had he met such august and imposing individuals.

"I am Father Dietmar," said the priest, "Grand Fjaron of our Lord Krone. And this is Mother Encarra. We are the temple high elders. How may we assist you, Mr. Tate?"

Dharmen blinked. "Forgive me, Mother and Father. You know me?"

"Your reputation precedes you, Lieutenant Commander," Grand Fjaroness Encarra answered. "We've known of the Seventh Order's fieriest soul for a while now, but your recent actions over the Abyss have made you renowned in our Lord's eyes, and in the temple council's. And surely you've received much recognition on your home base?"

"I have, Mother." Dharmen couldn't help but notice the extra attention he and Theus were getting after downing the stolen ships, but he neither wanted the praise nor expected it to spread this far.

A faint smile penetrated the woman's kind but forbidding surface. "But you're unsure of your purpose here, or more to the point, you question your ability."

Dharmen felt flush. "Elders, I haven't been to temple since I was an SR. I'm . . . not worthy of our Lord's attention. I'm not even sure if it was right for me to come here."

"Never doubt your worth, child. Your honor is your one and only qualification to enter Krone's presence," said Dietmar. "You are a man of courage, conviction, and strong will, but you must recognize this in yourself if you're to achieve what you seek."

"I beg your pardon, Father?" Dharmen asked. He sensed the Grand Fjaron wasn't referring to prayer.

Dietmar regarded him through a battle-scarred face. "Only your honor and your best effort as a soldier will defeat the enemy: the one across the Great Void, and the one here in the Hidden Realm."

Dharmen opened his mouth but wasn't sure how to ask the question.

Encarra leaned closer. "You'll need strong resolve and unclouded judgment to defeat Lieutenant Commander Armetrian and his co-conspirators. Empty your mind of undue fear, embrace your strengths, and concentrate on your task. Only then will you be able to fight, and only then will Krone assist you."

Dharmen's heart skipped a beat. "I . . . I will, Elders. I promise you both."

"Promise yourself, child, before any other," Dietmar said.

He and Mother Encarra nodded simple goodbyes. Dharmen did the same, saluting as they silently left along the curved way. Swallowing the lump in his throat, he entered the empty chapel with newfound courage. The oval room was brighter than the larger sanctum. The simulated fires of wall torches and a growing stream of natural light through an oculus in its corbel-vaulted ceiling made it oddly inviting. Dharmen took the elders' words with him to the center of the chapel, lowered his head before the altar, and sat cross-legged on the floor in front of it.

He cleared his throat. "In the name of Our Majesties who shine brightly upon us each day, and of all their holy offspring, I place myself before them and you, Lord Krone," he recited, surprised at his sudden recall. "I apologize, Lord, for not having entered your presence for so long. It's been . . . You know how long it's been.

"First, accept my gratitude for keeping Will and me safe to this point. We've had some scrapes, but I have to believe that your hand shielded us in each one." He paused for a few pensive seconds that took him around his thoughts and back again. "Second, forgive me for questioning your will in choosing me for Negara. I didn't understand at first, but now I know why you sent me there and why you put me in the forest that night. You clearly have a purpose for me. For God and Realm, I will uphold my honor and see my duty through to the end, which is why I've come.

"I know I haven't done everything as I could have, and you know of my bad temper. I'll handle my shortcomings on my own, but beyond that, I need your help. Lord, I'm no hero. I'm not important or remarkable in any way. Angolin has my father for that. I'm only a man and my friends and I are few. We cannot protect our homeland alone, and

I humbly ask for your assistance. Give us strength and guidance to defend Angolin and defeat its enemies, and help me to stop Armetrian and his filthy bunch of—" *Don't swear!* "—his associates from destroying us from within. Help me think and assess more clearly to make sound judgments, carry out my duty, be a better soldier, and be . . . a better person."

He stifled a tear at that, thinking it inappropriate to show such weakness in the temple of the god of war. He straightened, deepened his voice.

"Finally, Lord, open my people's minds, and give them the tools they need to handle this. We Angolinians are isolated, unaware, and misguided in our notions, but we're good people who mean no harm to anyone. Most of us, that is. Help us to take this challenge head-on. If we can rise to your occasion, meet us halfway."

Dharmen rose and recited parting prayers, sighed relief, and headed for the exit but then slowed. "One more thing, my Lord," he said, turning back to the altar. "If possible, please wean Lieutenant Tarkala away from the East Vales. He spends more time in Nieuw Kered than on base. We don't want the enemy attack to catch him with his pants down. Literally!"

He stepped out into the passageway's low light, wondering if his words befit a soldier of the Guard. He considered that Krone knew his full mind regardless and moved on, rounding one of the huge dome-shouldering piers, and smacking into another worshipper.

"Lieutenant Commander! I'm sorry, I didn't see you," said Leatra.

"That's all right, Shipman Vinc."

"I've never seen you here, sir. I didn't know you came to temple."

Neither did I. "We all have to go sooner or later." Dharmen realized the example he should make as a midlevel officer. "Especially nowadays."

"Of course, sir," Leatra said shakily.

"Is there a problem?"

She opened her mouth but looked around before speaking. "Sir, I must talk to you about that night at Port."

"Yes, that was a near one, wasn't it?" Dharmen said restfully to calm Leatra and keep her fear from subduing whatever she might tell. "Has your stun wound healed?"

"It has, but . . ." She put a hand to her abdomen and frowned. "The pain from that blast shot through my whole body. I've never been that uncomfortable."

"We haven't quite reperfected the technology yet. Stuns will do that," Dharmen said. "Anyway, you had something to say to me. I'm listening, Shipman."

"Sir, I saw the thieves, nearly all of them. They used maintenance synths to load the containers onto the ships. I couldn't make out what was in them, but it wasn't hard to figure out after that first smuggling attempt."

Dharmen eyed her so sharply that she stepped backward. "Your duties carried you nowhere near that landing berth, Shipman. What were you doing there?"

"Why, snooping of course!" Leatra said. "If you had a hunch that something was up, wouldn't you?"

"Before you were hit, did you make out any faces?" Dharmen asked. "You said you saw most of them."

"I couldn't make out every face, and I definitely wouldn't have known them all. Some of them were port personnel. But I did see the one who shot me. It was Sublieutenant Ciros."

Dharmen lifted his eyebrows in the dim light. "You sure it was him?"

"I'm positive."

"This all happened two months ago, Vinc. Why didn't you come forward with it earlier?"

"I was afraid to," she answered. "I've heard a few conversations on Bemin and at Seventh lately about helping the enemy. Ciros and his friends are all part of it, and I wasn't sure who I could trust. I didn't want to risk telling what I knew to a traitor."

"You thought *I* might be a traitor, Shipman?" Dharmen said. "After all I did to stop them that night?"

Distress tinged Leatra's round face. "I truly apologize, sir, and I mean no offense at all. But this situation is so sensitive; I needed more time to—"

"Don't worry," said Dharmen. "I'm actually glad to hear you're this vigilant. It'll help a lot."

"Right, sir, thank you. But there may be someone else involved. I'm very worried . . . about my brother."

"Continue!" Dharmen said, unable to hide his surprise.

"Well, Irzek spends a lot of time with Ciros and Narond now. He used to hate them. Now suddenly, they're his close friends? I didn't understand it at first, and every time I asked about it, he got angry—told me to mind my own business, stop playing the twins holo, and let him be a man. He's going off base with them after morning muster."

Dharmen wanted to laugh. *Irzek Vinc a man?* "Where are they going?"

"To the Falconerplein, sir. There's an antigovernment protest there today. I overheard Irz talking about it."

Dharmen snorted through flared nostrils. He still didn't want to outwardly show his anger, but how dare a Guard recruit betray his honor to attend a rally against his own government!

Leatra shrank a bit at his reaction. "I've been past the square during a few of them. Lots of angry chants to overthrow our leaders. They get really intimidating at times."

"I know. I've heard about them," Dharmen grumbled. "I'm trying to take advice and stay clear of trouble. I haven't actually seen one yet, but I'd definitely like to at some point."

"Be careful, sir. I don't think the students would appreciate a uniform hanging around, from what I've seen."

"*They* need to be careful, Shipman, not me," Dharmen returned. "At least that's what my Willem would say, but don't worry. I'll blend in somehow when the time comes."

"If I may, sir, what's happening to us? What's all this anger about? I'm a soldier. I'm supposed to be tough, but this is the scariest thing I've ever seen."

"It's the scariest thing any of us have ever seen. For now," Dharmen said. "But whatever's coming, we'll match it. I don't care if some of the traitors *are* only students, I'm not willing to just hand Angolin over to the Carmis. I hope you aren't either."

"Certainly not, sir! Whatever you do, count me in." Leatra stopped as Guard uniforms approached from Krone's shrine. "I have to go. I have muster, then morning duties. Then I told Irz I'd meet him after his thing's over. I just hope he's alone. I don't appreciate his choice of company lately any more than they appreciate me."

"Good luck with that," Dharmen said.

Leatra hastily saluted and turned to leave.

"And Shipman . . ."

"Sir!"

"Krone be with you."

"Krone be with you also, sir." Leatra quickly crossed the sanctuary floor and left the building.

Dharmen went back into the passageway, away from the approaching worshippers. He found a quiet nook to duck into. "Forgiveness, Lord, this can't wait." He blinked his comm to activation. "Priority zero seven one Victor four. Authorization: Tate five seven nine five. Secure channel." At Rem-E's prompt, he continued. "Tate to Gennet."

"Gennet here."

"General, I need to place an arrest order."

"For whom, Lieutenant Commander?"

"For Sublieutenant Ciros, sir. I've just received information on his involvement in the last gun smuggling attempt from Bemin," Dharmen replied. Request approved, he made another. "And sir, send the security detail to the Falconerplein. About four hours from now, that's where they'll find him."

"WE NEED TO TALK, TATE! Right now!" said Armetrian.

Dharmen turned, found a pudgy, snarling face a meter from his own that was ready to interrupt his brief Ergive class-time break. He snorted at the unpleasant air accompanying the man. "Never a moment's peace. Something I can do for you, Lieutenant Commander?"

"Matter of fact, you can," Armetrian said. "What gave you the right to have Ciros detained? I know he was picked up on your order."

Hmmph, way sooner than I thought. "You can answer that on your own, but if you really don't know—"

"I read the warrant, soldier. I asked what gave you the right? You just had a good officer locked up. Guardsmen don't book their own!"

"Really? Ciros was witnessed as part of a weapons smuggling attempt. That's gunrunning and larceny. When discovered, he blasted the recruit who witnessed his actions. That's assault. We don't shoot our own either, *at least not off of Negara*," Dharmen said. "And today, Ciros was in the Falconerplein. A Guardsman has no business at a rally protesting the government he's sworn to protect. And as for *good officer*, your man is the worst I've ever seen in or out of my command."

"My man? What does that mean?"

"Ciros is a traitor, working under you. What else could it mean?" Dharmen prodded an angry finger into Armetrian's chest and kept it there. "He and the rest of your goons just happened to find themselves under me when I never requested them. You did that to get them to Port. Then right away, we had not one but two weapons thefts." Armetrian rolled his eyes away, and Dharmen's followed the evasion. "Do you honestly think you're fooling anyone, Armetrian? By now, half the Guard knows you're behind this."

Armetrian smacked Dharmen's hand aside. "Guess I shouldn't be surprised at how much your kind likes touching other men, should I, Tate?"

"Sorry to break it to you, mate, but nothing about you appeals to me. Good men, honorable men, *real men*, Armetrian—that's my type. So unless you suddenly grow into that and lose the beady eyes, bad breath, and bad attitude, I don't think I'll be bothered, will I? Your necro bag is the only part of you I want to get my hands on. Don't doubt that for a second!"

"How does so much mouth come from such a dry, useless excuse of an officer?"

"Got plenty of idiots like you to practice it on."

"Say what you want, but what's coming is coming, and you and your friends won't be able to stop it," Armetrian said. "Watch yourself, Tate, before things get ugly for you—"

Dharmen grabbed Armetrian by the collar, yanked him close. "And you watch who you cross while you're betraying your own people!" he growled with spit flying into Armetrian's face. "I haven't spent the better part of my career fighting for Angolin so lowlifes like you can tear it apart!"

Armetrian tried to free himself.

Dharmen grabbed his neck and slammed his head against the wall. "And you're right, Armetrian, it is ugly—real ugly!" he snarled through his teeth. "And it'll stay ugly until each and every one of you scum are gone, 'cause if you think I'm going to just stand by and watch, then you"—he gave Armetrian another hard head slam—"have to be"—and another—"fucking kidding!"

Dharmen had never gripped anyone so hard, and he had never seen anyone look so petrified. He glanced to his side and found his entire class and a good part of base watching in amazed silence. He looked back to Armetrian and shoved him to the floor. Armetrian coughed, red-faced as he scrambled to right himself. He took a swing, missed. Dharmen's didn't. Armetrian staggered back. Dharmen heard gasps and chattering around him. He stood ready for more, and he didn't care who or how many watched. But Armetrian had no more. Glaring, he straightened his tunic, rubbed his jaw, and limped away.

Dharmen's students filed in around him with a collage of expressions: supportive perhaps, hopeful maybe, confused. And on some, seethingly resentful. That arrest order was never going to sit well with everyone.

"You won't learn the ancient battle arts standing out here!" he boomed. With hands in the air as General Gennet often did, he ordered his dumbfounded Ergive aspirants back into the gym.

Class ended later with Dharmen still stamping out the flames of his anger as his students drifted out of the room. Footsteps halted behind him. He turned from the gym's main upright, expecting to find Armetrian or one of his cronies. He did not expect Irzek.

"Problem, Shipman?"

Irzek's thin, acne-scarred lips quivered. "H-he's right, you know. About Ciros—"

"Address me properly, soldier!"

"Sir! Apologies."

"That's almost more like it. And regarding Sublieutenant Ciros, just what was Lieutenant Commander Armetrian right about?"

"Permission to speak freely, sir."

"You've already done that, Shipman. May as well continue."

"Lieutenant Commander, I don't understand why you had Ciros arrested. He did nothing wrong."

"Oh, he didn't? And how do you know that?"

"I just know, sir, and . . . and what evidence do you have against him? You can't detain someone without proof of—"

"We need some discipline at Seventh. Since when does a recruit tell his CO what he can and can't do?"

"You granted me freedom to speak, sir."

"I didn't grant you freedom to forget who's in command, here or at Port. There've been two weapons thefts since we put boots down, and when I receive information on anyone possibly involved, I'm obligated to act. Anyone at all, Vinc. Don't forget it."

Irzek curled his lips into the same sickly sneer that Dharmen had grown so accustomed to from the man he had just sent hobbling away. "Permission to continue speaking—"

"You seem to have no trouble at it, Shipman, why bother to ask?"

"Why did you send MPs to the Falconerplein to spy on us to begin with? They walked the whole square before they found . . . Well, we know it had to be on your orders."

"Spy on you?" Dharmen hissed. "You and your cohorts—no one needs to spy on you. I was told some of my people were going where they didn't belong to take part in a treasonable situation. You've undermined the honor of the Guard, and mine for that matter. You're lucky I didn't have all of you brought in." Dharmen took the fear on Irzek's face and ran with it. "When your motives are right and you uphold your honor, Vinc, you don't have to hide anything. Tell that to Ciros and Narond next time you see them, and tell it to your boss who was just here at class break."

"But, sir—"

"Dismissed! Get back in uniform and attend to your duties before you find yourself in more trouble than you're already in. Because I'm just getting started!" Dharmen barked. "And if you can find time between protests, think about how to become a better Ergive student.

Concentrate on what goes on in here, Shipman, not on what's happening in the Falconerplein!"

Irzek flipped a salute above eyes pooling hatred, turned, and stormed off. Dharmen watched him leave and refreshed the main upright. He studied the class data uploads but ruminated beyond them. Why couldn't he follow the general's example and keep his mouth shut? And why did he always let even the slightest person affect him? "I didn't handle that well at all, did I, Lord Krone," he grumbled to himself.

Unsheathing metal and rushing boots filled his ears. He instinctively wheeled and leaped away, evading his attacker. Years of training and experience kicked in; he grabbed his own sword handle, yanking it from its scabbard.

Irzek's blade flew past him, hit the upright, and sent cascading ripples through its holo-imagery. Wild-eyed and oblivious to his blunder, Irzek turned and lunged, bringing his blade down in an offensive maneuver he'd been instructed in numerous times.

Dharmen was more than ready for it. He met the back end of Irzek's thrust, blocked the blade, and punched him in the side of the head. Irzek stumbled but regained his footing and lunged again, throwing rage into his movements. Dharmen handily dispatched each one . . . and he felt contact between metals that he hadn't experienced in years.

"That's not simulated, Vinc, that's real. Where did you get it?"

Irzek said nothing but breathed heavily. Anticipating the recruit's next move—and thankful that he had ignored or forgotten instruction against betraying intentions with facial expressions—Dharmen readied himself. Irzek rushed him. Unsuccessfully. He made more adrenaline-guided thrusts, each one skillfully met.

"Who are you to question my honor," Irzek grated. "You think being a general's son puts you above everybody else? I'm as loyal to Angolin as anyone!"

"We'll debate that one later," Dharmen said. "And haven't I warned you repeatedly about overextended limbs? If you want to continue this, tighten your stance before you lose an arm!"

Irzek apparently heard nothing through his crazed fugue. He made another long thrust—arms extended outward as he had done since day one against all tutelage. Dharmen evaded the inept move and parried with a force that sent sparks across the clashing blades. Taking advantage of Irzek's surprise, he twisted his own blade, attempting to wrest the other's sword from his hand. Irzek kept hold of his weapon but badly fumbled a countermaneuver. Dharmen repelled it, wrenched Irzek's sword from him, and sent it clanging across the floor.

Dharmen drew back, glanced down at his own blade. Blood ran along its edge and dripped onto the floor. Irzek's face changed from anger to fright at the sight of his badly slashed forearm.

"Be glad you still have it," Dharmen said. "And if you'd spent more time learning from me instead of Armetrian, you'd know how to use a sword by now, traitor."

He scooped the pilfered weapon from the floor and opened a channel to security, but before he could utter a word, Irzek reached into his cargo pocket and produced a gun, fumbling through his injury before aiming.

Dharmen held fearlessly still. "Put that away, Shipman."

Footsteps scrambled from behind. Dharmen looked around to a gym refilling with uniforms.

Leatra barreled through the onlookers. "Irz, by Krone, what do you think you're *doing*?"

"Defending my honor, Sister. What else?" he said emptily, holding his bleeding forearm with one hand while fingering the sidearm's trigger with the other.

He flinched, stiffened at a gun barrel pressed against his temple.

"You heard the man, Vinc. Drop it," Theus ordered.

Irzek didn't comply.

"Now!"

Irzek held firm, but the gun was snatched from his hand before he could fire. Dori backed away with it, deactivating its power cell as MPs stormed up behind Irzek and restrained him. Blood ran down his arm and dotted the gym floor as he was led away through the reassembled crowd.

"Right on time, mates," Dharmen said to his rescuers. "And curiously so. Thanks for the assist."

"No problem. Glad we could be here," Theus replied.

Dharmen ignored the agitated conversation crackling around him. His life had flashed before his eyes more than once in his career, but never from one he had worked so closely with and so hard to instruct. He looked to Leatra. *How has it all come to this?* his expression silently asked.

She said nothing. A strained sigh, head hung low, and eyes clamping shut was her answer.

CHAPTER 8

SUBTERFUGE

"**F**ile transfer complete, Nijs. You have all requested data. Confirm."

"Confirmed, Rem-E. My user should find them of benefit. With that, I query: Lieutenant Tarkala has expressed concern for your user's well-being. As the humans would say, how is Lieutenant Commander Tate *doing* at the moment?"

"*Unsettled* most accurately describes his mean emotional state over the previous 10.25 months in particular. At the moment, he is oddly and very much at peace."

❂

DHARMEN CLIMBED THE STAIRS AND stood before the towering doors. Flanking marblite likenesses of the Hidden Realm's founders greeted him in caryatid force. He ignored the door wardens' stiff stances and smug faces. Again. He had already toured most of the complex, walked the plein out front, and admired *The Crew*: a meters-long relief sculpted in tribute to the ancients' first starship complement. This was his third time entering the building. Willem's meeting was taking far longer than promised.

Dharmen didn't care. Not once did he check the time or pace about, swearing and drawing attention to himself like he normally would. Let them take all day. He was blissfully unconcerned about it. And blissfully unconcerned felt marvelous for once. Surrounded by his ancestors' achievements, tucked in the Alkmaar Range's green vales and folds, nothing ever troubled Dharmen when he came to the Great Hall.

He entered the building, looked up and around. Piers matching their exterior buttress counterparts supported a simply designed wood-beam ceiling. Its wide planks, carved and painted with scenes from the ancients' home worlds, seemed to shoulder the heavens. The octagonal forward hall's broad arches dwarfed the space behind and pulled his eye up to the building's dome. Beyond the arches, an ambulatory led out of the building to the rest of the sprawling, mostly hidden stronghold-turned-mountainside conurb below, and its satellite buildings on tree-shrouded, cliff-edge terraces. Far from the airy sleekness of Angolin's newer built environs, the Greathall district was a muscular place of purpose and built to last. For a time.

Dharmen found it hard to believe that every structure in the original compound including the Great Hall itself was originally intended to be temporary, and that the ancients had planned to dismantle the entire stronghold before leaving the planet. But they stayed, and their work endured for nearly a millennium.

And for Dharmen personally, something else endured. Now, as always, he sensed it: a warm, bright energy enveloping him. Physical, metaphysical, ethereal—he couldn't quite place the uncanny sensation filling him, or the gentle motion of his hair and cloak even indoors out of the wind. Or the voices, if that's what they were. Here and nowhere else, he sensed an *other* accompanying his every step, other and emotionally nourishing, though eerie . . . "Impressive," he breathed wistfully of the whole experience.

"Very!"

Inner peace held his upward gaze in arrest. "Dori. Thee. Interesting meeting you both *here*."

"I'd ask if you're all right if I thought I needed to," Dori said to the back of his head. "Never seen you so content. It makes a real change."

"Everyone has a place that speaks to them, Commander." Slowly, he turned from the Hall's heights. "I've been expecting you two."

"Really?" said Theus.

"Yes. You were there to put Vinc down the other day when neither of you had ever come to observe my class before. Now you're here keeping me company, and you're not even Great Hall enthusiasts. Coincidences, mates?"

"You saw us trailing you through the mid hall gardens, didn't you?" Dori frowned at Theus. "I told you we were too close, Lieutenant."

"There was that too," Dharmen said. "That, and Rem-E detecting your internals close by. Forgot that little detail, huh?"

"You of all people went before Krone last week. If you can suddenly find religion, so can we," Theus said.

"This isn't a temple, Thee," Dori said. "But Dharm, just think of us as angels of Krone, if you would."

"Angels of Gennet, more like," Dharmen said.

"Is there any part of this you haven't figured out?" Dori asked. "The general asked us to look after you and Will. We're on the clock for you, but we'd gladly do it on our own."

"I know, Commander," Dharmen said. "My household security upgrades are at maximum efficiency, and General Gennet has a detail watching our pod now. I figured you two would join the effort. We'll have more tenders than Lenan royals soon, but thanks for being part of the team."

"Where's your other half?" Theus asked. "We're botching this already. We know you came together."

"Will's meeting with the conurb mayor," Dharmen replied, "for the day, by the look of it."

"With Mayor Maur? Really? What on Tentim for?" Dori asked.

Dharmen's unusually placid, restful expression soured. "Among other things, to discuss lifting Gallin's diplomatic immunity and having him arrested."

"At Greathall? Why not talk to South C?" Theus asked. "The attack happened on your canal. They'd be the district to report it to."

"He has his reasons," Dharmen evaded, "and he knows Mayor Maur personally. I guess he thought it best to start here."

Silent, stony faces met him.

"Don't look at me. I told Will I don't want him in this further, but he insisted, said he's already deep in it, that he has every right to seek justice and won't be able to if he doesn't speak up soon. And he's right."

He calmed himself, not wanting to be angry here. Dawn Fire could try for him all they liked. He could handle it. He was *ready* to handle it. But his partner was another matter. "And Gallin," he took a deep breath and continued, "better hope the conurbs find him before I do. I can't take it much longer. I'm about ready to march back up to Mount Condorcet and yank him out of his hole."

"And create more trouble, Dharm," said Dori. "Definitely seek justice, but beyond that, leave well enough alone."

"I'd be glad to if it were well enough!"

"Have you discussed any of this with Gennet to start with?" Theus asked.

"I have. And I can't do anything—I gave the general my word. *Yes, Thee*, we discussed it, and Gennet doesn't like it either, but he can only restrict *me*. He can't control Will's choices."

Dori straightened her uniform and threw back her cloak. "Will can take all the legal steps he needs to while you beat the Lenan senseless, but I'm afraid you really will have to find him first. After your little shootout above Kleve Park, Gallin is still nowhere to be found."

Dharmen's glare could have whittled the Hall's pillars to dust finer than the ancients' Tentimly remains. "Seriously, the man's got immunity, why even bother to hide? He could dance rings round us, and we couldn't do anything."

"I had a long talk with Aremel last night," Dori said. "She told me about him, and about Balaneth and his harem of sorts. Did you know upper-class Lenan men are allowed to—"

"They're polygamous, Dori, I know. What did she say about Gallin?"

"Well, when Aremel told me about Balaneth and how she may take him back, I warned her about his aide. I gave her the full account of Will's incident and told her to be careful. 'Anybody intent on forcible kidnap should be kept clear of for starters,' I said, 'and with Balaneth's immunity covering anyone working for him, who knows what else Gallin might do, even on your property.' I didn't mention your run-in with him up the mountain. That would've thoroughly frightened her."

"And what did she say to all of that?" Theus asked.

"You know Aremel. She shrugged it off, or she seemed to," Dori said. "That woman's got a smile for everything, just like her cousin. Must be a Hanne trait."

"You've obviously never seen Will's father," Dharmen muttered. "Old Henk's stare could still every tree in these mountains. I'm surprised upright generators don't fry when he's on the NewsMesh."

"I do believe Aremel understood me," Dori continued in an unmoved tone, sidestepping Dharmen's venom. "She didn't quite say so, but then she told me that Balaneth is returning to Mount Condorcet, without his attaché of course. But that doesn't mean Gallin won't turn up at some point."

Dharmen cast his eyes downward and sighed. "I'll let the general know to redouble his efforts in our protection. I'll reinforce my own measures too."

"No need, I've already briefed him on everything," Dori said. "I also suggested posting a detail around Kleve Park, but it's a big place. I doubt it would be completely effective."

"*I* doubt Gennet can scrounge up enough people who can be trusted with that." Dharmen gave her and Theus a shoulder clap each and paced between them, crossing his arms and looking up to the flickering holographic flames in the Hall's enormous chain-tethered candelabras. "So we've got two attempts on me, one on my Willem, and now the traitors' head Lenan is on the loose. What a gods-forsaken load of—"

"Will! Good morning!" Dori cut in.

"Dori, Theus," Willem approached and greeted. "What brings you two here?"

"Oh, we wanted to join you both today and take in the sights of—"

"I was kidding, Thee. I overheard about Gallin," Willem said. "So he's out there where no one can find him, and no one's looking either. How convenient."

Dharmen put an arm around Willem's shoulder. "We'll get him, love. Don't worry."

"I'm not. I don't really have to be. Immunity's as new as diplomacy in Angolin; it won't cover everything he's done. It's Gallin who should be worried, and I think his disappearance says he is."

"Is that what the mayor thinks?" Dori asked.

"That's his take on it, yes."

"Can he act on that take? Can anybody?" Dharmen knew the answer to that.

"He's looking into it. I can't divulge more."

"Will, you know we'll do whatever we can, regardless," Theus offered.

"Right, Thee. Will you two excuse us for a minute?" Willem took Dharmen's arm and guided him toward the ambulatory.

Dharmen stopped beneath one of its high arches.

"Not far enough," Willem said.

They left the Hall and descended a long flight of stairs to one of the fortress's many hanging garden terraces. They passed through an opening in a high, centuries-old hedge to a secluded spot beneath a canopy of mature, static trees. A waterfall rushing down from the heights masked their words perfectly.

"So what did Maur say?" Dharmen asked.

"I already told you. I can't say much more than he's with me on the immunity situation."

"I figured as much, but what did he say about the other matter? Do you think you'll get the position?"

Willem frowned and tightened his lips, a face he rarely made. "Probably. He's definitely interested in bringing me on, but . . ." He looked around even though they were clearly alone. "When we were finishing up, he said, 'We can't be too careful, especially nowadays.' I'm not sure what that's supposed to mean."

"I think you do, love. You just don't want to say it: Treason has reached local governments too. It's not just a few bad officers anymore. It's spreading."

"You and your flag of truth, Dharmen. Don't you get tired of waving it? No, I don't want to say it. I don't want to think about it, either."

They looked to the patches of sky peeping through the tree canopy. Its soothing purple brightened to a sickly yellow as the Cloak whisked above. Dharmen took Willem's hands, and they held each other for a few minutes.

"It'll be all right, love."

He received a message prompt, released Willem, and listened.

A half minute later, Dori and Theus found their way down to the shrouded enclosure. "You two sure know how to find privacy," Dori breathlessly puffed. "A few more steps would've taken you back to Nieuw Holland. Did you get the general's order, Dharm?"

"Affirmative, Commander." He gave Theus a pressing look.

"I'll see Will back to the Centrum and meet up with you both right after," Theus said in response. "Probably better this way. We'll be able to take separate ships. The three of us shouldn't travel together at this point."

Theus and Willem climbed back up to the Great Hall's front plein.

Dharmen and Dori took a less public way. And he grunted in disgust at the thought: he was about to leave his favorite place unexpectedly for his least favorite. "At least we'll get Bemin over with early today, if nothing else."

DHARMEN COULDN'T REMOVE HIS EYES from the spectacle. "Who on Tentim are all these people?"

"Open Port Day participants, who else?" Dori answered from the ground below.

Dharmen was too busy gaping to follow her off the gunship.

"Today is the annual event for outside visitation. You were briefed on it when you took the posting, remember?"

He had remembered: this was Bemin's welcome to scientists, Guard top silver, and (unfortunately) politicians from all over Angolin for tours, panel discussions, and anything else to get in the way of his duties. He vaguely recalled having the thing described to him, but the last two months' calamities had pushed it cleanly out of his mind. *And no one said there would be this many participants!* Port looked more like a swarming hive from above. The sight on the ground was much worse and of no help to their current situation:

General Gennet's message reported a small Carmogen force over the Abyss—far out but closing. Sensors had detected archaic fighter planes in an approach vector bringing them directly to Bemin. And then sensors curiously became inoperative.

Jammed, and internally, Dharmen thought. Mainland and Port defenses were raised, and all Guard bases and sensitive installations placed on high alert. He had expected to arrive to another lockdown. So why this ridiculous security risk? Having the Kraal and the Ministry of Science send all their people at once was bad enough. Couldn't they recall at least some of them and let him and his people do their jobs?

"General Gennet told us to keep our eyes open," he said as he joined Dori in the human tide. "Carmis headed in this direction is serious. How can we possibly secure Port with all these bodies here?"

"With our best effort," Dori replied mechanically. "Station, Lieutenant Commander! I'll be in Main Command if you need me." She disappeared into the sea of wide-eyed, ambling groups.

This was no time for his usual ire. Dharmen forced patience as people practically fell over him for better looks at anything and everything. Even the roving maintenance synths seemed put off. And after several minutes of what felt like navigating the Centrum at High Holidays, he understood: enemy ships were approaching, and every beaker twirler and grandee in Angolin was packed into Port all at once. The gods weren't sporting coincidence on this one. He shook his head as he spotted Theus coming toward him. "Mind accompanying me, Lieutenant?"

"Through all this? To where?"

"To section Delta-56, Heavy Artillery Storage. I think we'll find something of interest there. I'm sure of it, actually."

"Don't you have afternoon muster first?"

"We're early, Thee, remember? Transport from Seventh isn't due for another two hours, though who knows? Some of my company might be here already."

Theus nodded. "You suspect—"

"Uh-huh."

They carved a burdensome path. The ogling, mesmerized multitudes challenged every step, unaware that they might be in the way. Even Dharmen's hard stares weren't enough to part them. Being a hidden society even to your own people meant extreme curiosity when they were actually shown something. "Make way, please. Make way! A meter for your trouble," Theus snapped at the stupefied faces. "And don't look at me with your mouths wide open. Some of us are actually working, you know!"

"Nice, Thee. Badass 101, I'll teach you yet!" Dharmen received a communiqué that was coded and marked Personal. He entered the security decryption, and the caller's voice filled his earplant. "Understood, sir. Tate out."

"Now what?" Theus asked to his frozen look.

"That was Gennet. He says Armetrian's disappeared. No one's seen him since yesterday, there are no log entries for him since the night before, and he didn't show up for duty this morning. And not just him, Fifth has an AWOLer too."

"What about his internal? A scan of it must've turned up something."

"Negative. According to the general, his internal's untraceable and not answering summons."

"Hacked into and disabled, just like on Negara?"

"Yep, and likely for good this time," Dharmen replied. "Did you look over the files I had Rem-E send Nijs? I think we'll be using them."

"Affirmative, but are you certain it'll work? TS is shaky enough technology. I'm not so sure about mobile suppression via internals. This kind of thing is normally done by more advanced equipment."

"You were the developer-specialist in your enlisted days, Thee, you tell me if it'll work."

"Well, both of our internals acting in concert might be enough, provided anyone using TS is close enough to detect. We'll need to maximize field strengths to increase range. But, Dharm, even if it works and if anyone's here, how will we find them in this crowd?"

"Set dampening to short interval bursts and keep your eyes peeled for distortions, Lieutenant, that's how. We have to neutralize their PTS gravity wells without compromising any port systems."

They navigated the mass, watching and scanning. The painfully slow-moving throngs weren't helping either of them focus sights. Dharmen's mind numbed at the thought of a missing traitor—two missing traitors—to contend with. He contacted Dori for official instructions.

"As you were, Lieutenant Commander. Nothing we can do about Armetrian from here," was her order before signing off.

"You realize he could be anywhere besides Bemin, and he probably is," Theus reasoned. "Armetrian's not stupid. If he's been gone over twenty-eight hours, who knows where he might be? Gennet will have half a unit looking for him."

Dharmen stopped. The distortion in the corner of his eye was just enough. "Won't be necessary, Lieutenant. We've found him."

"What?" Theus followed his gaze to Armetrian, standing across the tarmac. A woman appeared beside him. Her PTS had undoubtedly also been affected by the makeshift dampeners. Armetrian glared defiantly at Dharmen until his companion grabbed his arm and yanked him away. They disappeared through the crowd. "Dharm, we've got to contact—"

"No time!" Dharmen unholstered his sidearm and dove into the crowd with Theus behind him.

Through hordes of dumbfounded faces, he glimpsed his targets. He yelled at onlookers to clear the way; somehow the sight of his drawn gun hadn't done the job. He shoved bodies out of his path and ignored the protests. Theus and Dharmen reached the spot where he initially spotted the pair, stopped, and scanned. Their targets were nowhere to be seen, and there were too many people to visually sift through until Dharmen located another mark: a head of dirty-blond hair flying in the winds blowing in from above the Abyssal ceiling.

Armetrian's dull features blended him into the crowd, but Vara was readily noticeable. She and her fleeing companion were having as much difficulty getting through the masses as their chasers, tripping up and knocking down the unwary as they ran. They scrambled and disappeared around the corner of a hangar. Hovering maintenance synths swerved to avoid them.

Dharmen and Theus rounded the structure, crossed its forward tarmac. Tour groups continued to abound, and Dharmen wondered to the Netherlords why they were allowed in a restricted area. But at least there were fewer of them here to deal with.

He spotted Armetrian running fast. Alone. "Get down!" Dharmen bellowed. Heads turned, then vanished as everyone in his line of fire dropped. He tightened his finger across the trigger, pressed—

A flash blinded his sight, followed within a fraction of a second by a hard thrust to his chest.

"Dharmen!" Theus yelled.

Dharmen barely heard him. His attention was on the familiar sensation of the particle shot, and his body hitting the ground. He was aware enough to comprehend that Armetrian continued to flee while Vara lay in wait for him to round that blind corner. He had taken that bait too easily.

"Dharmen, are you okay?" Theus crouched beside him. "Sound off, Lieutenant Commander. Speak to me!"

Dharmen's eyes opened and blinked. "I'm fine, Thee," he said in a strangely leisurely tone. "I hope."

"Krone's balls!" Theus stared, stumped. "That weapon either wasn't set to stun or didn't have the feature. The beam was too intense. How can you possibly be . . .?"

Dharmen got up, partially undid his tunic, and reached in to examine the hit. Nothing. "Thee, I'll explain later. Let's just try to get them. And this time, let's stay sharp!"

Looking around and finding no sign of Vara or Armetrian, he ran in the direction where he'd last seen the latter. Theus followed.

They didn't get far.

The ground rumbled with the force of heavy antigrav drives. One, two, then three massive starships were rising above Port. The sight was amazing. Nearly two kilometers in length each, they were gigantic. Dharmen had seen them on the ground in shallow hollows turned berth-sets, but never in the air. HRA-20 heavy cruisers they were, fresh out of workups and built for deep space travel. But these ships left at too low an angle for orbit. And their pilots weren't bothering with stealthtech. Port sensors must have been thoroughly scrambled.

"Maybe they're carrying some of the VIP groups back home. Those are passenger ships, aren't they?" Theus asked.

"Oh, they're for passengers, all right," Dharmen answered. "Passenger *crew*. Hundreds at a time for space exploration, and not just going back to Angolin." He turned and headed toward one ship's vacated anchorage.

"Where are you going?" Theus called after him.

"Fill Dori in and get to MC, quick! We have to get a pursuit force after them!"

"But Dharmen—"

"That's an order, Lieutenant!"

DHARMEN ARRIVED AT ANCHORAGE SIX, the closest berth-set for one of the escaping cruisers. The tour groups along the way had nearly evaporated, but he barely noticed. He moved stealthily to the anchorage's control tower, ducking behind building supports and equipment stands to dodge roving security synths. He had the distinct feeling of being watched, and not by artificial eyes or internal tracking. But he couldn't use PTS and his dampener simultaneously, and if Armetrian's ground people tried to escape under PTS, he had to keep them visible.

He reached the tower entrance and allowed himself to be scanned. No other choice if he wanted access. The door slid open. He entered the small vestibule. There was no guard, flesh or synth. Towers were priority-one secure sections. Why was no one here? He went to the lift and let its sensor scan him for entry; there was no choice if he wanted access. Then he left the lift for the stairwell. No sense in getting trapped like that.

He climbed, the dizzying sensation from the upward twisting turns feeling too much like the point-blank particle hit he'd just taken. Laser focus kept him from vomiting. He reached into his tunic and felt around more thoroughly. Still no sign of blood or any wound at all. *That idea worked. Hope it'll continue to,* he thought.

At the top of the stairs, Dharmen paused. Curiously, there was still no one to be seen, but he knew his every move since entering the tower had been monitored. He reached the control hub door. Gun in hand, he commanded it open and burst through.

Someone rushed him faster than he could turn and fire, kicking the sidearm from his hand. His combat instincts took over as a fist flew at his face. He blocked the punch and landed a bone-crushing one to his assailant's jaw. The attacker lifted his pulse rifle but got a hard, swift knee to the abdomen before he could fire. He fell to the floor groaning, and his weapon tumbled from reach. Dharmen unsheathed his sword, held it to the other's throat.

"Morning, Shipman. Interesting to meet you here."

Stunned eyes went to the rifle.

"Don't even think about it." Dharmen pressed his blade tip deeper into the shipman's flesh and said, "Turn over now or lose your head!"

Looking mortified, Narond capitulated.

Dharmen pulled two sets of manacles from his belt pouch, placing one set across Narond's wrists and the other across his ankles. Both sets activated the instant they were laid, their end sealers quickly finding their targets and tightening their grip.

Port Security arrived in force. Their lead asked for the manacle key codes. She wanted to put the prisoner into her own restraints and free his legs for transport.

Dharmen refused. "I'll collect him and take him back to Seventh later, much later. In the meantime, let him hop his way to your brig!"

DHARMEN ENTERED MC, IGNORING THE harried faces turning to him from workstation uprights.

"Report!" Dori ordered.

He complied, beginning with Armetrian and Vara, and ending with Narond's capture. "I got the first half of that from Thee," she said, "and I have a portwide lockdown in place till we can get our bearings. We're in pursuit of the stolen cruisers. As for Armetrian and his friend," she paused at his expectant look, "we'll keep searching for them now that we have partial sensors. Theus is scanning for their internals' signatures, but he's coming up blank. They must have escaped on one of those ships."

"*Partial* sensors," Dharmen said and threw up both hands. "After having been saboed. Of course! Why not? Thee, is there any way we can boost the scan range to—"

"Ma'am, the pursuit force has located the stolen cruisers," came a report to Dori from a monitoring station.

"Where, Petty Officer?" Dori asked.

"Bearing north five seven east, less than fifty klicks out. Our people have overridden and patched into the cruisers' navigation systems, strangely without resistance. They'll auto-land them back into their berth-sets. ETA, six minutes."

Dori ordered a cadre of security to all three anchorages with Dharmen and Theus added to the force. Monitoring the situation from MC would never satisfy Dharmen, and Theus was the best possible accompaniment against any more rash behavior. Dharmen understood his superior's purpose perfectly.

They joined the Anchorage Six detail after its cruiser was remotely brought to landing. The port grid's sensor effectiveness was still spotty; sniffer synths were sent in first to scour the capital ship for its thieves and any hidden surprises they might have laid. The security lead, the very same one who allowed Dharmen and Theus to pursue the last set of stolen ships, ordered his team to stand ready to storm it. He acknowledged Dharmen with a sideways wink through an overfriendly smile, one of too many lately. Dharmen ignored it.

Synths and uprights relayed initial reports, but the host of mobile sensors indicated no life aboard. Dharmen readied for a gun battle anyway. The lead gave the signal, and his people poured into the ship with Dharmen and Theus in-stream. The deck-by-deck search of the vessel took nearly an hour. Dharmen ground his teeth through every minute of it. He had hoped to find someone—anyone—onboard, but sensors had been correct, the cruiser was empty. The same was reported of the other two ships. The team's last effort was recombing the bridge deck and examining the duty stations' post-liftoff command entries.

"You thinking what I'm thinking?" Theus asked.

"That these ships were decoys? Definitely," Dharmen returned. "All tower-controlled, while the real carriers escaped under full TS." He went to the helm-right and accessed the conn logs. He wasn't familiar with the new ship's instruments, but it didn't take long to find what he needed: extraneous navigation commands spliced in with the original threads, hiding some portions and replacing others. "Narond's smarter than I ever gave him credit for. Most of this is irretrievable, but he left just enough behind . . . along with a personal access trigger." *Nice work, Shipman*, he thought. *Enough to detain you on grounds of treason. That'll be one down!*

The security lead reported new information: the port sensor grid was slowly returning to normal function but with the range limited to Bemin's immediate vicinity. Dharmen was unsurprised at the rest: other ships—more heavy cruisers—were missing. And at present, four weapons depots in section Delta-56 had been despoiled of their contents, with more compromised stores expected.

Pain splashed across Dharmen's face.

"You realize there was nothing more we could've done, mate," Theus offered.

Dharmen stood wordless, thinking of the immediate future. He had already begun mentally crafting the report to General Gennet, who would not be pleased at all. But that was the least of the problem. An arms stockpile great enough to outfit a decent-sized army was on its way to Carmogen, likely delivered by two AWOL traitors and any number of minions working for them. Armetrian and Vara were being searched for, and at least one accomplice had been caught. But what was the use? They had already succeeded beyond imagination.

Dharmen roared a litany of curses, kicked a container of scanning equipment across the metal floor plating, and slumped into the helmsman's seat. He looked around through the sudden silence to find Theus and the rest of the bridge staring wide-eyed at him. Burying his face in his hands, he took stock of the situation. *I'll settle with Narond later,* was consideration number one. The next was the hard reality of Dawn Fire's latest win. And despite every countereffort, Armetrian's elaborate subterfuge had worked.

CHAPTER 9

COURIERS

re we out of her ship's sensor range, Cor-GON?
Affirmative, Lieutenant Commander. And all onboard signatures, including my own, are masked as ordered.

Excellent! Vara's a stealthtech expert, I can't be too careful. Now, if I can only see the second *half of this mission through . . . What's that signal, Cor-GON? Are you getting that?*

I am, sir.

We're nine thousand kilometers from Angolin. There aren't even rises, let alone civilizations out here. Who's sending it?

Unknown, but I can easily determine that. The signal is a hail. Shall I respond?

Negative. Maintain silence. Whoever it is, this is no place for hi-theres.

❂

A YEAR OF HARD WORK, and now it's all falling apart! Estes stood on his live-in terrace staring blankly in the direction of Fifth, his thoughts eating him alive . . . "I can smell your perfume. I know you're there," he said softly out into the night.

Coraia stepped out and joined him. "You've been far away all evening. You hardly spoke at all through dinner. What's the matter?"

Life! And it's burden enough. Do I have to talk too? "Base business, as usual. Nothing to worry your pretty head over."

"Twenty-five years of marriage to a senior Guardsman has taught me a few things, Eldric. Fifth practically runs itself. Something else is bothering you. What's the news from our Eastern friends?"

Estes ground his teeth behind closed lips. "There is none. That I know of, anyway. We had regular contact until a few weeks ago, and it's been quiet since."

"There's an entire void between you and your contact, literally. But you established and nurtured the first ever relationship across that distance. Lord Naul must appreciate that."

"I don't know what Naul appreciates. He *understands* results and only results. There were too many failures before this latest weapons lift, and he was angry then." Estes lifted his eyes to the heavens. Night sky peered back with no solace to give. "I know I promised you, Cori, but our plans are in limbo right now. Armetrian vanishes, and three shiploads of Bemini weapons vanish with him? That was my project to implement—and mine to lose apparently. It's all finally happening but without me. I'll admit that for what it is, I have no other choice."

"Choose patience then," Coraia said. "What we're doing is highly delicate. Blood, sweat, and a lot of hours are what power and prestige cost. This isn't over by a long shot."

Estes turned, pulled her close, and wrapped his arms around her. "You more than anyone would know, Cori. Your family's been doing this for ages. How many unsuspecting backs have you all stood on to get ahead?"

"Each and every one that got in our way. You know my answer. But that's gotten us nowhere lately."

"Your uncle is the president of Angolin. Doesn't that mean *something* for the Prinsen clan? It's more than anyone in my family has achieved, especially my gods-damned excuse of a father."

"Your father did gods-damned well enough from what you tell me, though thank Lothnë that your mother took you and escaped him, or your life would be vastly different now," Coraia said. "But president or not, my uncle is the family outsider. Angolin elected him and forgot the rest of us. Now we're outshone by one do-gooder who clawed his way up through the Kraal but can't be bothered to honor his own flesh and blood's—"

"We can't worry about that, Cori. We have to think of ourselves. Vieron has us in high-flyer sights now, and this latest situation could expose me. I'll have to lie low for a while, not that I have much to lie low for at the moment."

Coraia smiled that smile of hers: pleasant and tranquil on the surface, and hiding calculating thoughts beneath. "You aren't through yet," she said. "There's still a chance to recover this alliance. Armetrian doesn't have your years of experience; he'll slip up eventually. Be ready when he does."

Estes nodded. Coraia's clear-minded resolve in ever-deepening unseen layers never failed to astonish him. Neither did her beauty. Tonight, she wore that long, shimmering gold dress that made her smooth deep-brown skin all the more stunning, and the moonslight of Kiern and Dasha bathed her in a soft glow, pierced by the sparkle in her dark eyes. He silently undressed her.

"Husband, I'd love to indulge you, but—"

He hushed her with a kiss, moving from her lips down the nape of her neck.

"Please, we mustn't."

"Why not, Cori? We used to do it out here all the time."

"You forget that we're expecting someone."

"She's not here yet!"

"She's due any minute, and you know we need the information."

Estes wanted badly to ignore that. But he stopped, gently resting his forehead on hers.

"We're building a new order for Angolin with us at the center, Eldric," Coraia said and leaned backward. "A union with the most powerful people on the planet is my family's only hope. The Hannes will never top us again, and neither will anyone else with the Carmogen behind us. Sex can wait."

The front door chimed. Estes sighed, followed Coraia inside to the foyer. She dismissed the butler and opened the door herself.

"Good evening, Lieutenant," she said.

"Come in," Estes ordered. "We have a lot to discuss."

"Yes, General, but first . . ." The visitor undid a hidden trouser pocket. From it emerged a small, spherical robodrive, rising to rest in midair before the trio. "As agreed, sir."

Estes retrieved it, held it between himself and Coraia. He ordered it to display an upright and accessed its files, unwilling to risk downloading them to his internal. The nanosystems swimming through Guardsmen's bodies were military property, subject to review at any time. Face-to-face dispatch and physical, stand-alone data storage only, for now. He poured over the information line by line . . . and smiled.

"Maybe things are looking up after all!" He sighed in relief, eyes shifting to his messenger subordinate. "You've done excellently, Vara."

SICKENING ODORS AND BADLY RUTTED roads, the reality of primitive overland transport, defied Armetrian's wildest dreams. As if the smoke and fumes that smelled oddly like the Abyss weren't enough, the boxy contraption he'd been collected in didn't hover but rolled instead across bare ground—on wheels, like those he had seen on toys as a child. In museums. But the ride would have been equally miserable had the road been smooth.

The outside landscape was gray and formless, beyond a few scrawny trees seemingly too nutrient-starved to move, and surrounded by clusters of ramshackle lean-tos. And they were just that: barely standing makeshift structures with sullen, emaciated people loitering around them.

The sky above it all was dim, partly from the eastern hemisphere's low sunlight, mostly from the brown-gray haze filling the air: smog. Armetrian had heard of the pollution on this side of the world but never gave it a second thought. The vehicle's interior view was just as dismal, if not downright unnerving.

"I am surprised to see *you*, Lieutenant Commander," said Naul, sitting between his two aides. "I finally have what was promised, though I never expected a courier to accompany the shipment."

"I keep my word, even if it means seeing to things personally," Armetrian said. "I came to prove that Angolinians are capable of delivering, even if one in particular wasn't. I apologize wholly for General Estes's inept and inadequate—"

"Forget him! Once my people verify the shipment's full working order, you will become my sole partner in all matters. The Ninth Army will do well with you in that position." Naul shifted in his seat and breathed a strangely disappointed sigh. "Pity though, you came alone. I know Vara worked with you on this. I would love to have seen her again."

Armetrian let a wince escape. He and Vara had left their cruiser in separate sloops to rendezvous back in Angolin. Her disgusted expression before departure indicated that she hadn't trusted him. *She's smart if nothing else,* he deigned to admit. She had likely sidestepped his sensor jamming and tracked his sloop's flight path, so she had to know he changed course and headed back to the escaping cruisers. But never mind that, what about that odd hail over the Abyss? He couldn't tell who had sent it and couldn't trace its source, and neither the ship's database nor his internal's had a listing of any entity this far out. But the frequency used was definitely Angolinian, and the hail greetings oscillated between Dutch and English, the ancients' chief languages. It was all too strange, but there was no time to think more on it now.

"Vara had little if any part in this, Lord Naul. Her involvement was minimal."

"Really, Lieutenant Commander? Was it not she who had Bemin's tracking equipment jammed? Were the decoys that allowed your escape not her idea, along with the interestingly covert devices that allowed you both to walk the spaceport unseen—the very same devices that let your army fight unseen on Negara much of the time? Do my conclusions bear accuracy, or am I remiss in my understanding?"

Armetrian held in a gulp. *How in the Netherlords . . .?* "You aren't remiss."

"To say that I have a vested interest in this endeavor would be the grandest understatement, Angoliner. I see far more than you imagine."

Armetrian wanted to crawl beneath his seat. Naul was as annoyingly apt and informed as usual, his inner voice told him this, though he was loathe to acknowledge the facts. So what if it was Vara who insisted on PTS for the mission and knew how to hack internals to deactivate trace functions. So what if Narond remotely piloted the decoys under her instruction. And who cared if Vinc got all the right access codes for the weapons stores?

He suppressed all of this too, peering at the world beyond the transport-on-gummy wheels. Naul said earlier that they would travel through the capital and not waste time circumventing the huge city. They must have been getting close. There were more dilapidated shelters now with more dilapidated people milling about them. Most of the inhabitants appeared the same: very tall, though severely back-bent. Detached gazes pooled in bright-yellow eyes, sunken in bony, gray faces. They were elderly. *How anyone of advanced years can exist under these conditions . . .* Armetrian looked closer. They weren't old, just incredibly overworked, likely over their entire lives.

The vehicle passed an abode with a large animal standing beside it: a meler, or an eastern version of the species. Two humanoid legs protruded from beneath it. Armetrian frowned in shock at the emaciated skeleton of a man drinking from the beast's teats.

"Do people not avail themselves of milk in the West, Lieutenant Commander?" Naul asked, breaking his fugue.

"Well, yes. But definitely not right out of—"

"What is unacceptable to your people is more than fitting for these wastes of skin out here," Naul said. "They are from the Trogenlands on the rise slopes beneath the empire. They breathe the Great Nothing's gases with some ease, so we use them to mine our most prized possessions." He held up a hand, admired the large gemstones set in rings on his long, tentacle-like fingers. "So much beauty from the empire's nastiest wretches and lowest profession. Ironic, no?"

Armetrian was too put off to comment. How could anyone call abject slavery—scratching worthless stones out of gas-filled tunnels for thankless masters—a *profession*?

"These are the dregs, the refuse. The workforce's unfortunates," Naul continued. "Only the sick and permanently injured are permitted to live outside the capital wall. We tell them it is in honor of their long years of service. Truthfully, it absolves us of decaying bodies littering the city's streets when they die. A conveniently sanitary arrangement."

The ice in that candor lanced Armetrian. *Will my people's lot match these "wastes of skin" if plans go wrong?* He ignored his contrary inner voice once more, but he couldn't ignore what lay beyond the window. So this was poverty. He knew nothing of it beyond rumor, legend, and a few lectures by bleeding-heart professors back at the academy. It was amazing. He pictured his instructors' reactions if they could be here now. He also wondered how ordinary Angolinians would react to this life. The Carmogen Empire lay comfortably in bed with disparity and suffering, relished in it apparently. In Angolin, poverty hadn't been invented yet.

The vehicle approached a high, stone barrier. Armetrian stared at it. What he initially thought was smooth, well-formed material was covered in graffiti and riddled in the pockmarks he remembered to be primitive bullet holes: the Wall of Gragna. Now and thereafter, he had scarce seen anything more frighteningly imposing.

Naul explained the wall's intendment. It was built centuries before to repel invaders. Now, as Armetrian understood, its sole purpose was to keep its inhabitants *in*, and it was only the outer barrier. The city within was divided into hundreds of tightly sealed sectors and subsectors, housing every race, caste, type of worker, type of ensnared foreigner, everyone in separate pens to be used, monitored, and who knew what else. Mobility was controlled and restricted. Only high military officials with the right shade of gray skin could move between sectors at will. Armetrian wrinkled his nose at the notion: neat, efficient partitioning for the empire's unending array of peoples and uses for peoples to be exploited—and violated— as the Lescainate saw fit.

"We Carmogen are the world's most effective race at utilizing the lesser ones," Naul said in a self-satisfied tone.

"An open society never hurt my people any," Armetrian considered aloud before he could stop himself.

"You Angoliners and that pale-faced Lenan scum may find such living amusing, but we do not let everyone and anyone mix so freely here," Eldo sneered from Naul's left side. "The way you Westerners let the inferior intermingle is disgusting!"

Armetrian stared the man down—what a different specimen from his master. Perhaps Naul had simply been expert in hiding this world-view. Or closer to the truth, it had never arisen. Gunrunning and multiculturalism weren't exactly compatible conversation topics. "I've never been put out by it. Never know till you try."

"Keep that to yourself, Angoliner," said Daio. "All our master requires of you is your cooperation. Do not expect to survive long here without it." He clipped his words as a blade was put beneath his chin.

"Mind your place, before I pin your hide to that wall out there," Naul threatened, with his eyes on Armetrian. "Ignore my servant's poor manners. He knows only the ways of his caste."

The vehicle slowed. The city wall ahead met the road with a broad opening, framed by two smaller ones: a checkpoint. Throngs lined both sides of the wide, traffic-filled pavement. From the opening on the left, handfuls of workers were leaving the city with the most contented expressions Armetrian had seen on anyone since his arrival. It appeared that the collage of imperially committed faces could be something beyond sour after all. People looked nearly relaxed as they made hobbling but hurried tracks away from the razor-wired exit gate.

Before the right-hand gate, people stood in long lines divided by metal chains. Each line contained a different kind of person: some darker-skinned, some lighter, some interestingly colored, many gray with the telltale Carmogen ridge atop the skull, many others just as gray without it. Heads bent downward before the armed troopers flanking the slow-moving lines.

"Our subjects are returning home from the day's work that God wills for them. Nice, very nice," said Naul.

Armetrian found nothing nice about it for the "subjects." But the troopers found their own amusement by shoving, hitting, and spitting on their helplessly constricted victims. Two deep-brown-skinned men closely resembling General Gennet argued with them. They were pulled out of line and shot. Armetrian flinched. His travel mates didn't. Neither did anyone near the victims.

So this is what happens when you defy authority in the empire, he thought. *Better to be military here.* Naul muttered something about the race being consistently problematic. Armetrian understood why: The Kay Allendë were the hemisphere's strongest people before the Carmogen conquered them. Fiercely resistant and hard to subdue even under total subjugation, their reputation was well known in the

Angolin Guard and their cause for freedom championed, though from the well-shrouded distance.

"They resisted the Carmis for decades with a lot less tech than Angolin, and absolutely no help," Armetrian had heard, mostly from the likes of Dharmen Tate. *"If they could fight back, so can we."* But the greatest of the Eastern cultures was still defeated. Anyone who couldn't remain strong was fair game, and without their technological advantages, Angolinians were anything but strong. Armetrian smiled. *An Angolin weakened by Carmogen occupation will be that much easier to administer . . . with me as its ruler, if I set it all up right!* Fear of everything he had witnessed drifted away; he was suddenly glad he had made the long trip.

The vehicle lumbered on to the semblant cheer of one roadside and the contrasting misery of the other. It traveled in a lane obviously dedicated to VIP traffic and was quickly waved through the checkpoint. The troopers tried for a look into the tinted windows. They drew back when Naul partly rolled his down in subtle but effective warning. Armetrian soaked it all in as they sped through a short tunnel. Beyond it, the opposing people traffic switched sides.

They drove freely down traffic-choked streets shrouded in a haze visible down to the potholed pavement. Their path was completely unobstructed, demarcated from the rest of the crowded avenues with broad white stripes. The VIP lanes apparently continued through the city, separated by a graphic divider of fear. No other vehicle dared enter them despite the horrendous gridlock.

They passed an interruption in the tightly crammed abodes: an open plein surrounded on three sides by dull wattle-and-daub buildings. A crowd gathered around a raised platform. On it stood a decently dressed gray-skin Carmogen man beside a family: man, woman, and three small children. Each was tethered at the neck by a chain, and each looked frightened as their holder yanked their fetters and animatedly took bids from the screaming audience. A Carmogen slave auction. Armetrian couldn't help but gawk.

His rolling vantage took him from the for-sale chattel past more grim buildings. Home was his only basis for comparison. Every built part of Angolin (that could be seen) gleamed, glistened, and invited. Centrum and South C skyscrapers gave shows of light, color, and in some cases, particle manipulation to move and dance to tenants' and onlookers' delight. The East Vales' entertainment districts quadrupled the theatrics, and in the quieter residential areas, pod houses came and went, interlocking in clusters to form new, fluid communities.

There was no such innovation or whimsy for its own sake here. Every structure passed Armetrian's eyes in horrible condition. More bullet holes and more graffiti than before, and if even one building stood firm without great cracks, a pronounced lean, and complete threat of collapse, he had yet to find it. And the sheer size of Gragna awed him as much as its destitute physical state. The urban sprawl hadn't subsided even after nearly an hour of driving through the gargantuan, festering city-slum that was nothing like Angolin's loosely connected, fastidiously maintained conurbations.

In front of hardscrabble hovels stood hardscrabble life—people seemed permanently affixed to the dirt-packed frontages. Kay Allendë inhabited one sector, Trogen miners filled the next, and other sectors held races Armetrian had seen as combat conscripts: blue-skinned folk covered in spines, and people with multiple limbs ending in appendages that might have been hands. He had seen the *Handies*—as Guard soldiers called them—used as laborers on Negara, and he couldn't believe his eyes then.

The next sector took him by surprise. He thought he'd imagined, but he hadn't. The pale, fur-faced inmates were definitely from north of Angolin. Lenans were unmistakable in any environment.

Wherever the people hailed from, their lot amazed Armetrian. No one wore anything beyond rags, mismatched shoes, or no shoes. Some simply went naked, literally unclothed. And why not? They regarded themselves no higher than their society did by the look of it; why bother to dress living uselessness? And everyone was filthy, caked in the refuse of who knew what. It seemed every "profession" involved grime and was performed on hands, knees, and faces. *And is anyone here wholly intact?* Armetrian wondered. There was no lack of blood-soaked bandages, eye patches, missing limbs, and limbs held in slings or aided by makeshift crutches.

He sealed his disquiet beneath a tight lid, but every sight imprinted onto his mind. Battered, soulless living flotsam. *How do people live like this?* He promised himself to keep the same from happening in Angolin when he came to power. *And I will,* was the more personally satisfying sentiment he squashed his remorse with.

Most of the living tide was male. A few lifeless women clung to doorless entries looking forlorn and spent, with mucous-faced children milling around them. Common sense warned Armetrian to keep quiet, but the preposterousness of it all overcame him. "Not much warmth in the neighborhood, is there?" he said. "And how do they keep from freezing with no doors or windowpanes?"

Wordless, Naul looked to his right-flanking aide.

"Who should care?" Daio said. "Only the up-castes are entitled to privacy. Why would lower peoples have doors? How would that serve them?"

To keep from being easily assaulted, robbed, taken at will. Armetrian's mental comeback streamed unending reasons beyond weather. And it didn't take long to see one in action. Ahead, four armed troopers entered a dwelling. Seconds later, they emerged with a struggling, bawling, unclothed woman. A teenager followed them out and tried uselessly to stop them. He was knocked to the ground and beaten senseless while the woman was hauled away. *She must have done something moderately serious,* Armetrian thought, then realized she likely hadn't. Weakness and vulnerability were her true infractions. That seemed to be the only real transgression in this society.

The three men seated across the vehicle floor chatted idly, oblivious to the misery around them. Armetrian's usual mindset didn't include sympathy, but he couldn't help but wonder at their indifference. He also couldn't help but wonder at the noise coming from up ahead and silently queried the gods on just how many more nasty surprises they would fill his trip with.

Explosions rattled the surrounding buildings. Rapid gunfire followed. The driver stopped as hordes fled down a cross street. A mass protest gone wrong, it had to be. Angolin had experienced plenty of them lately. And Armetrian reveled in it. Angry students would bring revolution, but unlike here, the conurbs rarely intervened in protests, and they would never do so with violence. That was an advantage to Dawn Fire's designs.

And this one was violent. Troopers appeared seemingly from nowhere, herding the running crowds and cutting off all means of escape. Gray, brown, and blue bodies fell trampled and bleeding from gunshot wounds all around the creeping vehicle. Naul leaned across Daio for a better view. He had caught sight of something that either pleased or angered him. "What in the empire are these *women* doing out here?"

A trooper caught sight of Naul's vehicle. "Lescain passing. Hold fire and give him way!"

Naul lowered the glass. "As you were, Commandant! You keep on firing. Show these animals the meaning of reprisal!"

Armetrian withheld another flinch as Naul removed his shoulder-holstered sidearm, pointed it out the window, and fired into the fleeing crowd. Bodies lurched in midstride and wheeled to the ground. The driver accelerated, intentionally striking a few who had escaped. He passed the protest site with crowds fleeing alongside now. Naul reloaded and took down more, then suddenly holstered his weapon. Before Armetrian could blink, the door beside Daio was unlatched and thrown open. It caught a fleeing woman. Naul quickly jumped out and grabbed her. She struggled to free herself to absolutely no avail. One angry punch sent her to the pavement. He reached down, seized a fistful of her hair and dragged her into the vehicle.

She screamed in a tongue that Cor-GON's lingua mapper couldn't decipher. Naul backhanded her with a grisly thud harder than any Armetrian had ever heard one person inflict on another and then clamped a hand around her neck.

"Females are not permitted in public. Where is your husband? Do not tell me you were *both* protesting."

She began to sob but otherwise had no choice but to remain quiet. Her tears wet Naul's fingers.

He yanked her face to his. "You were a part of it. Answer!"

She crimped an affirmative nod.

He slammed her head against the window, cracking the glass. She put up a weak fight that was extinguished by more punches. The last one sent her to the vehicle floor, her face twisted as she lay prone between Armetrian and his escorts. Naul reached down, cursing at the woman as he ripped away bits of clothing that looked to Armetrian like little more than soiled dinner napkins. She rallied and desperately struggled. Naul's aides answered by stomping on her limbs. Daio's knee to her stomach ended the barrage.

"Wait," Naul ordered. "Do not damage my new acquisition further." He looked to his left-flanking man. "Eldo, if you will . . ."

Armetrian put all mental energy into masking his horror. His Angolinian sensibilities weren't prepared for *this*. He stared forward, up to the ceiling, out the window, anywhere but down.

"Problem, Lieutenant Commander? You do not approve?" Naul asked him with hardly a notice to the scene at his feet.

Eldo took his seat and nodded: the captive would meet his master's tastes. A small gesture of such leisurely detachment—Armetrian would never forget it. He shut his eyes but saw clearly: absolutely no one in this land—and definitely not its legions of powerless souls—defied military rule without cruel consequence.

OUTSIDE THE WALLED, DECREPIT CITY-PRISON, the quartet and their whimpering captive were driven along stately tree-lined ways devoid of the haggard shanties and ruined lives gracing its opposite end. Armetrian tried to appreciate it. Did. It was a welcome change from everything he had witnessed that was unfortunately imperial life. He stared out the window, marveling at the landscape's sudden lushness. Naul informed him that they were nearing his compound. Armetrian needed no such notice. Gragna hadn't sported so much as a blade of grass anywhere. The explosion of leafy, unpeopled pleas-antness enveloping him here was cue enough.

THE GROUNDS OF NAUL'S COMPOUND went on forever. The man-sion within could have held fifty M-7 gunships, and there were seem-ingly more attendants than Seventh's entire complement. Armetrian was astounded. Nothing like it existed back home. Angolin knew the meaning of refinement, but accumulation and display of wealth on this scale just wasn't part of the culture. Even Hannes and Prinsens weren't this lavishly housed. He inhaled it all, thoughts racing as he pictured himself living this life.

"One of the weapons delivery's first uses," Naul said casually without the same stars in his murky eyes, "will be to put down insur-rection. You just witnessed the threats we face, even within our own borders."

Armetrian nodded restrained agreement as a servant entered the out-door patio with a round of unappealingly cloudy drinks. He was relieved to be away from Gragna and thankful that Naul had thus far made no hint of using his newly acquired arms against Angolin. Whatever manifestation this alliance took would go smoothly if his host didn't overstep.

"And the second most crucial use, Lieutenant Commander, involves the partnership you spoke so passionately of last year, and the ending of your people's isolation. Our collaboration demands that vision."

"Partnership is my mission," Armetrian said, "though I can't speak for the rest of Angolin."

"How is that so? I recall that you swore to force your people's cooperation if they did not offer it willingly."

"Lord Naul, what I actually meant was—"

"*We will break Angolin,* is how you so enthusiastically put it then. Never underestimate a Carmogen's memory, and know that in spite of your retreating intentions, mine rest firm. That is my promise to you." Naul leaned across the patio table. "You bring guns and ideals. I appreciate that. But there is one more item in your technological arsenal that I require."

"And that is?" Armetrian asked warily.

Black-flecked yellow irises drilled into fatigued, bloodshot blue. "Something minor—a trifle. Something I saw on Negara—*or did not see*, as I should put it. Your troops and equipment have the convenient ability to simply disappear from existence."

Armetrian inhaled. He hadn't noticed Naul moving closer to him. They stared at each other over half a meter—the closest he had ever allowed a Carmogen to get without blasting him. Naul's eyes were relentlessly patient and focused. Armetrian's were fearfully evasive, and he knew it.

"If you're referring to cloaking tech, Lord Naul, we haven't yet agreed—"

"I recall you offering to give your realm's technology *willingly* back on Negara. And cloaking is only part of my wish. You have something far more valuable that allows your people to appear in one place one second, and elsewhere the next. That, I will have."

Stealthtech! Where on Tentim does powder face get his information? "M-my Lord," Armetrian said, quivering as he tried to figure out how to steer the conversation, "weapons are easy, relatively easy, to deliver, but we've had no discussion on cloaking, and as for—"

"And as for TimeSpace, as it is so interestingly termed, all in good time and with your full cooperation. General Estes briefly mentioned it. I know you will expand on that."

Estes! Idiot. Gods-damn him! Armetrian wished he could have said that out loud. "That technology . . . is unreliable. Even we can't quite master it. Whatever the general revealed, it's not on the table."

Naul's gray face was expressionless. "If you intend to further this alliance and the continued fortune of your people, Angoliner, see that it finds its way to the table."

THE NEGOTIATION THAT ARMETRIAN KNEW he'd botched ended an hour ago, though it seemed longer. A servant had escorted him from the patio to the guest apartments. The way in, the way through, the way up—the grandeur had defied expectation. *I want this life. I want it now.* The thoughts filled his mind as his quarters' splendor filled his eyes. But pain and suffering back home would be needed to buy it. He didn't care. Empathy even in the slightest wouldn't fulfil his wishes. *Will it be enough?* he mused. *Angolin, my people, will you do this for me? Will you?* Even through his wearied stupor, it became clear that this was the beginning, for better or worse, of something from which there was no turning back. He would have to maintain control of the situation. His dreams—and remaining alive to live them—would require more from him than running guns and technology. An Angolinian niche into Carmogen world order would need to be carved, if with bare hands.

There was a knock at the double doors. Servants thrust them open, quietly stood aside as Naul entered. "Lieutenant Commander, how do you find your accommodations?"

"Better than anything I could've hoped for. My Lord is gracious."

"It is beyond grace, as you call it. Carmogen vocabulary does not include the word," Naul said. "It is *sklarvro*—total power—and it can be yours if you are truly willing." He cast proud eyes around the room. "All of this has been paid for time and time over. I was a lowly conscript, snatched from a hut in Gragna when I started. With this shade of skin, I was never supposed to do more than fight and die quickly for the empire. No one in my caste is. But I excelled, worked my way upward, and cut a path few could dream of to get where I am. I have pounded men into the dirt to secure my place in the Lescainate! Your path will be no different if your ambition is as I see it."

"Maybe, but things work differently where I come from."

"Things move at an excruciatingly slow pace where you come from, with no glory or reward in return. You know this. You brought yourself to this point knowing it," said Naul. "And morals, principles, fairness, goodwill—none of that will elevate you. If you are willing to take what you do want and accept nothing less, you will grow great. Avarice will envy your achievement." He turned to the doors. "Enter!"

Eldo appeared with the woman from the transport. He held her by a chain fastened to a collar around her neck. Its metal shank sported a blackened join and a newly etched Carmogen number. Tears ran down her cheeks onto her exposed breasts. Beyond a swollen eye, she surprisingly showed no other blemish despite the beating on the way in, and what had likely happened again since. In combat, Armetrian had seen and done more damage to people with fewer, lighter blows. These men knew exactly what they were doing.

"Now finally," Naul beamed, "take this beauty as the first of many gifts you will receive in service to me. She is a fine fruit. I tasted her myself while you settled in. I would normally ask that you not use her up too quickly, but I have many others."

As Naul and his aide left the room, Armetrian's forced smile that had concealed his disgust evaporated. He looked at the woman. She immediately looked down. He turned to a window, hoping the sight of the painstakingly manicured, bucolic grounds would ease his mind. But his new life that he had cultivated since long before Negara, the one he had just knocked Estes out of contention for, demanded more. *No room for weakness. None.*

He summoned callousness beyond normal even for him and stretched his entire body to wring himself free of fear. He turned to the woman. She dared catch his eye, murmured pleadingly. His internal had begun to decipher her language, and her words relayed to his earplant.

"Have mercy, please," she was saying. "Do you not see the pain I am in? I can . . . no more. I will . . . anything you ask if you spare me . . . please . . ."

He looked down to the floor. His inner voice telling him not to go through with this was overpowering. But he managed to squelch it. *Do it, or you might as well go back home now. No room for weakness!* He looked up and refused to take his eye from her. She began to weep again, backing away from him as he stepped closer and undid his belt.

CHAPTER 10

CLOSEST FAMILY

Ma'am, my link to Fifth Command has been severed again.

Has it, Lun-AE? I wasn't aware.

It was ma'am who severed it. And it appears to be permanent.

Perhaps.

Will it be reestablished, Lieutenant?

It may. It mayn't. That depends on your cooperation. Finish your search for Cor-GON's ID signature, I want to know where his user is and what he's up to. After that, question me no further.

❂

"OH, I THINK IT'S ABSOLUTELY *splendid*, Dharmen," Aremel gushed. "My cousin thinks the world of you. He'll be so pleased!"

"Pleased?" said Dharmen's image floating in front of her. "I'm not asking him out to a school dance. I need more than pleased."

"Well, *certainly*, dear. But why consult *me* of *all* people? What about his parents?"

Dharmen's upright-generated eyes rolled behind half-shutting lids. "Talking to them isn't an option. If they despise Will, they hate me. I wanted to ask his closest family, his *real* closest family." His image leaned forward. "That would be you."

"Ah yes, of course," Aremel sighed, "and what a *shame*! I don't believe Will's ever known real love outside his relationship with you. It's not a typical Hanne emotion, at least not from that segment of our clan. My parents are a tale unto themselves, but *his* . . ." She put hands to hips and looked around, flustered. Her farthest gardens' wilting, undertended perennials were about as comforting as the conversational tangent. "They haven't said a word to him in years. Heavens to Lothnë, I *do* wish they'd put stubbornness aside and see *reason*."

"They're not made for reason, Aremel, they're made for politics," Dharmen grumbled. "Will sidestepped his father and chose the career *he* wanted. Do you think old Henk Hanne would ever forgive him for that?"

Aremel frowned. "I really *must* get the gardeners back out here. These haven't been micronourished in days. Such poor maintenance is simply not suitable for an estate of *this—*"

"Aremel!"

"Oh! Oh, I'm *so* sorry, dear. Do go on. *I'm listening.*"

"I have no more. Do you approve?"

"Most *definitely*. How could I not? And by the *grace* of Kleve Park and from deep within my heart, I wish you both the *best*! May you *flourish* in the Lady and Lord's light. I *know* the Heaveners smile *brightly* upon you and—"

"Thanks, Aremel. It means a lot to me. To us, really . . . What's that awful thing behind you? I've been staring at it for the last few minutes, or rather, it's been staring at me."

Aremel swung around to a marblite statuette on a squat podium. "That? Oh, it's one of my family shrines. Note the Hanne coat of arms near the bottom. They absolutely *litter* my gardens like fruit flyers in the night. Hadn't you noticed any of them on your visits here?"

"No."

"Dear, one would think you don't enjoy my hospitality. *Do* impart more *vigilance* to go with that severe uniform."

"More vigilance? Me?" Dharmen retorted. "And is there a shrine to the goddess of horticulture to go with your family ones? She must be offended. That's probably why your flowerbeds are so sparse." Aremel lowered eyes to the plant life around her, so nutrient-starved as to not bother with the friendliest of tendril wraps around her ankle. "Sorry," Dharmen said. "And thanks again. Will looks up to you. I wouldn't even attempt this without your support."

Aremel's smile was as incandescent as the afternoon suns. She was clueless to what she was being partly cozened into. "You two will have a *wonderful* life together, and my Balaneth and I won't follow far behind."

"What about his other wives?"

"Oh, them. *Well*, I'll deal with his, uh, *ladies* in due time. His spouse collection isn't the problem, if you can believe that. It's that *aide* of his that has my back up."

Dharmen's simulated eyes flickered. "You mean Gallin?"

"*Yes*! And I hope they . . . *I hope you* get him soon!"

"So he can be brought to justice?"

Aremel peered at the curiously inquisitive image moving ahead of her steps. "No! So he can reassume his duties, and Balaneth can dismiss the candidates for his job. Do you know the Lenan government has seen fit to send only *female* applicants for the vacancy? By Lothnë, I'm sure that's Princess Nien's doing, snotty little bitch that she is."

"Maybe, but Gallin's a dangerous man. He did try to kidnap Will, among other things."

"Oh, I know that. Let a lady squeeze a bit of *fun* from difficult circumstances, why don't you? I don't *really* want him back here, and he *won't* be, of course. But I want a suitable aide for my Balaneth—*a male one*, not these skinny, winking sluts that Lena keeps shuttling down. And our Will is none the worse for his ordeal. I'm *most proud* of him. I think he handled Gallin *quite nicely*, don't you?"

"He did, at that," Dharmen replied. "But what would help now is your family's involvement in the search for Gallin. The Guard has no leads, and the conurb police aren't exactly investigators, but we might just catch him with Hanne weight behind the effort. Pass that one by good old Henk next time you see him, won't you?"

"Uh, *right!*"

Dharmen's straightening semblance sighed. "I know you prefer the peace of your gardens to detective work, Aremel, but think about it. Not just for me and the Guard but for Will." A stern, insistent face suddenly waxed warm. "Tate out."

Aremel flattened her lips, perplexed as Dharmen's image vanished. Perplexed because for the first time, she thought she actually saw him—

"To answer your question, yes. I do smile," Dharmen's image reappeared and said. "When it suits me!" He flashed a wide grin, then vanished for good.

"Well, haven't *I* just been put right?" Aremel said at empty air as she withdrew to her favorite, more secluded gardens.

She passed through the concealed opening of a tall hedge, elated with Dharmen's news even if she could find no joy in her wonderfully fragrant but withered . . . "You. What are you doing here?" she asked her startled pilot, who stood at the leafy space's opposite end. "This is my personal enclosure. It's off-limits to all but the gardeners and myself. You've no business out here. Shouldn't you be in the carriage hangar seeing to the—"

The rustling behind her bore no resemblance to the tittering of the small creatures inhabiting her grounds or to the natural movement of the hedge itself. She wheeled on a man watching her with pale, cold eyes. Peeved curiosity evaporated as she realized her presence was equally unexpected. Absolutely frightened, she inhaled for a scream. Hopefully, someone in the house would hear—

"Do it, Miss, and I'll slice it from your throat!" Gallin threatened, whipping out a knife and pressing it to her neck. Her pilot's gloved hand covered her mouth from behind. "That's better," Gallin said. "Now I'm afraid you'll be coming with us. We quite insist, and oh, I'll take that." He snatched her necklace away, including the small comm discreetly chained into it. "We can't have you calling your Guard friends for help, now can we?"

"A DOMESTIC SERVANT? WHY ON Tentim do we need one of those?" Dharmen asked. "I know this is South C, but who in a pod house this small needs that kind of expensive help? You should comm your cousin. She has half an army standing by doing next to nothing all day. Maybe she can loan us someone. Temporarily."

"Dharmen, you're a midlevel officer now, and I'm a senior civil servant. We have the means," Willem rebutted.

Dharmen snorted at the annoying sensibility of that. "Between both our jobs, and Dawn Fire's attacks on us lately, making this a normal home is a challenge. Do we really need somebody else living with us? I just had a huge weapons complement get snatched on my watch, and now you want me to come home at night to a boarder?"

"Not exactly a boarder. Not so much."

"What does that mean?"

Willem's face formed that placid, hunched-brow smile that Dharmen never liked. "Well," started the unpleasant news, "no one would really consider a synth to be a housemate."

"A what?"

"You heard me," Willem said too calmly. "With everything going on lately, I didn't want to risk bringing a stranger into the house, so I'm having the cleaning service send us a synth."

"But I hate synths, Will! We have them on base. We have them crawling all over Bemin too, as if the place isn't crap enough on its own. Do I have to put up with one in my own house?"

"I know you don't like external AI, especially the walking kind, but believe me, it's better than—"

"Better than what? The most advanced ones can't do a thing without mindlessly specific orders, and the ones I put up with on a daily basis are useless. And spooky."

"No spookier than having a sentient nanite floating around inside you," William said. "You have your internal to keep you company anywhere, anytime. All I have are walls to stare at."

"That's different. Rem-E's my combat assistant. He's Guard-issue, tailored to me. I need him to get my work done."

"You need *him* to get it done? *He's* as artificial as the help you want to deny me. Why bother to assign the thing a gender?"

Dharmen was silent but unrelenting.

"I see this won't go well no matter how convincing I try to be, Dharmen, so let me put it plainly. You're gone all day and most nights, and lately, most week's ends. And I'm getting busier too. We need someone, or something, to do the work around here that isn't already automated."

That's not the real reason, love. You already betrayed it, Dharmen thought. *But I'm not about to sacrifice my last shreds of home life.* "Most of the household chores are automated at this point, and I can program the rest to be. I can even fix it so you never have to feed yourself if you don't want to. Why bring some walking gear job in here when we're stressed as it is?"

"Patronizing aside, thanks for finally saying it out loud. We are stressed, aren't we?" Willem put back. "But in different ways. You're away more than you're here. It gets lonely, *very lonely,* especially after dark, and don't forget I was attacked right on this canal on one of those nights. If anything like that happens again, I'd prefer to have another presence in the house, one that might even provide protection if I order it to." He looked down, sighed. "I remember when we lived on your base. Soldiers and their families everywhere, everyday—I used to wish for solitude. And now that I've got it . . . well, it's getting to be like your time on Negara all over again. Nine weeks with no mate and always wondering if you were still alive. The Netherworld couldn't have been worse!" He went to the dine-in window and stared into the night sky, arms folded across his chest. "I nearly went mad before you came back. I'd rather not repeat it so soon."

Dharmen moved behind Willem and wrapped his arms around him. "I'm sorry about that, love, you know I am. And I've apologized a hundred times since, but you know it couldn't be helped."

Willem turned around with a wan look.

"Life was so different then, before that night in the forest especially," Dharmen continued. "I had a career, a wonderful man at my side, we'd just left base together to settle down here, and then came the war down in the Vresel. Then the traitors shooting up so many good people . . ." His eyes twitched, then stopped after Rem-E's prompt for immediate CSD therapy. "And now they're targeting us personally. Negara wasn't pleasant, but it was simple. I knew my purpose. I thought if I survived, I'd come back, and you and I would plan a great future together, and we will. But Armetrian is trying to destroy that. For everyone, actually."

Willem's expression brightened a bit. "Everybody wants something out of life, Dharmen. Armetrian's no different. He wants something too. Even if it's evil and delusional, he's trying his best like anyone else. Do what you must to stop him obviously, but don't be so quick to judge. Underneath it all, Armetrian is no different than you or me."

Dharmen chafed at that one, but as usual, Willem had a point. His insight, his temperament—the whole suite of his wisdom and positive energy delved deep beneath life's most asinine situations. It was what made him so special. "You really do see the good in everyone, don't you?"

Willem smiled serenely. "As much as you see the bad in them." He lowered his head the few centimeters that separated them in height and kissed Dharmen. "Come up to bed soon. Don't stand down here all night in front of the foodkeep stuffing your face and plotting how to get rid of our house synth before she even arrives." He patted Dharmen's firm but expanding midsection.

"She? Assigning it a gender, are you?" Dharmen quipped.

"No, but the service is. All their staff is made to look and feel as real as possible. They say it promotes easier acclimation of client to domestic. I hope they're right about that. See you upstairs."

Dharmen commanded the lights off as he watched Willem climb the steps. His silhouette was illuminated by window-formed moonslight before fading into the loft level. Warmth settled into Dharmen that he hadn't felt in a long time. *I love him. I know I do. I've always known it. And no matter what they throw at us, there's no sense waiting . . .*

Willem came back down, feet hurriedly pounding each step as he commanded the lights back on. The look in his moistening eyes was urgent.

"What is it now?" Dharmen asked, clamping a hand to the nemurite bulge in his cargo pocket.

"I just got a message from Kleve Park, that's what," Willem answered. "Mel's been kidnapped!"

"IS THAT A DIRECT FEED to the proceedings?" Gallin's voice sourly asked from the dine-in doorway.

His unending nosiness had tried Vara's last nerve every day of her stay. "Shhh! I'm trying to hear."

"That answers my question," Gallin said. "This is supposed to be a safe house, Lieutenant—we can't have the Guard tracing your illegal patch-in to their judiciary."

"Relax, man. I have the feed cycling at random intervals and the signature masked at this end. No one will discover it."

"What's that, then?"

Vara looked back to the upright. A red warning beacon floated beneath it accompanied by a low chime. "Damn it!" she hissed under her breath. She reached into her cargo pocket for an old datapad and tapped furiously at its display. The warning disappeared. "It was nothing, Gallin, trust me."

"Nothing? They're tracking your hack. I don't call that *nothing*. Your internal AI would've intervened immediately. Too bad you can't risk using it."

"They haven't located the source, so just forget about it."

"Haven't located it *yet*, you mean. Your military runs continuous covert communications scans for just this sort of eavesdropping lately, and you know it. They'll locate it," said Gallin. "When that happens, woman, you'd better know how to counter it, or you'll expose us and lead them right to this house."

Vara made no effort to cooperate. Gallin moved toward her. She backed out of his reach.

"You can get the proceedings from the Guard CentraMesh and find out about your stupid little friend there. Now give me that!"

She withheld it.

He grabbed her by the throat. "I run this house. If you can't get that through your thick Angoliner skull—"

Cold nemurite touched his chin. His stare was prickly. Hers was an empty, expressionless dare of a gaze, infused with the only thing on her mind: "I'll fire in a heartbeat and think nothing of it." He relaxed his fingers.

"Back off," she said, deadpan, "or die and bequeath your new home to me. Neighborhood's a bit crowded and trendy for my taste, but I wouldn't mind a cozy little house to call my own even if it means burying its current occupant beneath it next to the previous one."

Gallin finally let go. "When they read the verdict, disconnect the patch-in and shut that off. I mean it!" He glared a bit longer and left the room.

Vara reholstered her sidearm. She cursed at having missed a good portion of the proceedings. They had hardly deliberated and were already at sentencing. "This thing's moving fast, kid. They're going easy on you."

The presiding JAG officer tapped his podium slab, cleared his throat. "Irzek Albren DeMeer Vinc," he read with the cadence of authority, "by the judgment of this general court-martial, you are found guilty of the following: possession of two stolen weapons including one sidearm and one Ergive sword, nonregulation use of said weapons, and endangering the life of a Guard officer with both. The charge of attempted murder has been dropped due to lack of evidence. This lessens your sentence from life imprisonment to a much shorter incarceration period, the term of which shall be decided in tribunal. In light of . . . verdict, Mr. Vinc," he crackled through a short lapse in the feed, "you are hereby stripped . . . your enlistment in the Angolin Guard."

The chamber murmured as Irzek's rank and insignia were removed, and the court reporter bot ordered to enter the dishonorable discharge into the record.

"Believe me, Vinc, you're better off," Vara said dryly. Day by day, she felt less need for the Guard. Surely the rest of Dawn Fire must have felt likewise, and if not, they should have, in her opinion. Armetrian cared nothing for the Guard. It was the one thing they agreed upon, though he was the last person she wanted anything in common with.

But regardless, Vara still wondered what his little deviation from their plan was about. *What's he up to, exactly?* That question increasingly circled through her mind.

The court chamber camera tracked Irzek as he was led from the room. She noticed him darting unfriendly eyes to an officer at the next table sitting stone-faced with arms folded.

"And you! I don't know how you continue to survive, but you won't the next time if I have to see to it personally," she muttered at Dharmen's image. "I'll have you if it's the last thing I ever do, Tate. That's a promise!"

Gallin's head poked in the doorway. He pointed at the upright and made a quick cutting gesture beneath his chin.

"Fine!" She prodded at her pad again, severing the patch-in and pausing Dharmen's incensed visage.

Footsteps approached the dine-in, soft and timid. Aremel came spiritlessly to the table and took a seat. Gallin went to the foodkeep, removed a bowl of stiff, greenish cold soup and shoved it in front of her along with a plastiform spoon and a threadbare napkin. Aremel took a few sips and stole a quick glance at Vara.

Unaccustomed to more than a few seconds quiet, even under her current situation, Aremel said, "Good afternoon."

Vara stared enough venom to frighten her back into silence. She wondered which scared the annoying socialite most: her new situation or Gallin's shabby house. The posh woman had probably never been in such digs. "So far from home and away from your element, Miss," she tsk-tsked, slowly shaking her head. "You poor little high-mountain thing!" She turned on Gallin. "And you accuse *me* of security breaches. Why the blazing suns did you bring her here?"

"Worry about your own matters, Lieutenant. Let me handle mine."

"We have enough to deal with as it is, which you and Armet"—Vara glanced at Aremel—"*our colleague* constantly remind everyone of. Do we really need to have to look after her too? A Hanne? Every security force in Angolin's looking for her, and the Guard's just steps behind us now."

"I know. That's why I don't want you patching so carelessly into their communications mesh! Why not just put a beacon on my front door and be done with it?" Gallin watched Aremel sip her soup as she was argued over. "She's Tate's manfriend's first cousin. We can use that."

"You're already using it to justify letting her stumble onto you so easily. If it hadn't been for your lackadaisical Lenan alertness, we wouldn't be in this now."

Gallin looked down at the prim, tidy woman. "The lieutenant's opinion aside, *you* won't get away from me the way your cousin did."

Aremel finally broke. "But I've cooperated, haven't I? I've minded myself, kept *mostly* quiet, and done everything you've asked. I hold to my word, and I told you I wouldn't betray you if you let me go. You have no further reason to keep me."

"Save it. We've heard it every day since you got here," Vara sniped. "Don't think for a second that you're going anywhere."

Aremel's eyes pooled with newfound courage. "I come from a brave and noble family. We Hannes are made of stuff stouter than the nemurite beneath the East Ranges. Holding me hostage won't get you whatever it is you're after."

"Fancy you saying that now," Vara put back. "You weren't so *brave and noble* the night you were brought in crying like a schoolgirl. If every prominent family in Angolin is anything like you, my work will be easy."

"And just what work is that?" Aremel boldly snorted. "Lying? Stealing? Kidnapping? Oh, my *dear*, if you want to consider yourselves gallant, you'll have to do better than snatching people off the ways or out of their gardens at night. But far be it for little *me* to talk while *cowards* cloak themselves in the guise of the spirited!"

Vara glared, snatched Aremel's half-full soup bowl, and threw it at her. "You wanna keep mouthing off and find yourself dead alongside Tate and your cousin? Right now, if necessary? I'm just in the mood to take out two filthy faggots and their rich hag-along!"

Gallin moved beside Aremel, who was still seated but turned away with her arms covering her head and soup splattered on her sleeves.

"Look, for our own safety, you need to get her out of here!" Vara growled at him.

"For *our* safety? I told you there would be no violence in this house. Do what you want outside, but while you're here, you will not harm my prisoner."

"I can find a place for her," said Ciros, coming in and heading for the foodkeep.

"You mind your own business!" Vara snapped.

"No need to bother, Sublieutenant," Gallin said. "Our other location is nearly ready. When it is, I'll transfer her there with the rest."

Ciros found whatever he wanted and left. Aremel stopped wiping soup from her clothing to stare at Gallin.

"You have fast reflexes," he said. "One second more, and that bowl would've found your head. Go to your room. I'll bring the rest of your lunch later."

Aremel rose, made a few defeated steps from the table, and finally saw Dharmen's paused image. "Just *what* do you mean to do? I thought you said you *didn't* want to harm anyone?"

"Unless you really want to find out, keep quiet," Gallin threatened.

"Oh, but you *can't* hurt him," she pleaded. "Will would be devastated! *I would be devastated*!"

Vara pulled out her gun again, held it up for plain view. "What does it take to shut you up, lady?"

Gallin moved between them, facing Vara. Oh, how she wanted to blast both away in one shot! His style irked her more than his cold, inscrutable eyes. He talked only when provoked but was quiet—too quiet—otherwise. It made her flesh crawl. She never could stand introverts, and Gallin was the worst kind: inward, aloof, secretive, calculating. When everyone else was busy talking, he was busy *listening*. Silently, he edged eyes to her weapon.

Glowering back, she stowed it.

"You. You're done." Gallin swiveled on Aremel and said, "Go back to your room, like I told you."

"But I—"

He grabbed her by the arm and shoved her to the doorway. "Go!"

Passing embittered glances between her captors, Aremel left and climbed the stairs to the guest room she had called home for the past several days. Vara rounded Gallin and left also, scowling as she passed him, scowling as she entered the live-in to overhear the silly teenage conversation that, as usual lately, was about her.

"Take my advice and set your sights elsewhere. She's too much for you, any idiot can see that," she heard Ciros say. "Which is why you of all people ought to see it, Kerbi."

"Come on, man. That's not what I want to hear," Kerbentha said, too self-absorbed to take the insult. "Now work with me, Ciros. Be on my side for once. Do you think me and the lieutenant—"

"Don't even consider it," Vara huffed.

Kerbentha jumped up from his seat.

Ciros grinned.

Vara ignored his ugly, slack-jawed face and focused on his near-ceiling height companion. "Listen, I've got a job for you."

Kerbentha flushed with glee until her barbed stare squashed it.

"And this time," she continued, "you'll get it right!"

CHAPTER 11

NOW IS THE TIME

Sir, you are shaking again.

It's not that, Rem-E. It's nerves. It happens to people at times, just ignore it. I don't expect to rely on you for everything.

"Nerves" is a human-contrived malady. Sir's mental and physical health—

Are fine. This isn't from combat stress. It's this evening that I'm worried about.

❋

DHARMEN WATCHED THE RIJKSFONTEIN'S CENTER spray shoot two hundred stories into twilit sky and drop its waters in artful, force field-constricted cascades onto the Emblusplein, the great circular common anchoring the Angolin Midways. From it, the west avenue led to the Parliament Pavilion. The east way wound into the mountains above Mid Realm. The north road went toward Greathall but never found the hidden folds beneath. And the south Midway faded into the Centrum's skyline, towering over the surrounding web of conurbs and public gardens.

Tonight, Angolin's formal center swarmed with people on their way home from the Kraal, on their way to a late dinner, or simply admiring the fountain. Couples strolled arm in arm beside its marblite embankment.

Nüren leaned over. "It's called the Fountain of Beginnings for a reason, you know."

Dharmen met him round-eyed, hoping no one else had heard.

"I proposed to his mother here," Nüren dashed that hope and beamed to everyone.

Dori and Brona glowed. "Young Miss Enri must have been absolutely delighted by that," Brona said.

Willem was more subdued. Brona and Yos went back to gazing into each other's eyes. They had been doing so all evening; something was budding between them. Theus watched them dejectedly as he had all evening.

"You never told me it happened here," Dharmen said to Nüren. "You just said it was by a fountain."

"I said it was by *the* fountain. Listen to your father now and again; you might just pick up a few things," Nüren said with a smile and a few quick taps to his snow-white temple.

"Is that any way to talk to your only son who just treated you to a birthday dinner at the best restaurant in Angolin?" Dharmen chided.

"At this ripe old age, you talk as you like. You'll understand one day."

"Sir, you're far from old," Dori said. "Dharm's already there ahead of the rest of us, but not you . . . And what's all this?"

A crowd appeared, large, noisy, and suddenly. They were university students from the looks of them, and sticking out like painted tarocs, wearing all the wrong gender colors and making a huge ruckus. They banged synth drums and chanted slogans, some against the government but more deriding the Guard.

"Good thing we're off duty," Dori said. "Aside from this bizarre affront to the Heavenly Pantheon, uniforms wouldn't be good here."

"What's that? You afraid of protesters, *Commander* Secár?" Dharmen bellowed.

"That'll do, Dharm!" she returned.

Dharmen read one of the revolving holos. "The Guard is the hatchet of Parliament and accomplice to enslavement of Angolinian society" was its floating message. "See that, Commander? Good thing we *are* off duty. I wouldn't want my slaving ways to offend these people!"

The holo bearer peered ferociously from beneath a bright-orange hood. He tapped a field on the holo. A smaller one materialized right in Dharmen's face: "Demand peace. Dismantle the Guard."

Dharmen backhanded the message with a look that dared a response. "Forget service and loyalty, let's all walk the midways yelling and broadcasting treason. What I wouldn't give to be a bored teenager with nothing better to do."

"I'm not a teenager," the other snipped. "I'm twenty, for your information."

"I have eyes, kid. What the Netherworld difference does that make? Stupid is stupid at any age," Dharmen shot back. "And while you're *demanding peace*, you'd better learn to defend your hide too, 'cause it'll take more than slogans to fight the Carmogen . . . What was that? I didn't quite hear. You got something to say, speak up!"

"I said take your atrocities elsewhere. We don't need them in Angolin. We want a free and peaceful existence without military oppression and warmongering."

"Atrocities?" Dharmen said incredulously. "You want atrocities? I'll tell you about atrocities. Men like me spending their lives protecting boys who don't appreciate it is an atrocity. Watching your comrades get killed in front of you while kids back home walk around with name-calling holos is atrocious."

"Easy, son. He doesn't know what he's saying," Nüren said to Dharmen. "Like any other misinformation acted upon, it'll pass."

Dharmen's blood boiled; he hadn't taken his eyes off mister "I'm twenty for your information" for a second. "This man spent his entire life protecting Angolin," he said, motioning to his father. "Without him, you wouldn't have the freedom to mouth off to your elders and float signs around. Are you telling him all his years of service were atrocities too?"

"I want what the Outside World has to offer," said the young man. "I don't need isolation, and I don't need old has-beens. None of us do!" He muttered something else under his breath at Nüren.

"You wanna say that loud enough for everyone to hear?" Dharmen said and stepped closer.

"No. Not really—"

Dharmen yanked him by the collar. "Then say it to me, just me, because I want to hear it!"

Tumbling water was the plein's only sound. People stopped to watch; even the other protesters were silent. Dharmen understood he had lost control. He didn't like it, but he wasn't about to let anyone insult his father's honor, and definitely not an anti-Guard, civilian little—

"Lieutenant Commander, stand down!" Dori rumbled.

"Let him go, Dharm," Theus said at his side. "He's not worth it. None of this is worth it."

Dharmen let some of Theus's calm wash over him. He bored eyes into the young man and then shoved him backward. What little force he gave it was still enough to send his skinny frame to the pavement. He got up with a belligerent glower that Dharmen's outmatched and scuttled back to his holo-wielding friends. To Dharmen's mild surprise, they began slowly moving away. Onlookers threw words at their backs, told them to do something useful with themselves, or be off.

"Guess I'm not the only one not having any of it!" Dharmen yelled after them.

Nüren leaned in and whispered, "Temper, temper, m'boy. Don't you have something much more important to concentrate on tonight?"

Dharmen eyed him, nearly forgetting what had just happened.

"He gets it from his mother," Nüren said to the rest of the group. "She was no woman to be trifled with, let me tell you!" He ushered everyone to pleinside benches, well out of Dharmen's reach of any more flash protesters.

Dharmen sat brooding. There were more and more demonstrations lately, and some got out of hand. This group was harmless, but its antigovernment, antimilitary, anti-Angolin babble rattled him. So much disregard from those just old enough to begin enjoying everything he and others fought to maintain for them, but too young to understand or appreciate it. He breathed hard through his anger. *Just what do these kids want?*

He watched the loud, postadolescent interruption to an otherwise wonderful evening pass on. Normalcy slowly returned with no more chanting death to the Realm and antagonizing the gods. Women warmed the night in honor of Lothnë the Great, and men cooled it in Rior's glory: Angolinians living as they always had. He caught sight of a woman coming from the direction of the Kraal. Blonde, middle-aged, short, and plump, though with an upright, dignified, purposeful gait. She looked over kindly as she headed east. It wasn't Aremel (she would never be out and about walking alone), but she bore a striking resemblance. Dharmen glanced to his side. Willem was watching her too, his eyes lowering as she left sight.

"We'll find her, love, don't worry."

"I know," Willem replied, upbeat. "Tonight's for celebrating anyway, not worrying. Happy birthday, Nüren! Hope you enjoyed dinner. And the Plein—great choice for an after-dinner stroll."

Nüren smiled. "I'm not the one who chose it."

Dharmen blushed and stood. Better to do this himself before his father did it for him. "And now . . . now I hope to make someone else even happier." Ignoring the bemused looks, he moved over to Willem and bent down on one knee.

Dori and Brona stifled excited wails and embraced each other. The evening's apparent competitive détente on Dori's part seemed to be continuing.

"Will. Love," Dharmen started, "I just want to say that . . . well, we've been through so much together, and outside my family, I . . ." He had to catch his breath. His heart pounded harder than it had during his minutes-earlier run-in. "I know I'm the *storm in your calm* as you once put it, and other things get in our way these days, but I won't face whatever's coming unless it's with you. I've always loved you, and I always will. Will you marry me?"

Willem gave him a dauntless but teary smile. Like a cloudburst through sunshine, the water left his eyelids. "I sure will, soldier!" He bent down, grabbed Dharmen's face, and kissed him.

Cheers and applause filled Dharmen's ears. Lots of them. He rose, holding Willem's hand. He knew it was Angolin's largest gathering spot, but uplords, what an audience! Strangers came over for rounds of handshakes. He couldn't believe the moment's goodwill. He felt pride in his people that he hadn't felt in ages. And then he realized something that heartened him more than anything could: the love of his life had just said yes!

A raucous pack of athletes came by from the direction of Mount Innsaec Arena. The evening match had just ended. "You'll make him a happy man, right mate?" one of them yelled to Willem.

"Definitely!" he yelled back. "What was the score? Did we win?"

Nüren gave Dharmen and Willem vise-like hugs. Dharmen hadn't seen his father like this since his mother was alive. "I didn't see a ring, son."

"That'll come later." Dharmen's eyes were sly. "But one thing's coming right now."

Willem shut his eyes as Dharmen picked him up and carried him to the fountain.

"You've lived on a Guard base, Hanne," Dharmen said, "you know the drill . . ."

Willem hit the water with a screaming guffaw. The others howled as he reached down and hurled handfuls of water at them. Brona and Yos were taken completely by surprise until Theus explained the quirks of the same-sex Guard marriage proposals he had witnessed. Dharmen laughed as Willem threw water on him. And then he mounted the embankment.

"Son, what kind of a bizarre proposal is this?" Nüren asked.

"Any kind but a hetero one, Father!"

"But—"

Dharmen dove in. He and Willem splashed around playfully before climbing out and dripping all over the mood pavers. Puzzled onlookers laughed and chatted with them. Another group of protesters came by. Dharmen ignored them. *Nothing*, he thought, *is going to ruin this moment.*

DHARMEN WALKED THE DARKENED, NARROW loft corridor to the guest sleep-in. He could hear clanking synthware being arranged for deactivation downstairs. He shut the sound from his mind. The evening had ended awesomely, and he didn't want his new, unwanted housekeeper interfering with that. He stopped at the door and knocked.

"Father?"

It slid open. "Oh, thank Krone, it's you, m'boy. I thought it was that blasted synth woman. Never could get used to those things, even back at the First."

"Right. Have everything you need?"

"Affirmative."

"Father, I need to apologize for tonight." Silent eyes met Dharmen, evincing understanding well beyond his notice. "That little shit got to me, but I shouldn't have picked a fight to begin with. I went too far too fast. I dishonored the Guard, myself, and you."

"Nonsense, son! People get angry. Give yourself some shred of credit. Krone has no rule of honor that says a soldier can't lose his temper once in a while, especially at a silly kid intent on provoking it."

"Maybe, but with me it's all the time and beyond Rem-E's help. I don't know what to do about it," Dharmen sighed. "It's like a monster living inside me. I wish I had a cool head like you, and just about everybody else."

"Well, there's no rule that says a soldier can't be himself either. You're a good man, Dharmen, but one who tends toward hotheadedness is all." Nüren leaned forward. "But save it for the enemy. I don't think the Carmis or the traitors are much of a match for your kind of . . . *spirit*. I just wish we could harness it in some usable form and fix it to a gunship. That would be a weapon to contend with!"

"But, I . . ."

Eyes kind but sharp let Dharmen know the conversation was finished.

"Sleep well, Father. I'll see you in the morning."

The door shut. Dharmen went to the main sleep-in and found Willem already in bed. "Are you happy, love?"

"Infinitely! But I have a question."

"A question." Dharmen looked around as though to imaginary people in the room. "I propose, I get soaked for him, and he has a question."

"Why tonight, Dharmen?" Willem asked with a marginal, placid smile. "Why now, in the midst of everything?"

"Excuse me?"

"It's not a complaint. I was just wondering."

"Look, I know you're worried about Aremel. I'm worried about her too, but we'll find her."

"It's not just that. I want to know why you chose this moment. You're so careful about nearly everything, I'm surprised you picked tonight and didn't want to wait."

Dharmen thought about it. "I wanted to do it months ago, the night our dine-in was nearly blown up. Then I wanted to right after we shot down those stolen ships from Port, and then you were nearly kidnapped—odd time to ask your partner to marry you." He sat beside Willem. "And Kleve Park would have been perfect, but we were too preoccupied with Gallin."

"So you chose your father's birthday celebration instead?"

"It was a good try at a cover, as much as Father let it be." He took Willem's hand and put it to his chest. "Think about it, love. When would be the right time? There's never that for us anymore. But you are the right man for me, that's what matters. If we can get past all this and be happy together, *now* is the time; and regardless of what comes next, we'll face it as a team. Promise?"

Willem leaned over and kissed him. "You've made me the happiest man in Angolin tonight, Dharmen. Anything you want is a promise!" He reached over, pulled at and loosened the tie in Dharmen's night trousers. Dharmen began pulling them off . . .

There was a knock at the door. Dharmen groaned. He knew it wasn't his father—the raps were too evenly spaced, too mechanical.

"Come in," Willem ordered after commanding light output higher. He remained in bed, but Dharmen got up and barely managed to pull his pants back up before the door slid open.

It walked in. Dharmen gave it his usual wince, a gesture only a real person would perceive. The artificial woman stood obliviously beneath its flowing brown hair and inhumanly tranquil demeanor, devoid of emotion or reaction to emotion. *Advanced particle manipulation and AI neuroscience,* Dharmen thought. *I'd love to find the engineers who reintroduced that combo to Angolin and throw them off the fjord line!*

"Sirs, if you do not require my service further tonight, I will retire downstairs for regeneration," it said, monotone.

"That'll do just fine, robot," Dharmen said. *It even sounds real.*

"I am called Clera 6, sir," the other dispassionately corrected. "I introduced myself with designation upon my arrival. And I am particle synthesized. I am not a robot."

"Is that a fact, *robot*?"

"Yes, sir. Perhaps you have forgotten."

"Perhaps I haven't."

"First names are fine, Clera 6. You may call him Dharmen," said Willem.

"You may continue to call me sir, robot," said Dharmen. "And what's with the *six*, by the way? Where are Cleras 1 through 5? Got fancier gigs up in the Condorcet Estates?"

"They were desynthed, sir."

"All of them? Really?" He scrutinized the simulated woman darkly. "Doesn't bode well for *you*, does it?"

A foot shot out at Dharmen from beneath the bedcovers. "Thank you, Clera 6. We'll see you in the morning," Willem said.

"Shall I see to General Tate before I go?"

"No!" Dharmen answered in Willem's place. "Father is already asleep. He goes to bed early. That'll be the case every night while he stays with us, so leave him alone."

"Of course, sir." It smiled factitiously.

Amid its correctly upturned lips, Dharmen noticed a twitch in the synth's expression: a smallish muscle glitch, if the thing had anything resembling muscle tissue beneath its particle-constructed skin. It wasn't meant pleasantly, whatever it was. The unreal woman backed out of the doorway, and it slid shut behind her.

"That thing's too damned quiet. I didn't even hear it climb the stairs," Dharmen said.

"That thing has a name," Willem said. "And please try to make this work. I've already explained a hundred times why we need her."

Dharmen ignored that. He went to the chair near the lavatory door and readjusted his uniform hanging across the seatback before commanding lights off and climbing into bed.

"So did you tell anyone else what you were planning tonight?" Willem asked.

"Only Thee. I didn't bother with Dori. She would have given it away."

"Mmmm. And your father?"

"No, but he knew anyway. He always knows what I'm up to. You can't hide anything from a Tate."

"No argument there!" Willem said.

"Speaking of which, let's try to keep it down tonight. I don't want him hearing us."

"And spoken by the loud one himself," Willem said with low brows above slyly smiling eyes.

"Hmmph, doesn't matter anyway," Dharmen grinned. "Knowing my father, he'll ignore his hetero side and listen at the wall."

"With your moaning, he won't need to," Willem said. He pinned Dharmen down, gently kissing his neck, and slowly moving those kisses downward . . .

They made love once, then twice. And *almost* silently.

Dharmen shut his eyes for sleep after some of the most powerful and potent sex he'd ever had, but Willem's voice forced them open. "So who chose tonight for your proposal? Whose idea was it really?"

"Are you really not ready for bed, after all that?"

"Whose idea was it? Theus's I imagine."

"Actually, it was your cousin's. You can thank her when she's safely back with us, which she will be." Dharmen leaned over for a long kiss, noted Willem's surprise-widened eyes afterward in the dim but waxing moonlight, and smiled. "Good night, love!"

WILLEM TOSSED AND TURNED. HIS partner had just become his fiancé, and his favorite cousin was missing. Who could possibly sleep through any of that? He reached for Dharmen.

He wasn't there.

Across the argent-lit room, the lavatory doorway was dark. *Another late-night snack raid downstairs,* Willem assumed, sitting up. *Rior, do I need to put a lock on the thing?*

The sleep-in door slid open. A figure stepped in from the blackened corridor. Willem sighed contentedly . . . until he saw the hand lift, and the faint flash of metal in the moonlight.

The blast lit the room like a white fire. Willem had never heard a gun fire in his life; the sound of the particle beam pierced his ears. He stumbled out of bed, heart pounding. "Lights!"

Clera 6 stood in front of the sleep-in chair. Seemingly unaware of anything else, it stared blankly at Dharmen's tunic and the smoke curling from it. Slowly, its head swiveled toward Willem. He noticed for the first time just how mechanical the movements were. Fear froze him as the gun arm swiveled to him.

The room blazed again with another ear-splitting shot. Shrapnel flew. He crouched for protection, and was surprised to find himself whole. How had it missed? He looked up. The answer emerged from the lavatory doorway with his own sidearm pointed at where Clera 6 had stood. Scorched simulated bone protruded from the remains: the low stumps of two shoe-fitted feet. The rest lay in charred, smoking pieces around the room.

"You okay, love?" Dharmen asked.

Willem rushed over, stared answerless at what had been his new housekeeper. He hugged Dharmen so tightly that he forgot his fiancé was holding a gun.

"Well, that's one way to cap an oversynthed synth," Dharmen said, nearly as passionless as the synth he'd just destroyed. Willem had never seen Dharmen in combat mode before. He was quietly amazed.

Feet shuffled up the corridor. Dharmen shoved Willem behind him and aimed at the door.

"What in Krone's name is going on in here?" Nüren demanded, barging in.

Dharmen gestured to the sizzling synth remains and the smoking seatback beside them. Nüren eyed the dinner-plate-sized hole shot clean through it and the tunic, and went speechless.

"Look what she did to my chair!" Willem finally noticed. "That was a gift from my brother Naeus. It's the only real furniture piece I own and . . . Oh, Dharmen, my gods! She must have thought—"

"Didn't do my uniform any good either," Dharmen said. "I guess it thought I like to sit in the dark fully dressed. Good thing I don't!"

Willem watched Dharmen's eyes flutter. He knew Rem-E was prompting him. Dharmen had programmed heat and motion sensing into every meter of the house, inside and out. A proximity alarm must have been tripped.

Dharmen activated an upright and requested a diagram of pod and grounds. He shook his head at the results. "Right on time. Excuse me a minute."

Before anyone could ask, he threw his gun-free hand into the bureau, yanked out another tunic, and darted from the room.

QUICKLY BUT STEALTHILY, DHARMEN LEFT the house, leaving the door open for two Guardsmen rushing in from a patrol sloop exiting TimeSpace across the canalside way. He went around podside. In the small rear garden, he found what he expected—and *whom* he expected.

The enemy fumbled with some kind of odd device, furiously tapping buttons on an attached datapad, trying to get it or its dependent unit to work. "Rior damn it, what's wrong with this thing?" The lanky, floppy-haired youth was too engrossed in his problem to see Dharmen walk right up next to him, even beneath the floating porch light. He turned his head to a gun barrel.

"No help here, eh?" Dharmen said, snatching the PTS generator stuffed into the other's trousers, stupidly blinking standby. "And if I were you, I'd drop that and get my hands up."

Still startled, Kerbentha let the controller fall to the ground and grabbed air.

"It's been a while, kid. I wondered when you'd be back. Nice of you to drop in and pay us a follow-up!" Dharmen heard boots round the corner.

Sentinels moved in, flanked Kerbentha, and forced him to the ground. The young woman affixing his manacles gave Dharmen a quick salute.

"Didn't know the general had a Vinc on the watch effort. Nice to see you, Shipman."

"Likewise, sir," said Leatra. "Though he didn't assign me. I volunteered."

Willem, Nüren, and more uniforms entered the garden. "Father, look after Will tonight." Dharmen shot a hard look at the arrestee lying on his face, shivering on the dewy turf. "I've just been given some early morning business to attend to."

THE SUBJECT SAT FIDGETING. DHARMEN watched, pleased. Perhaps the floating bots hovering overhead with their small but bright klieg lights menacingly shifting beams on him from multiple angles did the job. Or maybe it was the two uniformed men sitting across from him: one white with sleep-tousled black hair and looking thoroughly incensed at having sacrificed the wee hours of his morning over a saboteur, and the other, an older *Yoruban,* as Black ancients once self-identified, looking equally unrested and just as intimidating. Dharmen and General Gennet tapped at uprights and discussed him as though he weren't present. Until Dharmen looked up with a long, dark gaze.

Kerbentha avoided eye contact by staring down at his clamped arms and at another small, conical robot floating around the interrogation room. The detention monitor bot frightened him. Dharmen saw that through the put-on, cocky face the kid wore.

"Right!" Gennet boomed so loudly that the youth jumped in his seat and yanked his restraints. "We're ready to begin. Release the prisoner."

The metal confinement chair's arm clamps desynthed. Kerbentha rubbed his wrists and stood.

"Sit down!" said Gennet. "You will not leave that seat until this session is over. Do not get up until we tell you, and don't even think of trying to run out of here."

Kerbentha's rear end hit the chair before the order finished. "How long will this take?" he asked in a timid trill that betrayed his on-again, off-again tough front.

"We ask the questions here! And until we do, keep your mouth shut!" Dharmen barked. Through shadowy, unblinking eyes, he watched Kerbentha fixate on his hand resting casually on his sword pommel. He wore it scabbardless in his belt—its long, naked threat fully displayed and its tip scraping the floor.

"I was told I'd get counsel," said Kerbentha.

Dharmen glared fire. He rose, circled Kerbentha slowly.

"You'll have representation at your hearing," Gennet said. "Until then, the monitor bot is your counsel. It'll record everything said and done here before it returns you to your cell."

"I'm allowed one communication," Kerbentha said, defying Dharmen again.

"You're also allowed to keep quiet when told," Dharmen said from behind him. "As for your comm, you've already made it. Thought we forgot that quickly? Its destination was traced, including any mesh shunts. We'll have that information soon enough."

"And I made mine before you were brought in here," said Gennet, "to your parents."

The room's bare nemurite walls magnified Kerbentha's gulp. "They'll bail me out. I know they will."

"You're here for sabotage and attempted murder," Dharmen said, "of me, a Guard officer, which makes the charges much more serious. No one's going to bail you out of anything. Put that out of your hopes."

He watched that erode Kerbentha's facade. The kid's eyes misted.

"But how long you remain in detention, *and where*, depends entirely on you," said Gennet. "Your cooperation will determine how this goes."

"Wh-what does that mean?" Kerbentha asked.

"It means you can either stay here on this base where you'll be treated *properly*," said Dharmen, "or we send you to Northrealm Lockup."

"The inmates up there are the Realm's most hardened. They hate Angolin, but they hate its traitors no less," said Gennet. "The prisoners we've sent there lately have been beaten and occasionally worse."

"But I can't go there!" Kerbentha gasped. "You have to protect me. You can't just put me with dangerous men and look the other way!"

"Sure, we can," Dharmen said, leaning into his face. "You caused me and my family a problem tonight; I might like to cause you one."

Kerbentha tried to look tough again but apparently couldn't form the face.

"What's wrong?" Dharmen asked. "Don't think you can survive up there on your own?"

Wide, terrified eyes answered.

Gennet remained silent, and Dharmen joined in the deliberately long moment. They watched their prisoner's face revert to its fearful baseline. "If you want to make it through this, you will give us answers—truthful, complete answers," Gennet finally said. "And only when asked. The lieutenant commander has told you twice now to speak only when requested. Keep disobeying him, and you'll find yourself up north before daybreak."

Through hard sniffs, Kerbentha nodded acquiescence.

"State your full name for the record," Gennet ordered.

"I already gave it when I was brought—"

"Give it again," Dharmen demanded. "Give it a thousand times if we tell you to."

Kerbentha rattled his full name in Angolinian fashion: given, middle, mother's family, father's family.

"Very good," said Gennet. "See how easy it is to comply? Remember that, and things just might go well." He waved his upright aside and reached down to a rectangular case beneath his seat.

"What's in that?" Kerbentha asked in a panicked heave. "You two aren't going to torture me, are you?"

"Would you like us to?" Dharmen dryly retorted.

Gennet produced the improvised item confiscated at arrest. "Tell us what you were doing with this before you were apprehended."

"I . . . I don't know what that is."

"Of course you do. And so do we," said Dharmen. "It's an anthrosynthetic brain—or part of one—taken from a synth similar to the one working in my house. You had it in your possession. Don't forget that I caught you with it, and a Guard-issue PTS generator. Where did you get it?"

"I created an uplink. That's all."

"Yeah, I know you did. Where did you get it?"

"It's for a new game I'm designing. I didn't expect it to cause anything bad to happen."

Dharmen noted the red beacon on his upright, identical to the one flashing on the hovering monitor bot. It mattered little. "You're telling me you were standing behind my pod at 0200 gaming? What's the game called, *Murder in the Night*? But you still haven't answered my question. Where. Did. You. Get it?"

Kerbentha didn't answer.

"We've already analyzed this item," said Gennet. "Your uplink was to the housekeeping synth. Don't try to deny it, because even without the monitor bot, we can see through you. You're as bad a liar as you are an assassin." He held up and shook the evidence for emphasis. "You were caught using this brain part, rigged as a master to send commands to the Tate house synth."

Dharmen would have smiled had he not been so peeved. Kerbentha was trapped. He had gotten away the first time, so capture never occurred to his young mind on this one. He had no alibi ready.

"All right." Kerbentha broke. "Yes, the brain part is nearly identical to the one in the housekeeper. The datapad controls the uplink. With it, I could program the synth to do whatever I—"

"You wanted it to kill me—or someone wanted me killed, more like," Dharmen said. "Which brings me to my original question that you *will* answer because I won't take a fourth round of silence. Where did you get this? And who are you working for?"

Silence. A fourth time.

"And with this kind of advanced anthrotech knowledge," Gennet interjected. "Who gave you this part and this datapad? These are not items that fall into a teenager's lap so easily."

Kerbentha's eyes wandered faster than the klieg beams. Dharmen could almost read his feigned search for thought. "Uh, it's from another general," Kerbentha prevaricated. "I've only dealt with him remotely. I don't . . . I don't know his name."

The monitor bot and uprights registered more falsehoods, though it made no difference. The answers given really didn't merit need for sensory lie detection.

"You're saying someone you never met gave you these items?" Gennet challenged.

"You may be handy, but you're no engineer. Someone gave you these personally, showed you how to use them, and on whom," Dharmen said, resting casually against Kerbentha's seatback. "And it wasn't some general, remotely or in person. There's someone else more directly involved here."

Kerbentha said nothing.

Dharmen shot around into his face. "Enough of this—give us names! Give 'em now!"

"I don't have names," Kerbentha muttered, trembling. "I'm working alone."

"Alone! Your teleconned general suddenly doesn't exist," Dharmen shouted. "And you expect me to believe a teenager half my age, whom I've never met before, is out to kill me all on his own? Just what kind of taroc crap is that? What do you take me for?" He took Kerbentha's fright and ran with it. "I know a lie when I hear one. I was lying before you were born, and I was better at it then. Now do we get the truth, or do we ship you to lockup right now and get the information *after* you've been served up a dozen times? It'll be easy once you've been softened."

"You . . . y-you won't do that," Kerbentha spluttered.

"After surviving two of your attempts on me, I most certainly would!"

"You can't. I don't believe you. You don't have the right. This is Angolin, we're a democracy! People don't get p-put in prison that easily here. You're j-just threatening me with all of this to s-scare me."

Dharmen's rabid stare morphed into a dark grimace centimeters from Kerbentha's face. "Maybe I have the right. Maybe not. Do you really want to find out?"

Kerbentha looked ready to vacate his skin.

"Never underestimate the *Hidden* Realm's ability to keep secrets, and not just from the Outside World," Gennet said in the deepest, calmest tone Dharmen had ever heard from him. "You have no idea of what goes on all across Angolin that no one ever sees or hears of. Things that democracy never finds."

Dharmen reached into his belt pouch. Kerbentha closed his eyes, began hyperventilating, and braced. He opened them. Dharmen held nothing beyond a casual ruse. He retook his seat and tapped his upright. In the empty space beside the trio, a holographic scene appeared in miniature, full of people, lights, and music: the Zuidenmarkt. A figure ran through the crowd, towering over everyone he shoved out of his path.

Dharmen paused the holo. "This was retrieved from a public surveillance cam-bot five months ago. Take a look at the face and hair. That's you, making your escape."

Kerbentha started a denial, but Dharmen stomped on it.

"Tall. Gangly. Ugly! The computer easily matched every feature with yours, from every visible hair strand to that burn I blasted across your ear. Note the time stamp. It's 1942, four minutes after my dine-in was bombed. Now look again." He resumed the holo, paused it at another figure running eight seconds behind. "The stunningly handsome one chasing after you is me." He sat back and folded his arms. "The DNA on your controller matches that from my dine-in windowsill: solid evidence linking you directly to that night's events. You didn't complete the assignment of killing me the first time, so you were put up to it again—"

"But this can't be happening!" Kerbentha shot out of his seat and interrupted. "Armetrian said South C would have easy escape paths.

He never said anything about cam-bots! He told us we'd never get caught, and if we somehow did . . ." His eyes fluttered.

The men opposite him sat like contented stones, watching him as the roving monitor bot recorded his words.

"Armetrian," Dharmen mewed. "I wondered when that name would come out. Now we really *are* getting somewhere. Sit down before I knock you down!"

"I'm not working for him. We're friends! W-we've known each other for many years."

"You don't have *many years* under your tunic, kid, skip it!" Dharmen pointed to the seat, watched Kerbentha collapse into it and stew in his own lying juice. "Now, we know you're working with others because my esteemed colleague, Armetrian, didn't give you this brain part any more than some general did. And he didn't teach you how to program it either because he knows even less about anthrotech than you do. I actually have known him for years. Getting under people's skin and treason are all he does. But I do know of someone else who's skilled in these areas, someone from the same order your confiscated items came from. Their serials weren't properly erased, so she must've had to get them to you in a hurry."

He watched Kerbentha squirm, unable to contain himself under the bright lights and the pressure. Or contain his bowels. Krone, what a smell!

"We'll get to all your accomplices one by one," Dharmen continued. "But first, you'll stop protecting this person and give us her name, you'll give each and every detail of Armetrian's involvement, and whether you want to or not, you will tell us everything we want to know."

CHAPTER 12

THE FALCONERPLEIN

Week's end leave, Qi-VOS, a full one. I wonder how long these will continue?

Do you believe General Gennet will grant fewer of them in the future?

Yes. Any trouble we don't get from one end will come from the other.

Ma'am, several Dawn Fire members have been apprehended recently, including the teenager who attempted to murder Lieutenant Commander Tate. We may be winning the fight. Your misgivings are likely unfounded.

I very much doubt that! I also doubt I can keep Dharmen in line, even if you're right. I know him. All this pressure will get a reaction from him, and soon.

❀

"WELL, I CAN'T SAY I'M surprised," Yos's image said.

"No?" said Dharmen.

"*No.* Neuroscience in anthrotech is still highly misunderstood. It's hard enough to design a synth's primary reasoning functions, let alone more advanced behavioral safeguards and protocols."

"But synths are as forbidden to harm people as robots are," Theus said. "Regardless of any interference, that's their prime instruction, the very first one programmed into them."

"Nonsense," Yos said. "No system is completely tamper-proof. Anyone with the proper skills can bypass whatever instruction they wish, including the prime. Once that's done, AI is capable of inflicting whatever damage it's ordered to."

"Yos, as fascinating as this is, you realize that thing tried to kill me the other night?" Dharmen said.

"Not really. The kid controlling it tried to; the synth was just obeying its new programming. And you dispatched both nicely. Between your housekeeper and that shot you took at Port, the collaborators must think you have the gods shielding you."

"Certain physicists shielding him, more like," said Dori. "And you still haven't told us how Dharm survived that hit."

"No, I haven't."

"Yos, come off it. We know you and Brona gave him some sort of protective device," Dori said. "Dharm's as tight-lipped as you are, but it was definitely your handiwork."

Yos kept silently to his detached, mellow cloud for just a few seconds. "It's nothing particularly mysterious or profound. It's just a little something I designed with Brona's help, and a bit of engineering assistance, that's all."

"A little something that deflects particle fire and is portable," Dori said.

"Not just deflects. Absorbs and redistributes. Matter dispersal is still tricky, and energy consumption and transference difficulty make widespread personal use prohibitive. But give us time. We're working on it."

"Is that all you two are working on nowadays?" Dori said.

Yos's image angled its head and smiled. "Have a great lunch, you three. Andren out!"

Dori frowned at the holo disappearing from in front of them as Dharmen cued Rem-E to close the channel. "We'll deal with him later," she said. "It's too much bother for such a beautifully perfect day. Can't beat a full summer for a change. 'Bout time it warmed up for good."

"It's too crowded for me," Dharmen said. He and Willem were South C locals now. If the heat of his least favorite micro season didn't try him, the crowds it pulled into the neighborhood from every nook and cranny in Angolin did.

"Maybe some sunshine and purple skies will make up for that and AI gone wrong," Dori said, "if you're willing to let it. I can't help but notice the uniform. Don't you know the meaning of *week's end pass*? We don't get many of these lately with Bemin constantly falling apart. I should think you'd want to take full advantage of—"

Voices suddenly roaring in the distance silenced her. They were coming from the direction of the Falconerplein.

"That'll be another student protest," Dharmen said. "Bask in the suns all you want, but do it fast. Warm days won't prepare us for the enemy, including the ones up the street."

"We have three days off with no responsibilities and no orders, Dharm," Dori insisted. "Let up enough to undo your collar at least. It's twenty-eight degrees Celsius today. Even with enviro-control, you must be baking in there. Thee, you've said nothing outside the subject of mad synths all morning; help me. And my eyes are up here, Lieutenant! Save the ogling for your tarts Up East. I know all about your Nieuw Kered hops; don't think you were hiding anything from me."

"You've got Nieuw Kered going on right there, Commander," Dharmen said, eyeing Dori's cleavage. "You really expect the lieutenant to keep his eyes to himself? You're out all over the place. The heat is no excuse to be nearly as naked as Thee in an East Vale—"

"He's seen me in a dress before. It may be a tad low-cut, but I'm not as underclothed as you claim. If either of you in your own ways could appreciate a real woman, I'd fall over flat!" Dori tugged at her rather low neckline. "Next time I go out with you two, I'll leave my

snag-a-man-in-public outfit on base, but at least I'm not scaring everyone away with a sword and a sour face on a day like this. Invasion's
not coming right this minute, Dharm. Couldn't you have left that at
home?" She stopped grimacing at Dharmen's weapon for a moment
to admire the planter bordering the sidewalk. The mood pavers' warm
glow beneath her matched the blooms.

"I'll take my sword over second summer any day. We all know
what's coming, Dori. If the Carmis attack tomorrow, what will *you*
do? Hit 'em with flowers?"

"No, but I might hit you. And can we say goodbye to paranoia just
this once?"

Booms brought the whole way to attention. An outdoor café server
bot fumbled with a beverage tray at the drums and shouts filtering
down.

"Let's turn at the next corner," Dori said. "I'm in no mood for
Angolin's problems today. I'd rather go around that business than
through it."

"I'm not going out of my way for that lot. Let them do the detour-
ing," Dharmen said.

"Ditto me," said Theus. "Running from protesters isn't what I
signed up for."

"Look, you two, we're on leave. This is no time to stir up your usual
testosterone-driven trouble," Dori said.

"Thanks for the compliment, Commander, but we don't intend
trouble. We aren't afraid of it either," Theus said. "And we're meeting
Will on the other end of the plein in a few minutes—why let a bunch
of traitors in training come between us and lunch?"

"Listen, Thee," Dori said, "the general is still on me about that last
weapons theft. And after Dharm assaulted Armetrian during his class,
he'll be lucky to escape a JAG review, so the last thing I need as your
CO right now is either of you throwing yourselves into . . . Dharmen?"

She looked over her shoulder, found him already half a block away, running toward the Falconerplein. "Oh, damn, damn, *damn*!"

IT WAS THE LARGEST, LOUDEST assembly Dharmen had ever seen. The crowd spilled into the surrounding ways, hardly contained by a pitifully small police presence. He carved through it as carefully as he had through the Negaran jungle. But it was useless. The thirty-six-year-old in uniform stood out too easily among the chanting, sweaty students. Faces turned to him and hardened. He wasn't afraid, but he did begin to realize what an affront he was.

"Who invited you, soldier boy? Go home!" someone yelled.

"Abolish the military; abolish it now, beginning with this one here!" yelled another.

Dharmen stopped. "Got any more? I'm listening!" The hecklers clamped shut. "Challenge then retreat when the challenge is met. In my line of work, that's a coward."

With more students suddenly supporting them, they told Dharmen what he could do with his line of work. At his back and from a distance as he moved on through the crowd. With every step, stares and taunts vied for attention. His expression silenced most of it; no one dared challenge him directly just yet.

The platform speaker paused his tirade. Drums resounded in response. Yelling, stomping, and fist shaking erupted around Dharmen and joined the remarks resuming at him. He continued forward, suffering no intimidation and ignoring his CSD. The earsplitting noise ceased.

"You all know why we're here! Our government's lies bring us together today," the speaker—a short, flush-faced kid with big bushy hair—said into a hovering mouthpiece. "We sit in classes studying for meaningless professions while our leaders plan our futures—futures that benefit them, not us!" The audio bot followed his back-and-forth march across the platform. "I don't know about all of you, but I'm not having my education wasted by old people in high places. They say the Outside World is evil. I say that's an excuse to keep us cooped here like ancient zoo animals while the rest of the planet lives free!"

Dharmen shut his eyes at the screams and drumbeats reverberating on the surrounding buildings. He couldn't figure out which was worse: the noise or the untruths he was hearing. He partly understood the frustrations fueling them, but expressing them like this was a sure path to insurrection. As Rem-E began an antistress treatment, Dharmen did his best to calm himself and focus.

"He's a well-spoken young man. Misguided maybe, but bright and certainly enterprising," a familiar voice said beside him.

"Enterprising?" Dharmen turned and hissed hotly enough to wipe the flippant smile from Dori's face.

"Our government has been at this for ages now," the speaker bellowed. "Centuries of withholding the Outside from our reach has taught them exactly how to control us, but there's more to life than this tired little land stuffed between its mountains and lakes!" He moved to the platform center, close to where the three officers stood. "We can't get what's out there from this cage, we need to let Parliament know that the days of suppressing our rights are over and tell them where they can put their isolationism. We have the right to live our lives and go about *our* world as *we* see fit, and if freedom is denied us, then by the gods, we'll take it!"

The crowd roared. Dharmen narrowed his eyes at the noise and nonsense. *How can anyone demand something they know nothing at all about?*

"There's no truth to any of this," Dori said, hushed and more seriously now. "Is he leading a protest or trying for a riot?"

The speaker continued . . . and spotted Dharmen. "And what about our fine military? Will we let them dictate our freedoms? They're the government's henchmen. When we rise up, will they put guns to our heads for it?" he said, pointing at Dharmen. "And will they conscript us men to fight imagined enemies across the Abyss while you women wake at night to find soldiers like this one climbing into your beds, with your scared little children made to watch?"

"Right!" Dharmen snarled. That one completely tore it. He shoved bodies aside as he carved a path to the platform.

He heard Theus yell after him to stop, but the jeering and booing made him too angry for that. He reached the platform, climbed the steps. A burly youth in a Mid Realm team tunic blocked his path. Until Dharmen's punch sent him sideways. Barely slowing, Dharmen walked right up to the speaker. He and his big hair backed away as the maddened Guardsman took his spot.

"Give me that!" Dharmen snatched the audio bot controller from the kid's belt. The tiny device floated to him. He faced the crowd. "Okaaay!" he yelled too loudly for the hovering robot to handle. "You've all had a great time chanting death to the Realm and listening to taroc crap. Now you'll listen to me!" He had never addressed this kind of crowd, but that didn't stop him. "I've served Angolin my whole adult life, and that includes every one of you—yes, you! And in all that time, I've never suppressed anyone's freedom," he glared at big hair, "or assaulted anyone. Loyalty, protection, and service to Angolin, that's my charge."

Theus and Dori moved closer to the platform. But Dharmen was too engrossed in the angry remarks flying at him to notice.

"Maybe that works for you, but no soldier's going to tell me what I can and can't do," someone yelled. "You're the government's strong arm, and you know it! You think you can just barge up there and feed us all this? I'm not bowing to our leaders, and I won't bow to you either!"

"Do I look like a Lenan king to you? Who asked you to bow?" Dharmen yelled back. "And who said you aren't free? You kids are so busy spreading lies that you can't think straight!"

Booing hit him like synth oven fumes.

"Listen to me—the Outside isn't what any of you think," he said, making a sweeping motion toward the East Ranges on his left. "Out there, hate is the only rule of law. The Carmogen control their people with everything you accuse me of. You say you're cooped here against your will. Would you rather live life desperate and afraid instead? In Angolin you have homes, school, every enjoyment possible, and safe streets to enjoy it all in. Try getting that across the Abyss!"

The boos and jeers rose again.

"I don't need your protection, and I don't believe any of this!" a woman yelled. "If you and Parliament are so concerned for us, why keep us here and force us to stay hidden? If we're free as you claim, then let us leave!"

Dharmen stared incredulously at her. "You really think you'll just march across the world to welcoming arms? You think it'll be that easy? And do you all think they'll let any of us live freely when they come over here? The Carmogen have no pity at all. I know. I've fought them, and I have the battle scars and dead comrades to prove it!"

"How can you possibly understand us?" someone else yelled. "You Guard types get to go to war and leave when you please. You aren't stranded here like the rest of us!"

Dharmen needled him across the distance. "*Get to go*? What do you think Negara was, a camping trip? *We're stranded* risking our lives to fight for people too dumb to appreciate it!"

A horde of angry faces and shout-backs answered that.

He tried to smooth his tone. "Look, I don't like isolation either, but I know the alternative, and so do our leaders. If the Outside were livable, Angolin would have opened up long ago. But Tentim is not a friendly planet. Don't believe everything you're told, and don't think the gods will hand you an easy life in unknown lands just like that."

"Do you really expect us to listen to you just because you wear a uniform and knock out anybody who gets in your way?" said the speaker from behind Dharmen. "All we want is what's waiting for us. You won't stop us with any of this!"

Dharmen eyed him, tired to Krone of it all. "Kid, you're incredibly naive. Don't think for a minute that wealth and power are coming to you on the fast path, because that's what this is about, isn't it? You and this mob want it all, right this minute, and you'll drag your homeland down to get it. You don't even know what's out there, but you'll rush out after it anyway. If you had real knowledge of the Outside, you'd hide in your parents' pod forever!" He meant that for the speaker, but the audio bot was close enough for mass broadcast. "But don't worry. When the Carmis get hold of you, they'll find you a nice place on a rock pile out in some field. Or maybe in some old Lescain's sleep-in with a chain round your stupid neck!"

Big hair glowered. The crowd ranted.

Dharmen turned back to them unfazed. "Parliament and the Guard do everything they can to protect what our ancestors gave their lives to build," he said, still trying to get his message across. "I get that you're angry and feel unjustly locked into Angolin, but that's not the complete truth. Do you really want to throw everything away, just to satisfy—"

His vision flashed. He stumbled, looked down at the fist-size stone coming to rest at his feet. He put his hand to his head, felt blood on his fingers followed by pain. The projectile had shattered his patience more than anything else. He leaped from the platform to the ground and marched up to the shouting assailant. A hand reached out and shoved him. Enraged, he withdrew his sword, thrust its tip at the other's face. "I don't know what's worse," he growled, "the war that's coming, or the one you people are starting right here!"

"Drop your weapon!"

Dharmen turned to that oddly familiar voice. Scowling at him through ice-cold gray eyes was Lieutenant Vara. She was dressed in Military Police camos, which she most certainly was not, and her side-arm was drawn. Two more MPs flanked him. *Probably real ones,* he considered, *and does it matter?*

"I said drop it!" Vara repeated.

He eyed her. He was about to defy her, and had every right to. But what an opportunity, and interestingly timed. *It's worth the risk,* he decided. He acquiesced and tried to resheathe his sword.

"No! On the ground! On. The ground!" Vara gestured downward with her sidearm.

Dharmen lowered his sword to the pavement. One of the MPs stamped on the blade and wrenched it from his hand. The other secured his hands behind his back. It felt witheringly ironic to be on this end of a detainment.

"What's going on here? Explain yourself, Lieutenant?" Dori demanded as she and Theus made it through the cheering, onlooking mass.

Vara studied their Guard holo-badges. "This one has violated code," she answered, glancing at Dharmen. "We're taking him into custody, and you two are stepping aside."

Theus was closest. Vara tried to push him back, but he deflected her arm. "Forget it. Don't even try to give us orders until you tell us what this is really about," he said.

"And code says nothing about a soldier acting in self-defense," Dori added. "You're blowing this way out of proportion, Lieutenant. Just where did you get your MP training, anyway?"

"Where, indeed?" Dharmen dared to quip.

Vara ignored that and huffed at Dori, "We have jurisdiction here, not you. This officer is under arrest, period. Interfere, and you'll join him, Commander. Superior or not."

"Regardless of what offense you *think* he's committed, the lieutenant commander is a fine officer. Treat him with dignity and respect," Dori said, reinforcing Dharmen's rank in the wild-eyed woman's mind. "And don't expect to have him long."

Vara gazed menacingly at Dori for an insubordinately long instant. "Take him," she ordered her people.

"This won't stick, soldier. You'll be all right. We promise!" Theus said as Dharmen was whisked out of the crowd toward a Guard patrol sloop.

"I know I will. Got no reason to think otherwise," came Dharmen's reply over his shoulder with a wink. He shot eyes at his captor. "Isn't that right, Lieutenant?"

Theus and Dori watched helplessly as Dharmen let himself be led away in uncharacteristic obedience to the taunts and jeers swirling around him.

AN OLD, HEAVY WOODEN DOOR was opened into a dimly lit, rock-walled chamber. Before Dharmen could size it up, he was led inward and thrown onto soft ground. He rose and stumbled, sloshing through several centimeters of water as the door slammed shut. He hadn't expected a cozy brig cell, but what his dilating pupils revealed vaulted his grimmest imaginings.

Light from ancient wall torches revealed a muddy floor, rutted with wide, puddle-filled holes. The cave walls around him writhed, and he heard the din of tiny wailings.

"Micromice. *Nice.* Lords and Ladies in Heaven, you do make it pleasant!"

Thankfully, the mud provided a barrier. The last thing he wanted was thousands of fingernail-sized rodents threading his pant legs. High above their reach, crystalline walls glittered as they vanished toward a shadowed ceiling. A deep-purple opening hovered in it like the oculus of a high dome. It darkened by the minute: a natural sky-light in what was probably the west face of a mountain, judging by the angle of the fading sunlight filtering through it. A downward-flowing breeze too cool and fresh to be from the lowlands on such a warm day pierced the cave's dampness. Dharmen caught a familiar, pungent scent. Saaryl pine grew only in the East Ranges. This place was nowhere near any built-up part of Angolin, and it was definitely far from South C. Even if by the grace of the gods he was found, it would take a long time.

A faint glint of metal—no, marblite—caught his eye in the low light. He squinted. It was a human bust, a Hanne shrine like the one in Aremel's garden. The head had been blown off, the stonework over-flowing the shoulders melted by particle fire.

"Krone, what is this place?" Dharmen put a hand to his aching face.

The pain went from his jaw to his half-closed left eye. He had been clubbed with pulse rifle butts in transport. "You just struck a restrained prisoner. You'll pay for that when we get to base, Lieutenant," he'd said to Vara, mostly for his own benefit. He knew neither Fifth nor Seventh was their destination.

Her kick to his groin made him slump to the patrol sloop's floor, arms tethered behind his back and unable to reach out and right himself. Before he could pitch another remark, she seized a fistful of his wavy black hair and yanked his face up to hers. "You're already in deep. Keep talking, and we'll end this here and now!"

Dharmen's head had been clamped between her grip and the blade of his own sword, held beneath his chin. The two petty officers that aided in his arrest—real MPs or not—were in the cockpit flying them to who knew where. On either side of him were two noxiously familiar faces.

"Five traitors for three. Must've been a sale. And I guess I shouldn't be surprised to see *you*, Shipman." He rolled eyes from Narond to

Ciros. "I'd assume he escaped detention no thanks to you if I didn't know the JAG better."

Fists answered that. The pummeling he took in the back of that sloop was worse than anything he had ever experienced in combat.

He tried to access his internal as he watched the flickering torches. Nothing. Vara had gone over him with an improvised, datapad-rigged scanner and managed to deactivate Rem-E's principal functions: trace, communications, personal interfacing—everything. She hadn't detected the beacon floating through his bloodstream independently of his now painfully silent combat assistant. Theus was tracking his position, but there were no guarantees. This hadn't exactly been the plan.

But Yos's experimental antiparticler, however, had been found and confiscated.

He tried to move his wrists, but the manacles held firm. The muddy cave's moldy stench and the blood running down his face filled his nostrils and made the situation clearer. He'd assumed earlier that he would get out of this safely, if only just. Bad call! *Father always says a good soldier knows when and when not to fight*, he thought. *Was one stupid protest and the wish to catch Dawn Fire's hatchet woman worth losing your life? And destroying Will's happiness?*

He hung his head, wanting to cry. He actually found himself wanting to crumple to the mud and drown himself in tears for the first time in his life.

"How did I bring it to this?" he asked upward toward the Heavenly Pantheon.

He looked around for an escape. The skylight was too high and there was nothing to reach it with. The door was the only way out . . . Footsteps approached it from the outside. Its antiquated lock clicked, echoing through the cave before it swung open.

"So now that you've had a taste of reality, I trust we'll have no more mouthing off," Vara said, sauntering in as though into her own live-in. Ciros and Narond filed in behind her, carrying a camp chair each. The three remained at the front of the cave for the moment, avoiding the mud farther in. Vara set up and took one of the seats. "Bring him forward."

Dharmen was grabbed by the arms and thrust in front of her. She glanced stone-faced at her subordinates and, with a flick of her wrist, pointed downward. They knocked Dharmen's legs from beneath him, forcing him to his knees in the mud. He knelt with his head held down by cold, hard hands. Metal passed beneath his eyes; his chin was drawn upward with the tip of his sword. Unskilled in even the simplest Ergive form, Vara fumbled and nearly dropped it.

"That's heavier than it looks." Dharmen dared a look up at her. "Novices are instructed to use two hands, before they learn to—"

"Shut up!" The vitriol that Vara channeled into her clumsy movements put a deep gash into his jaw. It warmed with blood. "This isn't a training session! And you can forget those outdated combat tactics. The New Order will have no use for them."

"New Order? And what's that, if I really need to ask?"

"You'll know soon enough. All of Angolin will."

Dharmen hadn't heard that voice in a while but wasn't surprised by it. "Lieutenant Commander, I wondered when you'd make it here. This smelled of you from the start. Everything since Bemin has."

Armetrian set up a seat beside Vara.

"Welcome back," she sneered at him. "Didn't think I'd see you again after all these weeks, though I s'pose we'll never know where you went."

"You know where I went, Lieutenant. Why waste the sarcasm? And that's a dangerous weapon. Put it down if you don't know how to use it." Armetrian reached over, snatched the sword from her, and thrust it into the soft ground beside his chair. He edged eyes to Dharmen, looked his wounds up and down. "And be careful, all of you. I don't want him dead just yet. And you," he said to Dharmen's steely glare. "How you managed to outlive every attempt on you has to be the Hidden Realm's greatest mystery, but you're a sight if nothing else."

Vara nudged him, handed him the confiscated antiparticler, and explained it to him. He studied it, whistled astonishment. "You've got a lot of lives in you, Tate—three and counting thus far. Now I see why."

"Four and counting. You can't add," Dharmen said. "And you might've succeeded if you hadn't put two kids on the job, one of whom couldn't wield a sword if his life depended on it."

"If you mean Shipman Vinc's little tantrum, he did that on his own," Armetrian said. "You have enemies everywhere, Tate. Even my lowest boot wanted you out of the way."

"Just get to it, Armetrian. What's all this about? Vara could easily have killed me and dumped me somewhere. But she didn't, so why am I here? What do you really want?"

Armetrian rose, paced to the door and back. "You know what I want, and you'll give it."

"Give what? You and your three goons here are riding high lately, handing all our asses to the Carmis. What could you possibly need from me?"

Armetrian bent down and cocked his head. He grabbed Dharmen by the collar, pulled his face close. "You really should stop asking so many questions." He let go and strutted proudly around the cave front. "You're smart, Tate. More so than I ever gave you credit for. Base top silver thinks so too. You made lieutenant commander in half the time I did, and you've got the general in your hand. That's what got you to Negara."

Dharmen widened his uninjured eye at Armetrian.

"Then there's that night in the jungle. Plans were set and would've been underway so much faster if you hadn't interfered. How long had you been hiding in the shadows that night? How much did you overhear before we discovered you?"

"You know what I heard. You didn't bring me here just for that."

Dharmen watched Armetrian's nostrils flare. He braced for the blow. And it came with quick-fire rage: the kick to his chin slammed his teeth together. He fell into the mud, managed to right himself in spite of pain and bound wrists.

"You don't do this well at all, Armetrian, and you haven't from the beginning," he gurgled through the blood filling his mouth. "You should have killed me in that forest when you had the chance. You botched that and every attempt since."

"Soon enough, soldier!" Armetrian retook to his seat. "But now, you're going to stop babbling and tell me what I want to know. What did you overhear that night, and how much of it have you told Gennet? I hear you've met privately with him at least once, and you've been talking to others in the Space Commission and at PDP. Don't think I don't know where your friends are."

Dharmen answered nothing. It would take more than a few broken teeth to make him.

"I'm just as impatient as you are, so you'd better stop wasting my time and give me the information you've been spreading all over Angolin. I've come too far to let you people ruin everything for me."

"For us!" said Vara. "You're not the only one in this, Lieutenant Commander. We've all done more than our share of—"

"You talk too much, Lieutenant. Learn to shut it once in a while." Armetrian snorted before pointing furiously at Dharmen. "He's the one I want talking now!"

"She's just like the rest of you scum, Armetrian. How do any of you expect to rule Angolin someday if this is the best you can do for teamwork?" Dharmen expected another hit, but Armetrian stared at him instead.

"You never learn, Tate. Don't you ever get tired of causing trouble?" Ciros said. "Like having Gennet send MPs to arrest me. Did you really expect that to change anything?"

"Taking part in an antigovernment protest is a Code violation, Sublieutenant. You looking for me to apologize?" Dharmen threw back.

Armetrian ignored all of that. "I'll ask you one last time, Tate. What do you know, and who have you been talking to?"

Dharmen let fiery eyes speak for him.

Armetrian inhaled, looked to Narond. The recruit unstrapped his pulse rifle and slammed its butt against the side of Dharmen's head. Pain seared. Ciros struck him in the back next.

"Ready to talk now, or should we continue?" Armetrian said. "I don't have all night, and neither do you."

"I've got . . . nothing to tell you," Dharmen gasped, forcing himself to stand.

Ciros and Narond secured his arms as Armetrian rose again. "You sure about that?"

"You'll kill me whether I talk or not, so forget it. I have nothing to say—take that down to the Netherlords with you!"

Armetrian punched him hard in the gut and followed it with another. Dharmen tumbled over.

Narond moved in and kicked him in the side. "You thought you had me beat back on Bemin that night, didn't you? Didn't you?" he yelled. "Well, look who's got the power now, filthy man lover! Look who's got the power!"

The kicks and the clubbing sent blood tracking through the muddy water. With his arms fastened behind his back and in excruciating pain, Dharmen couldn't defend himself. Armetrian ordered Narond to stop. In a burst of rage, the Shipman gave Dharmen one last hard kick to the chest.

Dharmen's groan filled the cave as he felt his ribs crack. Panic was ready to overtake him, but CSD got to him first. He rolled over in the mud and lay, his eyes dithering and his whole body shaking violently. "Rem-EEEEE!" His internal had always been there for him. The silence was frightening.

"Don't bother, Tate. It'll do you no good," Vara mewed. "Your combat assistant cannot *assist* you at the moment."

Her tone and the grinning sneer on her face gave Dharmen just enough impetus to sit up. He spat blood all over himself while trying, but he wasn't about to let her win easily. *Damn it, Thee! Where are you?* He painfully shifted his weight, moved his arms . . .

His heart skipped a beat. One of his wrists was loose in the manacles. The beating must have damaged them. Pain shot through every part of his body, and his vision clouded, but he forced himself to focus. He slid his wrist out the open cuff but kept his arms behind his back.

"This isn't getting us anywhere," Vara said to Armetrian. "Beating him to a pulp's not getting him talking. Can't you think of anything else?"

"Why don't *you* think of something instead of yapping! And for your information, I do have something else." Armetrian turned to Ciros. "Sublieutenant, make yourself useful and return to South C immediately. Go to the lieutenant commander's house on the Heiden Kanaal. Arrest both occupants and bring them here. The younger one won't give you any trouble. He's an even bigger faggot than his new fiancé here." Armetrian eyed his battered and bloody prisoner coldly. "I'm aware of your marriage proposal, as if you two will make it that far."

"Just what do you intend to do?" Dharmen wheezed as Ciros followed orders and left.

"I think you can figure that out. I need to know what you know and what you and your friends have planned. If you won't see reason, maybe your husband-to-be will." Armetrian paced the wet floor again. "And if he won't cooperate, then I'll work on your father." He leaned in, leveled his eyes with Dharmen's. "I know he's still visiting you two. It'll be three for one when they're brought here."

"Your score is with me, Armetrian. Leave Will and my father out of this. They've done nothing to you!" Dharmen gurgled through the blood pooling again in his throat.

"He has a point there, at least," Vara said. "You can't bring Nüren Tate here. People are getting suspicious as it is. If he disappears—"

"Oh, but I can," Armetrian said, still staring Dharmen down. "I didn't see it before, but if my trip taught me anything, it's that success demands risk. Having old General Tate in our care will create all kinds of opportunities for us." He began to rant about what a shame it was that the best military leader Angolin had ever known had a homosexual for a son, and how that would soon be *corrected*. "You and your kind," he spat at Dharmen, "don't deserve the skin you run around in, much less the right to live among normal, clean-minded people. I can't wait to see the Lescainate roast all of you on a spit!"

The hate coming at him for no reason shocked Dharmen. But through his pain, he could contemplate just one thing: his father and Will were about to be pulled into this. He couldn't let that happen. He searched feverishly for options, any at all.

"But you're right about one thing, Tate," Armetrian continued, strutting now with his back to his captive, "I shouldn't have been so soft on Negara, I should have killed you then and there. Letting you live and get away was a big mistake."

Not your biggest, Dharmen thought. With what strength he had left, he whipped around and leaped toward his weapon, still stuck in the cave floor. Vara tried to intercept him, but he knocked her aside. Narond moved in from behind in nearly the same instant. Dharmen reached his sword, wheeled, and thrust hard into his assailant. The blade shattered Narond's spine with a *crack* as it ripped through his body and exited through his back. An arm tightened around Dharmen's neck, pulling him from behind and choking him as he looked into the recruit's dithering eyes. They closed as he collapsed, impaled in the mud.

Armetrian wrestled his captive, but Dharmen gave him a backward elbow and broke free.

"Hold it!" Vara yelled.

The door was close, but it was no use. Dharmen stared across the barrel of her pulse rifle. The torch flames leaped in her eyes, wide and glassy as synth saucers.

"I don't know how you broke free, but you'll join Narond in a second!" She reached over and snatched the antiparticler from Armetrian's pocket. "You survived on Bemin because of this. But you don't have it now, do you?" She raised her rifle, pressed the trigger—

A blast came from behind Dharmen. Vara lurched backward, her own weapon discharging upward as she went down. Smoke curled from her pierced skull.

Dharmen looked around, saw Dori's red hair and drawn rifle. Heat rose visibly from its barrel.

"Stay where you are! And hands up," Theus bellowed at Armetrian while rounding Dori.

Armetrian slid his hand to his sidearm. Theus's warning shot nearly scalped him.

"Hearing problem, Lieutenant Commander? Put 'em up!"

Armetrian raised hands, and uniforms rushed in and secured him.

General Gennet came through the doorway. "Are you all right, Tate?" His expression told Dharmen that he realized he'd asked too soon.

"*I couldn't be better.* But sir, you have to stop Ciros. He's headed to my house!" Dharmen replied, terrified. "Armetrian just sent him after Willem and my father to have them—"

"He won't get that chance, Dharm," Dori said as she eyed Armetrian. "Will and the general are back at base."

"We met up with Will right after they took you," Theus added. "Dori saw him and General Tate safely to Seventh while I tracked your signal to here. Your father insisted on being part of the rescue, but our general wouldn't have it."

"That was absolutely out of the question, Lieutenant," said Gennet. "We had no idea what we'd find here, and I couldn't risk General Tate's safety." He narrowed his eyes, turned on Armetrian. "You! How could you destroy your honor like this? Kidnapping, beating, and plotting against your own people on top of all else you've done. Do you have any idea of what you've become, soldier?"

"A visionary if anything, General," Armetrian snarled. "Angolin is old and sick. It needs to die and all of you with it if you can't see past this useless little land. And if I'm the one destined to make that happen, then let it be!"

"Illuminating perspective! And the last one you'll ever give as a free man, Lieutenant Commander. But save it for your court-martial." Gennet's eyes flickered in the dim light. "Get him out of here! And you two," he said to Theus and Dori, "excellent work. Absolutely outstanding! Now get Tate and the others back to base and to the infirmary. I don't want to lose anyone else tonight."

Dharmen reached down, ripped his sword from Narond's limp body, and nearly fell over from the pain shooting through his own. "Glad you finally made it, Thee," he gasped, needing to be held up. "I was just about at the end of my . . . Others? What others?"

"You're not the only inmate here." Theus's tone was morbid. "We've found three dozen so far and not all of them alive. But guess who we did find safe and—"

"Oh my *goddesses, Dharmen!*"

Dharmen looked to the doorway and couldn't believe his sight. Caked in mud, looking otherwise no worse for wear, Aremel came in and ran through the muck with tears streaming down her face. She went to hug him but stopped at his appearance.

"By Lothnë! What have they *done* to you?"

"Nothing I couldn't handle." Dharmen began to feel light-headed. "I'm glad to see you, Aremel."

"We're glad to see you both!" Dori said as she and Theus helped him to the door.

"Commander, I know I . . . made a mess of things . . ." The rest of it left him. It took all he had just to stay conscious and standing.

"Later, Dharm. Right now, let's get you patched up and back to base before you bleed to death," Dori said.

Before they got him through the doorway, Dharmen turned. "General," he addressed weakly.

"Yes, Tate? Make it quick."

"Send that detachment to my house. Sublieutenant Ciros . . . is still on his way there. We can't let him esca—"

In his friends' arms, Dharmen closed his eyes and said nothing more as everything went black.

CHAPTER 13

BALANETH'S CHOICE

em-E? Rem-E!

    I am here, sir. I am online.

    Thank the uplords. Where . . . where am I?

In transit, sir.

Again? How? Armetrian and the others—

Are all in custody. You are safe. They can do you no further harm. But you are far from well, and your memory is clouded. You must not overexert yourself with worry.

Taroc balls, Rem-E! The traitors . . . Will and my father, I need to make sure—

Sir, for the first time ever, I must give *you* an order: Silence your mind. Rest!

❂

"COMMANDER, THERE ARE TOO MANY people in here," Theus insisted. "Dharm's under intensive care. They don't allow more than one visitor at a time for that. We should leave Will and him alone and come back later."

"We won't be long, Thee. I'll take responsibility," Dori said. "And he's in delta sleep. We could throw a party on him, and it wouldn't wake him. Sorry, Will."

Willem was far away. His thoughts and emotions danced painfully to the music of one question: why? Everything from a year ago, months ago, *three nights ago*—why? He said nothing.

And as far as he or anyone knew, Dharmen heard nothing. He lay peacefully on his back, fitted with an army of medi-synths and biopresses. Collaborating under Rem-E's close supervision, they ran tests, repaired tissue, and administered treatment for the rebuilding of his badly damaged body. Beeps indicated stages of bone repair. A flicker of light now and then signaled ocular and nerve tissue regeneration for his nearly shattered left eye and root strengthening for broken teeth. Natural microbiome replenishment commenced silently. Mattress membrane sensors worked with nanites swimming throughout his bloodstream to scan and heal internal injuries while surface bruises and cuts were covered in refurbishment wraps. All activity was reported in uprights surrounding Dharmen's infirmary bed that had served as his convalescent haven all week's end.

"Now, as I was saying," Dori continued, "of everybody we apprehended in those caves, eleven worked for Aremel, including her pilot, kitchen staff, and most of her gardeners. How's that for household loyalty?"

"Is it any surprise? Look where they put their operation," said Theus. "I still can't believe that in all of Angolin's tucked away places, Dawn Fire chose the caverns under Mount Condorcet for their ops base, right above Aremel's estate! Dharmen wondered what Gallin was doing up there. Now we know."

"The hideout was still being established. The general's search teams assessed as much," Dori said. "Aside from Gallin and his Kleve Park cohort, the larger traitor network hadn't been there more than a week when we found them. They definitely started elsewhere, and that base likely still exists."

"It actually makes sense," Willem said through a mournful sigh. "So much of Angolin is unknown and uninhabited. No one thought to look beneath their own noses. The Condorcet caverns are endless. Every Highland family has spelunked a few, but no one knows how many networks there are or how extensively they reach." He turned to the window, looked past the confines of Seventh and Nieuw Holland Valley to the unending line of snow-capped peaks beyond the Great Lake's opposite shore. The morning rain had diminished to drizzle, but fog continued to mantle the mountains' faraway feet. "The East Ranges are perfect for the collaborators. I just wish they hadn't infiltrated my cousin's home. Blasted! If only she hadn't been in her gardens that night."

"Gallin had scouted and recruited the household staff for some time," Dori said, "though it appears they didn't need much coaxing. Aremel would have run into them eventually; she couldn't have avoided it."

"Yes, yes, I know all that."

"She's safe, Will. That's what matters," Theus said. "So is Dharm now, thankfully."

Willem turned around. "Why did Dharmen go with them?"

Theus gave him a forlorn look. That and his lack of answer were too much.

"You heard me, Thee. Why did he go? He knew who Vara was. He told me about his run-in with her on Negara."

"We don't know why he did what he did," Dori said. "I intend to find out when he recovers, but I wish, for your sake and his, that we knew more."

Willem glowered. "Everybody always tells me how calm and peaceful I am, and I've managed to remain so thus far. I stayed calm while the love of my life was away at war, I stayed calm when some kid tried to blow up my dine-in, I didn't say anything when I was nearly snatched off my canal just steps from my own pod, *and*"—he brandished a finger at both of them—"I kept my wits about me when my house synth shot up my sleep-in. Now four traitors—*four of your colleagues*—just beat my Dharmen to within a centimeter of his life, so I want you both to stop feigning ignorance and talk to me.

"Dharmen knew exactly what would happen, so why did he agree to go with them?" The brittle silence beyond the infirmary's instrument chimes was more than he could handle. "I'm easygoing most of the time, but that ends right now, and believe me, you two don't want to see a patient man lose his patience! Now for the love of the Heaveners, tell me!"

"Dori doesn't know why Dharm went," Theus said, "but I do. He wanted to draw them out of hiding and expose them."

"Thee, what are you saying?" Dori asked, incredulous.

"Dharmen wanted to go traitor hunting when he discovered them, and more when they started harassing him. And he would've done it in his usual knock-'em-down-first-ask-questions-later way, but Gennet demanded caution and wanted things handled quietly."

"*General* Gennet's purpose was to locate and apprehend as many of them as possible. And mind your place, Lieutenant," Dori said. "Casting a net takes time and care. The general thought it better to surround a whole hive at once rather than stir them up too soon and scatter them. I know this because Dharmen certainly wasn't the only officer recruited to work on the problem, and despite what's happened, I support the general's strategy."

"So do I. But it's easier to stomach from a comfortable office than from out in the field every day," Theus flatly replied.

"That and your tone are insubordinate, Lieutenant."

"I apologize, ma'am, but with permission?" Dori's raised eyebrows barely granted approval. "General Gennet is occupied with base business most of the time," Theus continued, "and I know part of that involves monitoring the traitors now, but he doesn't have to deal with them constantly, face-to-face like us, and he hasn't had to put up with them trying to kill him like Dharm and Will."

Theus laid a hand on Dharmen's shoulder. "He towed the general's line for as long as he could. But he just wasn't having it, not the first time someone targeted him and Will, not the second. And after that house synth incident, he'd had enough. He wasn't about to wait for more attacks and risk having one actually succeed, he wanted to flush them out. He insisted we try to find Dawn Fire's hiding place, so we started planning. Then Vara came along and gave him the opportunity. Dharmen knew I'd track him, so he took it." He lowered his eyes, shook his head. "But damn it, I should have recognized her sooner."

"What do you mean, Thee?" Willem asked.

"I mean, it was Vara who helped Armetrian get the weapons off Bemin. She shot Dharmen and would've killed him had he not been wearing Yos's antiparticler, and it all happened right in front of me. Didn't Dharm tell you about that?"

"No, he didn't! He tells me less and less, lately. He thinks he's protecting me. If only I could tap into that internal AI of his." *And if only I could tap into my fiancé's mind. One nasty surprise after another, and now, Dharmen is the one creating them!*

"Well, Vara must've been as shocked as I was to find she hadn't killed him then, and wanted to finish the job when she caught up with him at the protest," Theus said.

"She nearly did, no thanks to Dharmen, himself," Dori grumbled. "And Thee, you should have filled me in on all this en route up to the mountain. I knew there was more to it."

Footsteps approached the doorway. "Ma'am!" Leatra said.

"At ease, Shipman, but you can't stay long," Dori said. She shot Theus an impish eyebrow. "Too many people in the room."

"Commander, if I may," said Theus, "Dharmen would want her here."

"Aren't you the one policing the visitor count, soldier?" Dori said. "The lieutenant commander needs his rest."

"What happened to *I'll take responsibility*?" Willem wanly chimed in.

"Oh, all right, Vinc, stay a while!" Dori said. "How's your brother doing?"

"I wish I knew, ma'am," Leatra answered. "He won't talk to anyone since his court-martial, and our parents aren't having an easy time with him at home. Mother says she preferred him back at school, running his mouth and getting in trouble, to having him quiet and sad around the farm every day. He spends most of his time out in the fields or with the animals, as far from people as he can get. It's hard for him, being under house arrest with a disappointed family."

"House arrest and far from the house. Angolinian justice at its finest," Dori moaned. "The punishment never matches the offense in this land."

Leatra wrinkled thin eyebrows. "Ma'am, permission to speak freely."

"I did say *at ease*, Shipman. Say what you need to."

"Aye, Commander. I overheard Gallin's name before I came in. What little Irzek's had to say lately has included him."

"What has he told you? Excuse me, Dori," Willem said, having ripped the question right out of her mouth.

"I don't know if you've gotten this from interrogation yet," Leatra continued, "but Gallin has a safe house in South C. That's where Dawn Fire started. Irzek went there several times."

"No, we hadn't gotten that, not from anyone," Dori said, wide-eyed. "We only knew they were all working for Armetrian. No one's mentioned Gallin before now."

"This place is in South C, you say?" Willem asked Leatra.

"Yes. On Niro Way, near Ursula. Irzek tried to keep quiet about it whenever I asked, but I'm good at making him slip up and talk."

"Niro is just down the hill and beyond the market from me and Dharmen," Willem said, astonished. "Every morning, I go to work and look down that way, and all this time Gallin was right within sight!"

"Shipman, we've got to get you to the general. He needs this information," said Dori. "Who knows what we'll find in that pod. If we can get there soon enough, it could turn this whole investigation around. Thee, comm his staff assistant and set up a meeting, stat."

"I'm on it, Commander." Theus activated his internal and left the room.

Dori folded her arms, lifted one to rest her chin on her hand. "Tell me about Armetrian," she ordered Leatra. "Your brother's already given several statements on his dealings with him, but I want to know what you know."

"Well, ma'am, Armetrian's biggest—his *only*—duty for Irz, far as I can tell, involved that last Port incident."

"You mean the one where my Dharmen was shot," Willem put in.

"Yes, sir."

Willem managed a slim smile. "She's *sir*," he said, glancing at Dori. "You can call me Will."

"Well, Mr. Hanne . . . Will, Armetrian had the weapons theft carefully planned, ever since . . ." Leatra peered at Dharmen and lowered her voice. "Ever since Lieutenant Commander Tate and Lieutenant Tarkala took down the one before it. I think Armetrian needed a successful one to maintain his reputation with the enemy, but he couldn't just walk in, grab the arms, and go. He needed authorization first, specialized authorization."

"And that's where your brother came in?" Dori asked.

"Yes, Commander. Irzek's job was to obtain the access codes for heavy weapons stores and report on the standard security rotations guarding them. His duty station was in the ops hub, so he had ready access to the information."

"Why, Shipman, didn't you come forward with any of this before?"

"I didn't think I needed to, ma'am. Irz had been detained for a while. I assumed you'd gotten this already."

Dori shook her head. "And before now we'd scrutinized Armetrian and Vara the most. How did we not catch any of this? We should have broadened our scope from the start." She went to the foot of Dharmen's bed, shifted her weight to one booted heel. "Vinc got difficult-to-obtain access codes to restricted stores. Narond created the diversion, then was somehow released from confinement. It's amazing how an operation's biggest parts are made possible by its smallest players."

Theus returned, gave Leatra a sharp nod to the doorway. She saluted Dori and left the room.

"My internal recorded that conversation, Will," Dori said when she was out of earshot. "Once I turn it over, Gallin's as good as caught."

Willem sat at Dharmen's bedside and took his hand, resting peacefully beside him. "Think so?"

"I wish I could say I know so. But this is the breakthrough on that part that we needed to—"

"*Indeed*! And if *you* don't find that Lenan thug, *I will*!" huffed a big voice from a smallish woman storming in past Theus. "We Hannes have our *own way* that's *far worse* than *anything* the Guard will do to him, and if I ever see Gallin again, I'll . . . Whatsamatter? High flyers got all your tongues?"

"Aremel, how did you get up here?" Dori asked. "Security has been lax as it is. Don't tell me no one's guarding the lifts."

"Why, my dear, I am the *queen* of *resource*. Precious little holds *me* back!"

Willem nodded to that. Half-heartedly.

"There are too many people in here," said Dori with a raised eyebrow for Theus. "I know, I know. My responsibility. I'll handle it!"

Aremel bent down and gave Willem a brusque hug that pulled him out of his seat. Her eyes went to Dharmen's massive injuries and attending devices. "*Lothnë's grace*, how *will* he come through this?"

"He'll be fine, Aremel. Every part of him is being worked on," said Dori. "He's way better than he looks, at this point."

"*Oh!* Well, can't we wake him then? You know, I'd *so* like to *thank* him from the depths of my heart for *everything* he's done."

"Absolutely not!" said Theus. "His father woke him this morning, *early* this morning, and the medi-synths had to backtrack and restart every treatment."

"He has to recuperate, cousin," Willem added just as forcefully.

"Well, *pity*! He's done so much and been through so much—*oh,* and my Balaneth wanted to come and give *his regards* to one so *honorable,* as he so rightly put it. But he had some other business, left me in a hurry this morning saying he had *justice* to serve. I have absolutely no *idea* what that could be."

"Cousin! Everyone, actually," Willem said. "A moment alone, please?"

"Why certainly, Will," Aremel said. "How utterly *selfish* of us all!"

Theus shot Dori an exasperated frown that said, she's calling *us*—

"Come along, you two," Aremel directed. She bid Willem goodbye with the customary Angolinian right-left-right cheek kisses before ushering Dori and Theus out the door.

Willem sighed hard. It felt as if the weight of the world was leaving him. Marginally. He turned to Dharmen. "I know why you did what you did, I just wanted to put feet to fire. But guess what? You're not a young bachelor warrior anymore, you're with me now. And what about your father? Nüren would be crushed right now if you hadn't survived. Even leading the Guard couldn't prepare him to lose his only son—and I've got news for you, every conversation you and I have had about you dying in combat hasn't prepared me either. I'm not ready, Dharmen!"

He wanted to go on, but he couldn't. Tears blurred his vision and poured down his cheeks. He buried his face in his hands, cried so hard that he felt mucous run through his fingers and join the watery torrent in an emotional outpouring stronger than the roaring falls beneath Greathall. The gush stole his words. He could do nothing but expel and let every bit of despair drain from him completely after having held it all in for so long.

"We have a life ahead of us," he finally sputtered between sobs. "Damn the Carmogen and damn Dawn Fire. I need you with me safe and sound!"

He stopped, looked at his hands and down his front. He moved a step toward the room's lavatory, wanting to clean up. But he leaned in close to his fiancé's still face first. "Promise me you'll think twice before risking yourself like this again," he said softly, "because I don't know what I'll do without you." He left Dharmen's side, went into the small chamber, and shut the door.

DHARMEN WAS ALONE NOW IN the room that had for days read his neural activity, took medi-synth directives, and adjusted everything in measure: temperature, humidity, light, sound filtration, and all else accordingly to aid his healing and comfort. Amid the pulses and sensations coursing through his body, his good eye twitched, opened slowly. A tear ran down his face and stained the regeneration wrap covering the gash to his cheek from his own sword.

"I promise, love," he mouthed lightly to empty air. "I promise."

FLANKED BY TWO BODYGUARDS, LORD Balaneth stood silently just outside the doorway to Gallin's emptied sleep-in. He watched as the man was obviously preparing a hasty departure, and completely unaware of the other Lenans present. He sighed disappointment, but Gallin was too frenzied to hear and still hadn't turned around.

"Norgods! How much longer?" Gallin grated as he rummaged through a packed bag overflowing with disheveled papers and old Angolinian datapads. A robodrive sat connected to one of the pads protruding from a side pocket, and in no apparent hurry to complete its download. "I need an independently mobile, untraceable backup. Now move!" he muttered at it.

"Are we off to somewhere?"

Gallin wheeled, knife in hand. His face changed as he tried to hide his shock. "Maybe I am."

Balaneth entered the room with his bodyguards following. "And taking all evidence of your disgracefully clandestine affairs with you to wherever you're moving your double life."

His men moved in.

"Keep your places," he commanded with a leisurely raise of one hand. "My former aide and I are about to have a discussion."

"Only if you make it a fast one," Gallin said and resheathed his weapon.

"My apologies, Gallin. You're in a hurry." Balaneth fingered his snow-white goatee. "From this interesting living space, unknown to our diplomatic corps. And in the South Centrum of all places, though it's a bit dark and drab for such a tony neighborhood."

"It's a space worthy of a man and better than the cubbyhole I had under you."

"Why, Gallin? Why this betrayal? What would make you turn on your own people and the trust of Angolin, for that matter, to work for our enemies? They'll enslave this entire planet, including you. Can you not see this?"

"Betrayal? Who's here to betray? *What's* here to betray?"

"You can't be serious. Angolin has been as fine a home to you as Lena."

"I require something finer. We all do. I need more than spending the rest of my life serving an old man like you or in a dying nation's brigades. Even if you did sponsor my admission into the officer corps."

"You aren't thinking clearly," said Balaneth. "Lena may not be as big as Carmogen or as fierce as Kay Allendë once was, but we've grown great in our own right through honor, not conquest. Every loyal Lenan should be proud of that."

"I'm not highborn. My place in the dominion doesn't allow me such vain notions. I need more from life than other people's Northern pride."

"But you were a submajor and a very young one at that, and then an ambassadorial attaché. You chose an honorable path. Had that continued, you would've enjoyed an exceptional life."

"Exceptional for *me*, you mean."

"Don't be so quick to assume you'll do better in the East. You've not invented restlessness. Many before you have taken the same easy way, and every one of them found a Carmogen slave market soon enough."

Gallin gave that a few choice Lenan curses. He walked across the room and looked out to the rain-washed way below.

"And you've done none of this alone. Who, might I ask, are you working with?"

"No longer for you, which means you have no right to question me."

"Humor an old Lenan then."

Gallin turned on him. "You already know who. With fortune only the Norgods could've given, I found Armetrian. He's the only person I've met in this hidden cesspool of a society who sees his destiny as clearly as I do. He's the only Angoliner with true vision!"

"I've heard of him before."

"You heard of him after Tate was recovered and the questionings begun. That's what brought his and my name into this, and that's what brought you here."

"You see much as always, Gallin. You excelled in my service because of it. Pity it's been so squandered of late."

"That's the first time you've ever given me such credit. It must be painful."

"Credit? Oh, I've given you far more than that. Your OC sponsorship aside, I offered you a top position in my service when every one of my peers told me—implored me—not to. But I chose you over hundreds of candidates from high families. What a mistake it was to elevate a commoner and assume he'd prove a loyal dominion subject and not some ungrateful, change-mongering traitor, not to mention my beloved's kidnapper!"

"*One* of your beloveds, and it wasn't intended," said Gallin. "And don't think the highborn are free from *change-mongering*. Highborn money has financed me from the start."

"And continues to, with my pay in your pocket now! But no matter. The Angolin Guard is aware of you. They'll weed out all of you to the last and least, and so will Lena."

Light, dim but noticeable, swept across the floor, shaped by the sleep-in's windows. It intensified, then faded to nothing.

"The suns are coming out. The rain has stopped at least," Balaneth digressed.

"You know full well that wasn't sunlight. These people are doomed, and fancy cloaking technology won't save them. The East will overrun Angolin, and once they—once *we* do—we'll settle up with Lena. Try to find a new mindset when the change you're so afraid of makes its way north!"

The robodrive beeped and detached itself from the datapad in Gallin's travel bag. It floated upward and stopped beside him, download complete. He reached down and busily shifted things around in the worn sack.

"So instead of lecturing me about honor," Gallin continued, "I suggest you, your high-mountain bitch that your other wives will never accept, and her man-loving cousin and his interfering mate prepare for the New Order. Carmogen's armies are massive. Now they have advanced arms too, and neither Angolin nor Lena is ready to take them on." He smiled. "It's unstoppable. Live in your fantasy world if you want, but don't pretend not to know that—"

A low rumble shook the building. The floorboards beneath their feet jolted. Balaneth steadied himself as his bodyguards flitted confused eyes around the room.

"So I was correct," Balaneth said. "This is a mobile house."

"What would you know about that?"

"I've been ambassador to Angolin for two years now. I've learned a few things, even about these pod houses." Another rumble rattled the sleep-in's walls. "That's the ground-level propulsors firing. You don't intend to run. You're having the house take you to wherever it is you're going. So why bother to strip the place? Some bizarre housekeeping ritual you learned from your Eastern friends?"

"You did nearly deem me intelligent just now."

"They can track something this big and slow easily. You'll be tractored and trapped like a hunted borbol when they do."

"You underestimate me still, my Lord."

"Ahhh, I see! You're only taking it a short distance. You'll set down somewhere else and then make your real escape."

"That's right. Now you really *have* got it correct."

"Even moving the house to the next way would throw them off your trail. The Guard would arrive here to find nothing, and arrive there to find nothing, wasting all that time while you escape. Such a surreptitious move, it's worthy of a—"

"Of a mercenary?" Gallin eyed the burly men just behind Balaneth. "Yes. I know!"

Balaneth swung around to the man on his left. "Get downstairs and see if you can shut down—" Metal sliced into the man's neck, spraying blood. He fell with the thrown knife still in him.

The other guard lunged for Gallin, but not fast enough. Gallin had already yanked out a gun from his open bag and fired. He fell dead beside his counterpart, the gaping hole from the beam pouring his innards across the sleep-in floor. Balaneth could do nothing but stare down the barrel of Gallin's pilfered Angolinian sidearm.

"They make efficient hand weapons here. I'll give them that," Gallin said. "Let's see how well they fight their own creations when the time comes." He reached down, fastened his bag, and pulled the strap over his shoulder with his free hand. "Now if you'll excuse—"

Balaneth moved to block the doorway. The hard face he put on trembled with the rest of him.

"Trying your hand at honor, are you?" Gallin said. "And it couldn't be more absent."

"You may have successfully betrayed the West, and you may have fooled me for a time, but you won't get out of this house if I have anything to do with it!" Balaneth charged, made a foreshortened move to grab Gallin's gun. He tried to recover the botched lunge even as he quivered with fright.

Gallin dodged it and clubbed him on the back of the neck. Balaneth stumbled. Gallin landed a sharp kick to his head, sending him to the floor in a sprawl. Balaneth shut his eyes; the pain was excruciating. He felt himself being pistol-whipped as he lay prone. Afraid but daring to open an eye, his blurred vision made out Gallin backing away and heaving heavy breaths.

The house shuddered again, harder this time. Then came the whir of fully charged propulsors. Through his pain, Balaneth felt the floor press beneath him under the pressure of lift-off.

"You have the rendezvous coordinates," he heard Gallin say to the hovering robodrive. "Go!"

The small machine swiveled and floated out the window. A beam shot upward at it, Balaneth saw that much. It was thin, probably from a stun weapon. The robodrive swerved but was hit by a second shot. He felt another shudder of a different kind. Propulsor antigrav was cycling down, the house was descending. With a great thud, it resettled into its base.

Balaneth was fading, but he was aware enough to hear the front door burst open downstairs. He watched Gallin hastily activate something on his belt, something Angolinian in appearance.

"Guard sensors better have as much difficulty detecting this frequency as you promised, Vara," he heard Gallin mutter.

And then saw the man's entire bag-and-body turn toward a dark corner and disappear with one temporally adjusted step. Uniforms stormed into the room at nearly the same instant. He saw Gallin reappear briefly as he quietly darted through the doorway behind them and down the stairs.

Balaneth lay limp in the Guardsmen's path, drifting in and out of consciousness and wishing he could alert them. Hazy vision caught heavy boots attached to black-and-gray-clad bodies, and pulse rifles methodically aiming around the room.

"Sir, in here! We've got three, all down!"

More boots approached. Uprights materialized above Balaneth and his felled bodyguards. "These two are dead," said a rather familiar voice. "And uplords, look at all the blood."

"Lieutenant?" Balaneth managed, trying to open his eyes further. "You must . . . stop—"

"Remain still, Ambassador, and try not to talk." Theus knelt, examined Balaneth's bleeding head. "Get a medi-synth in here, immediately!" he ordered the rest of his detail. "And get reinforcements to this area. Two platoons. We'll need a ten-klick-square cordon, full TS scan. His wounds are fresh. Whoever did this can't have gotten far."

"YOU HAVE TEA, LIEUTENANT COMMANDER. Drink it," Gennet ordered, more paternally than militarily. "You've progressed tremendously with infirmary AI help, but this will speed your recovery naturally."

Dharmen took the steaming cup from the general's desk as though it might bite him. His father swore by saaryl pine tea for its supposed healing properties and made him drink it whenever he fell ill as a child. He winced at the green-black swill and took a sip . . . The tea was as horrible as always. Three weeks of invasive machines and wraps hadn't been so vile! He returned it to the desk. It was thankfully too hot to gulp.

"If it isn't boiled to the extreme to rid the roots of their acids, it'll burn your stomach lining."

"I know, sir, I've had it"—Dharmen reached for the cup and forced another sip, gasped in disgust—"many times before!" He put it down. Two tries were enough for now. "Sir, you were telling me about Armetrian."

"Ah yes, Dawn Fire's coleader. He's finally revealing his involvement, albeit slowly. And what a history!" Gennet tapped his desktop, pulled up interrogation files. "Established a relationship with the Carmogen long before Negara, funneled weapons to them in light quantities before increasing the supply, helped run the Niro Way safe house, recruited several new members in and out of the Guard to gain information, and—"

"And to get rid of me." Dharmen grunted. His broken ribs were mended but not fully healed. "Pardon my interruption, sir."

"He would have succeeded at that, had he done the job himself. I'm surprised he didn't, considering your fondness for each other," Gennet said. "His converts' ineptitude kept you alive. Mr. Vinc aside, young Master Duraan's inattention to detail and inability to fully manage a task didn't match his technical knowledge. The lieutenant commander trusted him with work he deemed too marginal to handle directly, but it was still too much for the kid."

"Really? Killing me himself wasn't high on Armetrian's list?"

"It was, but weapons smuggling was higher. Armetrian master-minded the last Bemini theft, and"—Gennet paused, gave a more pointed look—"he delivered the shipment to the enemy personally."

Dharmen choked. Hot tea burned his fingers; he wished he hadn't chosen this moment for another nauseating sip. "He went to Carmogen? *That's* the trip he mentioned under the mountain?"

"And met with the very same Lescain you found him and Vara meeting with on Negara, yes."

Dharmen took that wide-eyed. "All this would be enough to have Armetrian's head this minute if we had a death penalty like the Lenans do."

"If we were so inclined, lots of heads would roll in coming days."

"Sir, you said Armetrian was coleader. Was Vara or Gallin the other half of that?"

"No, they were his lieutenants more than anything. Someone else brought him on to help funnel weapons initially." Gennet sighed gravel. "An old friend of mine, I hate to say."

"Who, sir?"

"My Fifth Order counterpart."

"General Estes! So Kerbentha wasn't lying after all?"

"Not fully. Kerbentha worked for Armetrian; he'd heard about the general and saw him a few times remotely, but that was the extent of it."

"General Estes is married to one of the president's nieces," Dharmen said. "If high government leaders are involved in this, possibly even the president himself—"

"Don't assume that yet. I don't doubt we'll uncover government involvement, but my gut tells me President Prinsen's not of that ilk. His niece Coraia is another matter though. I wouldn't count her ambitions out of this for a second." Gennet's eyes ghosted over. "No. Eldric and Armetrian are our chiefs, with Gallin the second now that Vara's out. Shame, really. I commend Commander Secár on her quick action, but we could've extracted much information from the late lieutenant."

"I can't imagine Miss I'm-smelling-something-bad-and-it's-my-own would've volunteered much, though she must've had plenty," Dharmen grumbled. "Probably as much as Armetrian."

"Well, of everyone's involvement, hers went largely unnoticed. From what I've put together, Vara was groomed for this by General Estes, likely before Armetrian came on board. But actual traces of her work didn't manifest until Bemin, when she and Armetrian disappeared. General Estes tried to hide that from me, but as I said, I've been watching. And I've managed even after the Condorcet sweep to keep her death a secret for the time being."

"Sir, I don't understand at all. Why would you—?"

"She's a vital piece to this puzzle, with connections reaching well beyond the Guard and at Port," Gennet answered. "Her dealings may have undermined our security in far worse ways than any stolen weapons, and I know those dealings included the general secretly. Even Armetrian didn't know she was working directly with Estes, and if I'm to get *him*, I need to keep his right-hand woman's demise quiet. I can't have him panicking and slipping out of our hands like Gallin has." His eyes lowered, shadowed. "All in good time, old friend. And as soon as you present me the opportunity."

"Sir, if I may, we've moved carefully and quietly for a long while now, but isn't it time we act? Not just in apprehending traitors but in defending Angolin against invasion. Just because we have Armetrian and a sloop load of others doesn't mean we can rest. I know I'm bordering on insubordination, but I'm sick of playing games with them."

"Insubordination? Nonsense! And yes, it *is* time for action. That's why I called you here."

Dharmen sat still, brows lifted.

"Interrogation information to date corroborates intel from our monitoring of Carmogen military installations. They've been retrofitting their fighter planes with Angolinian arms: pulse cannons, particle emitters—every type of microprojectile system found on Bemin, some with energy signatures matching those of the stolen weapons. We're also seeing a massive troop, assault craft, and materiel buildup, and the number of energy weapons we've detected is much greater than what they received from over here."

"My gods, sir!"

Gennet nodded confirmation. "They have our combat tech. Now they've begun reproducing it themselves—successfully or not, we can't yet determine. But one thing's for certain: Carmogen is mobilizing, and in far greater ways than we've ever seen from them."

Two feelings battled in Dharmen's aching body. One was afraid for Angolin. But the other wanted to finally engage the enemy after so much prancing around. "Where does this lead us, General? What's our next step?" he asked and rose too quickly. Sharp pains checked his enthusiasm and returned him groaning to his seat.

"Careful, mister. And it's interesting of you to ask. I've had several discussions with High Command lately, and your East Ranges episode, though completely reckless, has pushed our case far forward. My superiors are still skeptical, but with the intel we've gathered and Mount Condorcet's flushing, we've been given the go-ahead."

"Go-ahead for what, sir?"

"The Guard is ready to report all we've obtained on the threat to Parliament," said Gennet. "HC needs its authorization to build defenses further and prep for combat operations. A joint war readiness committee has been established. I received word this morning: we've been summoned to present to them all our findings."

"*We* are meeting with them? You and I?"

"I have last-minute data to compile and briefings with others ordered to testify, Lieutenant Commander. After that, you and I will head over to the Parliament Pavilion."

Dharmen sat frozen. He had spent his entire career either appreciating his government or disapproving of it but always defending it. Now he would meet with it face-to-face.

"Tate, this is the moment we've been waiting for. Don't go mute on me now."

"I'm sorry, sir. I don't quite know what I'll I say. That I haven't said already."

"You're prepared, soldier. Don't think otherwise. Of everyone involved in this, *you* are beyond ready. The hearing is in two days. We'll meet again tomorrow to prepare. After that, you're on."

Dharmen deadened his face to hide his fright.

"Any questions before then, Lieutenant Commander?"

"Not as of yet, sir."

"Dismissed."

Gennet's calm gave Dharmen slight comfort as he gingerly rose, saluted, and hobbled out of the office. He moved slowly down the corridor, ignoring the looks from every face he passed. Bemin and now Mount Condorcet had made him top celebrity on base, and it was great to be recognized for once for his own ability and not for being Nüren Tate's son. But right now, the future displanted all else in his thoughts. *My Lord Krone, you have our troubles lined up and waiting, don't you?*

CHAPTER 14

DISHONOR

Magnificent!

Sir?

The scene, Rem-E: The government buildings, the monuments, the crowds rushing to and from it all. No entertainment centers or markets or mood walks for the Netherworld of it, just loads of forced perfection dipped in grandeur. Utopia, and it's not for everyone. No wonder so many people here want something, anything different.

Sir, the pilot is cycling to retros. We will land in Daehira Square in ten seconds.

Right in front of the Capitol. Think they're ready for me, Rem-E?

Are you ready for them, sir?

●

DHARMEN AND GENERAL GENNET WERE guided down corridor after long, lofty corridor: formal conduits through architecture that proclaimed, "This place is important; make no mistake of it." Stares followed the pair. Their militarily composed unsmiling faces peered back, with movements matching their stony expressions. Quick, thudding boot falls announced every step beneath prim service dress uniforms and presence-expanding cloaks. It was a countershow of force, however unintentional.

Dharmen had prepared to be a spectacle when the gunship rounded the Rijksfontein and joined the civilian air traffic up the Kraal Midway. He prepared more when the war-battered conveyance touched down in the Daehiraplein and stopped the entire square in its tracks. The Guardsmen had created anxiety upon arrival; now it was their turn to be anxious.

"This isn't the way to the committee chamber. Where are we going?" Gennet demanded of the closest escort.

"You are meeting with the joint committee," came the answer a lazy second behind the question. They halted before a set of high, burnished metal doors. The escort waxed official. "Within a full session of Parliament."

Gennet regarded him unblinking and shot Dharmen a glance of mute surprise. Dharmen's heart fell to the polished marblite floor. He and the general were originally intended to address the committee only; no one said anything about the full assembly! The doors slid open with a rush of air that heralded the influence within. With no more time to think, wonder, consider, or find a corner to hide in, Dharmen and Gennet entered.

The Parliament chamber was a great oval, ringed by audience galleries staring down on the austere space. Dharmen's eyes went to them first, but eventually he had to lower them to a far more unnerving sight: the rows of high seatbacks, each framing the head of a councilor, and most of them turning with a look saying, "*We* are important. Make no mistake of it!"

The Guardsmen walked the center aisle beneath a bright light wash and a conversation shower ebbing like a wave rushing out to the Great Lake as they passed. The creeping silence felt to Dharmen like high flyers swooping in from the Abyssal heights to snatch away his nerve. Alerted, Rem-E instructed him to control his breathing. He obeyed. Fainting wouldn't do here. He mindfully put one foot in front of the other as aisle-side eyes probed, constricting him as if between high, close walls.

He and Gennet left that gauntlet for a floating table slab on a dais, just beneath the presiding officer. And *facing* the assembly. Opposite theirs, an identical table housed at least a dozen generals and legates in service dress bearing hefty assemblages of medals donned only at official functions. Their cloaks hung on hooks hovering behind them. Dharmen was cowed as he sat. These men and women, leaders of the Guard, had summoned him. They would require (demand) his utmost cooperation. He wondered if he would have theirs.

"The committee's added another member," Gennet said, while holding the mute button of the tiny audio bot hovering near his face. At the committee table sat a woman at the upper levels of middle age like himself. She smiled and nodded. "At least there's one new face I know we can trust," he said and nodded back.

Dharmen looked closer. He knew her—well, knew *of* her and certainly should have. Had he been so completely nervous as to not recognize General Caevon Sajeva from his enlisted days back at the Second Order before he, Theus, and Dori were transferred to the newly created Seventh?

Session was called to order. Gennet straightened as he and his subordinate were introduced. The chamber's parliamentarian center groaned. Dharmen wasn't surprised that Angolin's most patrician citizens would frown upon a Guardsman of barely intermediate rank, but he was still irritated. *Feeling's mutual, mates!*

Gennet spoke. Militarily precise in tone—commanding but respectful—he started with Dharmen's presence, outlining in detail events on Negara that had pulled him so deeply into matters that "beyond any doubt, will change Angolin forever," as he put it. Not asked to speak even though he was ready to talk now, Dharmen sat pinned in mind-numbing reserve as Parliament and committee bombarded Gennet with quick-fire questions. From him came information on missing Guard armaments on Negara and a relay of everything he had witnessed as he and General Estes commanded forces battling the enemy, and soon, each other.

An elderly councilor questioned the veracity of Gennet's statements and said outright that Negara had not been necessary. The first Conservative of the day, Dharmen marveled more at the man's ignorance than at his party's entrenched hold on government. Gennet deflected the remarks with his own sage reasoning of why Carmogen forces had come so close to Angolin and why they had to be engaged. The aged councilor backed down, either content with Gennet's preparedness or put off by it. Dharmen hoped his own communicative ability would match the general's *if* he were ever allowed to speak.

Questioning switched to events on Bemin. Gennet reported the two unsuccessful weapons smuggling attempts and, to Dharmen's amazement, others prior to his posting that he had never been apprised of. He outlined Dharmen's involvement in downing the second major attempt over the Abyss. Chamber chatter kindled at that as hot as Dharmen's flushing face. General Sajeva trained eyes on him, her head angled in curiosity.

"Lieutenant Commander Tate, I commend your actions at Port"— she was far more pleasant than he expected or remembered—"but let's go back to Negara for a moment, to the night you discovered Lieutenant Commander Armetrian and the others behind enemy lines. Tell us about that. Start from the beginning."

He swallowed the lump in his throat and recounted everything from losing Theus in the bush to the cold swim across the Nabreac River beneath Armetrian's badly placed shots. General Sajeva seemed thoroughly immersed in the account. She must have known most of it, but she appeared intent on having his personal narrative above hearsay.

"Mr. Tate, I understand that Negara hasn't ended this for you, that it was only the beginning, in fact. I want to know about that first attempt on your life, the one that occurred in your home."

Dharmen described his dinner table explosion and emphasized the likelihood of a civil servant, three Guard officers, and a renowned former Guard leader being killed had the attempt succeeded. She delved into the rest of the deadly events. He gave more: every detail of Willem's near kidnap and of the house synth incident. He was questioned on his encounter with Kerbentha Duraan that night. The committee faces were wide-eyed at his capture of the repeat saboteur. He was glad for that: the information and improvised device extracted from that incident were real evidence supporting his own treason claims, and he was happy to report it here.

More fact-finding questions came from the committee—and then a terse, completely anticipated remark from an all-too-familiar voice: "This is all fine for the sake of trivia, but we've heard these accounts! They have little to do with Angolinian security or any of our purposes here."

Sajeva and colleagues exchanged annoyed glances before looking up behind them. Dharmen didn't bother. No need to see the speaker; the bombastic rant was clue enough. He had watched the man on the NewsMesh often. He knew it was Willem's father. *I'm surprised it's taken you this long to open your mouth,* he thought. Through the scalding tirade that followed about the *mendacity* and *utter useless-ness* of Guard testimony, he felt the old councilor's eyes disapprove of him with every word.

"But apparently, reasonable answers are beyond military capability, so if you insist on wasting this body's time, Lieutenant Commander, do find the courtesy to prattle quickly!"

Good old Henk Hanne in the flesh! Dharmen wanted to say it aloud to the man who hadn't just ignored Willem's long-term relationship with him but had also not spoken once to his son in a decade. A loud rap filled the chamber.

"Order!" the presiding officer gaveled.

General Sajeva continued her query, now on to Dharmen's captivity beneath Mount Condorcet. He relived it, "arrest" to discovery. His jaw twitched. CSD therapy hadn't fully eased the memory for him. Rem-E intervened with a medication and subliminal white-noise cocktail.

The committee sat hushed. Seats complained beneath anxiously shifting rears as he described his beating in transit and the more brutal, near-fatal ones afterward.

A legate whose name he had forgotten leaned forward. "No offense to the esteemed councilor," he said in reference to Henk's outburst, "but it appears that the root of treason has been laid bare here, left to wither beneath Lothnë's gaze. With all due respect to the assembly, I say we must proceed with great prudence in Angolin's safety and commit ourselves to action."

"Oh what nonsense, man! Action toward what?" Henk said, lifting his rotund, elderly bulk from his seat. "These two come here to feed you a line, and you swallow the whole boat! Our loyal citizenry is as pure as North Ranges snow, and with good reason. Why would any wish to betray the very government that has looked after them for so long? Talk of treason is as ridiculous as talk of space travel or digging up old technology that we have no use for. Our forebears—may the Pantheon keep them—sought a simpler existence after they settled these valleys, and we've enjoyed the fruits of their wisdom and run our realm successfully for centuries since. No one should want more than we provide, and whoever spreads the absurd notion that the Carmogen Empire has the faintest ill intent toward us only seeks to stir misplaced passions and sow discontent. We overreacted in dispatching forces to

Negara, which I warned the assembly against from the beginning. Let us not continue to overstep reason by blindly accepting as unvetted truth the hysterical wares peddled to us by every uniformed bounder and ingrate who comes to us bearing lies as boldly as they bear gunships and weapons!"

Dharmen and Gennet locked bristling eyes. Gennet turned to his audio bot. "Madam Speaker, permission to address the assembly?" Request granted, he looked upward. "Councilor, I have been in military service nearly as long as you have been in government, and never in my time has anyone accused me of hustling information. Lieutenant Commander Tate and I have done nothing to deserve your insults, and I daresay your disrespect undermines the honor demanded of us by the gods, the Realm we serve, and this body."

"I call things as I see them, General. Take what insult you will." The corpulent old Conservative's backers chuckled around him. "And if a few mindless pranks against your officer are what constitute evidence of treason in your field, then I suggest you save the matter for the conurb courts and leave your Parliament to its rightful business!"

Dharmen could hardly see through the haze of his anger. He didn't request permission to speak. "Councilor, sir! Your *rightful business* is the protection of your constituents, and whether you understand it or not, so is ours."

Henk's wild-eyed glare threatened more than anything Dharmen had experienced from his worst enemies. Neither Armetrian nor Vara could have matched it. He stared back unintimidated.

"You claim protection too easily, Lieutenant Commander," Henk berated. "Were you in full protective mode at the Bemin Spaceport on the evening of 26 Kronaas, when three weapons-packed ships were stolen? Those ships were taken under your command, Mr. Tate. Perhaps then, as now, you were in too great an insolent huff to see your own failure."

"Those ships were already airborne when discovered, Councilor. What was my officer to do, jump up and snag one with his bare teeth?" Gennet interjected across the verbal pounding Dharmen was ready to salvo back.

"I say, why on Tentim not? He more than exhibits the mouth for it!"

Dharmen shot up so hard, his chair sailed backward. "Councilor, you're fortunate to hold position high enough to freely abuse those charged with your safekeeping. But since I'm made to fight abroad *and at home*, I'll speak for Angolin's security rather than for its continued stagnation beneath Conservative rule!"

"I object to this, wholeheartedly!" Henk bellowed, his jowly cheeks quivering as he rose again, peering around to his supporters.

"Sustained!" returned the presiding officer. "And be seated at once. Both of you!"

They complied. A hateful smile formed on Henk's lips. "Madam Speaker," he began, "the lieutenant commander is quite out of line. Perhaps his case is not as airtight as he presents it."

"It is you who has been out of line from the beginning, Councilor," said the presiding officer. "I urge you to remain quiet and composed as the lieutenant commander continues his testimony, provided the assembly can remember it over your antics."

Dharmen blinked in astonishment despite his knowledge of Parliament's reputation for bare-knuckled verbal brawling. "Thank you, Madam Speaker," he continued, peeved and barely noticing Gennet's cautionary look. "Esteemed representatives of Angolin, can you not see what's happening all around you? The threat's already out there with the Carmogen, but an even greater one exists right here. Look on your streets, in your conurbs, and on the NewsMesh. Look at your youth—they protest against you every day now."

Words from the assembly—supportive and otherwise—pelted him.

"And most threatening of all is some of our own soldiers who plot on the battlefield, steal weapons, and gather secrets from all over

Angolin—from the Space Commission, the Protection and Defense Program, the Ministry of Science"—he squared eyes on Henk—"and possibly from members of your own assembly."

That reignited the chamber. He heard Gennet's pained sigh but didn't care. He was tired of accusations and evasions, and tired of having his and the general's reports discounted by those with the greatest power to wield but the least ability to listen. So many representatives, so many deaf ears to navigate. The assembly was again gaveled to silence.

"If the traitors succeed and Angolin falls," he continued, "then we will all have failed—not just Parliament, every one of us. I respect our ancestors as much as anyone; they worked hard for our continued survival. But I'm sure they never intended on complete isolation and ignorance of the people. Angolinians have every possible comfort and convenience, but they aren't truly free. Centuries of confinement policies have some ready to rip Angolin apart for that freedom now. Do any of you consider that *running the Realm successfully*, as put earlier?" He paused at another regatta of loud, combative outbursts. More gaveling. He went on: "I've been in the Guard for fifteen years. My loyalty and duty is to honor and truth. I have no use for games, deceits, or *peddling*, as my work's been called once today, and definitely none for petty politics."

"I underestimated you, Lieutenant Commander. You are quite a debater," said Henk in defiance of the presiding officer. "But histrionics will not move your Parliament to rash acts. This is a legislative body, not an army base, and contrary to your upstart wishes and heated rhetoric, the Conservative Wing will not allow a few brazen officers like you to bring Angolin into conflict. We will not authorize a declaration of war, as you and the committee so intend."

"And what about the *defense* of Angolin?" Dharmen put to him. "Whether you authorize it or not, how will you respond when war comes to us? When the Carmogen arrive to blow Angolin to bits with its own weapons, will you and your colleagues have the Guard sit and watch?"

Henk's gaze smoldered as much as his own, but it didn't stop Dharmen from continuing.

"I wouldn't want that any more than I hope the Conservative Wing would. And neither would your youngest son, Councilor, who was nearly abducted by the very same people you feign ignorance of. An attempt, I might add, that received no attention from you or your most prominent family, even at Aremel Hanne's insistence right after her own abduction and rescue."

"This is outrageous!" Henk stood and roared over the pings of outmoded datapads flying from his table to the floor. "In the name of Rior, I never—"

"Councilor, you have been warned," said the presiding officer.

"But Madam Speaker, this man and his inflammatory words are a disgrace to our assembly. You cannot expect us to simply—"

"Councilor Hanne, sit down at once!"

Quaking with rage, eyes blazing Lothnian fire, Henk plopped into his broad chair. The distance couldn't hide the sight of his silenced lips, white-pressed in a blood-reddened face.

"These proceedings will continue properly," said the presiding officer. "Any further outbursts from the assembly will be viewed as contempt of Parliament. We move now to our next agenda item: the joint committee's report on the latest Carmogen military movements."

CLOSE OF SESSION SENT DHARMEN and Gennet to the chamber antewings. Attempts at one-on-one discussion were interrupted by passing councilors and top silver with congratulations and encouragement on what would become everyone's newest charge: working together to thwart invasion (in spite of the Conservatives). Dharmen had never said "Thank you, sir/ma'am" so much in his career. It tired him more than the three and a half hours of questioning and deliberation before it. He wanted to lie down on the floor, curl up, and sleep, but there was no chance of that.

"Gentlemen, my compliments to you both. That was quite a show you put on." General Sajeva was affable, though she was as equally imposing as Gennet.

Dharmen had lived in fear of her as a private and avoided her back at Second—easy to do as a grunt, even as a Tate. She was different now. Older, formidable as ever, her face was age- and wisdom-lined, but through that redoubt, she was oddly accessible. He thought it due to his higher rank. He didn't realize that the year's events had elevated *him* independently of it.

She scrutinized him, smiled. "And Lieutenant Commander, it's good to see you in action again."

"Likewise, ma'am. Thank you." Dharmen didn't smile himself, but he wanted to.

"General, Lieutenant Commander, I must be going," said Gennet. "I have a special meeting of my own now to attend to."

"So soon, Vieron? I was hoping we could have a late lunch—or early dinner at this point," said Sajeva. "We don't get to meet like this often anymore."

"We'll have to catch up later, Caevon. This absolutely cannot wait."

"I'll see you back at base, sir," Dharmen said to him. "I know we have a lot of changes to discuss."

Gennet narrowed his eyes, activated an upright. Sajeva strangely did likewise; whatever the comm was about had been expected. And unwanted. They deactivated their floating displays, frowned at each other like schoolchildren who had just been told classes would extend into second summer.

"By Krone, changes indeed!" Gennet rumbled.

Dharmen watched him turn on his heel and hurry toward two lieutenants waiting in the chamber doorway for him.

ESTES SCANNED THE ROOM WITH crazed eyes. He tossed the few items about that had been left behind. He was of no mind to try to place them, he was absolutely panicked. The house that had been Dawn Fire's main stone for months had been emptied and abandoned. Its occupant had cleaned it out. Or had the Guard? He'd heard no report of such, though being here was foolish regardless. But he had no other choice.

Vara wouldn't risk carrying the files around to lose, he thought, *and she can't store them remotely without detection, or anywhere at Fifth. She must have hidden them somewhere in this house. If the information is here, I have to have it!* He wished he could just ask, but he had neither seen nor heard from Vara *or anyone* in weeks.

Fright left him no more room for conclusions. The house was picked clean and its tenant gone. His most vital and, up to now, most reliable accomplice was likely gone, and his quarry's whereabouts were unknown. "Damn it!" he muttered. He searched the dine-in compartments, stabbing at buttons of doors not already sitting open. All empty.

He looked to the stairs. The sunlight at their base rendered them an almost cheerful sight. The grayness at their vanishing top was less inviting. He hurled himself upward and found the sleep-in door. It was partially ajar. He shoved it into its pocket and burst through.

Casting stress-narrowed vision across the forlorn room, Estes did not know where to begin. Underneath the bed seemed good. He went to it and searched. Nothing. The bureau next. He checked every nook and cranny. Empty. His eyes went to the floor, to blue-purple bloodstains a meter across. Markers were set at given points around them: standard crime-scene positioning for the remnant of either an extremely unfortunate accident or brutal murders. Of Lenans either way. He recognized the stains' sickly coloring. No further hint needed. It wasn't safe to be here, and he'd stayed far longer than he should have . . .

His stomach sank, and his already pounding heart pounded harder. He turned his head slowly and dejectedly. He could believe what the corner of his eye had just caught, but he didn't want to. Staring dumbfounded was all he could manage. His frenzied search had completely missed the man sitting quite still: legs crossed, elbows on the chair's broad arms, and chin resting peacefully in his folded dark-brown hands. Bothering with neither TS nor his uniform's camo mode, hiding in plain sight had sufficed. Pulse rifles appeared on Estes's left and right.

The seated man rose, ordered one of his people to retrieve Estes's weapon.

Estes sighed. He hadn't moved fast enough after all.

General Gennet reached into his breast pocket and pulled out a small robodrive. "I believe you were looking for this?"

GENNET WATCHED AS ESTES'S EYES flitted around to the room's uprights, to the two lieutenants from the Niro house flanking the office door, and to a third standing near his suit of armor display. "It's been a long while since you were here last. In our war room, if I remember correctly."

"For the Negaran Campaign strategy briefing. Of course you remember," said Estes. "As for me lately, I've seen better days."

"Everyone in Angolin has, though most outside this room wouldn't perceive that." Gennet reached over and closed some data windows on his desktop. "My wife, though, is as sharp as the peaks of the North Ranges. I haven't told her a thing, but she knows something's up. That's a woman, for you."

"A very good woman. I trust Audra is doing well? Taking good care of you both despite all this . . . alertness of your own?" Estes rolled his eyes at the room's humming, warbling fittings.

"She is, at that. She's asked about you, suggested having you and Coraia over for dinner soon. 'It's been a while since the four of us got together,' she said. 'I hope the Abyss hasn't swallowed them.' I think she knows it has."

Lifting and peering at his restrained wrists was Estes's response. Gennet accessed his internal's prisoner protocols. The sealers released and the manacles fell into Estes's lap.

"Thanks for that, at least."

Gennet swiveled around to his credenza, took the small sphere from it, and placed it on the desktop between the two of them. "Shall we get down to it?"

Estes eyed the damaged robodrive. "I take it the interrogation will occur here instead of in your holding area."

"After all the years we've known each other, I thought this would be preferable to Seventh's sublevels. For now." Gennet picked up the robodrive, examined it before releasing it, and let it float in front of him. "We barely recovered this. It was shot down just outside the Niro Way house. It didn't manage to escape, but its owner did. You know him."

"If you mean Mr. Gallin, I know *of* him, certainly. We've never met face-to-face."

"I know. But aside from your remote collusion, he's a countryman of yours, or more correctly, you two share the same ethnicity."

"Just what are you getting at?"

"Oh, come on. Haven't you kept it a secret long enough, Eldric *Moraneth* Estes?"

"I am General Eldric Estes of the Angolin Guard, Fifth Order. That's my proper title!"

"Not anymore," said Gennet. "Your rank you still have until tribunal decides otherwise, but Fifth is no longer yours. The Guard is seeking your replacement as we speak."

Estes took that with cold eyes. The information seemed to come as no surprise to him. "And so you've finally put my background together. Congratulations. Other than my beloved Coraia, you're the only one who's ever done so." Estes casually shifted his weight. "Gennet the Venerable, Commander of the Seventh Order, leader, fighter, and lately, astute investigator of his own, though this one took you a while, Vieron."

"It hasn't. I've always known. Everyone has, but you tried so hard to conceal it over the years that we just assumed not pry. Angolinian etiquette: preserve other people's hidings as well as your own, as well as your realm's. But the clues were there. Having only one family name, and your vehement refusal to have children even against your wife's wishes."

"I spared Coraia the indignity of mothering the lowest progeny imaginable," Estes savaged. "She would have loved our children to the fullest, but there's no way I'd ever father any with even a drop of Lenan blood."

"But that blood is in you."

"It's dirt! And the rest who carry it so gladly can stay up in the far northern snow where they belong, away from me!"

"We'll discuss your bizarre hatred of your own people some other time, Eldric. Being half Lenan in Angolin is no great issue. Betraying Angolin *is*."

"I haven't betrayed a thing."

"I'd say you have."

Estes sniffed at that.

"It was you, all along. You established contact with the Carmogen; you recruited Lieutenant Vara, Lieutenant Commander Armetrian, and countless others from nearly every order, including mine; and you had every one of them break their oaths of service and destroy their honor. I don't know why, and I'm sure you'll never tell me, but you single-handedly built the network and masterminded weapons thefts long before Negara, all the way up to Bemin. Dawn Fire has sprouted many heads under your guidance. They've all gotten away from you lately, but you were the architect, nonetheless."

"You're quite the sleuth, Vieron. Your intuition never ceases to amaze me."

"What amazes *me* is not the speed at which your effort spread but the treachery beneath it. Armetrian continued the gunrunning in your stead, but you found something much more valuable to the Carmis and absolutely dangerous to Angolin." Gennet reclaimed the damaged robodrive. "The TimeSpace data on this is harmful enough, but it also contains information on the Cloak—not just the science and engineering behind it but the locations of every generator station in Angolin and Bemin. The data was partially lost in the blast, but we were able to retrieve most of it. What's on here all but destroys our safety." He stowed the device in his pocket and clasped his hands on his desk. "But why bother to tell you any of this? You know it already. Weapons weren't enough—you intended to hand the enemy stealthtech and give them the best possible advantage over us."

Estes remained still and silent.

"What did you hope to gain, Eldric? What out there is so important that you would do this? Did Naul promise to make you ruler of Angolin once they brought down our defenses and marched in here? Is that what you want to see your own homeland seized over?"

Estes stared ahead, seemingly at nothing beyond his own thought. "What I want, you wouldn't understand," he said mistily. "Angolin is old and stale, but that's just part of it. You're encrusted in the machinery here and so am I. Well, I want no more of it. I'm tired of this isolated life. I'm also tired of living a boot's existence with a general's rank, while my wife and her family have all the preeminence. I need way more than what little I can get here, and as far as I'm concerned, it's not too much to ask!" His eyes flickered. "Had I been even half a day sooner, I would have succeeded."

"Speed wouldn't have benefitted you, Eldric. Your problem was planning. Lieutenant Vara was a good choice of accessory, but you should never have let her keep the stealthtech information. You should have demanded it the moment it became available and secured it somewhere. The robodrive files were loaded days before we got it, and not by her."

"Where is she now? Detained, I imagine?"

"No. One of my officers shot and killed her in defense of another whom she'd abducted and had nearly beaten to death."

Estes opened his mouth, but no words left it.

"I know she gave you a preliminary data set prior to that—delivered it to you at your door."

"I'm a general of the Guard, Vieron, and not subject to this level of scrutiny. You really have gone too far with this."

"That sentiment's as wide as the Abyss, coming from the worst traitor Angolin has ever known. You've dishonored yourself and the entire Guard, mister. Get used to a good hard look into every part of your life from now on."

"The truth isn't half of what you assume. You know nothing!"

"I know we'll defeat the Carmogen, no matter how much you've helped them. You, your minions, and your wife." Gennet cocked his head. "You didn't do any of this alone. Coraia's ambitions are in it too."

Estes's face twisted into something Gennet had never seen. He couldn't tell if a cry or a laugh was coming. "My darling Cori," the other softly murmured, "center of my life, gift of Lothnë . . . my everything." Estes looked up slowly. "Do what you must, Vieron. Investigate everyone if you like, because who's involved in what no longer matters." A low succession of beeps sounded from his vicinity. "Now does it?"

Gennet stared at him for a heartbeat before standing. He looked down, saw light flashing on a small device on Estes's belt. He had been thoroughly scanned. *Where did that come from?* His heart flew into his throat as he shouted. "Everyone out now!"

Gennet rounded his desktop and bolted out the door right behind the two officers who had been flanking it. They scrambled down the corridor. He heard the third officer's footsteps behind him—at least they had all gotten out—

He felt the floor leave him as the blast filled his ears and sent him airborne before dropping him on his face. Shrapnel rained. He could hear nothing now but a piercing ring in his ears that displaced all other sound. He rolled over and sat up. Two of his men stirred; they appeared unhurt at first glance. He got up and rushed back to the third, lying motionless on the debris-strewn floor. Blood poured from the man's broken skull. He hadn't gotten clear in time.

Gennet stood and peered through the smoke toward his office. The doorway was a metal-twisted chasm. Flames shot through it like the volcanic plumes dotting the Vresel. He covered his nose and searched the blackened corridor for Estes but didn't find him. He hadn't expected to. Estes was still seated when he triggered the explosion, he hadn't moved a muscle. Gennet painfully dammed his upset as he summoned emergency teams; there was just no time to think more on that now.

But the reality of it wouldn't go away: his longtime friend had given up everything for treason. Everything.

CHAPTER 15

GAMBIT

s that the entire weapons complement to date?

Affirmative, Commander Secár, though marginally greater amounts will be ready in time for combat.

Krone help us if it's the best we can do. And that'll be one thing; here comes another.

Ma'am?

Our genius brigade, Qi-VOS, they just arrived. They're practically one now. I'll be happy for them. I just hope she understands the load she's lifting. Honestly, between Yos's airs and Dharmen's constant grump fest . . . Men! Why on Tentim do they have to make everything so tedious?

Are you a man, ma'am?

❋

"UPLORDS, NOW WHAT? DAMN THIS equipment!"

Upright generation didn't hear Gennet and wouldn't have cared otherwise. It failed and reinitialized anyway. Base ops had installed everything he requested, but the underpowered temporary digs just couldn't support a mini command center. Main power failed days ago; now auxiliary threatened to go.

"Blasted basement conduits!"

He gazed around the tiny storeroom's windowless walls. The view was of no help either. It was mid-Vatternaas, second autumn. The trees swaying in the entrance court and across Nieuw Holland Valley were near peak, and he couldn't enjoy the sight from down here.

"Ahem!" Nüren stood in the doorway, white-haired and bent with age but sharp-eyed and with an air of rooted authority behind a disarmingly calm expression. He stepped in, allowed the door to slide shut at his back. The two saluted. "*Admiral* Gennet," he greeted. "It's good to see you again after all these years."

"And you, General Tate. Excuse my surprise."

"If you'll excuse my dropping in unannounced. I know you're busy."

"I wish busy was my only problem. Until my office is reconstructed, this is my roost, I'm afraid."

"Of course. The news spread through the GuardMesh like wildfires across the Southern Plains, even to us retired folks." Nüren shook his head and grunted through tightened, wrinkled lips. "A general of the Guard taking his own life, and in the most dishonorable manner possible. *Cowardly* can't begin to describe it. This would never have happened in my day."

"Neither would the treason behind it. Frankly, General, I wish it were still your day."

"You have new ones coming." Nüren shifted tack and beamed. "Your next office may sit beside the bridge of a deep-space vessel before long."

"Don't count on that one just yet," Gennet said stiffly. "I'll accept the rank conversions, but I can do without change for its own sake. Unless HC orders otherwise, my place is here at Seventh. Forgive me, sir. To what do I owe this visit?"

"There's no need to stand on that ceremony. We're equals."

"In rank only," said Gennet. "And I spent most of my early career under your wing, so it's hard not to still call you—"

"You know why I'm here, Vieron. I want to talk to you about my son."

And we're on. Gennet offered him the chair opposite his tiny desk. "What would you like to know about the lieutenant commander?"

"Whatever you can tell me. I don't need such an exacted briefing as you gave Parliament; I'll spare you a repeat of that. Just tell me about him, not as a Guardsman under your command but as a person."

"What can I possibly say that you don't already know?" Gennet said. "He's intelligent, driven, honorable, takes nothing lying down, and tolerates no taroc crap. He's easily riled, to put it no further, but I can manage that in him. Truth be told, I'm still getting to know your son, but you must see these things already, sir. You did raise him."

"Call me Nüren, Vieron. Please."

"I'll try."

Nüren sniffed. "His mother—may Lady Xoraen keep her—and I observed everything you describe in Dharmen his whole life. He was a bright kid and he excelled in school, when he got along with his teachers. And he was honest. He told the truth when we questioned him about a girl he snuck into the house as a teenager. Heh, and a boy he snuck in not long after. Any other kid would have fumbled lies, but not our Dharmen. He looked us both in the eye each time, admitted his mistake, and apologized just like that! Left us speechless. Later on, some boy twice his size tried to bully him over his sexuality, and Dharmen sent him to the infirmary with a broken nose. That was a trial, but the kid should've known better than to unleash the raging high flyer in my son. Even then, he wasn't to be trifled with, but I digress."

"Not at all," said Gennet. "I have a son too, as you know, though my wife and I don't have quite the same stories about him." He sighed, parental pride evaporating. "The boy's a cadet now. We'll see how that goes."

Nüren's eyes widened, made evident in the poor light only by the lift of his unruly eyebrows. "I don't have to tell you that Angolin has a major situation coming. Given what you've seen in Dharmen, how do you think he'll handle the invasion?"

"You doubt him, General?"

"Certainly not! I have utmost faith in him as a soldier and as a man, but I'm only his father." Nüren's gaze had been on Gennet, but it seemed far away now. "Dharmen's an adult, and he's become one right before my eyes! He has his own life now that I don't see half of. You're his superior. I want your professional assessment, that's all."

And I thought I was being spared another briefing! "If you want my view as a gen—as an admiral, your son is more than capable of handling the Carmogen. I wouldn't worry along those lines. As for my personal opinion of him, I've headed Seventh for over a decade now, and in that time, I've not seen a more determined, hardheaded, honorable officer here. Our lieutenant commander would give himself to the Netherlords before he'd submit to the enemy. I can count on him for that, if no one else."

"Which is why you placed him beyond the Negaran front line?"

"I apologize for any grief that caused you or Mr. Hanne."

"Don't. You needed something done and found the right soldier for it. I would have done the same. My wife—may the goddess of the dead again protect her soul—once said I was as stubborn as an East Ranges saaryl in a drought."

"In the lieutenant commander's case, the seedling hasn't crawled far from the tree."

"My reputation doesn't get my boy any extra leeway here, I take it?" The belowground room's lifeless quiet amplified Gennet's lack of reaction. Nüren's lips parted to form a toothy smile. "Right! From what I've heard of you since you advanced from my command, I didn't think so. And I wouldn't have it any other way. It hasn't crossed my mind once since Dharmen was transferred to this order."

"But?" said Gennet.

"But I do have one little—well, big concern."

"And it is?"

"As you said, you've seen his temperament."

"Who hasn't seen it? He overheats. Even at peace, he's a boiling synth cauldron."

"Exactly, and it worries me. Worries him too. He is what he is, but I don't want it to get in his or the Guard's way." Nüren left his seat and went to the damaged but defiantly displayed suit of armor propped in a corner. "Dharmen is midlevel now. He'll have far more boots under his command, and you and I both know the battlefield is no place for overemotion. The pressure on him will be fierce."

"You think your son won't be able to control his temper out there, General?"

"It's not quite that. On the contrary, I hope you'll help Dharmen see what an asset his particular talent can be if used wisely. And sparingly. I'm more worried about him getting hot at the wrong moment, than about him being . . . KIA."

Not a lie, not exactly the truth either, Gennet understood. "Aye, General, remove that from your worry cart. I believe the lieutenant commander's anger will bring results rather than cause problems. No one I know gets things done the way he does, especially when he's pushed too far. I think you perceive that without ever having seen him here."

Nüren nodded. "That, I do, Vieron."

"YOU'RE NOT REALLY GOING TO drink that, are you?" Dharmen said, watching the green, steeping liquid's vapor swirl into infinity above Centrum Gardens' outdoor café.

Brona took a tentative whiff. "It's only *kallam* root tea. It won't kill me. We have hard times ahead, and I need a soother."

"Was it on the menu?"

"Course not."

"That should tell you something. Father made me drink it once as a teenager. That crap's worse than saaryl; it nearly turned my insides out!"

"Oh really? And just what did you do to bring on that kind of punishment?"

"It was for a fight I got into."

"Is that so, Lieutenant Commander?"

"Hey, nobody calls me a girl among other things and gets away with it. The kid had it coming, and he got it, pure and simple."

"Dharm, you and your tales. Let the woman be and mind your own . . . whatever that is," Dori said from across the beverage- and confection-filled table. "You've seen the latest reports from Admiral Gennet on surveillance of Carmogen. We have to think defense prep. Who has time to dwell on other people's drink choices?"

"We've been preparing plenty well for that ourselves," Yos said with a squeeze to Brona's shoulders. They sat close enough to nearly form one person.

"In what way have you two been preparing?" Theus snidely asked.

"Brona and I have discussed bits of our plans with Dharmen," Yos returned.

Dharmen ignored Theus's and Dori's stares and remained silent, stuffing a small tart into his mouth and watching the vapor of his *Yngvi* Springs decaf briefly coalesce into a gelatinous ball before settling back into his cup.

"Look, we know they'll come over here with the weapons they lifted from us," said Brona, "and only the Heavenly Pantheon knows how many since the Carmogen have learned to duplicate what they stole."

"Where exactly do you two fit into that?" Theus prodded. "What plans are you talking about that Dharm here has kept secret up to now?"

"Oh, we've thrown together a couple of things," said Yos. "One is the personal antiparticler that he tested for us, which I'm glad was recovered. Our engineering team won't have time to make it available for general use with the Carmogen moving so quickly, but the other item we can utilize right now."

"Do continue!" said Dori.

Brona cleared her throat of the horribly bitter concoction that passed for tea and leaned across the small table. "Particle weapons emit radiation within a specific spectral range. This type of energy signature can be tracked. We've discovered how to distinguish and isolate particles in hostile fire only, and we've worked with our people in devising an energy emission detection system that can disable its source. Once the enemy fires any of our weapons, we can lock onto their signatures and send suppression commands to deactivate them permanently. They'd be rendered useless from then on; the Carmogen will have nothing more than elaborate toys in their hands."

"All right, sounds well-conceived. But how will you keep the command signals from being discovered and jammed?" asked Theus.

"By using airborne *microscopic* soldiers small enough to escape detection, and positioned much closer to their targets," replied Yos. "The Guard cannot perfect and construct enough nanites in time for combat, and the same goes for full-sized synths—you'll still need human fighters for that. But we can at least use what's available against the enemy's equipment like we currently do for the Cloak."

"They won't win the fight for us," said Brona, "but they'll give our side the advantage it badly needs, even if only slight."

"Gallin overheard some of this up at Kleve Park, remember?" Dharmen said. "I hope you've accounted for that."

"We have, and we've refined and added some safeguards to our work since," Yos said. "Regardless of anything he's relayed to the other side, we're ready. Trials are complete for the most part. We can deploy the micro-AI program once combat begins."

Dharmen cocked his head. "*For the most part*? We can't afford mistakes from undertested research, you two. No backfires—this'll have to work for us, not for the Carmis. The last thing we need is your little micro minions disabling *our* weapons."

"Lieutenant Commander Tate, do we look like the sort of scientists who skimp on research?" Yos joked. "Brona and I will have you know that all our backfires are top-notch and each one implemented to its finest half measure!"

Not even the slightest smile answered that.

"Trust us, Dharmen. It'll work." Brona grunted at her tea's sinus (and brain cell) clearing fetor. "We have a few tweaks to make to particle targeting systems to prevent just what you're afraid of. We've run dozens of simulations, and I can set up more trials to be sure, but Yos is right. The system's ready."

Dharmen nearly choked on his own reliquefied drink. "Simulations? It hasn't been tested on actual weapons?" He stopped short—laughed, actually, in a depreciative chortle.

"Sorry to underwhelm you, Dharm," said Yos.

"The Guard will want to run its own analysis before granting approval," Dori said, "and our Science and Engineering Division spends months testing new and revisited technologies. You can count on Carmogen arrival before there's any time for that."

"Then we'll need to step it up," said Dharmen. "Beginning with Admiral Gennet so these two can be given some real guns to work with soon. *Now*, frankly."

"Dharm, you know that's not in our purview," Dori said. "And do you really think the Guard would incorporate this technology so quickly, even if the admiral does throw his weight behind it?"

"Only one way to find out," said Yos, "which is why we're already working with Admiral Gennet. He's the most uncompromising man I've ever met—Dharm here notwithstanding—but we're fairly confident we have his support."

The table went silent. Dharmen hid his own amazement. He was learning not to underestimate Yos and Brona's determination when they got going on a project. "Admiral Gennet knows what's at stake. If he thinks the system is viable, he'll endorse its use."

"Fine enough, but there'll be tens of thousands more Carmis than us," Theus said. "Never mind who has what weapons advantage. How will we go up against them? We don't have the equipment or the man-power, human or AI. And even if we maintain superior firepower with this new particle isolation system, there just aren't enough personnel or heavy gunships to support a major defensive."

"Add to that the time it takes Parliament to decide on anything," Dharmen said, "plus the logistics needed to get battalions and materiel into place when they finally do. Bemin is already put to it constructing new, bigger gunships, but regardless, the Kraal hasn't even begun the slightest mobilization effort, no thanks to the Conservatives and even some HCers. If the enemy came right this minute, all we could do is spit at them."

Dori sighed. "Bleak picture taken, you two."

"Bleak but real, Commander," said Theus. "Despite every advantage, Yos and Brona's included, we won't be prepared when the time comes." He lowered his voice as heads turned from other tables. "If the Kraal even steps up."

"This is our home, Thee. We'll be prepared. We'll have to be," said Dharmen. "If you and Yos don't want to see a Carmi slave market up close, Will and me tortured and killed for who we are, and Dori and Brona . . ." He shelved that horribly unpleasant thought immediately. "Each one of us better damned well be ready to fight when the time comes, period."

Rem-E's incoming message prompt filled his earplant. He activated an upright and scanned the information. Dori and Theus did likewise.

"What is it?" Yos asked.

"News from our admiral," Dharmen replied. "Parliament is debating the Angolin Defense Act. I was wrong. Looks like we're about to *get* prepared."

"Are you that certain it'll pass?" Brona asked.

"No, but Gennet is if he's sending general comm on it."

Brona grasped her teacup and took a huge swig. She coughed and swore in a way that amazed even Dharmen before returning the cup to the table.

"This was fast, remarkably fast!" said Dori. "Recon reports enemy chatter about 'hidden aliens across the Abyss in need of remediation' and more intel on forces massing all over Carmogen. They'll be headed this way very soon. I'm guessing the act's about to pass, and Admiral Gennet will confirm such. He's called an AOM two hours from now."

Theus snorted hard enough to blow the hair on Dharmen's temples. Dharmen gave him a sharp shoulder pat to calm him. "Brona, whatever those final tweaks are, you two may want to get on them."

"Say no more. We're on it!" Brona took Yos by the hand and pulled him away from the table. He threw a hasty goodbye behind him as they left.

Dori watched them disappear into the Gardens. "Pains me to say it, but I think they'll make a fine couple."

I hope they get that chance, Dharmen thought. He looked to Brona's half-full teacup and decided on a small, precombat bit of courage. He reached for it, sniffed it, and carefully took a sip . . .

The foulness filled his mouth and nostrils and made his eyes water. He spat the putrid green liquid down his front and slammed the cup on the table. The whole patio stopped in midconversation at his cursing as Dori tossed napkins at him.

LOTHNË AND RIOR SAT ABOVE the rim of Centrum Gardens' rolling landscape when Yos and Brona reached the North End. Brona had wanted to get to work right away. Yos had insisted on a short stroll first, just the two of them. It turned out to be a long one. The day couldn't have been more perfect for it: cloudless purple skies pierced by the silver-white towers lining the great urban park above second autumn's enflamed foliage. Nearby, workers desynthing outdoor market stands clopped around in time-honored wooden shoes. The aromas of packed-away produce still lingered. Yos soaked it all in, determined to keep his mind at ease and off the coming threat. But at Brona's behest, *they talked about the coming threat.*

"The tea didn't help much, did it?"

"I'm not that upset, Yos, really."

"We've known each other for years, Bron. You think I can't tell?" He stopped their stroll, looked into her eyes. "And especially now?"

Brona sighed. "What do you really think will happen?"

"What do you mean?"

"You know what I mean, Yos. Stop being so glacial all the time. Invasion is coming, within days from the sound of things, and we might not be able to stand up to it."

"Ahh, but you and I have a plan," Yos said radiantly. "The great and beautiful Brona Devries has joined forces with Yos the Magnificent to come to the Hidden Realm's rescue."

"That's not the least bit funny! And what plan, exactly? Half of it's just an army of energy-detecting nanites. That's all. One suite of technology fighting another, and in prototype phase at that. And the other half . . . Well, *unethical* is the best descriptor even if the admiral condones it. This is no battle plan, and we're not warriors, Yos."

"Oh, but we are, *mijn liefje*."

Brona looked beleaguered. "You realize we're talking about breaching an alternate universe and pulling people into it."

"Enemy combatants, Bron, not people. We won't solve this by playing it safe or obsessing over ethics."

"I think Theus suspects something, and maybe Dharmen does too. We should have just told them the whole truth of what we're doing."

"Maybe later. For now, let's let them use their skill and brawn to fight, and we'll use what we have to offer. And if our solution is . . . creative, then so be it." Yos read acquiescence in Brona's gentle gray eyes. "And to your previous point, technology fighting technology is the way of the future."

"For our ancestors, it was the way of the *past*. We haven't reached their knowledge level yet; we might not be as fortunate."

"Perhaps. You have me there."

"You and that nonchalance, Yos. Does the house in your head ever catch fire?"

"You were just as calm once. What ever happened to that Brona, the one who was so free of worry, though no less lovely than she is now?"

Brona reddened and shook her head. "You're right, the tea didn't help." She looked upward, frowned at the sickly yellow-green hue of the Cloak racing above the day's mix of natural and human-made beauty. "I have to go."

"Now?"

"Yes, now. You heard the man. War's coming. We have to get our part of the effort working. I should run more tests and I have more than a few things to tighten up. We've wasted all afternoon in the Gardens as it is."

Yos grimaced. "Dharm's just being his usual alarmist self. Our systems will work whether you test tonight, tomorrow, next week, or not at all."

"You just don't want me to go, do you?"

"Of course not!"

"Look, Dharmen's right, despite anything," Brona went on, "and as for *alarmist*, I'll take his alarm over anyone else's ease any day."

"You like him, don't you?"

"Well, yes. I like all three of them now that Dori has let me in and Theus *has let me out*. Willem's charming too, and his cousin is fun. I think. What's not to like about any of them?"

Yos took her thin, delicate hand in his, caressed her fingers, and gently kissed them. "Do you like Dharmen as much as you like me?"

"Certainly not."

"Well then." He took her other hand and savored their closeness, covering up his own fear at once. "Whatever happens, we'll face it together. All of us and you and I, if you'll permit it."

Brona smiled her answer.

"Dinner later tonight then? My pod?"

"I can hardly wait." Tears formed in Brona's eyes.

Yos saw the joy-fear blend in them. She pulled him close, stood on her toes, and kissed him. "Goodbye, *liefje*. So cute and old-fashioned. I'll see you tonight."

She let go and headed up the way toward the AirTransit terminal.

Yos stood still in the middle of the sidewalk, oblivious to the swarms of people rushing around him. Heart fluttering, he thrust his hands into his pockets like a love-struck teenager and squeezed his narrow shoulders up to his ears in dreamful glee. Brona's face was stamped on his mind, and her exquisite features and the soft warmth of her lips that had just touched his branded his heart. A wonderful new beginning pushed invasion fears aside and held him in arrest.

He left the fugue long enough to watch her walk up the way, across from the gardens' fiery show. He studied every curve of her frame as she moved: graceful, beautiful, feminine, strong, and with the mood pavers glowing in soft-pink shades beneath her steps.

BRONA SAT AT HER WORKSTATION, lost in the hum of information processing around her. Data analysis, light-bending calculations, computers doing their work—nothing calmed her more during evening research. High up in the great bay's rafters, subgenerators 275–299 whirred on, now higher, now lower as they shunted and directed power. Then came the welcomed cascade sequence racing from one end of the array to the other. The entire building shuddered at the power reduction.

The PA system double-chimed its greeting: "All departments, stand-down procedure initiated. Confirm gridwide clearance and power relay disengagement."

About time, Brona thought, relieved. *I don't care how many primitive Carmogen satellites pass overhead or how many radio waves they bounce at us; we've only got two suns to draw energy from. Does the Kraal think we have endless power to keep running this thing? The Cloak is for our protection and only when needed. It's not for scared officials keeping us scurrying round like micromice at the least bother!*

She sighed, stared at her main upright. Beyond the sign-on icon, it was blank. Her trials, all of them, finished an hour ago. She had sat thinking blissfully of Yos since and wanted the eve-dream to continue. But she was too afraid for even the stand-down of Cloak to comfort her. She resettled her mind on Yos, picturing his long frame that could use a few workouts, his wispy hair that he constantly pushed out of his face rather than trim, and those calm eyes that always seemed to say, "All is good, and life is wonderful, no matter what."

And no matter what, I'm due for a love life. Overdue for one! She realized how long it had been since she had dated . . . and promptly put past boyfriends out of her mind. No use going there! Yos was the one for her. She imagined that people might mistake them for brother and sister if they didn't always hold hands in public. They looked alike, though they didn't think alike. She was serious about nearly everything, had more in common with Dharmen there. But Yos's even temperament had to be the greatest constant in the universe. It was refreshing. It got under her skin in excess, but it still brought her back from the moody, anxious states she had fallen into lately. *Brilliant man! Odd and hideously intelligent, but wonderful just the same.*

"Why, Brona! What the Heaveners are you still doing here?"

Ugh! And just when you think you're safe from your resident traitor. "I'm working late, Ian." She didn't bother to look up. "Should be pretty obvious at this time of night."

"Well, temper, temper," Ian said to her back.

Brona rolled head and eyes around at him. It was less peeve than she would like to have shown, but hopefully enough to get rid of him without being *too* unprofessional. It didn't work.

He rounded her desktop. She did her best to ignore him and feign attention to her long-deactivated testing and adjustments. But that uncombed yellow hair and oily pink pudge of a face kept coming nearer. Why could he never be content to bother her from the opposite side of the desk? And that breath. What on Tentim had the little cretin had for lunch? It resurrected queasy memories of bad food, binge drinking, and inevitable vomiting after party nights back at university. Funny how the man retained the stench. He was right beside her now, within kicking distance.

"The Gravitational Lensing Project's all finished, and the Cloak just went down. Major systems are idled, so what could you possibly be still working on?" Ian said. He could see that her uprights were blank, but she didn't care.

"Oh, this, that, the other. I'm absolutely rushed with research." She swiveled cold, unblinking eyes up to his. "And yet, there's nothing going on!"

Ian flattened his perpetually sneering lips. "What an effort at nothing. Have it your way, Bron."

Brona rolled her eyes again. "I've told you before: no one calls me *Bron* but my father." *And tall, handsome physicists with a penchant for know-it-all-ism.*

"Sorry. We've worked together for five years. I thought by now we just might be friends."

Brona tightened her jaws to keep from laughing in his ugly face. "Don't put yourself out on that one." She went back to her uprights, signed back on, and opened arbitrary files, anything at all except micro-AI testing or alternate universe shift calculations. From the tops of her eyes, she could see him studying her, the way unwanted men endlessly did. *Why do the wrong ones insist on that?*

"Speaking of which, we should go out sometime," he said, just like that. "Perhaps you could invite me to your pod for a quiet dinner?"

Now we come to it. Surprised it took you this long! "Perhaps not. Plumbing and electrics are working fine, Ian. I've no need for fix-its at the moment."

To that, Ian really did come to it. "I guess I'm not tall and skinny enough like that Yos friend of yours, am I?"

"No, but you're short and fat enough if that's any help."

"And you've brought him here numerous times lately. I can barely set a foot near your station, and I work here."

"That didn't stop you from accessing my personal files, now did it?" Brona threw back, boring her eyes into him. "It's been a year now, and I'm still trying to locate what you lifted."

Ian's permanently flushed face blanched. "We're on the same team. Our work is interdependent. I didn't know I needed permission to access what's rightfully the property of the entire program, frankly. I certainly wouldn't need it from anyone else here, Bron."

Bron. Bron! "You most certainly would. And access is one thing, appropriation is another. But you wouldn't need an excuse if your right was as great as your sense of entitlement to everyone else's projects that you consistently take credit for but never contribute to." It felt so good to say it after having held it in for so long. "And while we're on the subject, since when does your right include bringing military personnel in here to tamper with my files? Especially those who later kidnap and torture their own colleagues when theft and espionage aren't enough for them. That was your friend Vara's last act before she died, was it not?"

Ian snorted though his tiny nostrils. "You know a lot for a woman who spends all day aligning energy grids and scheduling power."

"You know damned well my job involves the science of the light-bending requiring the power. I advise the engineering teams on the needs, they do the aligning and scheduling. And it's a world away from what you're up to of late. You've done a good job of stealing information but a lousy one of covering it up. Let's see what it all gets you and how well you keep at it!"

Ian leaned forward with his sweaty palms on her desktop. "Oh, don't worry about me. Think more about covering up whatever these spacetime disruption effects are that you and your friend have been generating lately. I'll find out what that's about soon enough. Though it won't make any difference, no matter what it is you two are scheming or how many more people you have taken into custody here."

For a few heartbeats, Brona misgave her puzzlement. Dharmen did mention a traitor sweep after his rescue, and she had noticed a few of her colleagues missing lately, but she hadn't had time to give it any real thought.

"That's right," Ian continued. "Eight people from StealthOps Teams C and E were arrested last week and three from Central Engineering the week before. Don't tell me you weren't behind it. Well, once your witch hunt is over with, we'll see how you handle what you only *think* you know."

They stared heat at each other. If Ian wasn't backing down, Brona absolutely refused to. He raised himself sharply from her desktop, holding his glare as he left.

Brona heaved a sigh at the sound of his footfalls fading down the metal planks of the walkway that would take him out of the area. Beyond disgust, now she was even more afraid. *Fight, woman. Fight,* she told herself. She returned to her main upright, called up her files, and began programming another trial sequence, this time with a few enhancements in mind. She pictured Yos's face again during compiling and smiled, realizing her unpleasant night was about to vastly improve. But not before just one last round of simulations for the targeting scanners.

CHAPTER 16

MESSENGER IN THE NIGHT

need your help, Rem-E. I have one major task before the Carmis get here.

Sir, defensive operations are still days away, and deployment has yet to commence. We have already covered combat prep procedures and information made available to date.

That isn't it.

What do you require, Lieutenant Commander?

Connect me to Great Hall administration. I need to speak with their archivist.

❀

"DHARMEN, WHAT IS IT? WHAT'S bothering you that grochlaroot stew on a second autumn night can't fix?" Willem asked from across their dine-in table.

Dharmen's eyes were on his plate. His thoughts were so far away that he barely heard the question.

"It's about to start, isn't it? The invasion, I mean."

This broke the spell and got eye contact.

"You've been pushing your food around all evening, which is incredibly unusual for you," Willem said. "So it's either that or wedding jitters. Which is it?"

"It's definitely not the latter. You accepted, Hanne. Don't think for a minute that you can get out of it."

That got a marginal smile.

"Sorry, love. I don't mean to upset you."

"Don't be," Willem said. "We both knew this was coming, and I'm getting used to the thought of it now. As much as anyone can." His smile deepened, but Dharmen saw pain behind it. "And anyway," Willem changed tone and quickly rose from his seat, "I have to contact my brothers about the wedding—they've been asking me for details, surprisingly even more than Aremel. I just haven't had time to respond to—"

"You don't really intend to reach out to your family right in the middle of dinner," Dharmen said, "and you're not getting used to the thought of invasion either. But thank you."

"For what?"

"For trying to understand. For doing your best to in the worst possible situation . . ."

The front door chimed. Willem's eyes edged toward the live-in.

Dharmen's rolled to the ceiling. "Blazing suns, what now?" He threw his napkin onto the table, stood and gave Willem a quick, reassuring kiss on the forehead, and went to the door. He assumed it was the admiral's watchers having caught yet another saboteur trying to do who knew what. "We're nearly at marshaling, and they're still at it. Can't a man and his man eat supper without traitors calling in lost causes?" he muttered, checking his trouser leg pocket for his gun.

Rem-E: activate porch monitor.

"Krone in Heaven, what can *this* be about?"

Dharmen commanded the door open, ignored the pair of Guardsmen, and looked squarely at their captive.

"Sorry to bother you, sir," one uniform said. "We caught him in front of the pod, staring up at your door. Says he has something to tell you."

"We've scanned him, sir. He's clean," said uniform two.

"Good. Give us a few."

The sentinels eyed each other but obeyed Dharmen's sharp nod off his porch, pulse rifles out and flanking the path to the canalside way. Dharmen stepped out and let the door whiz shut behind him.

"Interesting of you to drop into the neighborhood. Can't get enough of South C, I take it? Is this a friendly visit, Vinc, or should I go fetch my sword?"

Irzek looked ready to jump out of his skin rather than speak.

Dharmen's glare roasted him for a new stew. "Bit late to be out while on house arrest, isn't it?"

"My . . . my confinement's ended, sir," Irzek stammered. "They said I behaved well, so the sentence was reduced."

"No surprise there. Try to kill your CO, get a comfortable stay at home, and not even a complete one at that. What would we do without the JAG's expert decisions?"

"But I didn't actually want to—"

"And I hear from an *almost* reliable source that you acted fully on your own. First thing you've ever done without someone else's help."

"Sir, I wish *sorry* could cover it," Irzek said in a youthfully urgent rush of emotion through breath visibly escaping into the chilly night. "I'm not even sure now why I . . . I guess I thought—"

"You thought taking me out would impress your new boss." Dharmen's tone could have been paternal had he not been so incensed. "Excuse me for beating you to it. I know how Armetrian and his grand talk affects recruits—or used to."

"I never really found it all that put on."

"Course you didn't, that's how he wanted it. But a meler in diamonds is still a meler, Vinc, as you more than anybody should know."

Irzek gave that the same flustered look Dharmen had become accustomed to from his twin sister. "I didn't come to talk about Lieutenant Commander Armetrian, I came to talk about the others. Sir, I have some information."

"On what?"

"On Dawn Fire's plans to get stealthtech secrets to the Carmogen."

Surprise escaped Dharmen's face before he could contain it, magnified by the bright porch light that exposed every error of self-control. "Stealthtech. Really? And just how did you come by this? Don't tell me Armetrian and Vara put that kind of trust in you."

"Not exactly. I accessed the encryption codes in Lieutenant Vara's file sets and managed to get past them."

"It's just Vara now, or it would be. She'd no longer be commissioned if she'd lived. Neither is Armetrian." Dharmen watched Irzek's eyes flicker. His designation was gone too in one of the Guard's shortest enlistments ever.

"In that case, I don't really have to call you *sir* anymore, do I?"

Dharmen met that unblinking and answerless.

"Look, *sir*, I'm telling you the truth. Honestly."

"*Honestly*, Vara's encryptions were incredibly complex and subtly constructed," Dharmen said. "We analyzed them. They were designed specifically to keep prying eyes from access, so how did you of all people— Oh, let me guess!" He put a finger to Irzek's bony chest. "From your duty station on Bemin. You could do more powerful decryption there than at Seventh. Well, at least you achieved something under my command! Now out with it, Vinc. What exactly do you know?" Irzek's tongue seemed to abandon its courage. He looked timidly down at his feet. "This is a long way to roll off a farm and end up on a cold night. You didn't airtram it across the lake and hike down here just to go silent on me now."

Irzek sighed. "Vara got stealthtech data from PDP that she was going to hand over to the Carmogen through General Estes." He backed away as Dharmen snarled hard and hot enough to scatter the chill from the night air between them.

"If that's all you've interrupted my dinner for, kid, you're late. A lot late! We confirmed Vara and Estes's involvement weeks ago."

"Maybe, but you and Gennet can't possibly know of everyone involved in places like PDP."

"*Admiral* Gennet has had a sloop's load rounded up these last few weeks. You're saying we missed someone?"

Irzek's narrow, acne-scarred face contorted into a wince beneath the bright light.

"Names, Vinc! Don't waste any more of my time unless you've got names to go with all this."

"There's a scientist . . . physicist I believe," Irzek started, "a Dr. Ian Folc. He does something with light-bending, or however the Cloak works. I don't know his exact function at PDP, but he shouldn't be too hard to find there."

"Go on, I'm listening."

"He was Vara's PDP operative, and with her gone, someone will likely take her place. Though maybe not a Guardsman this time."

"I've dealt with Dawn Fire for a while now, Vinc, I think I can figure out who's resurfaced for that job. I hope Folc likes the replacement because he's in this even deeper now."

"Right. And sir, Vara tried her best to keep the information from Gallin, but she didn't try hard enough. He gained access. I overheard him discussing her stolen stealthtech information with Armetrian just before . . ." He looked down. "Before our holo-gym situation."

Forget regulation Guard methods, Dharmen thought. *Nothing beats a jittery teenager to do on a cold night what weeks of interrogations couldn't. Armetrian's nowhere near this forthcoming!*

"We'll deal with the Lenan later. Do you have any real proof of Folc's involvement?"

"No, not really."

"Then you have nothing besides my time better spent eating."

"I know it's not much, sir. All I'm asking is that you and the Guard keep watch on PDP. Whatever that physicist is up to could leave Angolin defenseless."

"You've considered that, have you? Confinement's found your heart after all?"

Irzek shrugged. "I'm a civilian now. I guess I'm starting to think like an ordinary Angolinian again."

"Ordinary Angolinian? Nearly funny, that one, Vinc. A true citizen wouldn't have gotten mixed up in this to begin with. But keep up the reflection, it'll make a man of you yet! Is there anything more?"

Irzek returned the crestfallen look of a small child despoiled of candy. "No, sir. Just please look into what I've told you." After a few tense seconds and a frenetic dart of the eyes, he hastily said goodbye, left the porch, and scurried back toward the guards.

Dharmen turned to his opening door. Folc was the colleague Brona had told him about on Mount Condorcet. He had to inform Gennet, but why hadn't the admiral's sweeps snagged him with the others?

"And sir!" Irzek yelled from the street, stopping him in his doorway.

"Yes, Vinc?"

"Congratulations on your engagement!" He passed through the watching sentinels and hurried up the mood-paver-illumined sidewalk.

Dharmen sniffed. "Hmmph. Amazing!" He stepped inside from the chilly night and chillier information and let the door close behind him.

MORNING MET THE FJORD LINE with pale sunlight. Flat-topped in some places, craggy and jutting up like rocky teeth in others, the mammoth stretch palisaded the Hidden Realm's high perch from the Abyss all the way up to the Northern Passes. Upon it, Dharmen stood alone, a solitary figure revealed by retreating fogs.

Behind him, the Osterrand Plain's golden grasses swayed blithely in the gentle micro autumn breeze. Streams rushed down into the empty land from the East Ranges. Among them, downy *ganaal* flocked and rested their wings, and wild taroc herds faded in and out of sight. Their seasonal southward range from Lena's southern frontier had begun through the quiet, unpeopled haven between the mountains and the abyssal murk at the edge of which Dharmen stood and stared out.

"My apologies, Lieutenant Commander," said Father Dietmar's image rematerializing in front of him. "The Council of Elders is meeting soon. Minor spiritual matters. Now as I was saying, you are welcome to come to temple at any time, but the eve of battle is the proper time for a soldier to present himself to Lord Krone. For now, find some other suitable place for the guidance you seek."

"But where, Father? There isn't any place . . ." Dharmen stopped. For him, there certainly was.

"You, like everyone, have your own personal sacred space that brings you peace of mind and succors your soul."

"Yes, Father. And I'll come to temple afterward as you advise."

The image smiled. "And Mother Encarra and I look forward to joining the battle when it arrives."

"Only military units will deploy. I doubt that temple elders—"

"We, too, are military, and we will be there to fight in Krone's name."

Dharmen straightened, realizing that the idyllic surroundings had made him too lax for the occasion. "Of course, Father."

From the image came a familiar scrape of metal against metal. Dietmar's floating semblance raised its unsheathed sword. The blade glinted brightly even through the haze of comm interference. "Good fortune to you, Lieutenant Commander, to your family old and new, and to your comrades who fight beside you."

Dharmen lifted his own sword. "Krone be with you, Father."

"And you, child." Dietmar's image vanished as he closed the channel.

Near total silence followed. For a pensive moment, Dharmen heard nothing beyond ganaalsong and the gurgling streams in the plain behind. The morning had warmed, but he felt chill. He was afraid, had been on and off for days. Foreboding encompassed everything and everyone in his life: his fiancé, father, comrades, even his enemies—personal and traitor alike. And he wondered when on Tentim he had started considering the latter! He stared down the Abyss's throat, at the brown gas plumes dancing silent death below in their vast stretch eastward. *Gods bless Angolin,* he prayed, *and every one of its inward and thoroughly clueless—*

The sound of propulsors pierced the warbling, windswept chorus of nature behind him. The engines cycled to landing and sent the animals scattering. The vessel, just out of TimeSpace, was close enough for its draft to toss Dharmen's cloak about. Sword stowed, sidearm drawn, he turned. A small shuttle sat less than ten meters away. Unmarked and not emblazoned in Guard dun finish, it wasn't Theus, Dori, or any of the admiral's people. Dharmen stood ready for whoever had caught him alone in the most solitary and unlikely corner of Angolin. Running was no option. He aimed and waited.

The side hatch opened. Out came a single figure with the gait and frame of a woman, a vaguely familiar one. For an instant, Vara's image beneath Mt. Condorcet flashed through his mind. Rem-E went to work on his trembling. It couldn't be her, but he tightened his trigger finger regardless, ready for a firefight, until . . . "Brona? What in Krone's name are you doing *here*?"

"I should ask you the same question," she replied. "What brings you up to Helmer Fjord of all places? Bit out of the way for a morning stroll, isn't it?"

"I needed a place to think," he said, turning and looking back out toward the nothingness. He wanted to be friendlier, but he was too preoccupied.

"You picked the right location for it. I don't think there's a more isolated spot on this rise."

"There are plenty more isolated spots. This one just happens to be significant."

"If you say so. I can leave if you want."

"Don't," he said, still looking outward. "How did you know I'd be up here?"

"You briefly mentioned the Osterrand to Theus at lunch yesterday, right before we started discussing preparedness. I thought I might find you here."

He turned fully around. It was invitation enough to bring her to his side and stop their bellowing across the plain's peace. He glanced back at the expanse behind them.

"This is where it'll happen, you know: broad, reasonably flat, just outside the Cloak and completely visible to the enemy, and right on the edge of the Abyss. Not all combat scenarios indicate such, but this is the perfect place to start an invasion. Krone himself couldn't pick a better war theater."

"You think the collaborators told the enemy to land here specifically?"

"I'm sure at least *one* traitor suggested this spot to the Carmis, yes." He looked back to the gas cloud swirl.

Brona moved ahead of him and stepped closer to the edge. "It's beautiful."

"It's deadly." Dharmen watched her shiver as she searched out her footing on the rocks. It wasn't particularly cold. "And stay back. It's a fifty-thousand-meter drop to the bottom, though the gases would take you first."

"I was raised fjordside. I'm not afraid, never have been." She gingerly backed up the way she came. "I've always found it peaceful. It's what's coming from the other side of it that scares me."

"For your part in that, Brona, I'm very sorry."

"Beg your pardon?"

"PDP's been compromised, and I can't tell you everything will work out there or that we'll win this and go back to being the happy, hidden little land we've always been." Dharmen grunted at the notion of calling throngs of angry protesters and the traitors silently shouldering their cause *happy*. "I'd like to put on my Will's cheer and assure you that we'll get through this. Truth is, we're far from ready, and I don't really know what'll happen."

Brona looked as wan as the still-lingering fog trails. "Women don't need men to assure them, as I've told Yos many times now. I'm fine, Dharmen."

"Are you? *Fine* brought you up here?"

"Yes, actually. And I'll confess something: in this fun, well, interesting group, you're the one I trust to tell it like it is—no insincerity, empty encouragements, or patronizing evasions. Honest assessments, not meler crap. That's what I want as a researcher, and that's what you give every time."

"Thanks," Dharmen said. "And if you can handle more honesty, you said a while ago that you believe the traitors infiltrated PDP."

"That's right."

"What's Ian been up to, lately?"

"You remember what I told you back at Kleve Park about him, I take it?"

"I do, and I've just gotten new information on his Dawn Fire involvement. I relayed it to the admiral last night. He put out an arrest warrant immediately."

Brona narrowed her eyes as if to size Dharmen up. "You're sharp! Ian wasn't in this morning, though I don't think Gennet got to him in time. I think he's gone."

"Oh, I think he'll turn up. And we can guess when," Dharmen said, unsurprised. "I also spoke to Admiral Gennet about your detection system. He's impressed with the results. I think you'll have a go-ahead whether the Kraal likes it or not." He leaned closer, light piercing his black eyes. "But if in the midst of it all, we can't deal with your colleague—"

"I'll have to. Understood, Dharm, as always." Brona gave him a mock salute. "I just hope I can handle him when he makes his move. Yos and I will be busy. I won't have a lot of time."

"No one will; he's probably counting on that. But I've got a little assist in mind. If it works, we might not have to worry about him. Not too much, anyway."

Brona lifted her eyelids. "And if it doesn't?"

Grim silence.

"Right," Brona said through a dreary sigh.

Dharmen stared back out over the Abyss, noticing from the corner of his eye that he was being intently studied. *Sorry*, he thought. *The situation is what it is at this point.*

Brona threaded her arm into his. She rested her head gently on his shoulder and followed his gaze outward.

Caught off guard twice in one morning! He reached over and clasped his hand across hers as he watched the expanse, knowing the Carmogen would appear over it soon and hoping Brona wouldn't look up to see his flushed face. Yet.

"So," he ventured—*time to make someone else red.* "While we're talking, tell me about this alternate universe thing you and Yos are working on."

After nearly an hour of what looked like dawn rising in the middle of the night, we can clearly make them out: rows upon rows of orange lights. They twinkled innocently like family outing campfires at first, then they grew. The enemy bears torches, allowing the size of their army to be estimated. And it makes no difference. Their numbers are far greater than ours, thanks to all the wrangling back home on our expedition's size. Eight months on this bizarre spine ball of a planet has made my people excellent archers, sword handlers, and axe wielders, but our enemy has better skill, solid knowledge of the land—and no bureaucracy to hold them back. But there's no time to complain and no one to complain to. They're on us. Their flames and their chants fill the field before the West Gate now. The sound of their war cries, the sight of their fire, and the trees waving wildly around them put fear in us all.

I am resolved to fight. I hope my companies are too.

Cpt. Nolin Falconer
H.S.S. Stonewall
09-24-2397

Unable to absorb another word, Dharmen closed the centuries-old account of the ancients' first major battle on Tentim. He rubbed his tired eyes and looked down the long wooden table's length. Unlike the massive Great Hall built for the entire expedition, the old fortress mead hall served only the needs of Captain Falconer and his crew. Properly set, it could comfortably seat a hundred or cozily accommodate a choice few senior officers. Presently, it sat one.

The second autumn daylight that had blazed through the high, arched windows all afternoon was dimming. Warm but waning light touched the old parchments and journals left behind for the Hidden Realm's posterity. It was late. Dharmen knew he would be told to leave soon, but he was satisfied. He had done what he needed. Invasion was coming. What better place to spend the day than in the Great Hall's confines, and in the more intimate meeting space of its chief crew complement, immersed in the battlefield logs of the man who would later become the founder of Angolin.

He had read all he could of that initial crew's landing, their first fort's hasty construction, the captain's frustrations with having to debate every expedition detail with a government too distant in time and space to understand his people's immediate needs, and having to learn combat technologies very different from what they were accustomed to. Laying aside energy weapons to match the fighting methods of the planet at the time wasn't easy. Neither was the Battle of Sarneth Forest, whose outcome led to Greathall's planning and secret building.

Dharmen had seen all the holo accounts before; they were required instruction for officer cadets. But reading the originals written in Falconer's own hand was a prebattle experience like no other. He inhaled the information as deeply as he inhaled the scent of the paper it was written on, and he couldn't remember having ever been so inspired. These people fought an enemy five times their size that served an inaccessible leader intent upon altering timelines, and having the power to destroy their entire light-years-distant civilization in one stroke if they didn't succeed. War was coming to *them*—no collaborators, protestors, or hard-headed politicians to bother with. The Carmogen would bring a modern war, but the demand on mind and honor would be no different from nearly a millennium ago. Dharmen perused the journal spread.

"Krone, Lord, we'll do this. For the captain and for you!"

Footsteps filled the corridor outside. He took one last look at the history assembled on the table and built all around him. The heavy high-back wooden chair scraped the floor as he rose. He decided to spend his last moment at the windows. Beyond them, streams and falls hurried down the steep slopes, forming golden bands in the fading sunlight. The bright-orange cliffside trees that had mesmerized him on arrival were shadowed to deep brown now. Autumnal positioning had put Rior at the solar forefront, and the heavens were stained russet with Lothnë's last, lone vestige of light. Nights lately had been moonless, and already, stars awoke across the eastern sky.

Peace flowed on both sides of the crystal panes. Dharmen felt the lifeblood of his ancestors around him; he didn't need texts, real or synth, to sense it. And whatever force, whatever *other* that inspirited them and drew them to this sheltered spot permeated him now as it always had. He silently thanked Father Dietmar for reinforcing his wish to come here and promised Lord Krone to come to his presence at temple. Tomorrow, that would be the appointed time. Naul's forces were that close. He felt it in spite of reports . . .

The Hall's main door creaked open. "Time to go, sir." The calm earnestness in the voice communicated understanding of his personal mission. It wasn't the Great Hall archivist.

Dharmen turned from the sight before him. "I know, Thee. I'm coming."

THE THREE OF THEM WALKED slowly in the twilight along the tree- and hedge-shaded paths leading downward from the old stronghold. Dori had insisted on immediate departure, wanting to see her family one last time. Dharmen and Theus convinced her to share a few minutes of peace together. Only the gods knew when they would have another chance.

Descending the steep declines beneath the revered district, Dharmen glimpsed the far-distant profiles of the East Ranges' three tallest peaks: Hiver, Tenebraeum, and Condorcet held the day's last light above a darkening world. He was stirred and sensed brooding in his comrades as deep as his own. He said nothing and left them to it. The temperature was dropping. Mists from the falls wafted across the path, their droplets glistening on the hedge leaves beneath the waxing starlight and wetting Dharmen's hair and face. He adjusted his uniform's enviro-control to compensate. The extra warmth suppressed the early evening chill, but not the force surrounding him. They walked single file along the footpath atop a centuries-old weir and down to the marginal way far below the Great Hall's rear.

"So it was my turn to find you two and not the other way round," Dharmen yelled above the rushing water beside them.

"Beg your pardon, mate," Theus said. "I found *you* stuck up in old books. Any longer and you'd have become part of the print."

"Have a good read, Dharm?" Dori asked. "Shame that all of the captain's personal logs and journals aren't in the Hall archives."

"Commander?" Dharmen queried.

Dori gave him a low-lidded, fey smile. "I'll get you access to the others sometime later. After we come through this invasion, of course."

Dharmen opened his mouth in astonishment but said nothing.

Further along and into deepening nightshades, he stopped them, and got stares likely expecting more complaining about combat odds. He was sorry for that. He put a hand on each of their shoulders. "I don't say this enough, but a soldier really couldn't ask for better friends. I'm honored to face the enemy with you two more than anyone, and I'll be proud to fight beside you both. I wouldn't have it any other way."

They had a long group hug, a rare show of warmth for Dharmen that he soaked up, savoring the moment that could be one of their last. He led them to the bridge that would take them across the ravine to the landing platform. Tonight they were granted a special allowance: a few hours of personal time, compliments of Admiral Gennet. Dharmen controlled his breathing to calm his emotions and ordered Rem-E not to assist for once. Willem and his father were at home, waiting to say goodbye. Later that evening, the three officers would deploy to Bemin.

CHAPTER 17

LINE OVER THE HORIZON

"**Y**ou both have a monumental task ahead of you. I'm in awe of what you're about to do. I just wish I could contribute from my end."

"Your contribution will be human love and support. That I cannot give him, though I will assist his combat efforts to my last circuit's strength."

"I never knew AI could exhibit such compassion. You surprise me . . . Are you speaking to me with his permission?"

"Negative, sir. But in times like these, even *artificial* intelligence knows when to sidestep regulation."

"Of course, Rem-E. Thank you."

"You are most welcome, Mr. Hanne."

❹

A RAY OF PALE-BLUE SUNLIGHT crept across Dharmen's shoulder and extended on a widening angle downward across his knee. He didn't bother to turn and watch Rior peer over the Realm's edge through the gunship viewports. He knew day was coming. He had gone to temple to present himself to the god of war in the wee hours of morning. There would be no time later that day. He had asked Theus and Dori to join him the evening before. They had politely refused.

Theus said he would honor Krone in his own way, and Dori defied character and remained silent. The port barracks had been quiet as he went off into the darkness.

To each their own then . . . Dharmen's eyes bucked in the cabin's dim light at that thought. He wasn't peeved at all. He understood that maybe, just maybe, he didn't need to take issue with everything and everyone all the time. Progress? The gods would be pleased. So would Will.

It was images from two nights ago that ate at him. He'd only had a few hours to spend at home. His father understood, and with his only son in the Guard, from a family member's perspective now. Will had been braver than the first time Dharmen went off to war, but pain sat in his eyes. It pooled deep within, but Dharmen still saw it. He was sorry. It wasn't enough, but it was all he could offer. Beneath the sunlight filling the cabin, he hung his head.

He remained in that position when the ship landed, barely looking up when the deployment hatch desynthed and everyone else began filing out. Rising slowly, last to do so, he followed.

He stood on the tarmac as stunned as the youngest cadets recruited to make up for Negara's losses. Bemin was busier than he had ever seen it. Guard uniforms outnumbered station personnel at least three to one, with thousands more set to arrive. He wondered if Port could hold them all. Camos rushed about, conferencing on the move, receiving orders, and giving (yelling) them. Guardsmen helped Bemini staff shuttle light arms and equipment. In the distance, he could see the new Long-Gunners being inspected by frighteningly large, multilimbed robots and by port personnel on hovering maintenance platforms. The marshaling was on.

He kept out of the way of everyone darting around him. The day before had been an exercise in controlled madness from end to end. This morning was twice as frenetic. He dryly assured himself that the enemy would be equally awed. He pried himself from his safe spot at the first break in traffic and headed to his first set of tasks. Several interrupted strides later, he found Theus and Dori ready for bright-and-early morning mayhem and looking nearly refreshed from the haggard state he had left them in the night before. But he wished they were alone.

"Commander, Lieutenant," he greeted more formally than usual. The port security lead who had granted him and Theus a patrol sloop months prior to pursue escaping gunrunners made them a trio. Dori liked him. Too much. Theus trusted him too much, but Dharmen felt the station had enough assholes as it was. "Major." He briefly noted the new rank on the man's collar.

"Good morning to *you*, Lieutenant Commander!" the other said with that sparkle in his eye that Dharmen still couldn't quite read.

Dori had her internal transfer data to Dharmen's. She looked put-upon. Her silent, pursed lips amply introduced the problem. He activated an upright and scanned the information: instructions on his unit's formation positioning, complete with personnel roster. No issue so far, and he was glad of the names: SR Leatra Vinc in Alpha Company. Great. He would have had one of his company command-ers request her otherwise, and . . . "Theus, my XO. Excellent! But, Commander, it looks like we'll be separated from you."

"Not quite. My unit will be right beside yours," Dori said. "I'll have no trouble keeping an eye on you two, and Major Clouw here will be my XO, so both units will be in good hands."

Dharmen stared at her, dumbfounded.

"Glad to serve, Commander," the major said. "I'm up for the chal-lenge even if it is my first volunteer assignment." He edged eyes to Dharmen. "I didn't get assigned to Mr. Tate's unit like I requested, but no problem. We'll still see this through."

"You *requested*?" Dharmen asked.

"Yes, Lieutenant Commander." The major's eyes gleamed inscrutably.

Dharmen didn't like it.

"And from a Guard perspective, we're glad to have you and your weapons and equipment expertise onboard," Dori put in, "because beyond personnel, it's the heavier equipment, or lack thereof, that concerns me."

Dharmen returned to his upright and found Dori's issue. "Two hundred M-12 Gunsloops, sixty Robo-Interceptor Assault Vessels—impressive machines if they're up to the job. But only sixty? Even fewer High-Neck Gunners and none of the old LR-2 Gunships. Why aren't they listed?"

"That line is decommissioned, or it will be. That's all I can say," the major answered.

"Shame. I liked them. The ride wasn't worth a borbol's middle cheek, but they did what we needed them to." Dharmen read the remaining list items, winced. "And last, but not least, two, maybe three working Orbital Weapons Platforms. Think those'll be operable at go-time, Major?"

"We're not sure yet."

Dharmen's raised eyebrows requested something more truthful.

"Unlikely, in light of the problems we've been having, TimeSpace energy consumption for such massive structures being the greatest," the major admitted. "That, plus they've never been used. I wouldn't count on them."

Dharmen glanced at Theus, adding his comrade's earlier equipment concerns to his own. "You realize this won't do. This inventory's not nearly enough to engage the Carmogen war machine, which will be here before your beard grows in fully, Major." From his very first Bemin tour, he couldn't help but notice the port staff's casual appearance standards compared to the Guard's. The major was one of the worst culprits.

"You sure about that, Lieutenant Commander?" the other said. "We've had four micro seasons to build new assault and support vessels. You know that; you were present at most of the status meetings. Don't tell me it was all for nothing."

Dharmen returned steadfast silence.

"You may also have noticed that I've been promoted," the major continued. "As of two days ago, I'm in charge of Port stores and materiel, southwest quadrant. That makes me partly responsible for the combat equipment and service support we provide in this effort."

"Glad to hear it," Dharmen said. "And I apologize, Major, I think. Your hard work's not for nothing, but you know the enemy will be here with twenty times this complement, including a few stolen surprises from our own arsenal. Surely you can use that extra rank to scare up more resources." He flicked his upright around to the man's stubbly face.

"It is what it is, soldier. Show some faith," Dori said in her usual *Shut up, Dharmen* tone.

"Commander, there has to be more ships available beyond what's in this manifest. One quad section of Port alone houses enough to—"

"Work on that positivity just this once," Dori said. "It would be as greatly appreciated as more heavy gunners would be."

Leatra hurried up. "Commander," she saluted before initiating an upload from her internal to Dori's.

Dori surveyed the update, scowled. "Eechh! You two carry on with your duties," she said to Dharmen and the major. "Thee, Vinc, you're with me."

Dharmen watched them disappear into the uniformed tide. "You heard the woman. I have tasks to complete, and then I'm sure I'll have to assist with whatever that was about, which probably involves those fancy new Long-Gunners of yours." *And stop staring at me like that.* "Got work to do. I'm sure I have something—"

"Don't be so quick to run off, Lieutenant Commander," the major said too pleasantly. "Stay a minute and finish telling me how woefully unprepared we are."

"I call it like I see it, Major."

"Oh, I know that! I haven't forgotten the first time we met. You'd have knocked me halfway across the Abyss if I hadn't let you and Tarkala on that patrol sloop."

Dharmen rolled his eyes fractionally. "Even if we do get those Orbitals online, three hundred-plus birds won't be enough to match thousands of enemy fighter craft, no matter how primitive they are. You and your staff know this."

"I know that's all there is, regardless, unless you want to completely rob us of reserves. I'm sorry if you don't like it, but every legate at High Command has approved this complement, and it's all we have to work with. I can't pull more ships out of my ass, so when the time comes, we'll all just have to work that much more magic."

Finally, 'bout time we cut through some of the smarm! "I'm a Guardsman, Major. I'm used to settling, but you're right. I don't like it." Dharmen stepped closer to avoid being struck from behind by two shipmen carrying a particle cannon housing on their shoulders. Robotic support must have been stretched thin.

"Look, I don't want to be Carmi target practice any more than you do, but if you'll bear with me a sec . . ." The major activated an upright and joined it to Dharmen's for conference view. He called up a diagram of the battlefield-to-be, complete with full materiel emplacements.

Dharmen recognized the terrain. He'd just stood on the Osterrand Plain two mornings ago. The major showed him how ships would be deployed and how formations could be aligned and realigned to match the enemy's advance, including call-up reserves and equipment for a solid rear guard.

"We'll have every piece of light and heavy artillery loaded onto the assault vessels by shift change—Guard-issue and our own. And as for the Orbitals, instructions were transmitted to them last night. We'd like them up by suns-down so we can have time for workups, but that's a long-assed shot."

The major's enthusiasm was just disarming enough to quiet Dharmen. For the moment.

"Apology accepted, Lieutenant Commander."

Arrogant shit! "I wish I could say I'm impressed. I am, considering; I just don't want to say it," Dharmen admitted.

"I'll pretend I haven't heard it then."

"Just promise you'll get us what we need up there, Major."

"I will if you promise to call me Ilbron from now on, *Dharmen*. I never could stand all the formality you Guard types bring here."

There's that damned wink again! "Fine," Dharmen said. "On one condition."

"For you, anything."

Dharmen peered over his shoulder, nodded downward to his rear. "Lose the hand."

THE DAY DRIFTED THROUGH DHARMEN'S weary mind like fog over Nieuw Holland Valley at 0600. He moved mechanically through his duties, revising combat readiness preparations, finalizing his unit roster, and overseeing final shakedown exercises with his staff and their recruits aboard the new Long-Gunners that, as boasted, really did hold eighty LR-2's worth of boots and seemingly as many particle cannons. Necessity running on adrenaline carried him from one task to the next, and to the next.

Dori and Theus had scrambled equally. He didn't see them at all again until just before lights-out back at the barracks. Sleep was as unlikely as sweeping victory; before turning in, they stood on the walkway outside the GOQ, looking out over Port's lighted expanse.

"Dharmen, you were so short with Major Clouw this morning," Dori said. "I don't get why you don't like him. He likes you."

"Heh, tell me about it!"

"He did give us that patrol sloop when we needed it," Theus innocently threw in.

"I think you're jealous, Dharm," Dori said. "Of what, I can't say."

He gave her a nemurite-hard look. "Jealous? Of an upstart with no combat experience? Hardly! And why are you making him your XO? When the fjord line heats up, you won't have time to babysit him, Commander."

"We're working with a lot of new equipment, Dharm, and the major's expertise is unparalleled. We need him. We need everybody we can get, so overlook whatever your issue is. That's an order."

"Let's hope his expertise makes up for the numbers deficit," Theus said. "And Dharm's right. The man's untested. Who knows what he'll do up there." He gave Dharmen's arm a brisk nudge. "You might not have him under your skin for long, mate."

"Thee, that's the wrong thing to say the night before battle!" Dori said. "And after so short a time, here we are again. We've never done a thing to the Carmogen Empire; no one on this planet has. What do they want from us?" She turned and leaned back against the railing. "Still, after everything this past year between the Carmis and Dawn Fire, it's been interesting. Boys, no matter what anyone says, we've lived life."

Dharmen thought about it all: Negara, the traitors, every attempt on him and Willem, and of course, that night beneath Mount Condorcet. Even Rem-E's therapies couldn't fully wipe that pain from his mind. He rubbed his side, ignored the uncomfortable tinges that answered, and cut Dori an eye. "And some of us have had life lived *at us*."

At lights-out, Dharmen lay on his back, staring up at the darkened ceiling. He wondered how he could be so tired and wide-awake at once. He wondered what the next day would bring. And combat aside for a minute, how would his fiancé and father cope if he didn't return? How would *he* cope if he survived and either Theus or Dori didn't? And considering the odds, did any of this really matter? His eyes began to twitch and his limbs followed. *Damn it! Rem-E. One final round.*

Defying fear-induced insomnia and under CSD treatment, he closed his eyes. He remembered little of the night beyond those few moments and later wondered if he had slept at all. Though he would never forget the sensation of everyone else around him passing the night just as fitfully: not a single snore, just a lot of bunks groaning beneath tossing and turning bodies.

MORNING REVEILLE. *LIKE NO OTHER.* Dharmen took quick readiness reports from his company commanders, then with everyone else around him, he suited up for combat. He felt fried, as he always did when wrenched from sleep too early and when already underrested. And as always, he ignored it and kept working.

"Sir!" his XO greeted. "You ready?"

"Been ready forever, Lieutenant."

"Me too. So I'd like to think."

"We've done this before, Thee. Once or twice now."

"But never on home soil. The last people to fight here were the ancients . . . No, this one's different." Theus adjusted his combat gear and said no more.

Dharmen got the point but didn't mind the quiet. It let him concentrate on the next several hours. The joint Guard-Bemini force would be under the command of Admirals Gennet and Sajeva. Gennet had had most of Seventh deployed to Bemin while his counterpart, who had just recently taken over administration of Fifth, would have her order sent directly to the battlefield, largely as reserves.

Dharmen didn't like it one bit: fighting the Carmogen on one end and any traitors on the other who hadn't been scooped up in Gennet's sweeps. Krone knew what semper knifing straggled back at base. But it was HC's decision. He couldn't see either Gennet or Sajeva contriving such a naive plan, particularly with the latter still unfamiliar with her new post's personnel landscape—one she had acquired from a traitor. He ground his teeth at that as he performed one last check: battle armor integrity, Yos's antiparticler, internal interfacing, comm functions, geolocation, TimeSpace diagnostics, pulse rifle readiness, and ammo power cells. He changed the cells out for ones without curious scorings on their undersides that betrayed obvious tampering. He ordered his people to check theirs, stat, and relayed the situation to the other unit commanders.

Then he picked up his sword from the bunk he had bivouacked on for the last two nights. The chatter quieted. Eyes stared at the long, double-edged blade shining in the overhead light as he inspected it.

He looked slowly around the room, met every gaze. Everyone but Theus looked away immediately and went back to their business. Ergyres were requested to leave the revered but cumbersome weapons behind in favor of more practical particle weapons and assault knives.

"Taroc balls to that!" Dharmen muttered under his breath.

Captain Falconer and his companies had relied on theirs nearly a millennium ago, and so would he. And he knew he wouldn't be the only one. *Anyone wants me up close, this'll be as good as any pulse rifle,* he thought. He thrust the blade into its scabbard. Grinding metal cut the room's silence. Then, choosing to wear it as the ancients had, he flung his weapon over his back and secured the straps.

The PA call to arms swept the barracks. Camos sprayed out of doorways with platoon leaders bellowing behind them. Dharmen glanced over to Dori. She nodded crisply. He returned it as his staff ordered their recruits out into the black morning.

From the walkway above Port's widest tarmac, Dharmen watched the assembly. Ranks upon ranks stood before a line of Long-Gunners bigger than anything any Guardsman had gone to battle in, with their broadside deployment hatches opened to receive their armed but anxious living cargo. On the support buildings behind them, the Angolin Guard Jack fluttered in brilliant red and blue from newly erected flagpoles, each lit from below and giving a much-needed confidence boost.

Area klaxons sounded prompts. To the keenest of sight, bodies forsook military precision and trembled at the formation call. The air was charged with precombat emotion: exhilaration, excitement, tension, fright. Every bit of it filled Dharmen's senses. He took it in stride, concentrated on just those elements that would get him to the battlefield ready to fight.

He headed for the down ramp. Dori was waiting below. Smiling tightly, she stopped him long enough to hand him a folded cloth. He unwrapped it and put on the copper-colored armband that denoted him as a UC. It wasn't his first stab at leadership, but it was his first battlefield command, and he realized that the trepidation he had prepared for never really materialized. How had he come to such a composed mental place? He walked his unit's ranks, nodded to his staff, then to Theus before stopping front and center. Dori took up position in front of the next unit.

Standing at attention, Dharmen felt every man and woman's fear behind him. His gen-comm earplant activated. Recon reports were updated and verified. The enemy was closing. ETA: point-eight-five hours. He shrugged off the jitters loitering in his mind, hoped his people followed suit. *And maybe, just maybe,* he thought, *we could all use a quick uplift* . . . "Krone, give us will, Krone, give us strength," he prayed out loud, and was heartened to hear others behind him join in. "Krone, put your might behind each and every one of us. Hail the fighting Fifth!"

The whole unit repeated the prayer once more before the final signal came. Dharmen, Dori, and the rest of the UC line yelled a unified order to forward march. He advanced, and a massive rumble of boot falls advanced with him up into the gargantuan open holds, three thousand to a ship.

LORD NAUL WENT TO THE front of the fortress-bomber's main deck. Empty handed. He refused to read the prebattle speech the Lescainate had prepared for him.

"My finest achievement needs no forced prose!" he had spat at Daio earlier. "Angolin will be taken by nightfall. Who off the field has words for that?" He mounted the steps to his command throne, aides flanking, chained chattel quivering.

His assembled officers raised fists and shouted. Naul lifted a hand. The noise below him died.

"Fighters of Carmogen," he bellowed, "at last, we come to the task put before us by God himself: to rid this planet of the alien scourge that has infected it for too long. Here, I look upon the best warriors of the most powerful empire the world has ever known. Out there"—he pointed a long gray finger at the aircraft's forward viewport—"out there sits a mongrel horde from who knows where, trespassers against holy supreme design! This is our world. It is every gray-skinned man's duty to secure his birthright and put the foreign filth beneath his heels where it belongs! We are Carmogen, we are the master race on this planet, and no one lesser will outdo us!"

Naul paused to allow the hate thundering beneath the deck's dim lighting. "The Angoliners call theirs the *Hidden Realm*. That will change soon enough. We will render them weak as grazing ganaal after a day's flight, and once we cleanse the lands of the alien trash, we will turn our sights to Lena's pale pestilence. Our final victory and dominion over the West will be as the Great One dictates! Tentim is ours!"

"Death to the aliens," the men shouted. "Death to the trespassers! Death to the inferior! Death to Angolin!"

Naul's thin gray lips twisted into a dark smile. As he absorbed it all, euphoria gripped him and his insides soared as high as the vessel he commanded. He took his throne, arms across its gilded gold armrests and feet planted firmly on the metal floor plating. He reached over and grabbed one of his slave's chains, pulling her close. Looking out to the nearest high-caste officer, Naul ordered him forward. The man took the woman's tether and pulled her into the crowd, a prebattle gift of his very own.

Naul relished in the scene beneath him: a sea of gray-skin elite officers singing his praises and chanting destruction to the soon-to-be-conquered, and all amid the main deck's filtered air, with inferior nongray conscripts segregated in glassed-off anterooms. Their oxygen-masked overseers whipped them into joining the melee of praise as they gasped and choked on the Abyssal gases penetrating the rest of the aircraft's poor air-handling system.

The officers carried their noise to their stations. Naul swiveled his throne to the viewport. He expected to see the same cloud-and-sky expanse that had stared back at him for the last two days out of Gragna Airbase. He was as mistaken as the vessel's instrument readings.

Over darkened gas clouds, the first light of the Great One's lanterns unveiled a jagged line of dark green and gray capped in white above the misty horizon. The sight of Angolin's northernmost mountains moved his stunned lips. "And there, Lord in Heaven, sit another people who will find themselves in the maw of the Carmogen Ninth Army. There lies my greatest prize!"

ADMIRAL GENNET LEFT THE LOW stone he had used as a seat for much of the morning. Tired of haggling with HC over tactical strategies already covered ad nauseum, he had left Admiral Sajeva to her forte: dealing with thick-headed legates with less ability to listen to their field commanders than to plan. He ignored the giant upright, walked the low hill's crown, and stared downward. The command post provided an excellent overlook to the entire engagement area.

He had reviewed battlespace interest points exhaustively for days. Now he put the endless maps and data blocks aside and pulled out a careworn pair of antique binoculars given to him by his great grandfather. He wanted to see the dawn-uncovered plain with his own eyes: rear combat support sectors, touchdown sites, revetment shield positionings—every sustainment point. Beneath it all, the Osterrand sat ominously peaceful, a lonely stretch of land that was about to see its second run in history as a major battlefield.

He raised the eyepieces to the eastern horizon. Far over the Abyss, a line of small fires was erupting. He was cautiously pleased. Phase two of the plan was working, though he wondered just how many enemy aircraft would be struck down . . . and how many casualties might be prevented had phase one—nano-AI neutralization of Carmogen forces en route—been undertaken by the Kraal sooner to bring more than minor sabo. *Damned irresponsible,* he thought. *This war should be fought with machines, not boots on the ground!* He lowered the binoculars, returned to the upright.

Sajeva's face had calmed from its frustrated tightness. Her voice modulated now to a more conciliatory tone toward the images of the legates seated around their conference table. "Sirs, according to our data, enemy approach vectors will put them on the plain below us as the latest intel indicated."

"We haven't yet confirmed the exact number of downed enemy aircraft," Gennet added after examining data refreshed and split-screened on the meters-wide upright, "but so far, three hundred TimeSpaced LR-2 Gunships have been remotely crashed into the most heavily armed Carmogen vessels, and nearly as many mines have made direct hits. Synth drone squads sent in behind the enemy are commencing a second sweep."

"Excellent news, Admiral," said a flickering legate. "By that estimate, at least fifty thousand hostiles have been taken out of commission. May the Netherlords beneath the gases receive them well."

Gennet grunted closemouthed his concern for his own people that would soon die also. "Sir, regardless of initial successes, tens of thousands more have broken through our barricade. Forgive me and my colleague if we feel little inkling to celebrate just yet."

"And particularly since the Orbital Weapons Platforms are still nonoperational," added Sajeva. "If Bemin control doesn't get them up soon, there's no telling how this will turn out."

"We are well aware of that situation, Admiral," said one of the seated men on the upright. "Those who escaped will put down and begin amassing on the Osterrand fields below your position within the quarter hour."

Tate was right about that! His hunch beat Armetrian's confession on telling the enemy where to land. Gennet would have smiled had the coming situation not stolen it from his lips.

"But at the least, you have some help there with the enemy's stolen arms capabilities," said another legate, gesturing toward CP's two physicists at their monitoring station farther up the hill. Yos and Brona looked over at the mention, nodded to the hovering row of top silver, and returned to their work.

"The particle detection system has already proven effective. We cannot thank them enough!" Gennet lauded in their direction. "Our mining hit marks without fail, but once the drones exited TS and rerouted power to their targeting systems, the enemy had only seconds of particle fire before their rigged cannons were disabled." *And some of their pilots pulled into a permanent alternate universe holiday, if I understand Brona correctly. Tsk-tsk!* "Conventional fighters were sitting prey," he continued, "but a lot of it—too much for our equipment to get to."

"Well, you'll be pleased to know that we've finally received word from our Northern ally," interjected a woman from the legatine side of the conference. "Lena has promised to commit a task force. They'll arrive late, but we're thankful for their support."

"If all goes well, I'll personally thank Lord Balaneth myself, ma'am," said Gennet, hiding his surprise at the news. Even while recovering from his injuries, the ambassador had insisted from his hospital bed on soliciting military aid. The attack on him had apparently fired him up. But Lena was potentially as much a target as Angolin, and no one had expected the extra help.

"Ma'am, is there any update on your end on the Realm's Cloak status?" Sajeva asked. "I'm worried about the report of power fluctuations over the last hour, and oddly, we have no status readings at all up here."

"The Cloak is fully operative as far as we can tell, Angolinian grids as well as the Bemini systems," was another legate's rather stiff response.

Gennet winced. The distance between the hilltop post and HC couldn't mask the lack of knowledge, genuine or otherwise, from the other side of the upright. From the corner of his eye, he saw Brona look up. "Those fluctuations indicate a potentially massive problem," he said intentionally loud enough for her to overhear. "The Carmogen still have no idea of Angolin proper's exact location. That'll give Second and Sixth more time to secure generator installations, but if even a single section of our defenses is lowered . . . well, any victory up here would be useless if we find ourselves chasing Carmogen forces to our population centers, Greathall being the nearest."

"That's not your primary concern," said one of the legates. "You two concentrate on your objective. We will work with PDP to monitor the Cloak situation. Kronespeed to you both. High Command out!"

The alarmed looks Gennet and Sajeva gave the vanishing upright were burned into their faces as they mounted the hill toward Yos and Brona.

"Do you two suspect what we suspect?" Gennet asked, his breath forming clouds in the cold morning dampness.

"If there's bollixing back at PDP, I'll deal with it," Brona said.

"How, exactly?" Yos asked.

"However I need to, that's all I can say. That's all I know." She grabbed his hand, squeezed it, and beckoned him back to their monitoring.

The admirals left them to their work. "Please tell me she isn't our only hope in this," Sajeva hissed out of the physicists' and the rest of the post's earshot. "This Ian Folc that she warned us about has been missing for days now. If he's involved in even the slightest sabo effort—"

"Yes, Caevon, I hear you," said Gennet. "I'm handling that situation as best as I can."

"If even part of the grid or, Krone forbid, the shield layer beneath is compromised . . ." Sajeva frowned. "The Centrum, the Condorcet communities, Mid Realm, the Westermeer, and Nieuw Holland—every corner of our interior will be at risk! The Carmis may be primitive, but they're far from stupid. They'll find any weak spot Dawn Fire creates and spread from it like—"

The world rumbled, faint at first, then louder. It came not from over the Abyss but from the south. The entire post looked upward. The sky flashed. A long line of Robo-Interceptor Assault Vessels and waves of Long-Gunners emerged from TimeSpace and headed for the plain below. The RIAV cannons faced the eastern sky with the troop-filled gunners ready to deliver their ranks directly behind. The joint Guard-Bemini force had arrived.

Gennet sniffed. He saw Yos and Brona stare in wonder at the armada. Their friends—his officers—were on one of those ships. He sucked in his gut, summoned as much courage as he could, and channeled his experience from the final Negaran battle.

"Admiral," he said, "let's engage the enemy before they get that chance."

CHAPTER 18

THE OSTERRAND

S ir, your CSD symptoms will undoubtedly return. Severalfold.
I'll deal with it.
And your combat anxieties at this moment—
I'm ignoring them. You should too.
—are made worse by your worries over your father and fiancé. I advise you to put them out of your mind for now and focus.
I am focused, Rem-E. Let me keep to it!
Of course, sir. Krone be with you.

◉

DHARMEN LEFT HIS JUMP SEAT, reached for a rail beneath the Long-Gunner's low ceiling. He looked out the broadside viewport. Time to see the stage! A long RIAV line formed the Guard front on the grassland below. The enemy massed opposite, about five klicks away by his estimate, until the FOB reported it to be just three. He breathed hard and fast, heartbeat exploding in his chest, and Rem-E nagging.

The Carmogen force looked archaic as ever from the air, with its rotary-bladed copters and wheeled ground assault vehicles. But it was enormous. Lines of armored tanks mounted with pulse cannons (which Dharmen hoped would soon be disabled) rolled slowly in front of the greatest sea of foot soldiers he had ever seen. Column upon column of conscripts were positioned in front of single lines of gray-skin elite officers: standard Carmogen battle formation and easily fifty times what they had brought to Negara. Dharmen clamped his mouth shut to stop gawking at the spectacle ready to swallow him and his unit.

A flash swept through the Long-Gunner and the ground came instantly close. The ship had just exited TimeSpace. Far behind the RIAVs, he saw a line of High-Neck Gunners disengage stealthtech also, their power now focused on weapons. With artillery batteries flanking their bases and arrayed on their massive, high heads, they held position, ready to support the ground force about to be dropped in the broad, empty space between. The yellow land raced upward. Dharmen felt the tension within and around him as the ship descended.

"All units ready!" The battalion commander's voice rattled into his gen-comm earplant.

"Touchdown in T-minus seventy seconds," came the copilot's prompt.

Rockets fired from the Carmogen line over the shielded RIAVs and directly at the Long-Gunners. Dharmen's ship was pelted. The shields held, but hands on rails didn't—camos were thrown to the floor.

"T-minus thirty-five seconds!"

Dharmen braced. His whole body tightened as he tried to keep balance, stifle his fear, and keep his unit from seeing it. They would be on the ground soon, intact or in a blazing fireball. *Keep it together, Tate,* he thought. Rumblings in his hands traveled up his arms. Rem-E countered with treatment. *Whatever you do, just keep it together!*

"T-minus twenty seconds . . . eighteen . . . sixteen . . ."

The Long-Gunners descended in tight formation. Once in position between defensive lines, the forward revetment shield cascaded upward in front of and high above the RIAV line in a broad, raking arc, leaving rotating grid sections open for their cannons. In nanoseconds, the RIAVs dropped their own energy-sapping defenses and began bombarding the enemy air offense.

It worked. Partially. Copters fell out of the sky, and tanks slowed their approach, but they continued fire, pounding the revetment.

With Rem-E's aid, Dharmen controlled his shakes. He made one last round of eye contact with his company leaders and their platoons before they would be thrown into hellfire.

"Twelve . . . ten, nine, eight, seven . . ." Bodies swaying to the retro landing cycle faced the broadside deployment hatches. "Six, five, four . . ." Dharmen spread his feet on the metal floor plating, ready to go. The ship came to a hovering halt. "Three, two, one!"

The great doors desynthed. Daylight streamed into the cabin above grasses waving in the Gunner's propulsor wake. Ramps lowered from the ship's top level. "Units move out! Move!" shouted the BC.

Camos leaped out of the hold and stormed forward in swarms. Dharmen followed, monitoring as his staff herded their recruits to position. They were in the forward line, right behind the RIAVs and the secondary revetment shielding the ranks of boots on the ground. The emptied Long-Gunners lifted off and sped above the energy barriers, firing particle volleys at the enemy.

Dharmen hoped they'd return if the fight went badly. *The last thing we need is to be stranded out here!*

The enemy didn't cease firing for a second, though they took a pummeling. The secondary revetment hovered well above troop forward position, but all units still had to run for the protection zone. Camos flitting in and out of TimeSpace hampered enemy targeting ability, but not completely. The ground groaned from mortar hits. High-powered bullets whizzed over Dharmen's head, courtesy of copter machine-gunning. He recalled the sensation from Negara the year before, recalled that even then, stealthtech and exoskeleton body armor provided little protection.

A shell dropped dead ahead. Turf sprayed his unit.

"Keep moving!" he bellowed. He knew some had been hit even before falling bodies, screams, and flying blood droplets confirmed it. He glanced to his left. Synth lensing revealed Dori and her unit keeping pace. Same on the right; most were in step despite the strafing.

Howls of pain rang out. Anger and CSD tackled Dharmen, but his MedComp would have to handle the casualties—he and all survivors had to get to the shield line ready to fight.

Another shell struck. The blast threw him onto his back. His whole body shook violently. His instinct was to call out to Rem-E, but he ignored it, wrenched himself off the ground, and got to his feet through the smoke engulfing him. Floating gunpowder evaded his synth lenses and burned his eyes. Biting back pain and anxiety, he helped Theus see the remainder of their people safely beneath the revetment. The other units joined, boots down and more appearing as PTS devices were switched to standby.

They had made it. Theus called for casualty reports. Platoon leaders took quick head counts and rattled numbers. Reports came from other UCs via gen-comm. Dori had lost twenty-four to Dharmen's nineteen. He was surprised there weren't more and surprised that stealthtech held firm. No Guard campaign had ever been this large, and the power tax on battlefield mains was enormous. Forty thousand PTS generators in addition to heavy equipment and particle weapons demands couldn't be supported indefinitely, even with independent power generation and external solar help.

The frontline units held position as more filed in behind them. All around Dharmen, yellow-gray featureless camos stood ready. Shells rained on the revetment overhead. It shimmered and, in places, nearly buckled before power could be routed to compromised grids. Some found marks fore and aft of the protected zone, but the enemy fire was solid ordnance. Dharmen saw no particle hits. Yos and Brona's system was working. He hoped it would continue to. The shields wouldn't have lasted this long against Dawn Fire's funneled weapons.

The heaving ground upset the least experienced boots. "Tuyens, Haas, B'hrykhone, van Guilder, your platoons are chattering," Theus barked. "Shut 'em up before I have to! Have 'em un-ass their comm channels and perform gear checks if they have nothing else going on! Vinc, I can hear you all the way up here. Quiet!"

Dharmen went to the front of the unit. He nodded to his XO, muted his comms, and paced the forward ranks. Earplant commands wouldn't cut this one. "You are the Guard of Angolin. This is your home you're fighting for!" he yelled, looking into as many eyes as possible. "Don't let Carmi just come in and walk all over it—whatever he throws at you, put your fear to action and fight!"

"Sir! Yes sir!" Most of that chorus came at him from other units, lifting above the ranks and singing in his earplants at once. The entire formation roared. Either comm mutes had malfunctioned, or his voice carried farther than intended. He looked over at Dori who had also assumed the front. She nodded approval . . . and shot a gaze ahead.

The forward revetment buckled. With power reserves severely weakened by shelling, it came down. The RIAVs continued bombardment—their own shields once again their only defense, with just the secondary revetment in place to cover the ground force.

Then every eye drew upward.

Angolin's heaviest particle beams blasted overhead toward the Carmogen lines. Dharmen looked back and saw the heads of the High-Necks firing. Light gunsloops exited TimeSpace in echelon formations below their fire. The fury of assault from the rear line, the sheer number of ships entering the fight—the enemy was getting a pasting, and what an incredible sight! The opposing shelling stopped completely.

Dharmen straightened himself, his quaking limbs controlled, stomach unknotted, and every part of his body ready to float in hopeful wonder. *If it keeps up like this, we might actually win this thing.* The BC's call to ready wrenched him back to reality. He and Theus moved unitside, readying pulse rifles as all barrels trained forward. He held his breath for an instant. Now or never.

The secondary revetment shimmered. Its hovering robo-generators moved, advancing the protection line. "Forward!" the BC yelled.

Dharmen inhaled, and with the entire front line, his unit advanced. The High-Necks fired without resistance. He considered that the enemy was pinned. Then he saw his error.

Legions of Carmogen infantry were counteradvancing. "No firing till I give the order. Conserve your energy!" he commanded his people. "We want them well in range."

The enemy resumed shelling and machine-gunning. The few tanks that hadn't been blasted rolled ahead of running foot soldiers. The revetment was hit hard. It would lose power soon under the fresh assault. Dharmen was worried, but he'd seen it happen before. He engaged PTS, but at fifty percent output at random interval cycling, and he ordered XO-and-unit to follow suit. The mains would need all the help they could get.

The generator drones signaled the revetment shield's (hopefully temporary) deactivation. It would be down in one minute. Guard fire blasted the enemy's tanks and forward lines. Dharmen saw whole squadrons cut down in place like second summer crops in the Westermeer's farms. But they were too many to completely neutralize, even for the High-Neck and RIAV concert. He tightened his grip on his rifle and made ready.

The revetment dropped, and the hovering drones flew away. "Go!" Theus and a host of XOs commanded.

The entire force raced forward. Theus shouted range prompts per Dharmen's order to give every shot from their people the best chance to hit targets.

"Remember what we said in transit," Dharmen yelled through the raking assault into his unit-comm. "Target the powder faces where possible! Their conscripts will be confused without their masters to command them!"

"Belay that!" yelled the BC. "Those aren't your orders, Lieutenant Commander. Bringing down the leaders might panic the rest. There are too many of them, we don't want them rushing us like they did on Negara."

Dharmen peered ahead to a mass of enemy uniforms and guns evading the RIAVs and coming straight for them. "Captain, they already are!"

The Angolinian rifles fired. Dharmen hit four gray-skins and then had to take out any who got too close. He heard other UCs and XOs give fire-at-will orders. *Maybe that'll clue the BC in on reality and shut his mouth,* Dharmen thought, but he and Theus had no need to do the same. Their people hit hard and fast—particle beam against Carmogen, bone-shattering bullet against Guardsman. Dharmen wondered why body armor had even less effect now than a year ago. But his instincts had proven correct. The loss of their masters and the limb-severing, flesh-melting particle carpet scattered whole conscript clusters, sending them retreating into their own ranks. Enraged overseers gunned them down midstride.

Dharmen scowled. *What a way to run a command!*

A conscript platoon closed in, maintaining formation and being led by a large, black-skinned soldier: a Kay Allendë apparently intent on taking up his fallen gray-skin's charge. Dharmen fired, but his rifle gave a fraction of its energy. He tried to recharge the power supply, but the transfer was slow—too slow. Either the mains were overburdened, or patch-in was being blocked.

Not good!

Dharmen's nearest people covered for him, took down packs of conscripts before being struck themselves. Camos fell around him— camos fully armored. Why was that providing no protection at all? And why wasn't his PTS operating as programmed? Even at half capacity, it should have provided *some* cover. But it hadn't activated. Neither had anyone else's—too coincidental for a general power loss.

A bullet tore through his armor and pierced his thigh. He lurched in pain. His armor had been thoroughly checked—nothing should have penetrated it this easily, and definitely not so small a shell. Either the enemy had upgraded their ammo, or Dawn Fire had provided them with countermeasures. Yos's antiparticler was active but only around vital organs. Rem-E would have to handle the wound in lieu of MedComp. Right now, the Kay Allendë was closing, and Dharmen had no rifle power.

No time to query his internal for equipment or combat gear diagnostics. He flung his gun on its sling over his shoulder, and his fear and pain along with it. Bullets bounced off his personal shield. It held, but its power was limited.

The Kay Allendë looked confused, angry. He charged, turning his rifle butt forward.

Dharmen reached over his shoulder and snatched out his sword. The other made ready to ram him in the head. Dharmen dodged and swung—his best ever. The Kay Allendë howled as his forearms flew from their trunks still clasping the rifle and dropping with a whoosh into the tall grass. Another fast arc passed the blade clean through the man's neck.

The armless, headless sight falling to the ground made other conscripts turn and flee. A lone gray-skin bellowed at them to no avail. He responded with shots to backs, then looked viciously at Dharmen and began firing. No effect, the personal shield continued to hold. The Carmogen's weapon clicked away evidence of spent ammunition. He holstered it, drew a long, curved knife.

Dharmen readied sword and footing, ignoring the burning sensation from his leg wound as best he could. The gray-skin came with a battle cry, raised his blade. Dharmen blocked it. The Carmogen was nearly as big and powerful as his last opponent, but his blade-handling skills were no match for an Ergyre's. Dharmen anticipated every move. He tripped the man, who stumbled but tried for another lunge. Dharmen's boot to his stomach knocked him onto his back. He dropped the knife, tried to recover it. Dharmen slammed his heel on the man's wrist and felt it snap. Then he thrust his sword clean through the other's thinly armored vest. And just in time.

During the scuffle, the antiparticler had powered down and entered Yos's preset power-regeneration mode. Dharmen swung his rifle around for another check. Still recharging. He looked up to a half dozen gray-skins leaving their conscripts and charging him, guns hot.

They went down. Dharmen wheeled. Theus and Leatra were flanking him, rifles forward and apparently amply powered.

"Good news, fuckers! We came to kill!" Theus yelled, staring ahead.

Dharmen smiled.

A line of smoke trails sailed deep into the enemy columns. Massive explosions rippled through the ground. The High-Necks were firing their missiles now: standard energy-conservation procedure. Overall power supply must have been dangerously low.

Definitely not good!

Dharmen checked his rifle. It was back to full power, but for how long? And had field weapons lost power to sabo in addition to the drain on the mains? He had no more time to ponder any of it. The troopline secondary revetment was back up—temporarily—and raised long enough to scoop up and push forward a long turf mound forming a low trench for the ground forces. The enemy fired from opposite the shield-strengthened line as they sought shelter behind their ruined tanks.

Dharmen thought about the Kay Allendë he had just cut down, about their reputation as a people before falling to the Carmogen. He had respected them in the last campaign and respected them now, but battle slave or no, the other had been on the wrong side. *Kill or be killed.* He thanked Krone for giving him strength, but wished he and the Kay Allendë had been allies rather than enemies.

One of these days . . .

The soldier beside him lurched and screamed. She'd been hit. He hastily examined her. Petty Officer Tuyens had been struck *from behind* with a fresh particle blast through the back of her armor. Dharmen swung body and rifle around and laid fire faster than he could process the situation. More fire hit the traitors from his right. All of them fell, easily twenty to thirty total. He looked around wild-eyed. No more semper knifing to be found, at least not for now. Just others who had been hit, fighting the enemy only to be cut down by their own people. He moved from one body to the next, ordering anyone seemingly loyal to attend to the living until medics could arrive. And then he saw her.

Meters away, Dori lay on her side, holding her back just behind her armpit. She looked up as he reached her. "Qi-VOS says it's bad. Is it?" Her breathing was labored. "On second thought, don't tell me."

Dharmen examined the hole, the width of several fingers. Not the worst he'd seen, but it bled badly. He retrieved a large medi-patch from one of his belt pouches and staunched the wound until her internal could take over. "Gods-damned traitors. Krone, just give me a shot for every one of 'em," he muttered as he worked.

Bemini camos rushed up and knelt beside them.

"I'll see to her, Lieutenant Commander," said Ilbron. "You get back on the line."

"She's my superior and my friend, Major. I'm not leaving her to—"

"MedComp's on the way. I'll look after her in the meantime. She'll survive," Ilbron insisted. "Now go!"

Dharmen glared fire.

"Lieutenant Commander, you . . . heard him," Dori garbled. "Don't worry about me. I'm still in this."

Dharmen ground his teeth. He scanned the field for more would-be shooters and returned to the revetment line. At the front, he threw more rounds at the enemy, anger diverted to his trigger finger before all attention went to the sky.

From the northeast, a dark line closed like a massive high flyer flock in coordinated ambush: heavy Carmogen fortress-bombers, a fresh assault wave. From over the Abyss, they opened fire, hitting the revetment not with shells but with particle beams! And no visible spatial distortions pulled them from the sky. Brona did say great distance was needed for the AU plan to affect only the enemy. Dharmen's heart sank. RIAVs and High-Necks fired furious salvos, but he knew the effort couldn't possibly be enough.

"All units retreat!" It wasn't the BC's but Admiral Gennet's order over gen-comm. "Regroup on the southern fjord line and take immediate cover!"

Faces equally perplexed met Dharmen. No one wanted to cut and run, but no one wanted to disobey orders or die in vain either. He ordered Theus to pull the unit back. Fierce particle volleys came from both sides of the fighting even as the Guard-Bemini retreated. But the barrage from the reinforced enemy line came in too hot and fast. The revetments flashed violently, then collapsed. With both energy fields gone, the ground force was defenseless beyond what localized shield and firepower was left to it.

In the rear, explosions rocked the ground as the High-Necks succumbed to particle fire one by one. And it wasn't the force of the hits upsetting the turf beneath Dharmen's boots. He understood that as he watched the massive beam-severed head of one High-Neck fall . . . and as small black objects dropped into the grass. Exploding!

Dharmen trembled, but tried to ignore it. "Keep moving!" he yelled at his people as open gunships landed in a line ahead of them.

"Don't look behind you. Concentrate on . . . getting to safety and . . . keeeeeppp . . ." His rifle fell from his hands. His body hit the ground next. He groaned, shaking from head to toe. The sounds of grenades amplified in his ears, drowning out all else. He couldn't shut the explosions out any more than he could control any part of his body. Tears ran down his cheeks.

"Lieutenant Commander! Dharmen!" Theus's voice was barely recognizable, sounding low and hollow as though it came from the end of a long tunnel. Dharmen shut his eyes, held his head.

"Sir!" came a voice much clearer.

What, Rem-E? What is it?

"This is your most severe episode yet. Standard treatment is useless, but I have another, if it can be called such. One not approved by Medical."

If that's so, then . . . how . . .

"Relax, Sir. Administering treatment now. Breathe deeply."

Rem-E, what's going on. I don't—

"Breathe!"

In a fog, Dharmen complied as best he could. A new sensation swept through him. It felt like hot, stinging beads of water pelting his skin all over, then working their way inward and through his entire body. The sensation cooled. He was able to flex his fingers. His whole hands next. Now his feet. He moved his arms and bent his knees.

"Lieutenant Commander, sound off," he heard Theus bellow, loud and clear now. "Tate, respond! . . . *Dharmen Nüren Enri—*"

He opened his eyes, took in Theus. "I'm all right, Thee. For now."

Theus helped him to his feet. Dharmen was unsteady at first, but he shook it away and stood firm, gave his XO a nod.

Rem-E, he thought to his internal, *we'll brief on this later. And thanks!*

With rifles aimed at the Carmogen pursuit, Dharmen and Theus finally herded everyone to the ships. Behind Ilbron helping Dori onto the nearest one, they were last to hop on before it shot into the air and sped southward, cannons firing. Through his own cold sweat and the stench of wounded bodies filling his nostrils, Dharmen put his face into his still lightly trembling hands. Thinking clearly again, the enemy reinforcements hadn't panicked him nearly as much as their firepower. He activated personal comm.

"Tate to Andren."

"Dharmen? I'm glad to hear your voice—"

"Yos, what's going on? What happened up there? Your system's—"

"Dharm, our AI link's been interrupted, and backup isn't responding," Brona cut in. "Yos is trying to reinstate it, but . . ."

Dharmen could hear panic in her voice.

"I don't know how it's happening," Yos said, "but we're getting strong interference from somewhere, and not from the enemy. Whatever or whoever's causing it is also targeting the Realm's Cloak. That's been going on since early this morning. Power reserves are fluctuating, causing grid sections to temporarily lift in spots. South C NewsMesh reports people taking shelter in pod cluster sublevels in case the whole thing comes down . . . Bron, where are you going? Brona!"

Dharmen grunted. He hoped she could get to PDP and stop the sabo in time. Countermeasures had apparently done all they could, it was up to her now . . .

A beam hit the gunship's shields. The vessel descended to dodge fire. Dharmen looked out the open hatch. Bodies, broken and lifeless, littered the plain, their combat wear advertising both Angolinian and Carmogen service. Body still tingling from Rem-E's *treatment*, Dharmen put his hand to his mouth. He had never been so tempted to let loose his emotions . . . and never so resolved to fight temptation. He forced himself to choose strength over fear. *The ancients faced the exact same odds and never gave up,* he recalled. *Falconer didn't cave. He was in it till the end. And so am I!*

BRONA COMMANDED THE DOOR OPEN and entered. She looked down the metal walkway toward the power relay hub. If anyone wanted to damage the Cloak without being discovered, this would be the place, so she bypassed her workstation and came here.

She looked around, confused. She didn't understand it. With the battle of a lifetime raging up north and the Cloak destabilizing, the central power nexus should have been awash in engineering teams.

There was no one.

Not a single person to be seen or heard anywhere: no one working, none of the troops Admiral Gennet sent to look after Cloak operations, just the hum of the generators lining the cavernous, multilevel bay. She moved forward, chilled. Never mind the unnatural emptiness, she knew at least one other person was here.

She patted her pocket, felt the gun she had lifted from CP. She had gathered bits of the admirals' conversations. Things were going wrong, and she hadn't intended to be caught defenseless on that hill. The uplords would have to overlook her pilfering just this once. And she would have to overlook her own fear. If only all of this could have been avoided! And if only the mainland Cloak was as advanced and tamper-proof as Bemin's. Dark matter manipulation was still too misunderstood a science to hack into so easily (especially for a certain do-nothing-but-latch-onto-other-people's-work teammate). But greater Angolin was far too expansive for DM retrofits.

She stopped, listened. Quiet had never been so frightening. She pushed on. *I'd never do this in any other situation!* She put that out of her mind. No other situation had ever been like this one. She analyzed conditions: there were a few hundred workstations in the nexus bay, but only three prime level ones from which the power transfer grid could be fully accessed. He had to be at one of them. Stomach roiling, she clapped a hand to her pocketed weapon.

With micromouse quiet, she climbed a flight of narrow stairs to the first workstation, located in an upper loft. Far down the walkway, carefully checking passages between generators along the way, she arrived.

Not a soul to be found.

She activated the station's upright, signed on, and began a query of power grid functions. Access denied. She had proper clearance; the credentials should have been recognized. She tried a higher-level sign-on, one she shouldn't have had but acquired during her time in the program.

Locked out still.

Far across the loft, she saw the next prime level workstation. It, too, was vacant, and why not? These two were in high, cheerfully bright locations that a conniving sneak like Ian wouldn't choose. No, only the station in the darkest corner of the nexus's lowermost level would suit him and his purposes. *I should have thought of it sooner,* is what reason scolded her with. *Right, then. No other choice.* Stretching the tension and fright from her body, Brona pointed herself toward her next destination and walked.

Not wanting to risk detection by using the lift, she headed instead for the stairwell that would take her down to the sublevels beneath the relays. She reached it, keeping eyes and ears open for signs of life and for localized timespatial distortions just in case: still nobody but her, TimeSpaced or not. She might have been more curious had she not been so afraid. She descended slowly and softly. The third workstation was eight flights down, and the stairs were wall-less and exposed. She wanted more speed but couldn't risk the noise and definitely couldn't risk being seen. Patience, like it or not, went into every step.

She reached the bottom, to PDP's dimly lit, low-ceilinged bowels, looked around. She was still alone, but she heard uprights beeping error messages in the distance . . . and angry mutterings joining them. She moved, rounded a corner, then another. The light level dimmed with every turn. The transfer junctions were coming up. She passed them and carefully eased her head around the bend.

Ian had his back to her. The error messages she heard indicated he was trying to cut power to cloaking grids, and having difficulty dodging the myriad of security protocols never meant to be bypassed at his clearance level. That along with another clever little hindrance. As his stubby fingers poked at uprights and failed to produce results, he cursed a storm that would have put even Dharmen to shame. He wasn't having it easy, but he had been at least partially successful, and it was only a matter of time before he found a way to get through. Brona felt light-headed and could hardly keep from trembling. But she understood this was exactly what she came here to stop. She overcame her fear, reached into her pocket . . .

Ian wheeled his seat around quickly.

"Y-you," he stuttered with plump, flushed cheeks. "Wh-what are you doing down here?"

"Putting an end to what *you're* doing down here. Could it be more obvious?" Brona was surprised at how matter-of-factly it left her lips. "Our soldiers are out there fighting for their lives while you've been here interfering with the Cloak." She noticed his appearance was more disheveled than usual. "And all day by the look of it."

"Woman, you don't know what you're talking about!"

"Don't I? Grid power levels have been spiking since early this morning, probably since you started on that ganaal egg and *cryortlbeef* sandwich." She flitted a glance to the plate of half-eaten hardening food beside him. "Cloak energy output doesn't fluctuate on its own. It would only do so if someone were here trying to sabotage it from the nexus. And just where do I happen to find you?"

"I should have known," Ian growled. "You and your new entourage lately. It's taking hours to bypass security protocols, but there's one other thing in my way, one microscopic cousin of the trillions of nanites within the Cloak. Took me till now to figure it out, the signal counterblocks are so intermittent and subtly precise as to nearly not notice. It's some damned Guardsman's—"

"Internal AI!" Brona silently thanked Rem-E for its outstanding work.

"And granted full access to restricted systems. You realize the program directorate will have your head on a synth plate for this."

Brona raised the gun. "*My* head? Yours will be far more sought after for trying to bring down our defenses and put millions of lives at risk. That plate won't hold two!"

Ian's bloodshot eyes fixated on her weapon. "Don't tell me you know how to use that."

"Press and let it do its thing. Simple. What's to know?" Brona tried to hide her fear. She had never even seen a gun before today.

"Tate would've blasted me to vapors by now. You're bluffing and you know it."

"Do I?"

"You're no soldier. You've never fired one of those in your life."

"For a traitor, I'll gladly change that!"

Ian shot out of his seat at her. Brona panicked but in a split-second transferred that panic to her finger and pressed the trigger.

Nothing.

Her eyes flickered. Ian moved no farther. She expected him to at any second, but he curiously looked to her side. Brona pressed the trigger again. And again.

"Put it down!"

The metal against her temple was colder than that in her hand. Her own weapon was snatched from her grip. She swiveled her head enough to see two men. The neatly pressed black and gray and the demeanors beneath were unmistakable, but they had the situation all wrong. And why weren't they dressed for combat?

"I . . . I don't understand."

"You don't need to," snapped the Guardsman holding the gun to her head. "You don't need to be handling a weapon you don't know how to use either. You forgot to release the safety."

"But he's the one you want, not me!" she said, looking toward Ian. "He's been here all day trying to bring down the Cloak while you people were . . . Oh, I seeee! You're not the admiral's men. You're here helping my colleague."

"Who we are is no business of yours, Dr. Devries."

"Oh, I beg to differ. *It is.* If the Cloak lifts, we're through, including you three. But you wouldn't see that if you expect to be under Carmogen safekeeping, would you?"

No one answered her.

"What's wrong with you people? Don't you realize that if the enemy succeeds, they'll kill us all or worse? You don't really think you'll become part of their empire without gray skin and Carmogen blood in your veins, do you?" She hoped they would listen, or at least that her stalling might buy her time to figure out an escape. But how? She was outnumbered, cornered, disarmed. *What do I do,* she searched, *try and tackle 'em?*

"No lectures. You're coming with us." The other Guardsman grabbed her arm.

"To where?"

"To wherever we can keep you out of our way."

Not without a fight. "But . . ." She began to struggle.

Ian backed away hunched-shouldered and sat cowering at the workstation. The first Guardsman grabbed her chin and wrenched her face to his. "This will go easier if you cooperate. Don't make us have to plug you right here."

"Wait." Ian spoke softly, almost grinned the word. "She can bring down the Cloak right this minute and with just a few commands."

The Guardsmen eyed him.

"That's right. She's working with Tate. His internal AI is keeping me from disabling the relays. She'll know how to access it and sever its link."

The man gripping Brona's face unhanded it and stared into her eyes. "Working with Tate, huh? What a surprise! And since he's not here to disable his internal . . ."

Both Guardsmen pulled her toward the workstation. She tried to break free, gave it all she could. She loosed a hand, went for one of their guns. They countered. Now she was pinned completely. A scream was next, but who would hear her—

She yelped at the blast, and felt the pair of hands restraining her go limp as its owner collapsed to the floor. The other Guardsman fired down the aisle. A return beam nearly struck him. Brona took the distraction. She broke free and threw herself to the floor. Ian jumped up and ran. She grabbed his leg, but ended up with a fleeting handful of trouser. His pudgy bulk had too much momentum on her. He rounded the transfer junction array and disappeared. The lone-standing collaborator fired a few more shots before turning and fleeing behind him.

Brona looked up and saw uniforms fan out toward Ian and his cohort. And more uniforms coming toward her. She stood, shaking. *Not more of them, pleeease,* she pleaded to Lothnë. But she recognized combat camos. And faces. They were from CP, but she hoped that even these weren't traitors.

One of them examined the downed man.

She shivered. "Is he . . .?"

"Dead? Of course. There's a war going on. Who has time right now to make prisoners of traitors? Are you all right, Doctor?"

"For the most part." Brona wanted to be relieved, but she was still too afraid to let down her guard.

"Glad to hear it. We've got to get you back to CP. Your particle weapons detection system is still down, and the admirals need your expertise."

"It'll have to come from here, Lieutenant," she replied. "My boyfr— my colleague Dr. Andren can handle it on that end once I stop the jamming. Then I have a power grid to stabilize."

She took Ian's seat and accessed his work to see where to begin undoing his tampering. She could sense the officer behind her didn't like the situation, but when she turned, he nodded crisply without another word. Heart pounding but glad for the chance to right things, she put her disgust aside, ignored the dead traitor on the floor, and got to work. She undid Ian's poorly cobbled blocking commands and while scanning the grid maintenance records, found the sabotage she had expected. And more she hadn't.

"Well, damn it to the Netherlords. Who'd have given him the credit?"

She sighed away the digression and commenced the process of rerouting power to cover the spikes across the cloaking grid. The encryptions suppressing battlefield mains and TimeSpace generation would have to come later.

Yos would have their detection system back up in minutes. She knew once the interference was lifted, he would notice and be on it. As for the two fleeing traitors, PDP was a maze of labs, bays, and generator stations, with entrances and passages making the place as porous as the kallam root she had suffered through in tea form lately. She wanted to have faith in the CPers' pursuit, but it was too likely that Ian and his accomplice would slip away.

PUT DOWN, REFORM THE FRONT in the south, and await the two Orders due to arrive within the quarter hour. That directive ate away at Dharmen's conscience. The rout and regroup wasn't it: with all opposition speeding away, the East Ranges dividing the Osterrand and the rest of Angolin were left undefended.

Incoming fire jolted the gunship, knocked everyone off balance. In-flight stealthtech was inoperative. The only option was to return fire and land every shot. The cannon crews did their best. Dharmen shook his head. It wasn't enough, even for a state-of-the-art vessel packed with guns. Another jolt and a fireball. He shrank at the heat invading the cabin. A gunship to starboard was engulfed in flames. With an ear-piercing explosion, it fell from sight. He didn't want to think of all the lives that went down with it.

Enemy fighters came aft, port, and starboard: winged and rotary-bladed vessels with Guard pulse cannons attached by rough welds. The stolen weapons hit the gunship from multiple angles and with little rebuttal. The shipman on the aft cannon hardly returned a single shot that found its mark.

Dharmen watched. The ship's overcomplicated controls were the problem, not the recruit's gunning skills. Why did engineers always insist on mucking up the simplest designs? "Krone, damn these machines! Lieutenant Tarkala, go assist him!"

"I can do better than that, sir!" Theus relieved the recruit and assumed the station. He found marks after manually realigning scanners and retargeting cannons, and with well-placed shots, began taking down hostiles.

Dharmen was pleased for a heartbeat. *We might just live long enough to make it south. But what's the use?* He bit his bottom lip at his next thought. "Commander, we have to turn this ship around."

Dori dismissed the medic tending to her. "You're not serious. For what reason?"

Faces turned from the firefight and stared at Dharmen. "To defend the Northeast from the enemy, the one we just left free to roam where they please," he said. "It's our only real hope."

"Hope for what? We have orders from CP. Admiral Gennet wants us on the south line strengthening our reinforcements."

"Who won't do any better with us there," Dharmen contended. "Third and Fourth have as much firepower as we did. The south'll be covered, but the Osterrand foothills are defenseless now, and there's no way two admirals, a tiny CP staff, and one crazy physicist can counter the enemy if they decide to head in that direction, which they will."

Dori opened her mouth but said nothing.

"Think about it, Commander. Marchwarden Pass starts right behind our last position. It's the lowest, easiest way to cross the mountains on foot. With no one to stop them, those Carmis we ran from back there will find that pass and use it."

Dori gasped, held her side. "The BC is dead, and the admirals—"

"Those are the Kraal's orders, Commander, not our admirals'! Gennet and Sajeva are too smart for this taroc shit strategy. And we should've been able to hold out much longer back there. After what just happened, how do we know we can even *trust* High Command?" He hissed his last few words, though it didn't matter. He had the whole cabin's undivided attention now. "A couple hundred extra boots won't help the south line much, but we might just stop the Carmis behind us from filing into that pass and breaking into the Realm. We can't leave Greathall and the whole Northeast unprotected. It's a risk, but so was this whole thing to begin with. Damn it, Commander, we have to try!"

Dori's face hardened. She had never disobeyed an order, Dharmen understood that. But they had also never fought for Angolin's survival so close to its people. If there was ever a time to go rogue . . . She looked away from all the demanding eyes, activated her comm.

"Pilot, hard about and head back to the foothills. Take position four klicks north-northwest of CP."

Dharmen ignored the shoulder pats and hoots of support coming at him as she contacted CP to advise of their status.

And their trip back through the valleys tucked within the eastern folds came with a disheartening reply from Admiral Gennet—not a rebuke for disobeying orders but grim information: to Dharmen's intuition, the enemy had moved eastward the minute the gunships sped off. They had located the pass and begun to enter. With no ability to challenge hundreds, perhaps thousands of enemy conscripts, CP had relocated southward and cloaked its position.

"Keep us informed as we will you. Gennet out," said the admiral just before the channel was abruptly severed.

Dharmen made his way through swaying bodies to the aft cannon station. They were heading north with low shield strength and no light- or time-altering cover, completely in view and with the enemy now fore and aft. Forward and broadside cannoneers shot a path clean through the hostiles, while Theus kept busy throwing fire in the ship's rear. Dharmen stopped bothering to count how many enemy craft he took out. He peered downward through the open hatch. The rolling grasslands gave way to low hills dotted with bright-orange billowing trees. They were nearing Marchwarden Pass. He sighed. Shame that second autumn had to be met with this . . .

The blast threw everyone to the floor and nearly through the hatches. Dharmen got up and looked around. The gunship's port ventral section was a mass of up-twisted floor plating around a hole blasted clean through the hull. Bloodied, motionless camos surrounded the wreckage. Another shot jolted the vessel. The whir of the engines died; they must have been hit. Dharmen held tight as the ship lost altitude.

"All hands brace for impact!" the pilot ordered. As the treetops came threateningly close, Dori forewent her comm, stood in the center of the cabin, and yelled her orders: to the pilot to get them as close to the pass as she could safely manage, and to Theus and the other cannoneers to keep firing.

IT WAS A ROUGH LANDING, but everyone who had survived the initial blast was safe. Dharmen and Dori commended the pilot on her skill, and then formed the survivors into a company and ordered them to extract the wounded and all salvageable equipment possible. The dead would have to be left behind. Dharmen queried Rem-E for geolocation. No reading. Jammed, offline—Rem-E couldn't determine. Had the suns not shone in the late afternoon sky, Dharmen wouldn't even have been able to determine direction. His XO's internal had no luck either.

"Thee, if we can't determine field position, then we're in trouble. I have no idea where the pass is from here."

"We're not done yet, sir," said an approaching voice. "We're nearly at the pass, actually."

"Beg your pardon, Shipman?" Dharmen said. "You and your brother were raised way beyond the other side of the Great Lake. You familiar with this part of Angolin?"

Leatra rubbed a gash across her forehead. "My family used to hike these mountains all the time. I can navigate them in my sleep." She nodded to a grove of trees half a klick upslope. "We head past those and hang right. About seven klicks along the way, there's a stream. It leads up to where we want to be: a way into Marchwarden Pass near the stream's source."

Dharmen regarded her wide-eyed. Did she know of a particular feature of the pass that he read about in Captain Falconer's written accounts, one that would give them an incredible advantage?

"We can be on the pass in under an hour, though we'll need to get some shield strength going." Leatra looked back to the disabled gunship. "Hopefully, the portable generators are operable. The trees down here aren't dangerous, but they extend limbs far and fast. Irz nearly lost an eye to one once."

"It's not the trees down here that worry me, Shipman," Dori said as she came up beside them. "Even if we reach the pass, we won't last long once we're on it."

"Commander, respectfully, we can't stay here either," said Dharmen. "The enemy knows where we went down. They'll come looking for us—the ones already entering the pass or the ones behind us, either way. You know the Carmis don't like to leave loose ends. We have weapons but no PTS capability, and who knows what'll go next? We won't have a Netherworld's chance if we don't get moving now."

"Lieutenant Commander, I'm well aware of—"

A gunsloop appeared overhead and landed. Much smaller than the one they had crashed in, it only had space for a pilot, copilot, and a dozen or so extra hands. It couldn't provide transit for everyone, but it would just do as a medevac.

Dori ordered the most severely wounded to be placed aboard. She took Dharmen and Theus aside as Leatra and the others saw to it. "This isn't the worst plan in Guard history, but we don't stand a chance on that pass! Look at the shape we're in. If the enemy doesn't take us out, the trees up there will. Even with shielding, we'll be up against branches *and* guns."

Dharmen watched the groaning, swaying trees in the grove. "Neither will be a problem, Commander, because we'll get in way ahead of both."

Dori met that with a bewildered look. "How, exactly?"

"By using something the ancients knew of, but the enemy hopefully won't find. And if we move soon, we'll reach the other side of the mountains before they do."

Dori's eyebrows lifted. She apparently knew of what he meant.

Theus apparently didn't. "But I thought we were going to locate the enemy before they got too far and *defend* the pass. We can't walk its whole length, that's impossible! We're a sizeable group. Borbol troops might not attack a couple hundred armed people if we're lucky, but the trees up there are much stronger and heavier than these twigs down here. Saaryl pines can rip a man in two. Even the undamaged generators won't yield enough shield power to get us through them and still have enough if we reach the other side."

"Then we'll have to move fast and deal with the shield strength problem later," Dharmen said. He patted his leg and flexed it a bit. No pain. Rem-E's temporary medical treatments appeared to be working. His hands weren't shaking either.

"So that's your plan," Theus said, nodding understanding. "The enemy has no protection beyond bullets and maybe a few pulse rifles. You're hoping the trees and snow beasts—"

"Will weaken them, and then we'll handle what's left on the other side. And we'll move with shields only, Thee. No firing. We want every animal and tree we find, especially the biggest and strongest, completely intact and nicely roused."

Theus and Dori exchanged looks, but Dharmen could see they were with him on this. Dori informed the company of what, due to circumstances, it had no other choice but to do. Everyone was exhausted. Those not badly injured and haggard were just haggard, but Dharmen could feel their determination to go on and fight. And he felt for the first time ever that everyone was with him one hundred percent.

"Finish securing the wounded for dust-off," he ordered. "The rest of you ready the shield generators, the working portable cannons, and every hand weapon at your disposal."

Rior descended behind the highest peaks with Lothnë quickly following. The company made ready to depart under lengthening shadows. Dharmen ordered Leatra to his side to utilize her mountaineering skills. He looked to the faces behind him as he and the shipman headed the group, with Theus, Dori, and remaining UCs interspersed throughout. Will, his father, Yos, and Brona flashed through his mind. He wondered how they were faring, but he shoved that fear aside and concentrated on *everyone*—in this small band and at home well inland—who relied on this effort.

There was no time for a long pep talk with the enemy in front of and behind them, but there *was* time for honor. "Let's move out, people," Dharmen commanded. "We have a long trek ahead of us."

CHAPTER 19

MARCHWARDEN PASS

"Your user's condition has stabilized, Qi-VOS. Inform me if you require further assistance with her recuperation."

"Affirmative, Nijs, but it should not be necessary. Commander Secár is exhibiting great endurance, given the situation."

"Yes, though not as much as Rem-E's user. If I were human, I would be tempted to envy."

❂

DHARMEN WATCHED DAWN BREAK COOL and dim through thin clouds over the western issue from the mountains. The pass widened here but remained hemmed by low cliffs and overhangs clad in near-motionless trees. The company had traveled all night on a path that had been reasonably broad and flat in some places and narrowed to steep defiles in others. The saaryls higher up were stout and strong. Every step came with branches slamming the mobile shields so hard that Dharmen worried energy reserves would fail halfway through.

They didn't, though the mountain forest's attack had been unrelenting. And noisy. Mobile sensors and internals curiously indicated no other troop movements, Carmogen, or CP staff. But the enemy had to be right behind, and if nothing else, the boughs thrashing from one end of the pass to the other must have given the company away.

With Leatra's guidance, they did find their single saving grace. Even the ancients had no explanation for it: a spatial anomaly three kilometers below the summit line that with one step, led directly to the opposite side of the range. Angolin's very first soldiers had used this portal to avoid the snowy heights and all their living dangers: the *real* Marchwarden Pass that Dharmen counted on the enemy to miss in favor of a deadly combo of angry trees and frostbite. He thanked the gods for that advantage. But before and after the hidden doorways, the company had stirred the rooted mountain community, and the Carmogen remnant was following regardless. No need for sensors to indicate that. Good bait to draw the enemy in and finish them off, or bad bait that would lead them right to the Hidden Realm's doorstep—Dharmen couldn't be sure. He hoped to Krone and to every deity in the universe that he had made the right choice.

Communications followed sensors now. No dispatch could be exchanged with the reserves in the South. Nothing stood between the Carmogen and the entrance to the Realm's oldest marches but this one company. Dharmen knew Angolin's fate stood on the edge of a blade thinner than his own sword's . . . As they rounded a jagged set of low tors, he stopped, heartbeat pounding into his throat at the sight.

Not of the high valley of Vinalhaven that the ancients called Shadowvale, or its river cleaving through leafless woodlands blanketed in hoar frost, but of the Alkmaar Range beyond its opposite bank. Within its tree-covered profile, the Great Hall's nemurite-tipped dome shone brightly beneath the rising Lord and Lady of Light. And the enemy could see it just as easily.

Dori came to the front. "What is it?"

Finger shaking, Dharmen pointed. Dori stared at the iconic struc-ture in the distance. "Krone help us."

Dharmen went back through the company, checking sensors along the way. Still nothing. PTS next. Zero power—how unsurprising! "I get no readings on the pass behind us or anywhere else," he said when he found Theus. "I'm walking blind here. You?"

Theus queried Nijs, then furrowed his brows down to the tops of his eyelids. "Status unchanged."

Dharmen forced himself not to panic. "Then we'll need better cover quickly. This spot's too narrow and exposed for a solid defense," he said to everyone around them.

"There's no real indication that our sensors are inoperative. They just haven't picked up any other movements—Angolinian or otherwise—since 0100," Theus reasoned. "Your plan most likely worked and so did the anomaly. Carmi's probably up the pass in pieces, becoming saaryl and borbol pickings."

Dharmen regarded him unblinking. "You sure 'bout that?"

Bullets whizzed over their heads, hitting the cliffsides. Negligible energy strength made the company's shields as ineffective as Dharmen's now-dead antiparticler. The small shells ricocheted right through them.

"Take cover!" Dori yelled.

Dharmen and Theus scrambled behind a low rock. The others found what shelter they could, mostly with no option beyond throwing their backs to the cliff faces, with little ability to return fire. Dharmen looked up the pass. It and the heights on either side crawled with Carmogen conscripts, several hundred by his estimate.

"Maybe we can get one last bit of shield power from the portable generators," Theus said.

"Not possible, Lieutenant. Who has time to fiddle with spent generators through all this?" Dharmen swung his rifle around and fired at a group moving on the rocks above.

Screams preceded suddenly disappearing heads—he had hit at least a few of them. But he wondered what shape they were in. The saaryls must have had some effect, but if so, how had this many of them gotten so far so quickly? It was unlikely that they had found the anomaly. Its apertures were invisible to the naked eye and one had to either know exactly where they were, or locate them with finely tuned, advanced sensors that the enemy didn't have. So had they really been so determined to get over the mountains and into Angolin that they pushed on that much harder?

Stony shards pelted Dharmen and Theus from bullets grazing their rock cover. Dharmen's whole body shook. Rem-E intervened. "W-what do you think of my plan now, Thee?"

Theus said nothing through the shots gluing them to their spot.

Dharmen looked around, found Dori in the same situation with Leatra and others behind another large stone. "This won't do at all, Commander. We can't stay pinned here and let them just pick us off! We've got to move farther down and find a wider spot, or—" *No. It's too risky!*

Gunfire clipped Dori's reply. She and her group returned fire as best they could, given the constraints of their dangerously low perch.

Dharmen eyed Leatra. Between salvos, she shook her head negatively. "Sir, there's nothing below us but skinny trees and more rocks—not the cover you're looking for!"

A cloud of bullets had everyone crouched and unable to get off a single return shot. In a lull, Leatra raised her rifle and fired over the hostiles' heads, striking a large, loose stone in a cliffside cleft above them. Yells followed its fall. And they were quickly silenced—an excellent hit.

Dharmen peered at Theus, eyes glinting. *It is risky, but what's the alternative?* "If we can't go down . . . then the only way is up."

Theus sniffed. "Why did I know this was coming?"

Dharmen swiveled his head back to the women. "Cover us!"

"Aye!" Leatra responded.

"Tate and Tarkala! Don't you two even think of . . . damn!" Dori looked over to Ilbron and a group pressed against the rock face. "Get ready to lay covering fire! All of you!"

Dharmen found his target: an outcrop on the opposite side of the pass just low enough to reach if done quickly. "Ready, Lieutenant?"

"When you are."

"Then let's do it." Between bullet rounds, Dharmen signaled. "Now!"

They dashed. Leatra, Dori, and the others hurled particle fire up the pass and across the overhangs. Dharmen and Theus bounded the outcrop and ran upslope, hitting everything possible. Hostiles fell before they could get off a single bullet.

As Theus cut down every target on the left, Dharmen noticed Guard camos to his right firing across the pass from the opposite side. He made it a three-pronged offensive, mowing down all forward opposition. They reached what had been the core of the enemy's right flank and took cover behind tree trunks. Bullets flew across the pass at them, but on this side, all opposition lay dead. They had done it.

Dharmen examined the motionless carnage around him. Aside from fresh particle lacerations, every body was bruised and bandaged. Bloodstained rags replaced missing limbs and covered likely empty eye sockets. What a meal the trees and snow beasts must have made of the body parts and from all the conscripts who never made it down. *Not wise to roam the East Ranges unwary,* Dharmen thought. But what drove them on so? Or *who* drove them on?

"Good job, Shipman," he said to the young woman sheltering at the next tree. "But I thought I told you to cover us?"

"I did, sir, every step of the way," said Leatra. "But you needed more than two rifles to take this lot out." She looked around her. "Even if the upper forest did start the job for us."

The bullet fire began to move down the opposite side. Particle beams answered—coming fast upslope were Dori, Ilbron, and two platoons of camos, half visible through taroc fiber fear response.

"Now who has the upper hand?" Leatra reached into a belt pouch and retrieved a bipulse grenade. She moved around the tree and threw it across the low chasm. As it left her hand, a bullet struck her in the chest. She stumbled backward.

Double shockwave explosions rocked the opposite cliff. Melon-size boulders showered the pass below, along with limp bodies of conscripts. A short, surprised pause led to a bullet spray. Theus yelled as one struck him in the face.

"Krone be with me!" Dharmen gritted his teeth. He wanted to assist, but Leatra's chest wound was more serious. He managed to reach her position without getting hit. He took out a medi-patch, but before he could activate its nanoprobes, Leatra deactivated her armor at the entry point, reached in and pulled the shell out of her chest with her bare fingers. She groaned through her teeth as it popped out. Dharmen ordered her to hold still. He wanted to affix the treatment before her wound poured blood.

"Shipman, that was dangerous. Suppose your lung collapses now?"

Eyes tightened to wrinkled slits were her answer.

Gingerly, Dharmen removed his hand from the patch. He watched it pulsate and begin its repair sequence, glad that no blood ran from beneath it for the moment. "Looks like they've upgraded their ammo to match our armor. Hopefully, this'll hold, but if you have any trouble inhaling for even a few seconds, you let me know immediately. And don't try another stunt like that!"

Determined to be quick and not give the enemy an easy three-for-three, he moved to Theus, who had already patched his own wound. The bullet had grazed his cheek, but deeply. "You good?"

"Affirmative." Theus's eyes said that he was in pain but still in the fight.

"Great, 'cause before we can find you two a proper medic, we're going over there to help our people. We can't do any more from here."

"Sir?" Leatra questioned, shaking and with camo fibers slightly dimming her in response. "We can't get over there like this."

"This is still a battlefield, Vinc. Keep it together and don't lose your head."

"I'm trying, sir. I just don't want to get more shot up!"

"Would you rather see everyone die over there? And after that, watch the Carmis walk on through to Greathall? Our duty is to defend Angolin, to the very last if that's what it takes."

"This is as good a vantage as any, Lieutenant Commander," Theus said, "and the rest of the company's closing in—" He instinctively ducked as bullets hit the tree just centimeters from his head.

"With no guarantee they'll succeed," Dharmen said. "And when was the last time either of your internals had comm ability? No one can report, so we don't know the hostiles count over there. If they break through, we'll be fighting them over here again anyway. Alone!"

Theus and Leatra eyed each other.

"You two'll be staring at powder faces soon if we don't get moving. That's an order!"

Theus gave Leatra's chest wound an uneasy look. "You up for it, Shipman?"

She hesitated but nodded affirmatively.

"Then you heard the man, let's move out!"

The trio scrambled up the slope, firing. They came just above a section of the pass so narrow that the company had moved single file through it earlier. Dharmen took a running jump. Then Leatra, who stumbled on landing but stood without need of help. Theus followed.

They moved cautiously downslope. Within about twenty meters' sight of the enemy, they took what cover was available. Leatra pulled out two more bipulses and handed one to each of her superiors. Her wound wouldn't allow a decent throw. Theus activated his and lobbed it at a platoon, right toward its gray overseer. Dharmen sighted another gray-skin, cooked off his grenade to match the other's timing, hurled, and dropped prone. The explosion sets blew both captains to pieces along with most of their men.

The three Angolinians rushed the survivors, firing fiercely. They bolted and scattered, with some slipping past the trio's particle fire. Dharmen body-slammed one, then blew an abdomen-splitting blast into him. The three continued the downward advance, with the rest of the company hitting the enemy from the opposite end. Dharmen caught sight of a tall gray-skin, fired. And missed. He caught a glimpse of the face . . .

And almost didn't believe his eyes.

He had wondered if the empire would send the same commander against Angolin again. The choice didn't surprise him. Neither did the haggard conscripts' speed over the mountains now, despite every obstacle. *Makes sense*, he thought. *They're the work-taroc, here's their whip!* The gray man disappeared into a grove of static bushes. Dharmen recalled that every Carmogen force, no matter how large, had but one Lescain in command. This one had escaped the Guard once.

"Not this time, Carmi. Not this time!"

He followed, located his target for an instant through the brush. He fired, missed again. The rustle of branches faded as the other moved farther in. Beyond a few tossed stones with stunted trees growing among them, Dharmen came to the head of a wide clearing.

In its center, the other stood waiting.

Dharmen left cover, rifle trained. The man he hadn't seen in a year was still nauseatingly recognizable. Naul stood still, resting his pistol's long barrel over his shoulder. Boots scrambled up behind Dharmen. His peripheral vision caught Guard camos with Theus leading.

Dharmen kept sight on his target, who studied him and smiled.

"A rifle, Angoliner? Your weapons have already killed thousands of my men. I want something more honorable and true to my own bearing here. We will not settle this with guns." Naul dropped his pistol to the ground and kicked it away.

Dharmen held eyes on him, weapon still ready. "This is my fight, Thee," he said to his side. "But stay sharp, just in case."

The gray man stepped forward, hands outstretched. "Lieutenant Dharmen Tate, or Lieutenant Commander, I believe it is now. Congratulations to you."

"Been keeping up with my career, Naul? Since when are you in the business of following Guardsmen's lives?"

"I am a Carmogen soldier through and through. My enemy *is* my business!"

"And somehow, when all those heavy bombers went down over the Abyss, yours was conveniently not one of them. Why isn't that surprising?"

Dharmen's meaning was clear: protectively tucking the Lescain's vessel in the formation's rear just before battle was standard imperial practice. But only another gray-skin elite would dare mention such. It was execution-demanding slander coming from anyone else.

"You, of all people, understand reality, Lieutenant Commander. Life does not work so simply. It never has."

"Not for the rest of us, with you people turning this planet inside out for all you can get."

"You sound like the rest of your kind, Angoliner." Naul drew a curved scimitar. The script of the imperial warrior caste etched into it glinted.

Dharmen handed Theus his rifle.

"But true warriors do not talk idly, so stop wagging your immoral, man-loving tongue and fight like one!" Naul's dark smile degenerated to a snarl. He rushed forward.

Dharmen held his ground. Naul yelled, raised his blade. Dharmen threw his hand over his right shoulder, snatched his sword up and out. Sparks flew between the blades as they met. Naul's eyes bucked at the instantaneous block, but he wasted no time.

The blades locked again and again. The pair briefly drew apart. Naul was incredibly strong and half a meter taller. Dharmen was winded but only for a few heartbeats—an Ergyre knew the art of pacing a duel. He glanced around. Handfuls of conscripts came up on one side. Theus and lines of camos countered opposite, guns aimed from both camps.

"Stand down!" Naul bellowed at his men. "This is an exercise in courage. You will watch and learn, not shoot. If even one bullet is fired, its owner will answer to me personally!" He held black-flecked yellow eyes on his opponent.

That didn't intimidate Dharmen on Negara, and it didn't now. It didn't impress the conscripts either. Even from a distance Dharmen sensed their fear. With their overseers dead and their supreme leader in unexpected hand-to-hand combat, they were ready to cut and run. Naul was doing his boastful best to compensate.

Dharmen took the advantage. He rotated his long, straight blade skillfully in one hand, let its tip drop to within centimeters of Naul's face. "It's just you and me then."

Enraged, Naul skirted Dharmen's blade and lunged, stopping short for a feint before making a second true thrust. It failed. Dharmen anticipated the first and blocked the second. Clashing metal echoed on the surrounding stones. Naul closed. Dharmen thwarted what could have been a fatal slice through his chest, but Naul landed an elbow hard to his side in the pass.

Dharmen grunted. He didn't know which of his injuries were complaining: the ones from the battlefield and the gunship crash, or the still-healing ones from that night beneath Mount Condorcet. Or the ones in his mind transferring now to his hands. They began to tremble.

"You make this too easy, Tate. I could not ask for a greater insult! I had high expectations of your abilities. They have not been exceeded. Some famed sword handler—I should have known a warrior's match would be too much for a homosexual!" Naul looked around to his own men. "Someone find me a real opponent if this woman of one cannot stand up to a fight—"

Infuriated, Dharmen roared and lunged.

Naul tried to block, but the bitter animus was too much. The force nearly knocked the scimitar from his hand. He had unwittingly struck a deep, deadly nerve. The last man to insult Dharmen this way was painfully silenced, and he was always ready to put down the next. In another quick-fire move, Dharmen thrust his blade directly at Naul's head, ready to cleave it in two.

Naul backed away but not fast enough. The Ergive blade pierced his left eye with force enough to shatter the skull bone behind. He howled. A rifle clicked from the Carmogen side. "I said stand down!" He could barely fight off Dharmen's rage-driven thrusts. He blocked each one but only just and with strength fading.

Dharmen had never fought this hard in his life. He thrust, parried, and repeated the sequence faster and more times than he could keep track of. But he was tiring. The anger that had aided him began to consume him now. Along with quaking limbs.

No, not again. Not now! Dharmen glanced to his sword hand as it shook.

"Sir . . ." started his internal's prompt for another treatment.

Do what you have to, Rem-E, Dharmen commanded, *but I'm not out of this yet . . .*

Knees buckling, he stumbled and fell. Naul landed a hard thrust downward. Dharmen rolled. The curved blade pierced his lower side, just shy of his armor. He screamed in pain, but he threw his weapon upward and, forcing himself to get to his feet, wrenched Naul's blade from his hand. With one last burst of strength, he rammed his blade into his opponent.

Naul shuddered, screeched a stunted yelp as Dharmen yanked his sword out of his torso with an innards-slicing twist of his wrist. Dharmen backed away, hyperventilating as Naul fell to the ground. Sweat poured down his face through the green blood splattered on him from his victim.

"You couldn't . . . be satisfied with your own homeland. You had to come and . . . try for mine," he heaved across short, burning gasps at Naul. He saw rifles train on him from the conscript line and Theus and company readying. His head felt light. CSD was hardly the problem now—blood spilled from his wound. "You and your empire might win this fight . . . or you might not, but you . . . won't take Angolin without getting through me first. That's a promise from me to you, Carmi!"

"Save that for your own gods, Angoliner. I am here through trial put to me by the only ruler in heaven to claim my own," Naul gurgled through dark fluid spilling from his mouth. "These mountains . . . and that settlement over there. That will make a fine first cantonment for my army." He weakly pointed toward the Great Hall's dome in the distance. "Everything here belongs to Carmogen. It belongs to me!"

Naul tried to stand but fell to his knees. He looked up at Dharmen and spat blood at him. It landed short, with a dull splat across the Guardsman's boots. Dharmen lifted his leg and kicked the green plasma into Naul's glaring face. The brush rustled behind him. He turned, saw conscripts fleeing, though not all of them. Out of the corner of his eye, he caught sight of Naul grabbing the pistol he had tossed aside, but not in time to react—

"Look out!" Theus yelled and aimed.

Another beam hit Naul first. He fell limply into the grass.

Dharmen looked over, saw Leatra with rifle raised. Barrels from the enemy lifted. The Guard line fired. Dharmen thrust his bloodied sword into his belt and scrambled to join Theus, reclaiming his own rifle as they took hasty cover. Replacing his spent power cell with his last, he aimed for the enemy and let his trigger finger race. Fierce return fire pinned him and Theus down. He used the time to rip away his pant leg cuff and stuff it into the tear in his camos to stem the blood flow. Grinding his teeth through the pain, he made ready to leave his shelter for a particle run at the other side . . .

Great beams came from the sky. Blasts hit the center of the enemy position. Dharmen threw himself to the ground beneath flying, rocky debris. He looked up. A vessel appeared, exiting TimeSpace. Its underbelly bore the blazing red and blue of the Angolin Guard Jack, casting away fears of a particle cannon-rigged Carmogen copter as it landed.

Camos stormed out with their commanders right behind. Dharmen was amazed at the leaders: Admirals Gennet and Sajeva jumped to the ground, armed and ready, ordering the reinforcements toward the enemy remnant. He and Theus left cover. Gennet eyed Theus's patch, then Dharmen and his bloody hand holding his side. "Medics! Over here, now!"

Welcomed assistance and just in time. Dharmen had forced himself to stay standing through light-headedness, hoping he wouldn't collapse charging the enemy.

"Dharmen! Thee!" yelled a strangely skittish, excited recruit alighting the emptied ship.

"Yos? Is that you?" Dharmen said to the tall, thin man in ill-fitting camos.

"And suited up no less," Theus said. "When did you become a soldier, *soldier*?"

"They're for my protection. Your admiral's insistence," Yos returned. "He said the taroc fiber would give me some cover if I got separated."

Dharmen couldn't help but chuckle. "We're making a real man of you! But where's Brona? Please tell me she's back at PDP, and safe."

"She's still there, saving our skins at that end."

"If that traitor, Folc—"

"Don't worry. She's fine." Yos scanned Dharmen up and down. His peaceful smile evaporated.

Dharmen felt his unshaven face, eyed the green blood on his mud-blackened fingers. He grinned ruefully. "Never seen a soldier fresh from battle, huh? Not used to *this* Dharmen—don't I dirty up nice?"

Yos's lips quivered. "Dharm, if I've ever once questioned your . . . I'm sorry."

Dharmen lifted eyebrows at that.

"Why, Lieutenant Commander, I do believe you've been busy. And recently," Gennet said matter-of-factly of the soiled, naked blade hanging at Dharmen's side.

"As have you, sir, no doubt," Dharmen returned.

"How many did you take down, Mister?"

"Only three."

"Well, that makes four who've taken an Ergyre's blade in battle. That hasn't happened on this soil in nearly a millennium." Gennet looked to Leatra. She reddened. Unlike her superiors, she had taken the earlier recommendation and dutifully left her sword behind. "I only got one." Gennet reached over his shoulder and produced his weapon. The blade was notched. "Mine had a helmet. Midrate conscript—Trogen miner, by the look of him. Wore a light on the front of his head. Typical of the Carmogen to make men fight without proper combat gear, not that it would have helped."

Dharmen read despair in the admiral's voice. He understood. Gennet's pride was in defending Angolin, not in killing a man who had been more a slave to the enemy than the enemy itself.

"But suffice it to say, he no longer has it," Gennet continued. "Cleaved in two. And the helmet, well . . ."

"Sir, I won't brag, but mine . . ." Dharmen pushed the medics aside and darted to the area of trampled, bloody grass where his opponent had fallen. "Naul! Where is he?"

"If you mean the gray-skin who was lying there," answered Admiral Sajeva, "I saw him run when we touched down. Our people are after him."

Dharmen stared at her. "Ma'am, I ran him clean through! And Shipman Vinc shot him point-blank, there's no way he could have—"

"Never underestimate a Carmogen, Tate, not even a crippled one," Gennet said. "And definitely not one who's murdered his way up through the Lescainate like Naul has."

"But we can't let him escape, we've got to find him!"

"We will," said Gennet. "And if he's twice done in as you say, he won't get far."

The grass rustled behind the admirals. Dharmen did a double take at the white-haired man coming up beside them. "Father?"

Nüren's stony face smiled. He gave his son as brisk a hug as he dared through his injuries. Then he put his finger to his own lips to silence Dharmen's questioning as he activated his comm. "Will, I'm here and so is he! Alive and standing right in front of me looking like

Krone himself just appeared. Tell your cousin. I'll get him home as soon as I can. I promise!"

Dharmen stood stunned. Glad but astounded. "Father, you're a civilian now. What on Tentim are you doing up here?"

Nüren glanced to the admirals. To raised eyebrows and shaking heads. "I'm an old general, son, what did you expect? We just came through the biggest battle in Angolinian history, and my boy helped win it. I couldn't just sit at home through it all."

Dharmen eyed Theus, Leatra, Yos, the admirals. "Win it?"

"For the most part," said Gennet. He redirected his voice to the crowd of camos filing in from the opposite cliff. "The report came in from the south twenty minutes ago. Third and Fourth have secured the Osterrand. I'd like to say the enemy was routed, but unless they intended to leap the fjords into the Abyss, they really had nowhere to run. May the Nether Halls and their own god receive them well."

"It couldn't have been that easy, sir," Dharmen said as Dori came up, looking equally perplexed.

"It wasn't," said Admiral Sajeva. "When their second wave engaged our reserves, it looked hopeless. Most of the plain had already been taken, and we were about to lose Helmer Fjord and the entire south. But Third and Fourth fought as hard as you all did, and they might have been wiped out had it not been for all our additional help: the particle detection system and the Cloak's mending by your friends." She gave Yos a nod. "We can't thank you and your colleague enough, Dr. Andren. Admiral Gennet and I will see that you both get the highest recognition the Kraal can offer for this one."

"Add Bemin Central Command to that list," said Gennet. "It took them some time, but once they got the Orbital Weapons Platforms up and running, every airborne Carmogen vessel was downed in a matter of minutes. Without air support, they had no chance of a win. And our forces hit the enemy hard from the south while the Lenan brigades took them from the north." He looked across the clearing to troops funneling in with manacled conscripts. "Aside from this lot that splintered off and headed up the pass, the Carmogen lines were smashed to pieces."

Dharmen, Theus, and Dori congratulated each other at the news. Silently, with shoulder pats and slim smiles.

"But make no mistake about it, people, this day was dear-bought," said Sajeva. "We've lost nearly a third of every order and a sizable portion of Bemini staff." She glanced to Ilbron, whose head was hung.

Quiet bereavement started until more troops came in with a horde of war prisoners. The last enemy rabble was rounded up, sealing the victory for the Battle of Marchwarden Pass to join the south's. Cheers started slowly, then swept the assembly. They lifted higher at two more gunships touching down.

Dharmen wished he could join in. Everything had seemed so hopeless just days ago. But so many had sacrificed and died, and traitors had helped to hand every one of those lives to the enemy.

"The gods have smiled on Angolin. They've truly cast their love upon us," Nüren told everyone.

The crowd listened intently. Most were too young to remember his service, but everyone knew who he was.

"Never forget those who've fallen," Nüren continued, "but thank Krone and the Pantheon for what they've given us: Our lives. Our freedom. Our homeland."

Dharmen watched Dori and Theus listen teary-eyed, but he couldn't shed the water. Through the resuming hoots and shouts, he found Leatra wanly grimacing back, her face as absent of joy as his and relaying the same understanding: the battles had been won. What about the war?

And Naul? Plenty of powder faces were being hoisted onto the ships with no sign of him. Maybe he lay dead of his wounds somewhere.

But unlikely. *You were right, Carmi,* Dharmen thought. *Evil to your gray-over-green core, but right. Life doesn't work that simply, does it?* He let the sentiment find his lips. "And you better hope my people find you before I do."

FINAL PREPARATIONS COMMENCED: SECURING THE prisoners on the gunships, sweeping the area for further resistance, mending the injured, locating the dead, and making ready to depart.

"Sir," Rem-E began, "now may not be the appropriate time to discuss your CSD treatment, but—"

But it's only a treatment. It isn't a cure, Dharmen thought back.

"Affirmative. There is no *cure,* but more importantly, the treatment itself is not safe. It may only be administered a small number of times. Any more could cause permanent brain damage."

Why am I not surprised?

"Psychotherapy going forward is the best assurance of preventing future episodes."

Right, Rem-E, I get it. Sounds like this will be with me forever, regardless. Again, not surprised. Let's discuss it another time.

Dharmen dismissed the dreary notion of sitting on a couch and pouring his feelings out to the base psychologist, and concentrated on the joy still surrounding him. He tried to channel some of it; they had achieved the impossible, after all. He looked around, found one who had definitely lost the hour's pleasure. Admiral Gennet stared hard at an upright. He deactivated it, eyes looking into dead space.

"What is it?" Dharmen approached and asked, dispensing with protocol just this once.

Gennet's face was still. "Do you have communications restored?"

Dharmen queried Rem-E. "Affirmative, sir."

"Check your information."

Dharmen activated an upright and scrolled. A report had come in from Seventh. He read it, eyes narrowing at each word. He scanned the report one more time to make sure he had read the news of the jailbreak correctly. The duo stood solemn and quiet, two shadows in an otherwise bright, mirthful surge. With a regardful slap to his shoulder, the admiral left Dharmen to go and assist Sajeva in the departure preparations.

Dharmen strode over to and mounted a large, flat stone. He pointed himself westward, looked toward the Great Hall, and shook his head. *Krone, what next?* It was absolutely inconceivable. Lurking somewhere was the Carmogen Empire's chief warlord and Angolin's most dangerous threat. And soon, Armetrian would likely join him.

CHAPTER 20

A MORE USEFUL TOOL

He will excel in whatever comes to him, regardless of what the Carmogen have planned.

Yes, but it isn't just them that worries me, Lo-KAR. Life in Angolin is about to get very difficult. And from everyone's hand, to put it plainly.

Without a doubt, Admiral Gennet.

❀

GALLIN PACED AROUND THE LIVE-IN sneering at its lavish furnishings and artwork. "Waste, excess, and more waste—so Angoliner," he muttered.

"To each, his own," Armetrian said. "I'm just glad to be here and not still in a cage."

Footsteps announced the butler. A human one with a tray of fluted drinks. Armetrian decided he could use one even if it was barely midday.

Gallin peeked into the kitchen. More flesh and blood at work in there—not a house synth to be seen. "Wasteful again, though it's a change from the automatons running your everyday lives."

"It's a nice place, Gallin. Nice location too. Pocket vale, far from civilization, and concealed in dark matter. Lots of places in the Hidden

Realm to live comfortably but unseen." He could see that Gallin was afraid of the phenomenon, though Lena must have had DM pockets too. "Shame she had to move house so quickly, but it couldn't have put her in a better environment."

"One you never expected to find yourself in, though it's better than where I sprang you from." Gallin looked around with disdain. "Your next address won't live up to *this*. I'm not as well outfitted at the moment as our esteemed hostess."

"Nor as beautiful."

"Beauty isn't power, Armetrian. The woman may stop men in their tracks, but she couldn't have dispatched four brig guards with just a smile. You needed my skill for that."

"Her smile is just as effective. So is her family name," Armetrian said. "But this isn't the time to talk prison breaks, so for the love of Rior, keep your voice down."

"Keep it down about what?" their pudgy cohort asked, stepping in from the terrace with breath vapor swirling around his face as the door slid shut behind him.

"About nothing you need to know, Ian," Armetrian replied. He wondered how on Tentim anyone could sweat so much after having stood out in the cold.

"Really? After all I've done for this venture, I thought I was part of it. Forgive my presumption," Ian said.

"You mean after you trashed it," Armetrian said.

"Beg your pardon?"

Armetrian gazed around the room. He needed the extra seconds to calm himself. "You had the chance of a lifetime, many lifetimes, Ian. You could've gotten the Cloak lifted to let the Carmogen forces in, but after twenty-eight hours of whatever it was you were doing, you didn't bring down even one section of the defense grid, including those south of the Osterrand that you were instructed to disable first."

"I couldn't access those. I told you that," Ian self-defended. "Their security encryptions were too complex."

"So you tried the Cloak just about everywhere else?"

"Well, yes. And why not? What was so special about that location anyway? I thought we wanted to bring the thing down, period. Why was one spot on the fjord line so much more crucial than anyplace else?"

Idiot! Because I needed to control the Carmogen's entry into Angolin without them running amok and without them wasting themselves over the East Ranges, Armetrian thought. *How else was I supposed to make this work?* "That's my concern, not yours." *And you aren't worth sharing strategies with, anyway.*

"So you say. They found Marchwarden Pass anyway, at least," Ian said.

"Which you know is unshielded. Don't try to add that to your credit," Armetrian said. "That was the last way I wanted them to take. The force that made it through barely did so and was picked off bit by bit by my *favorite* little part of the Guard. Next time I see Tate and his friends . . ."

"We'll get him soon enough," Gallin said. "He can't elude us forever. Sooner or later, he'll slip up."

"Tate's irrelevant now," said Ian. "But for my part, I would've succeeded if it weren't for one of my colleagues. That Brona put her nose in everything she possibly could!"

"And she's working with Tate, who contrary to your uninformed, unscientific-for-a-scientist opinion is not irrelevant," Gallin said. "We'll have him, Devries, and Andren crying to your gods before we're done with them, Folc, but don't think we'll forget you either. Armetrian's right, the Carmogen should've had an easy in, and where desired. What they got instead was a frozen mountain pass full of deadly saaryl, with Tate-and-company waiting to finish off what the trees and borbols missed."

"I wouldn't have had to do anything if you hadn't lost the information I gave to Vara," Ian said. "You had stealthtech and nexus data months ago. It was supposed to go to our allies. Naul's forces could've had full access to any Cloak grids you wanted them to, but you let the Guard get it." He sighed stiffly. "I could've watched the invasion comfortably from my live-in upright, but no. I had to spend a night and a day trying to break through PDP's new Guard-installed security measures that wouldn't have mattered had it not been for you, Gallin!"

The Lenan eyed him coldly. "Most of the information you gave Vara was sabotaged. The initial files were clean, but once you were discovered, logic bombs found their way into them and scrambled the data. Thank Dr. Devries for that. Then there's Tate: it was his internal AI that blocked you, not Guard security measures. Not irrelevant, like I said. You won't admit that, so let me, and lastly, if after a year's worth of wasted work, all you can do is lie, fat little man, I'll gladly relieve you and find another PDP hack to work with." He drew a knife, leveled the blade with Ian's lips. "Let's see you keep talking without your tongue!"

Armetrian stepped between the portly physicist and the weapon waiting to send him to the Netherlords. "Enough! Let's just move on. Now, the weapons that I got to our allies—"

"Barely made a difference, no thanks to Brona and her new boyfriend," said Ian.

"I'd break your neck if I could find it," Armetrian said. "And we can't go back and change any of that now."

"Your ancestors could have," Gallin said. "They had time-travel ability, or so I've heard. Isn't that how Angolin came to be here in the first place?"

"That is completely out of our reach," Armetrian said.

"Not for long, it isn't," Ian piped in. "The ancients opened wormholes connecting separate points in spacetime. TS is only the beginning.

Once we determine the proper variables to create similar stable portals, we should be well able to—"

"Did anyone ask?" Armetrian snapped. "And even if Henk Hanne and the Conservatives approved it, we wouldn't regain that ability for decades." *I want to rule Angolin now, not when I'm ninety!* "Take your head up out of the Abyss and focus, Ian! Now Gallin here got me out of detention, and you did initially get us vital stealthtech information before Devries got to it. But regardless, we've hit a wall. We've lacked something through all this, and I haven't figured out what that is yet."

"I have," said their hostess as she entered the room. "Teamwork."

Armetrian waxed polite. "Gentlemen, let me introduce Mrs. Prinsen, our benefactor and widow to the late general. May Krone keep him."

"Mrs. Prinsen-Estes, if you don't mind." She took a flute of Vinalhaven Valley white, poured just for her by her butler. "But please call me Coraia." Ian went to take her hand for a kiss and stumbled over his own feet. She smiled with practiced patience. "Now, I didn't invite you three here to argue. We've wasted enough time dancing around our purposes, so let's try to recover them. Being at each other's throats won't get us what we want, any more than mislaid efforts will."

"Like your late husband's, I should say," Gallin interjected.

Armetrian gave him nemurite-hard eyes. Why did the man always insist on blunt truth instead of tact, when he actually *did* speak?

"My beloved did what he could for the cause, and he would have succeeded had Vieron Gennet not interfered," Coraia said, lowering her eyes. "He'll pay for my husband's death. So will his lackey, Tate, but let's forget them for now. In your own individual ways, you three have the skills necessary to expose Angolin and see to its overthrow. My influence can supplement you. No more sneaking around blowing up other people's dine-ins, or snatching them off the ways. Angolin's defenses are where we must concentrate—there and on the minds of its citizens."

"I don't follow you on that second point," Gallin said with a hair more civility.

Coraia activated an area upright. On it appeared a NewsMesh broadcast of a huge student protest. The camera panned to a young man threading the mass and going toward the stage.

"This is their biggest one yet," Armetrian said. "And surprising, considering what's happened."

The speaker cleared his throat, calmed the crowd's chanting and jumped into his talk. All of it blamed the Guard for bringing the Carmogen in arms to Angolin.

Coraia paused the broadcast. "Gentlemen, meet your newest associate, one who'll win the *people* over to our side and be a far more useful tool than everything you've thus far used."

"WE'VE ASKED WHY WE AREN'T allowed to leave this land. Now we know," the speaker bellowed. "It's our leaders' fear of us and what they know we could accomplish, and not anyone abroad, imagined and engineered to be our enemies. It's fear of what's right here at home that keeps us hidden."

Dharmen fumed at the face filling his live-in upright. It was the same brat who led the last protest he had found himself in the middle of. He shook his head. He couldn't believe the stupidity flowing into his ears. He was glad that Will had left long before the broadcast started.

"The Carmogen Empire was never the reason for our confinement here. They never intended any harm to ordinary Angolinians."

Dharmen grunted. "When they march across your quad and snatch you out of class at gunpoint, will you believe it then, you smarmy, self-entitled little—"

"Dharm, shh!" interrupted Theus. "I want to hear this."

"And up to now, I faulted our government for last month's incident that some say wiped out much of the Guard—yet another lie to gain sympathy for those who talk with guns. But I see now that it's actually, and again, our military heading up the problem!"

Dharmen clenched his fists. He wished the broadcast would end there, but he knew it was as far from over as the misinformed student movement itself.

The speaker elevated to a hoarse shout: "Our leaders are too old and complacent to govern, so they've handed control to the Guard. They are the ones who started the secret war down in the Vresel, they brought it up here, and it's they whom we must deal with if we're to end our imprisonment! We are Angolin's future. That makes us its rightful leaders, and I say let's end the tyranny and force our government to muzzle its butchers in uniform so we can live in the larger world as we deserve!"

The crowd erupted beneath pleinside cameras panning across throngs of raised fists.

Nostrils flaring, Dharmen wheeled, snatched up a chair, and made ready to throw it.

Theus grabbed the other end of the synth furniture piece headed for Dharmen's upright.

"You see what we're up against?" Dharmen yelled. "After all we've been through for Angolin and for every one of *them* who sat in school while we fought? A lot of good people died up on that field! How many did we see blown to pieces just so this little idiot and his followers could say it was all our fault?"

Theus met him with Rior's patience, his cooler head intervening as he removed the chair from Dharmen's grip and set it down. "They're kids, Dharm. They don't know what they don't know. This'll pass. It has to."

"But do you honestly see either of us as *aggressors*, Thee?" Dharmen grated across already strained vocal cords. "Aggressors against the people?"

"I see us as protectors, obviously. And right now, I'm protecting my friend from himself. You'll have a heart attack soon if you don't calm down."

Dharmen's eyes were as wide as Kiern and Dasha in the night sky at full. Red veins pierced rage-watered whites. He turned away, removed his dress cloak, and threw it across the chairback, then went over to a bureau, opened a drawer, and took out his sidearm.

"What are you doing?"

"Going down there. What else?"

"Really? And what would that achieve?"

"Thee, somebody's got to stop all this," Dharmen said, shaking a finger at the upright. "Somebody's got to intervene—get those people to see reason, once and for all. This whole thing, it's all just . . . madness!"

"So you want to revisit the Falconerplein and either crack open skulls or blast anybody who doesn't agree with you? And all by yourself?"

"If I have to, then yes."

"That *would* make you the aggressor and give them even more to yell about, now wouldn't it?"

Dharmen breathed a low snarl as he searched for a rebuttal.

There wasn't one.

"We'll deal with the movement later," Theus said, retrieving and handing Dharmen his cloak. "Put the gun away. Right now, you'll need this. You wouldn't want to be incompletely attired for your own wedding!"

THE GREAT HALL OVERFLOWED WITH people and chatter. And ears. Gennet and Sajeva found a spot away from it all in a side aisle. "No doubt, you've heard, Caevon," said Gennet.

"Heard what?"

"About the Pride of Angolin. She's receiving final fittings on Bemin as we speak. Word from the Kraal is she's due to leave Port for shakedown by month's end."

Sajeva sighed. "So after everything, HC intends to go forward with space exploration as if we have nothing else going on. Badly conceived and horribly timed as usual."

"I'm not worried about them asking either of us to command her. We've got our Orders to put back together," said Gennet. "But I know HC will snatch some of our best people. I hear they've tapped Tate and his combat unit XO for senior leadership, with Tate likely as captain. Lieutenant Tarkala's technical skills and, I daresay, cooler head will benefit the new ship, but Tate . . . he's the last officer I want to lose right now."

"The lieutenant commander has become an excellent leader, but he's not ready for that kind of elevation just yet," said Sajeva. "Though who is? Who outside Bemin knows anything about starships? It makes about as much sense as all those students haranguing the Guard on the mesh this morning after all we've sacrificed for them."

"I can't think about whining kids right now, I want to concentrate on our own more immediate future. Lift-off is weeks away—a lot can happen before then."

"You didn't bring us over here to discuss ships of the *present*, did you, Vieron?"

Gennet looked around them answerless.

"Then you think it's doable?"

"I don't know. I honestly don't," he said. "There are three capable of meeting our needs. The one hidden in the Shadowvale and the one concealed on Bemin are out of the question, obviously. Angolin needs their stealth systems and their 'staff' to help sustain our defenses. But the third is a possibility."

"It's the only possibility at this point," said Sajeva. "You know the Carmogen will be back to finish what they started. They've tasted our blood. No nation on this planet has ever resisted the empire for long. Our friends out in the Abyss are all I see possibly saving us now."

"Provided they still exist. And if they'll allow us to meet with them."

"If so, they'll be the best, most useful tool we can hope for."

Gennet nodded agreement. "Then it's settled. As soon as we can, you and I will take a patrol sloop—a fast one with the latest weapons and stealthtech—go out there and see about resurrecting *Sub Rosa θ*."

Chimes filled the Great Hall. Music of simple strings followed: a haunting but beautiful gentle melody to please the ear and at the same time politely say, "Glad you all could come. Please be seated." Admiral Sajeva and everyone lolling about hastily filled the rows, a monumental feat considering the sheer number in attendance. Admiral Gennet went to the front of the Hall.

ON THE HIGH PLATFORM BENEATH the synthed Altar of the Gods appeared Theus and Nüren. The younger man was steeled for his role in the ceremony. His elder was likewise, though a tear formed beneath one eye, and his lips quivered, imperceptible to all but the clerical quartet before them: the Priestess of Lothnë and the Priest of Rior for Willem, and for Dharmen, Father Dietmar and Mother Encarra, ready to hand one of their own to a life of matrimony in the name of Krone, god of war.

And to the front of the platform came Dharmen. He stood soberly austere in dress uniform with cloak outlining his form, right hand at his side, left palm on his sword pommel, medals shining on his breast, including his latest: the Falconer Star of Valor, awarded for his actions at Marchwarden Pass. He looked out at the crowd, eyes wide in amazement. The Hall was packed solid! He had never seen so many people in the massive space and never stood before so many in his life.

Earlier, he had found the mead hall just as he'd left it: comforting and intimate, the perfect preparation space. The Great Hall was a completely different animal. Dori had wanted to make his wedding a special gathering.

"Think about it," she had said. "This is the first military wedding or military anything since the Osterrand, and with spirits so low, this event might give our people a lift. Plus, it's a great opportunity to bring together all the parts of our effort: the Guard, the Bemini staff, and the Lenan brigades. We'll have to depend on everyone in the future, so why not extend a hand of friendship and solidify things now?"

Dharmen sniffed. "Commander, you've succeeded beyond your wildest—oops, getting looks."

He stopped talking to himself at the curious eyes from beneath the altar and stared back out to the peopled sea. Endless civilian faces greeted him, none he recognized, and multitudes of uniforms, including three full rows of pale, furry faces. Dori had made good on her word to extend the Guard's gratitude to the Lenans by planting them in his wedding. Whether they were here honoring the event or gawking at the incredibly un-Lenan sight of two men marrying, Dharmen really couldn't tell.

He lowered his eyes to the front rows: to friends, family, and his unit's survivors. Dori waved. Even from a distance, she looked elated enough to jump out of military form. She turned to the row behind. And turned right back on seeing Brona's head resting lovingly on Yos's shoulder. She found Ilbron, tried to get his attention, and failed, as he was trying for Dharmen's.

Ilbron lanced him with predatory eyes, and followed it with an air kiss.

Dharmen's stomach began to flutter, and not from the major's typically juvenile, untimely behavior, or even from anticipation of the co-groom. Much of the Guard, most of Bemin, and even the Kraal, from the look of things, had been emptied into the Hall. He began to see Dori's point. After Angolin had suffered so much loss, this *was* a special event. Maybe too special!

He saw legates and admirals with their spouses, many Guardsmen and Bemini he knew, and many more he didn't. Among them, newly promoted Shipman Apprentice Leatra Vinc radiated. Sitting beside her, Irzek looked about as comfortable as a borbol at a dinner party. And a few rows back . . . no need to focus for a clearer look, everyone in the Guard knew Coraia Prinsen-Estes on sight.

Dharmen did a double take at her. *Bereaved widow my ass. What's Traitor Prime's wife doing at my wedding?*

They locked stares.

Putting in appearances, Miss? Got anything under your gown evading hall sensors? He revised that notion. Coraia was of her late husband's cut, or he was of hers. She'd strike when least expected, she wouldn't try anything here. He pried his eyes from her, found his comrades again.

Yos was still with them. Why? What was Will's best man doing out in the audience? Yos met his confused look with raised eyebrows and his usual toothy, flippant smile.

The balmy, subdued string concert faded to silence. New music started. A choral ensemble, powerfully voiced in military cadence, but still ethereally toned and per Dharmen's design. Willem had wanted something livelier, but he had been overruled. Dharmen didn't want to risk the shakes at this moment! He straightened to attention, realized he had already been doing so. Aches and pains replied. The audience stood, with heads turning toward the Hall's rear.

The high double doors soundlessly swung open. Willem entered and marched slowly. His wedding raiment glowed beneath the overhead candelabras. He wore a gray coat edged in silver over an unadorned, collared white tunic. Over his shoulder hung a floor-length sash emblazoned with the Hanne family crest. At the front of his column, Aremel and family wore the same badge.

Dharmen was heartened. He was glad for the moment and proud of Willem's resolve; he *had* decided to honor his family in spite of his father's stubbornness . . . but Dharmen had been too fixated on his fiancé to notice Yos's replacement. He couldn't believe his eyes!

At Willem's side, Henk Hanne accompanied the son he hadn't seen in a decade to the altar. He stared ahead with the most severe, controlled expression Dharmen had ever seen. In tow behind them, Willem's four brothers—Naeus, Njorkela, Maarten, and Ulrin—were practically beaming.

Gasps rolled with the procession. Heads swiveled and bent to peer around other heads. Dori's spiky crimson locks twisted and turned as she chattered to her neighbors.

Dharmen smiled broadly in a way he rarely did. The procession of male Hannes reached the front row. Willem climbed the steps, came up to Dharmen's side with warm, bright eyes. They turned to the clerics, thrilled. Overjoyed. *Nervous.*

"Lieutenant Commander," Father Dietmar said, "I thank Lord Krone on the Mount for seeing you safely through battle." He looked to Willem. "As does Mr. Hanne, most surely."

Mother Encarra adjusted her robe and gave the couple a contemplative smile before turning toward the audience. A long, fresh scar graced her cheek. Dharmen assured himself that her Ergive blade met its adversaries well. "And now, by the glory of the Heaveners," she announced, "we will begin."

For the next half hour, the Fjaronate pair worked in tandem with the representatives of the Lady and Lord of Light before turning the final proceeding to Dharmen's commanding officer. With compassioned timbre, Admiral Gennet guided the pair in their vows, and with these final words: "May Lothnë and Rior above, our revered Lord Krone, and the whole of the Pantheon bless your union. Grooms, you may seal your bond with a kiss."

It was one order that Dharmen gladly obeyed. His and Willem's lips met in an impassioned kiss to cheers and applause sweeping the Hall.

AT THE END OF THE Arch of Swords, the doors opened. Dharmen and Willem emerged into the cold, clouded light of day to an earsplitting uproar. Cheers lifted from a crowd outside the Great Hall that was bigger than the one indoors. Swarming the space from the stone figures of *The Crew* in the forward plein's rear, all the way to the Hall steps, happy faces bobbed beneath waving hands. It was uplifting and unnerving at once. Above it all, a host of friends, family and Guard-Bemini bookended the newlyweds who stood hand in gloved hand.

Dharmen joined the cheerful conversations and jokes surrounding them, even laughed at some. He had forgotten how that felt. He heard Aremel's excitable voice tell Lord Balaneth and Willem's parents what a *"joyous* and *monumental* moment" this was. *Funny, I thought I was just simply married!*

"Will and I go way, way back," Yos garbled after having nipped a few wines before, and likely during, the ceremony. "But Dharmen's father is my mother's stepbrother's commanding officer's uncle's second cousin thrice removed, you know."

"And what does that make the lieutenant commander and you?" asked Lord Balaneth.

Yos's bright smile pierced the wintry weather amid his inebriated wavering. "Why, good friends of course!"

So much joy surrounded Dharmen that he wished he could seize it and never let go. But sadness sidestepped it and crept into him. It was like nothing he had ever felt. Not grief, it was deeper. Malevolent and thoroughly blackhearted, completely unlike the elusive but warm presence he normally sensed in the Great Hall. Inside, voices had spoken to him. He had eerily *felt* more than heard them, and they had comforted and encouraged him. Now, it was as though a North Lake serpent weaved stealthily in and out of his consciousness. He remembered one of Father Dietmar's comments to him on the Osterrand Plain days before battle: "The gods provide, take away, and provide yet again."

He looked around him. Theus and Dori looked downright gloomy. Nüren's dark expression delved deeper than his son's. Willem was euphoric, and Dharmen was glad for him, but neither he nor his uniformed companions could shake off the sensation beginning to overtake them. From without, from within, what was coming to Angolin?

Dharmen felt something sharp and cold on the tip of his nose. Snowflakes. He looked up into a gray-white stream that was nothing like the gentle, comforting snowfalls he remembered as a child.

"And just in time!" He said it jokingly but couldn't completely hide the premonition beneath.

Everyone on the Hall steps and the plein below pulled cloaks tighter and drew hoods as the clouds thickened, and the snow and wind picked up sudden intensity and swirled around them.

ACKNOWLEDGMENTS

Thank you to my editors, Christie Stratos and Elana Gibson, for their insightful manuscript review, and particularly to Christie for her patient, scene-by-scene examination of my work. *Angolin* would not be possible without these tireless efforts. My writing group, Longwood Writers, has also provided great feedback and moral support over the years. Grace Kuikman, our group leader, is a prolific writer with on-point observations and criticisms that helped me make this work shine. I thank her and all within the cohort.

I also greatly thank Dr. Sharon Bostick, librarian and friend whose comments and encouragements gave *Angolin* and its rather green author a great confidence boost, and my sincerest regards go to her husband, Oliver Pesch, for believing in me and my work, and for quietly putting me on the long and arduous, but fulfilling road to publication.

ABOUT THE AUTHOR

C. E. Taylor's fascination for science fiction began early as a child. As a nerdy, curious kid, he created his own worlds and realities and followed sci-fi adventures that captivated him. Instead of playing with toys, he created cities and, later, fictional societies and cultures on paper. Later in life, his interest in human culture and in urbanism let him to pursue degrees in Cultural Anthropology and Urban Planning, but his science fiction passion remained. His interest in other worlds, places, and times led him to write the first book of the Angolin trilogy.

By day he works as a planner for city government. His evenings and weekends are spent honing his story of a hidden society that is discovered by a dangerous enemy. Whether creating storylines, histories, and world-building for his novel series, or dealing with the inescapable real world, he finds a form of Anthropology in everything he experiences in real life, and in everything he reads, as even fiction provides insight into the human condition. C. E. Taylor lives in Chicago with his spouse.

IF YOU LIKE
C. E. TAYLOR'S **ANGOLIN**,
YOU'LL ENJOY
THE BUILDING THAT WASN'T
BY ABIGAIL MILES.

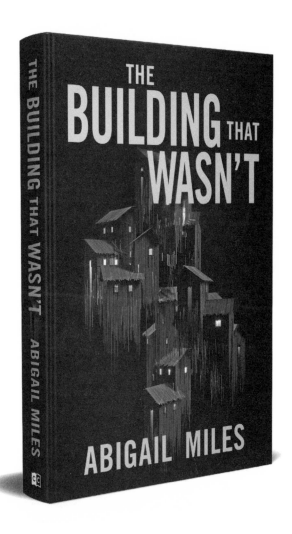

CHAPTER ONE

The room was white—almost blindingly so, with surfaces that had been scrubbed to a shine, so that by staring at the floor or a wall, it was nearly possible to see one's own reflection cast back. It was clean and fresh and sterile. The perfect canvas.

The most beautiful aspect of the white room was how stark contrasting shapes and colors appeared on the initial blankness. This was an aesthetic quality that the man found particularly pleasing to explore, and so he did as such extensively, to a near compulsive rate. He fancied himself an artist, with the borders of the room providing the ideal location to bring his masterpiece to life.

Keeping that in mind, and aiming for the truest form of artistic perfection he could conjure, the man gripped the tool in his hand—his paintbrush of choice—and hefted it before him. His arm fell down in an almost graceful fashion as the man completed a full swoop, similar in form to that of a baseball player setting up to bat. Then, pausing once to allow the moment to settle in its resplendent glory, the man slowly lowered his arm, tool in hand, and looked around at what he had created.

The white backdrop truly was perfect, he thought to himself. It made the red look so much fresher, more sharp and potent. And the shapes the droplets formed, the pattern they enacted across the room. Perfect. The man admired the final product and couldn't help but think that this may have been some of his finest work yet.

Not to mention the added pleasure derived from the screaming.

While some find the sound of a human scream to be unpleasant, the man found it to be more precious than music—a chorus of varying pitches and volumes coming together in a resounding crescendo at the final moment. He would do it all for that, for the symphony that was created as a result of the fear, the excitement. The pain.

That's why he was there, after all. To create such a stupendous pain in the people they gave him.

Well, that was not technically true. Technically he was there for many, many more reasons. Glorified kidnapper being one, rubber duck–watcher another.

But the pain. That was his favorite.

Though usually the pain was accompanied by a distinct factor of *more*—the unraveling of the universe and all that.

Not this time. This was only an ordinary body, with no spark of the otherworldly in sight.

The man didn't care.

Maybe others would, but he found purpose enough for himself in the beauty of what he could create there, with or without the ulterior motive. In some ways, one could say that having a secondary reason for the pain only tarnished it, whereas this belonged solely to him. This moment, right here.

The man took a deep breath, savoring the sensations that welled up within him, the complete ambiance of the space he was in, before he turned back to his subject and assessed his options once more. Settling on a different, more precise tool—one with a much sharper edge—the man once more lifted his arm, and continued with his ordained task.

The white walls, no longer pristine, echoed back the horrendous chorus that his work produced.

CHAPTER TWO

There was an elderly man whom Everly had never seen before standing behind all of the black-clad patrons, and his eyes had been focused on her for the duration of the service.

She blinked, and realized that wasn't quite right. There was an elderly man whom Everly recognized, as if from a dream, as if from a memory, lodged deep and low down in the recesses of her brain. She squinted at him, because if she could just . . .

She blinked again, and of *course* she knew him, why wouldn't she know him, why would she ever not recognize—

Blink. Everly shook her head. The man was still there, and she didn't know why a second before she had recognized him, because she did not, though she felt oddly unsettled by the memory of recognizing the man. Not as unsettled as she was, however, by his mere presence or by the fact of his staring at her.

He was too far away for her to actually see his eyes, to know for sure, but she could feel his attention pierced on her like a dagger through her spleen. The sensation was disconcerting, but in a strange way she appreciated the man and the mystery he presented. It gave her something to focus on. Something to puzzle over.

Someone to look at other than the laid-out form in the coffin on the elevated platform in front of her.

The man wore a bowler hat over his tufted gray hair, and a brown tweed coat, which worked even further to set him apart from the sea of faces that encircled him—the rest of whom were all adorned in shades of black or blackish blue, and were all at least a little familiar to Everly.

They were all the friends, the coworkers, the distant acquaintances and associates.

But not the family. There was no other family. None but her.

The preacher had finished speaking, Everly realized with a start, and was gesturing for her to step forward. She didn't want to. She wanted to go back to pondering the peculiar man in the bowler hat, trying to work out how he had found his way there, and why, but they were all staring at her, so she stood, refusing to breathe as she crossed over the distance between her chair and the platform ahead of her.

She couldn't look at the body. They had asked if she wanted to beforehand, to make sure he looked okay—like himself, she supposed— but she knew it would be no use. He would never look like himself. Never again.

It had been a car accident that had led her there, to that raised platform, in front of all the vaguely familiar forms in black and the solitary strange one in brown. Or at least, that is what they had told her, when it had been too late for it to even have mattered if the cause had been different anyhow.

(Like, for instance, if the cause had been a lethally sharpened knife, wielded gleefully in a previously white room.)

But according to them, it had been a car accident, and so he hadn't been quite right. Or his body hadn't been. They had told her it would be okay if she didn't want to have the coffin be open, but she hadn't been able to stand the thought of closing him up in there any sooner than she needed to. So even though she refused now to look, she kept him open. She kept him free.

Afterward, Everly was ushered to a dimly lit reception room, where she had scarcely a moment to herself before the other mourners came flooding in to report how very sorry they were, how devastating of a loss it must be, how much she would be kept in their prayers. Everly hardly heard any of them. She leaned against one of the whitewashed walls of the hall and crossed her arms, trying not to close her eyes, though she wanted nothing more than to shut out everything and everyone around her. She wanted them all to go back, to their lives and their families and their homes. She wanted to go back.

But back to what, she couldn't help but ask herself. Back to the empty house with too many rooms and the life that she wasn't sure she could picture any longer in his absence.

Her father's absence.

She was too young all of Everly's neighbors had tried to claim. Too young to be all alone. Nineteen was supposed to be an age of experimentation, of testing your wings, but always with the knowledge that a safety net was set up beneath you. They all said that they should find somewhere for her to go, someone for her to stay with, who could look after her.

But there was no one, and they knew it as well as she did.

She was on her own.

Everly considered leaving. She thought better of it a moment later, looking around at all the people who had come out to celebrate her father's life, but then she realized an instant after that that she didn't even care. None of them had truly known him anyhow. They had only come out for the cake, which was now set out on a plastic folding table by the door, the words *Our Most Sincere Condolences* traced out in poorly scripted black icing across the center of the buttercream sheet. They probably wouldn't even notice if she left, Everly knew, and even if they did, she could see no reason why she should care. No reason at all.

As she stood up from the wall to leave, Everly had the dizzying sense of doubling, like she had done this before, but different. Or would do it again one day. Her eyes again scanned the sea of vague strangers, and for a second she could almost imagine her dad standing there with her, watching the crowd by her side.

Almost.

She could almost see them being at a different funeral. Together. The type of funeral where they could leave with their arms linked together, rather than the type of funeral where she had to walk away, and he had to stay behind in a box.

Everly shook her head and pinched the bridge of her nose, trying to dispel the phantom image of her father standing beside her. Then she began to make her way toward the doors of the reception hall, trying to appear as nonchalant as possible as she walked between the so-called well-wishers.

Stepping out into the deepening evening air just beyond the doors, she paused as she caught sight of a blur of brown fabric far ahead of her. Straining her eyes against the dusk that was swiftly descending, Everly could just make out the shape of the strange man from before— the one whom she remembered and knew she had never met—as he strode off into the night, the shadow of his curved bowler hat protruding distinctly above his head as he left without so much as an insincere commiseration passed her way.

MORE SCI-FI READS FROM CAMCAT BOOKS

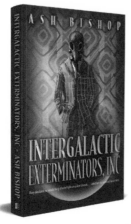

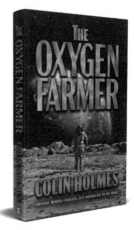

Available now, wherever books are sold.

CamCat
Books

VISIT US ONLINE FOR MORE BOOKS TO LIVE IN:
CAMCATBOOKS.COM

SIGN UP FOR CAMCAT'S FICTION NEWSLETTER FOR
COVER REVEALS, EBOOK DEALS, AND MORE EXCLUSIVE CONTENT.

CamCatBooks   @CamCatBooks   @CamCat_Books   @CamCatBooks